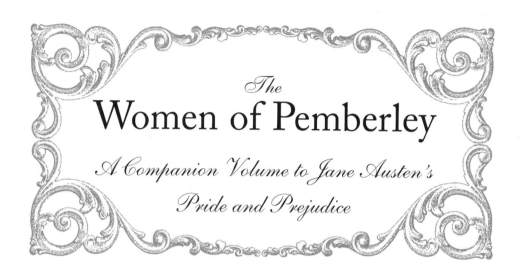

The
Women of Pemberley

A Companion Volume to Jane Austen's
Pride and Prejudice

DEVISED AND COMPILED BY

Rebecca Ann Collins

SOURCEBOOKS LANDMARK™
AN IMPRINT OF SOURCEBOOKS, INC.®
NAPERVILLE, ILLINOIS

Published by Sourcebooks Landmark, an imprint of Sourcebooks, Inc.
P.O. Box 4410, Naperville, Illinois 60567-4410
(630) 961-3900
FAX: (630) 961-2168
www.sourcebooks.com

Originally printed and bound in Australia by SNAP Printing, Sydney, NSW, 1998.
Reprinted in 2000, 2002, 2003, and 2007.

Library of Congress Cataloging-in-Publication Data

Collins, Rebecca Ann.
  The Women of Pemberley : The Pemberley Chronicles : Book 2 / Rebecca Ann Collins.
     p. cm.
  ISBN-13: 978-1-4022-1154-6
  ISBN-10: 1-4022-1154-6
  1. Female friendship—Fiction. 2. England—Social life and customs—19th century—Fiction. 3. Domestic fiction. I. Title.
  PR9619.4.C65W66 2008
  823'.92--dc22
                              2008004321

Printed and bound in the United States of America
VP 10 9 8 7 6 5 4 3 2

To the friends of my childhood,

with whom I shared the joys of discovering

Jane Austen

Contents

Acknowledgements

The author wishes to acknowledge her debt to Jane Austen—the creator of the original Pemberley characters—and dedicates this work to her memory.

Thanks also to Ms Claudia Taylor, librarian, for assistance with research, Ms Marissa O'Donnell for advice with the cover design, Ben and Robert for help with editing the material on her computer, and Ms Beverley Farrow for her patience with preparing and printing the text.

Prologue

ELIZABETH WAS HAPPY TO be going home to Pemberley. The Summer of 1847 was almost over. It had been a particularly pleasant Summer, spent only in the company of those she loved most.

A month or more had been taken up with travelling in the Cotswolds with Jane and Charles Bingley and their two younger daughters, Louisa and Sophie, followed by several weeks at Woodlands—the farm in Sussex—where they had been joined by her Aunt and Uncle Gardiner.

The farm, which Darcy had purchased for her, had become an absorbing hobby. She had come to cherish it as her own little corner of England—"a veritable paradise," as she had once described it to her sister Jane. Happily situated on the Albury Downs, its proximity to the town of Guildford, where Darcy and Mr Gardiner had established business contacts, was an added advantage.

With the help of a small, handpicked group of staff from Pemberley and the tenant farmers, who worked a part of the land, Elizabeth had transformed the grounds and refurbished the interior of the house. Informal elegance and comfort were now its most striking features.

The family and their closest friends, who were the only visitors she would ask to Woodlands, enjoyed the delightful intimacy that it afforded them and many happy weeks were spent there. Both Darcy and Elizabeth had already acknowledged that it had made a significant difference to their lives, left desolate after the death of their son William.

"I am very glad I let you persuade me that we needed Woodlands," Elizabeth said, as they took a last look before leaving, recalling her first reaction to his suggestion that he should purchase the farm.

"Indeed," her husband replied, "so am I. Judging only by the pleasure it has brought us, it must be one of the best investments I have ever made. Do you not agree, my love?"

"I certainly do and thank you very much for it," she replied.

They both understood how much the place meant to them.

Julian, still reluctant to leave the horses in the meadow, was finally persuaded to join them in the carriage, and they were soon on their way. It was to be a leisurely journey, breaking for the night at Banbury in Oxfordshire, but Elizabeth was keen to be back at home.

Returning to Pemberley after some time away was always a pleasure.

This time there was a special occasion, too, for they were soon to celebrate the christening of their first granddaughter, Elizabeth Jane, along with Julian's eleventh birthday.

Arrangements for the celebration had been meticulously planned in advance and left in the capable hands of Jenny Grantham—their housekeeper—and her husband, who was Darcy's manager.

Pemberley had not hosted such a gathering for quite a while and Elizabeth was anxious, but Darcy had complete confidence in their staff. "I have no doubt at all that John Grantham and Jenny will manage very well indeed. You have no need to worry, my dear," he said, and Elizabeth had to agree.

"Indeed, I do not. I realise it is foolish of me to be so anxious when everything has been so carefully planned. Jenny wrote last week that Mrs Reynolds is quite determined to emerge from retirement for the occasion, so I know nothing could possibly go wrong."

The following morning, they left Banbury after breakfast and Julian, plainly keen to be home, was rather restless and kept hanging out of the window. As they turned into the park, however, he sat down and was as good as gold.

Familiarity had not dulled Elizabeth's appreciation of Pemberley. The old stonework burnished by the afternoon sun, the wooded hills clothed in rust and gold, and the inviting soft green lawns aroused in her the same response of heightened excitement she had always felt as they approached the house.

Darcy helped her out—he understood and shared her feelings. Julian had already raced away in search of his dog.

Jenny Grantham came forward to welcome them. She had matured from the days when she had been Elizabeth's maid and was regarded by her mistress with both affection and respect. Her loyalty was without question.

"Welcome home, ma'am," she said, her face lighting up with genuine pleasure.

It was with a great deal of regret that she had agreed to relinquish her role as Elizabeth's personal maid and accept the honour of succeeding her aunt, Mrs Reynolds, as housekeeper of Pemberley. Young Susan, whom she had then trained with great care, held her in awe.

Still, Jenny jealously guarded her own privileged position—being always the first to greet her mistress, accompany her upstairs, and acquaint her with the latest news while she took a welcome cup of tea.

As Darcy had predicted, there were no problems—all arrangements were proceeding smoothly for the celebrations at the week's end. Jenny assured Elizabeth that it was all in hand. She had worried in vain.

Later, after the weary travellers had bathed and rested, she would return to discuss the details of the occasion with her mistress.

Much as she loved her little farm, Elizabeth was very happy to be home. Pemberley was very much the centre of her life.

Two letters lay on her writing desk, having arrived too late to be sent on to Woodlands. The first, from Charlotte Collins, brought news from Rosings, where Charlotte had been visiting her eldest daughter Catherine, who continued as companion to Lady Catherine de Bourgh and her daughter, Anne. What had appeared at first to be a matter of convenience for the de Bourghs had actually turned out to be quite advantageous for Miss Catherine Collins. Despite a seemingly impenetrable carapace of snobbery, Lady Catherine, it seemed, had taken a liking to young Miss Collins—her goddaughter—who was treated more as a member of her family than a paid employee and benefited considerably from being within the social circle at Rosings.

Charlotte's letter served to confirm this.

My dear Eliza, she wrote:

> *You may be surprised to receive a letter from me, since we are to see you very soon at Pemberley.*
>
> *I had thought to leave the news I have to give you until we met, but Catherine, ever conscious of the niceties of etiquette, was adamant that I should write advising you that she is engaged to Mr Harrison, the parson at Hunsford.*

Elizabeth had only met Mr Harrison once at Rosings and, while he had seemed pleasant and tolerably well spoken, he had not impressed her with his rather prosaic sermon in church. She agreed with Darcy that he was an improvement on Mr Collins. At the very least, Mr Harrison seemed able to conduct himself in society without appearing ridiculous, and that was a singular advantage. And, as Elizabeth said later to her sister Jane, Catherine was almost thirty years old and seemed unlikely to receive a better offer.

Charlotte was clearly pleased; her letter continued:

> *Lady Catherine de Bourgh has expressed her approval of the match, much to my relief, and has generously offered to host the wedding breakfast when they marry next Spring.*
>
> *I am not sure that I should accept. I feel quite strongly that my daughter should be married from my home. But there is the matter of Lady Catherine's continuing kindness and generosity to her.*
>
> *It may seem ungracious to refuse, and I am anxious not to upset her ladyship. She has been excessively solicitous and good to Catherine, since the death of Mr Collins.*
>
> *Dear Eliza, I am very keen to discuss this question with you and have the benefit of your opinion.*
>
> *Catherine and I look forward to seeing you and Mr Darcy on Saturday. Yours etc.*
>
> *Charlotte Collins.*

Mr Darcy came into the room just as she had finished the letter, and Elizabeth was so excited telling him Charlotte's news and discussing his Aunt Catherine's amazing generosity that she quite forgot about her second letter.

Darcy was of the opinion that Charlotte should have no compunction in accepting Lady Catherine's offer to host her daughter's wedding at Rosings. "Lady Catherine is very attached to Miss Collins—and since her own daughter is, sadly, an invalid with little or no chance of being married, this is probably an opportunity for her to play a role she has always coveted," he declared. Elizabeth was inclined to agree.

"It is not as if Lucas Lodge is available to Charlotte," she said. "With the deterioration of her relationship with her sister-in-law since Sir William's death, I cannot imagine she would want to approach her."

"Indeed not," said Darcy, "and since they are to continue to live at Hunsford, they may as well be married there." The logic of this argument was so clear that Elizabeth resolved to use it to set Charlotte's mind at rest when she arrived at Pemberley.

On returning to her sitting room, Elizabeth found her second letter, unopened and lying on the floor where it had fallen.

She could not recognise the unfamiliar handwriting, which was quite strange, though not ill-educated. It was also well sealed, in the manner of a confidential communication. When she had it open, the contents—two closely written pages—puzzled her even more. Turning quickly to the last page, she checked the signature, which made no sense at all, since she knew no one by that name.

However, on reading the letter, Elizabeth was so astonished at the news it contained that she had to read it over again.

The writer, a Mrs Brewerton from Norwich, was writing, she claimed, on behalf of Mrs Lydia Wickham, who was too distraught to put pen to paper.

The writer, identifying herself as "a neighbour and family friend of the Wickhams," wrote that Mr Wickham had been seriously injured in an attack upon him by a former officer of his regiment. Though she seemed reluctant to give any details, it appeared that the assailant had borne a grudge, which he had carried with him for some years, and on meeting

Wickham unexpectedly at a club, he had attacked him most violently, putting him in bed with a number of bruises and a broken arm.

While Mrs Brewerton appeared to be quite sympathetic towards Lydia and her children, she did not seem to waste any of her concern on Wickham himself, leaving the impression that the punishment meted out to him may have been well deserved.

> *We are all very shocked and sorry for poor Mrs Wickham, who is quite bereft. I have taken the liberty of writing to you, Mrs Darcy, because I am aware she has no parents to help her and only fair weather friends, who may buzz around her socially, but are unlikely to be of much help at such a time as this. She appears not to have much in the way of savings, either.*

Wrote Mrs Brewerton, who seemed particularly well informed about the state of the Wickhams' domestic and financial affairs.

Elizabeth sighed. No doubt, she thought, Lydia, with her usual lack of discretion, must have regaled her neighbour with all the details.

Shocked and embarrassed, for she had a fair notion of the reason for the attack on Wickham, she hurried out to find Darcy. When she found him in the gallery, she also found herself somewhat tongue-tied and had to be satisfied with handing him Mrs Brewerton's letter with very little explanation—so mortified was she by the situation.

Darcy had to read the letter through twice before the full import of the words sank in.

Watching him, Elizabeth saw expressions of bewilderment, anger, and exasperation chase each other across his countenance. The look of resignation that finally settled upon it suggested that nothing he heard about the Wickhams surprised him any more.

When he finally handed it back to her, Elizabeth asked, reluctantly, if there was anything that could be done.

Darcy shrugged his shoulders, and replied, "Probably not, and even if there were, intervention by us may not be welcome. Wickham has always had a degree of arrogance quite out of proportion to his capacity. He may well resent an offer of assistance. In any event, we do not know who his assailant was and how the attack came about."

Elizabeth was silent, not knowing how to respond, as he went on, "However, it seems to me your sister Lydia and her children may need some help while he spends the next few weeks in bed!"

Elizabeth, who over the years had never failed to marvel at Darcy's generosity to the undeserving and frequently ungrateful Wickhams, wondered aloud how she could help Lydia—especially in view of the celebrations at Pemberley, which would occupy most of her time.

Darcy was quick to reassure her, "You need not worry about it, Lizzie. I shall send young Hobbs over to Norwich with some money. Perhaps you could write a note in reply to this Mrs Brewerton and one to Lydia, which he could take with him.

"I shall ask Hobbs to make some discreet enquiries about the circumstances of this assault. Wickham may well have brought it upon himself—he has always had a reckless streak. I cannot believe it was entirely unprovoked."

Elizabeth hastened to agree and thanked him for what he proposed to do. "I'm sure you are right. Wickham has probably failed to pay a debt or outraged this man in some way," she said.

"Whatever the cause, Lydia and the children cannot be left to the charity of neighbours," he said and went away to find Hobbs, having both agreed that they would not speak of this matter to anyone but Jane and the Gardiners.

Later that night, as they prepared for bed, Elizabeth thanked her husband again. "It is truly kind of you to help them, dearest; I am sure they do not deserve it."

Darcy sighed, "I know they do not, my dear, but the children are hardly to blame for the stupidity of their parents. Moreover, whatever I do is for you, Lizzie, for your peace of mind; you know that to be true, do you not?"

"I certainly do, but I know also that your generous heart discounts the hurt that you have suffered at the hands of this wilful, incorrigible couple, and you continue to help them. I am grateful and I, too, worry about her children, I do not deny it; but Darcy, I am so ashamed…" Her voice broke, and she wept.

He would not let her continue, putting his arms around her. He was very gentle but firm. "My dear Lizzie, you have nothing to be ashamed of. Wickham and Lydia are as far removed from you as they could possibly be. You are not responsible for them and need never apologise on their behalf. I cannot forget that it was my reluctance to speak out and expose his true character that permitted Wickham to present himself to you and all of your acquaintances in Hertfordshire as he did. Had I done what I should have and the truth were known, your sister's disastrous elopement may never have happened."

With her knowledge of Lydia, Elizabeth was not quite so sure, but said nothing as he continued.

"While I have no desire whatsoever to meet Wickham, and will avoid any dealings with him, I shall do whatever I can to help your sister and her children. I realise that they would be in a parlous state indeed without some help from her family. He appears to remain as wasteful and feckless as he always was, and her lack of understanding compounds their problems.

"Lizzie, I have spoken of this to your uncle, Mr Gardiner, and he agrees with me. Indeed, he helps Lydia quite regularly," he said, hoping to comfort and reassure her. As she had often done in the past, she accepted his judgement and was content.

The following day, on a mild Autumn morning, the Bingleys arrived, early as usual. While the gentlemen were out talking to Darcy's manager, Mr Grantham, Elizabeth took Jane upstairs and showed her Mrs Brewerton's letter.

Jane was even more shocked than her sister had been.

"Oh! Lizzie, how could he be so reckless, so lacking in self-control?" she cried, even as she agreed that some help had to be sent to Lydia and the children. Jane would, as she had done many times before, send Lydia some money out of her own income.

When Elizabeth explained what Darcy had done, she praised his generosity. "Lizzie, to think that for a while we actually believed all the vicious lies that Mr Wickham told about Darcy—and yet he is such a good man. We must surely have been blind!"

Elizabeth had the grace to blush even after all these years.

"We were—at least I was, Jane, blinded by prejudice and my desire to believe what Wickham, who was flattering me at every turn, was saying about Mr Darcy, who had hurt my vanity. I well recall that you were never so quick to condemn him."

Jane would not let her sister blame herself alone, reminding her that all of Meryton had been taken in by Wickham's guile.

As they wandered downstairs and out into the garden, where a large marquee was being erected on the west lawn, Jane took a letter out of her reticule and thrust it into Elizabeth's hand.

"Lizzie, I am very sorry, but Emma will not be able to join us this evening. She is very disappointed, but it seems Mr Wilson cannot make the time—he is too busy with Parliamentary business to get away."

Hurt and surprised, Elizabeth opened and read the letter, written in Emma's pretty round hand.

My dearest Mama, she wrote:

I am uncertain if Mr Wilson will be free to accompany us to Pemberley for Julian's birthday party; he has urgent business at Westminster, and since he will not hear of my travelling alone—even with my maid—I may not be able to attend, either.

Please do make my excuses to dear Aunt Lizzie and apologise to Richard and Cassy for me. I am truly sorry to miss little Lizzie's christening on Sunday!

I had been looking forward to it so much, but I'm afraid I cannot see a way in which it can be done—unless I were to disguise myself as a post boy and hide away on the mail coach! I jest, of course, but only to hide my disappointment. Victoria and Stephanie are disappointed too.

I hope you will enjoy yourselves hugely. I shall be thinking of you every minute of the day and wishing I were there with you.

Your loving daughter,
Emma.

"Dearest Jane, I can see there is something wrong. What have you been keeping from me? Is Emma not happy in her marriage?"

At first, Jane seemed unable to speak. She was silent, but though there were no words, her eyes spoke volumes—showing pain and hurt.

Elizabeth took her aside, into a quiet grove, where they were well protected from interruption, and sat her down.

"Now Jane, I cannot bear to see you so unhappy and continue in ignorance. I must know if our dear Emma has a problem. Please, tell me what is wrong? Can we help in any way?"

Jane's eyes were filled with tears, and when her sister embraced her, the pent up feelings, the fears and anxieties, which she had shared with no one, not even her beloved Bingley, poured out.

As Elizabeth listened, unable at first to say a word so stunned was she by what she was hearing, Jane told of her daughter's unhappy marriage.

It seemed that Mr David Wilson had turned out to be both a jealous, domineering husband and an ambitious politician—a combination devoutly to be avoided.

As Jane told it, Emma had not been married long before she had felt the weight of both conditions; and yet, she had said nothing for years. "Lizzie, I cannot tell you how much I have suffered since she has told me what her life is like. She is careful not to let him find out that she speaks of it to me, lest he should become so enraged that he would forbid her to visit us. I cannot even speak of it to Bingley because Emma does not want her father to know. It would kill him to discover how unhappy she is.

"Yet, I have known since last Easter when she came to us while her husband was away in Europe. Lizzie, she would be totally miserable were it not for her two girls. Victoria and Stephanie are her only consolation. She lives for them."

Jane could hide her grief no longer. "Oh Lizzie," she sobbed, "I cannot think why this should have happened to our dear, beautiful Emma."

Elizabeth could hardly believe her ears. Even as she tried to console her sister, she could not understand how she could have hidden her sorrow and that of her daughter all these months.

The sound of a carriage coming up the drive heralded the arrival of more guests, and the sisters had to postpone the rest of their discussion. Moving towards the house, they saw it was Richard and Cassandra, with their children. Elizabeth hurried towards them and Jane, following slowly, could not help envying their joy.

Seeing the delight on all their faces as they alighted and embraced Darcy and Elizabeth and watching the carefree children run out onto the lawn almost broke her heart as she remembered her daughter, alone in London but for her two little girls and a houseful of servants.

Once everyone had exchanged greetings—some twice over—Cassandra and Richard brought their two boys, Edward and Darcy, over to meet Jane. They were both lively and affectionate children.

"We felt Elizabeth Jane was a little too young to come to the party tonight," Cassy explained, promising that her little daughter would be ready to appear at her christening tomorrow.

Richard was clearly proud of his two sons. Jane expressed surprise at how much they had grown since their last meeting. They were certainly good looking and well behaved children, and their parents beamed with pleasure as Jane hugged them both. Seeing their happiness, Jane fought to hold back her tears.

Why, she wondered, had her Emma not married someone safe and kind like Richard, instead of the ambitious Mr David Wilson. It had been considered a great match, at the time.

If only the truth were known.

Jane had spent a miserable summer, unable to confide in anyone—neither her husband nor her sister—because Emma had sworn her to secrecy. Fearful that her husband would discover what he would deem to be her disloyalty and forbid her to see her parents, Emma had begged her mother not to speak of her problems to anyone. Jane had heeded her pleas, until today. Forced to explain to her dearest sister the reason for Emma's absence, she had not been able to conceal the truth any longer.

Elizabeth returned to take them indoors and, putting an arm around her sister, she whispered as they walked up to the house, "Darcy and Bingley are riding out to Kympton later; that will give us time to talk of this again."

Perhaps for the first time in her life, Jane did not really look forward to a tête-à-tête with her sister. She was afraid Emma would be very upset.

Later, after luncheon, she was secretly relieved when the Gardiners arrived, together with Emily, her husband James Courtney, and their children—Elizabeth, William, and Jessica.

Their arrival kept Elizabeth occupied, while Emily, who had not seen Jane in several months, lost no time in engaging her cousin in conversation. Jane was eager to hear how Emily's children were getting on, and Emily, who had been blessed with three talented and good-natured children, was happy to enlighten her. Her natural modesty would not let her boast about their achievements, but she was happy to relate that Elizabeth, her eldest, was very bright and studious and could sing as well, while William and little Jessica had both shown an interest and ability in music.

"It is quite diverting to watch them help each other when they are practising together. But I am really pleased that William shows what his teacher calls a genuine talent, rather than mere precociousness," Emily explained, adding that Georgianna Grantley had also heard him play at a Pemberley children's concert and been very impressed by his performance.

It seemed to Jane as if she could not get away from all these happy, loving parents and their darling children while her own granddaughters and their mother languished unhappily in London.

Which was why the arrival of her son Jonathan and his wife Amelia-Jane with their three children brought so much pleasure. The warmth of their greetings and the joy of seeing her dear grandchildren brought some comfort. "Anne-Marie, how you've grown—quite the young lady, is she not?" said Jane, and everyone agreed that she was.

While her brother Charles was very like their grandfather—cheerful and friendly—young Anne-Marie Bingley was showing evidence of the beauty and poise that had characterised her mother at a very young age.

Turning to little Teresa, who was several years younger than her siblings, Jane picked her up in her arms.

This little girl was very precious, since they had nearly lost her at birth. Still rather frail, though remarkably bright and active, Teresa was her grandmother's favourite. Frequently, when her parents had to be away in London—when the Parliament was sitting—Teresa would stay with her at Ashford Park, while the older children remained at home with their governess. Consequently, a close and loving bond had grown between them.

Meanwhile, Mrs Gardiner, having spent the required amount of time with all her lively grandchildren, accepted her niece's invitation to rest awhile upstairs. There Elizabeth took the opportunity to acquaint her aunt with the troubles of Wickham and Lydia. Even Mrs Gardiner, who, like Darcy, was usually unsurprised by the behaviour of this recalcitrant pair, was shocked by Mrs Brewerton's letter and as censorious as Jane had been. She did confirm, however, that she and Mr Gardiner agreed with Darcy that not to help Lydia would probably leave them to the mercy of money lenders and pawn brokers, who would only drag them further down into the mire and damage their own families, as well.

Elizabeth accepted, without argument, the truth of this contention. "I accept all of that, dear Aunt, but it pains me to have to help them again and again while knowing that they are not only totally ungrateful, but given any opportunity, would not hesitate to abuse Mr Darcy or myself," she complained, and it was only Mrs Gardiner's unfailing good humour that saved her from sinking into a mood of depression.

The situation would not improve when Hobbs, returning later that week, reported that an unpaid gambling debt had been the cause of the fracas that left Wickham incapacitated.

When Jane joined them, Elizabeth asked for tea to be served.

Mrs Gardiner, who was their closest confidante, was informed that Emma was unlikely to be present at the weekend's celebrations. When she expressed her disappointment, Jane quite deliberately avoided the more harrowing details of her daughter's situation, referring only to the inability of her busy husband to accompany them.

Quite unsuspicious, Mrs Gardiner was disinclined to be critical of Mr Wilson. "It is quite understandable, dear Jane, that an ambitious young Parliamentarian may not consider an eleven-year-old's birthday party an essential part of his social life," she said. "However, it is such a pity the problem was not known to us earlier; Mr Gardiner was in London until Thursday morning, and he could easily have accommodated Emma and the two girls in his carriage, since he was travelling alone. It would have been quite simple for them to have stayed overnight with us and travelled to Pemberley today."

She genuinely regretted the missed opportunity, but Elizabeth, meeting Jane's eyes, realised that it would have been of no use. David Wilson would not have permitted Emma and the children to make the journey to Pemberley without him.

Even as Mrs Gardiner spoke, a hard, cold knot of fear had begun to establish itself in Elizabeth's mind. It was the kind of fear that she had felt once before—when the news of Lydia's elopement had reached her at Lambton, a combination of dreadful news and the realisation of one's total helplessness to influence the consequences.

If only Darcy could be told! She was sure he would know what to do, but Jane would not hear of it. Emma, she said, would never forgive her if her father discovered the truth. Poor, dear Emma and poor Jane! How deep must their suffering be? The sheer hopelessness of the situation horrified Elizabeth, who could see no way out for her niece, short of the destruction of her marriage.

The task of keeping the bad news from their aunt was made somewhat easier by the fact that Mrs Gardiner had some good news to impart. Her youngest son, Robert—who had gone out to the eastern colonies some years ago to work for one of the British mercantile firms—was returning to England. He was considering an offer of a position at the firm's head office in Liverpool.

Mrs Gardiner had brought with her his recent letters, which she read to her nieces with much satisfaction. Robert wrote of his success at two professional examinations as well as his plans to return to England in the Spring. Though it was more than six months away, Mrs Gardiner could not hide her excitement. Both Jane and Elizabeth were delighted for her, knowing she had felt her son's absence keenly.

Hardly had they finished congratulating their aunt on her excellent news, than Elizabeth's maid, Susan, ran upstairs to warn of another arrival. Being new to Pemberley, Susan had never seen one of the splendid vehicles from Rosings before.

"Oh ma'am, there is a great big fancy carriage, with four beautiful horses, coming up the drive," she cried, and in one voice the ladies responded, "That has to be the carriage from Rosings bringing Charlotte and Catherine," as they went across to the windows to look out at the approaching grand equipage.

Elizabeth and Jane went down to welcome them. They remarked not only on how well they both looked, but how much like Charlotte her daughter Catherine had grown. She had also acquired an enviable level of self-possession during her years at Rosings. Congratulations were in order, and these were received by Catherine with a remarkable degree of dignified restraint.

Jane and Lizzie, who could still recall with some amusement how they had reacted with almost unbearable delight on similar occasions in their own lives, were quite amazed at Catherine's lack of excitement. Remarking upon this to Cassandra, Elizabeth wondered aloud, "Could it perhaps have something to do with the fact that Mr Harrison is a clergyman?"

When Cassy answered, "It has probably more to do with the fact that Mr Harrison is a rather unexciting clergyman, Mama," her mother could scarcely restrain her laughter, especially when Cassy pointed out that their cousin Emily was certainly not similarly encumbered.

"No indeed," Elizabeth said. "James Courtney is popular with his parishioners and has never been considered boring." She then begged Cassandra to "make Catherine feel at home."

Cassy smiled. "Really, Mama, coming from Rosings to Pemberley should hardly present a problem to Catherine. We are far less preoccupied with the niceties of social etiquette than is Lady Catherine de Bourgh," she declared, as she went away to attend to her children.

The gentlemen, having returned from Kympton, had changed and were ready to go downstairs when a great commotion in the hall heralded the arrival of Colonel Fitzwilliam, Caroline, and their children. Isabella, the eldest, was a gentle, demure young lady with a fair share of beauty, but so unassuming that she was often overlooked. Her brother, David, was away at boarding school, but Amy and James, the youngest Fitzwilliams, were energetic children accustomed to treating Pemberley as a second home. They raced up and down the wide staircases and long corridors, quite oblivious to the treasures that surrounded them.

When Elizabeth and Darcy came down to welcome them, Caroline apologised for her children, but she was assured that they did no harm. Amy and James stopped in the middle of their play to affectionately embrace and greet their aunt and uncle. They were lively but delightful children, and neither Darcy nor Elizabeth minded their presence, although the maids, carrying tea trays laden with fine china, had been seen to flinch as they flew past on the stairs.

Colonel Fitzwilliam greeted Darcy, eager to discuss the political news, which his father-in-law, Mr Gardiner, had brought on his return from London.

Still gloating over the demise of the Conservatives, who had managed only one elected term under Peel, Fitzwilliam was triumphant that the popular Palmerston was back in power and in charge of the Foreign Office. He had endeared himself to the liberal middle classes with defiant statements of support for the Italian cause and condemnation of despotism in

Europe. Fitzwilliam hoped also for great things from him at home. "There is no doubt that Palmerston will be Prime Minister one day, Darcy. We can at least expect some progressive legislation soon."

Darcy was less confident. He reminded Fitzwilliam that Palmerston was once a Tory and "more of a Whig aristocrat than your modern democrat," he said, but Fitzwilliam was not to be denied.

The arrival of Anthony Tate and his wife Rebecca, both of whom took an active interest in politics, released Darcy to attend to his guests and provided Fitzwilliam with an even larger audience for his views. Having once been in Parliament, he could claim to have an opinion on all matters of interest. Indeed, so sincere and profound was his conviction on causes such as the ten-hour day or compulsory education for children, one could be forgiven for asking why he had ever retired from Parliament. But that was another story.

On this occasion, with Richard Gardiner and Jonathan Bingley as well as the Tates—owners of *The Review* and *The Tribune*—agreeing with him, Fitzwilliam was in full flight when the band in the marquee struck up a lively tune and demanded the attention of all present.

Julian, whose birthday had occasioned the celebration, was suddenly shy and had to be persuaded by Cassandra, his sister, to step forward and accept the congratulations of his guests.

His parents, whose lives had been devastated by the death of their elder son William, had promised themselves when Julian was born that they would not be excessively protective or possessive of him. They had endeavoured to give their son as much freedom as possible.

This liberality was probably responsible for the fact that Julian had a disposition as open and amiable as one could hope for in a young boy; his pleasing manners made him a general favourite. More mature than one would expect at his age, he seemed to take a greater interest in the estate and the people who lived and worked there than William had done, which was a matter of great satisfaction to his father. Cassandra, who had learnt a great deal from her father and his steward while Julian was still a baby, had made a point of teaching him all she knew. That he had no brothers and sisters at home had served to enhance his relationship with his parents, whose company and advice he sought often. They, in turn, gave him all the care and love he needed.

Though the years that had passed since William's death had not assuaged the pain Elizabeth felt, Julian had brought much lightness and pleasure into their lives, transforming the sombre atmosphere at Pemberley. Unlike William, Julian was eager to go to college—and in preparation, plans were afoot for him to be enrolled next year at a public school near Oxford, recommended by Dr Grantley.

With a perfect Autumn evening, a gathering of their favourite people, and all arrangements flowing smoothly, Elizabeth relaxed, confident that this evening at Pemberley would be one to remember with pleasure.

Just one shadow remained—the happiness of her sister Jane had been so deeply compromised by the situation of her daughter, Emma, that it preyed upon her mind. If only, thought Elizabeth, if only things could have been different.

While Julian's birthday party was in progress, with all the delights that children look forward to on such occasions—ample food, games and novelties, and, because it was also Guy Fawkes Night, a promise of fireworks to follow—the adults, who were staying to dinner, watched on indulgently or sat in groups on the lawn. They were all waiting for that magic moment when it would be dark enough to start the fireworks and light the Guy who sat waiting atop a bonfire in the lower meadow.

Darcy's steward had just indicated that they were ready to begin when a carriage was seen crossing the bridge and coming up the drive.

It was not a familiar vehicle—being modest though fashionably modern—and the late evening light glancing off its windows concealed the identity of the occupants until it drove right up to the house. A gentleman, who looked vaguely familiar to Elizabeth, alighted and helped Emma Wilson out, followed by her two little girls and their nurse.

Delighted, Elizabeth almost ran to her niece and Jane was not far behind. "Emma! How wonderful that you could come after all."

Elizabeth embraced her niece, and as she released her, Emma turned to the gentleman who stood quietly to one side and said, "Aunt Lizzie, this is Mr James Wilson, my brother-in-law, whose kindness has enabled us to be here today. When he heard that my husband was unable to accompany us, owing to his work at Westminster, Mr Wilson offered to bring us in his carriage," she explained, "and we are very grateful to Uncle James, are we not my darlings?"

Both her daughters indicated complete agreement with their mother.

Jane, who had arrived at their side, embraced her daughter and grand-daughters before turning to thank Mr Wilson, but he was unwilling to accept so much gratitude, insisting that it had been no trouble at all. "Believe me, Mrs Bingley, I had to travel to Derby tomorrow for a professional consultation with a client—all I did was leave a day earlier. It was entirely my pleasure."

Mr Darcy and Bingley had joined them and after greetings were exchanged, James Wilson was easily persuaded to stay to dinner. A quiet, cultured man, perhaps thirty-six years of age, well spoken, with an interest in public affairs, he was soon drawn into conversation with Fitzwilliam and Anthony Tate, providing them with news from Westminster. He was well informed on a variety of subjects.

There was a great deal of interest in the new houses of Parliament, which had replaced the old buildings destroyed by fire in 1834. James, who had been in London at the time of the fire, shared memories with Fitzwilliam and delighted Darcy with his knowledge of the work of Turner, whose paintings had immortalised the great conflagration.

Mr Wilson praised the new buildings, designed by the architect Charles Barry, pronouncing them to be elegant and impressive. "The Lords will soon be moving into their new premises, but regrettably, the new House of Commons is unlikely to be ready for a few more years," he said, agreeing with Mr Gardiner that the fire had probably hastened the demise of the old wooden buildings, which were in need of replacement anyway.

He won even more approval when he expressed support for the type of commitment to building communities that Mr Darcy and Fitzwilliam had been advocating for years and pleased Mr Gardiner with a clearly argued case for the promotion of freer trade between nations.

A Whig and a Reformist, he revealed that he had nevertheless agreed with Peel's abolition of the Corn Laws, arguing that Britain's advantage in being a trading and colonial nation would be lost by support for the extreme protectionist policies advocated by the Conservatives.

"You are a man after my own heart, sir. You must attend a meeting of our reform group when you are next in the area," said Mr Gardiner, plainly delighted to find a Member of Parliament who supported his views so wholeheartedly.

"Emma's brother Jonathan Bingley is a member; he can provide you with whatever information you need. I do hope we will see you at one of our meetings soon," Mr Gardiner added, and James Wilson was clearly surprised at the level of interest shown in his views, promising to follow up the invitation.

His kindness to Emma and her girls had already marked him as a favourite with the family. By the end of the evening, he had been pronounced a gentleman of the highest distinction and invited to dine with at least four of the families present whenever he was next in Derbyshire.

Jane, finding him beside her as they watched the bonfire in the meadow, thanked him once again for bringing Emma to Pemberley. "Mr Wilson, James, you must let me thank you for your kindness to Emma and to me, in bringing her and her little girls here today. I cannot begin to tell you how much it has meant to me and to all of us. We were so disappointed when we heard she was unable to come; you have made such a difference to us all today. I thank you from the bottom of my heart."

Jane spoke quickly, and James Wilson was a little disconcerted, but seeing tears in her eyes, he stopped and taking her hand, said, "Mrs Bingley, I want you to know that I would do anything to ensure that Emma and her children are happy. When I called to see my mother, who as you know is recently widowed, I found them all looking very unhappy. It was my mother who revealed the cause of their disappointment and, immediately, I saw that I could help. Pray, do not imagine that it has inconvenienced me in any way at all.

"I have heard so much about Pemberley—this beautiful house and its great estate—it has been a great pleasure to visit here and meet so many members of this distinguished family. Believe me, the pleasure has been all mine," he said, adding with a smile, "so, in truth, you have nothing to thank me for. Indeed, I am in your debt and Mrs Darcy's for a wonderful evening and such generous hospitality," he said with so much grace and sincerity that Jane was quite overwhelmed. Not for the first time did she wish that her daughter had married the elder and not the younger Mr Wilson.

Not long afterwards, he was preparing to leave and, though pressed to stay, insisted that he had to be at a meeting in Derby very early on the following day. Darcy and Elizabeth invited him to return and dine with them, while Fitzwilliam urged him most cordially to visit them when he was next in Derbyshire.

"Occasionally, I miss the cut and thrust of Parliament and would welcome some news straight from the horse's mouth," he joked, and Mr Wilson said he would look forward to their next meeting.

"I may even have some good news for you on the Public Health Bill," he said as he took his leave of Fitzwilliam, who had declared that it was a long overdue measure and a great scandal that sanitation was left to the whim of slum landlords.

Before he bade them all goodnight, James Wilson sought out Emma and arranged to call for her and her daughters after breakfast on Monday.

Elizabeth unwittingly overheard the end of their conversation:

"Are you sure we can stay until Monday?" Emma asked anxiously, to which he replied, "Of course, my mother will explain it all. David knows you are in safe hands. There will be no trouble, Emma. I give you my word."

Emma smiled and gave him her hand, which he kissed lightly, and minutes later, he was gone, leaving Elizabeth wondering how much Mr Wilson knew of Emma's troubled situation.

As she watched his carriage drive away, Elizabeth recalled a conversation with Jane, sometime before Emma's wedding. She had expressed a distinct preference for Mr James Wilson over her intended son-in-law, David, and when Elizabeth had queried her attitude, she had hastily produced a reason—it was simply that he reminded her of Bingley.

But it was not as simple as it seemed.

Elizabeth remembered her words clearly, as if they had been spoken yesterday, "Lizzie, not since that Summer when Mr Bingley came to Netherfield have I met so kind, amiable, and modest a young man as Mr James Wilson," she had said, with so much certainty that Elizabeth had been convinced that Emma was marrying the wrong Mr Wilson.

Now, almost ten years later, it seemed she was right. Unfortunately, it gave her no satisfaction at all.

CHAPTER ONE

Emma

AS EMMA WILSON TRAVELLED back to London, her mind was in turmoil. As for her heart, well, that had been left behind with her family and friends at Pemberley. Her two daughters, still weary from enjoying themselves so thoroughly, had fallen asleep. Their nurse, equally exhausted as her little charges, had nodded off as well.

While she was herself rather tired, she had stayed awake, trying to read, but the movement of the carriage would not let her concentrate.

Sitting across from her, James Wilson was immersed in his papers, which he had explained related to his client's business and were very dull indeed. Dull they may have been, but Mr Wilson applied himself to their study most assiduously, Emma noticed. There was little left for her to do but contemplate the passing countryside.

As twilight overtook them, even this was difficult, and Emma was wondering what she could do to pass the time when her brother-in-law put his documents away and said cheerfully, "It is too dark to read, so we may as well talk."

He changed his seat to sit beside her, and Emma, surprised and pleased, said, "What would you like to talk about?"

She half expected some polite enquiry about the children, and she was quite surprised when he said, without hesitation, "Tell me about Pemberley and your friends and family. I enjoyed very much meeting them on Saturday, but there was so little time and so many interesting people."

Emma laughed. "I thought you would have remembered most of them. They were all at my wedding," she said.

James looked abashed as he admitted that he was not very good at recalling names, and anyway, there had been such a crowd at that wedding, he would never have met them all.

"I was busy being best man, remember? I do recall Mr and Mrs Darcy very well—they are such a handsome couple—but hardly anyone else, except your parents and your brother Jonathan, of course. I had also met Fitzwilliam at Westminster when he was in Parliament some years ago; he was a member of the Reform Group. But you must tell me about the others. It is quite clear they all love you very much. They were obviously delighted when you arrived with Victoria and Stephanie. I was very glad I had taken you. I believe I acquired some immediate popularity with your family," he said lightly.

Emma smiled and acknowledged her debt to him, thanking him again for his kindness. "I cannot tell you how much joy you gave us, especially to my dear parents, who had quite given up hope of seeing us there."

James Wilson begged her not to thank him for what had been a genuine pleasure and asked only that she tell him more about the people he had met at Pemberley. "I can truthfully say I have never met so many attractive and interesting people in one place before," he declared.

Relating some of their stories, Emma was surprised at how much he had noticed in so short a time—like Fitzwilliam's obsession with Palmerston, Rebecca Tate's preoccupation with education for girls, the sound common sense of Mr Gardiner, and how deeply Richard and Cassandra loved each other.

"Theirs must have been a great love story," he said, and Emma agreed.

"What made it perfect was that it brought great happiness to everyone in the family, especially their parents, who are the closest of friends. Yes, Richard and Cassy are special," she said, a little wistfully. "Until their marriage, Pemberley had not shaken off the gloom of William's death. Even the birth of Julian, a few years later, did not seem to help much. William remained in all our thoughts each time we visited Pemberley. Aunt Lizzie certainly had not recovered from the loss; it was as if she would never stop grieving after losing him so suddenly.

"The wedding of Richard and Cassandra was the first occasion on which we noticed a change. They were so much in love and so keen for everyone to share in their happiness that it seemed to splash over all of us like the water from a fountain, and it brought back some of the magic that had been lost.

"I shall never forget watching them walk from the church through the crowds of people, frequently stopping to thank particular persons and then standing with their parents on the steps of Pemberley House. I thought at the time, 'Today is the day on which we can let go of our dear William at last and share the happiness of Cassy and Richard.' So you see, they are a very special couple and mean a lot to us."

"Indeed, I can and I understand why. I knew of William's death, of course, but I did not know how deeply it had affected the family," James said quietly.

"He was everyone's favourite—a very gentle boy, and with so much talent. He wanted to be a concert pianist. My parents were distraught, and Jonathan blamed himself for not having stopped the boys from riding out that day. You see, the Fitzwilliams lost young Edward on the same day. Oh, it was a dreadful time for all of us!"

Noting his grave expression, she stopped and said, "I did warn you they were not all happy stories."

"And your story, Emma, is it one of the happy ones?" he asked, quietly. Taken aback by his question, she was embarrassed and tongue-tied.

Seeing her discomfiture, he was immediately contrite, "I'm sorry, I did not mean to pry. It was not unkindly meant. If I have offended you, Emma, I apologise."

Emma found her voice in time to assure him that she was certainly not offended. How could she be? "I know you were not intending to pry, and I do thank you for your concern, but there is very little to tell. It was not very long after the deaths of William and Edward. I was very young, very sad, and rather lonely in London. I fell in love and married David. At the time, I believed I was the happiest girl in London. Everyone told me I was the most fortunate."

He persisted, though gently, taking her hand in his. "And are you happy now?" he asked.

One of the children stirred and glancing quickly at her, Emma gently withdrew her hand from his—but in that instant, meeting his eyes, she knew she could not lie. Uneasy, she bit her lip and shook her head.

His entire expression changed as her meaning sank in. Looking most concerned, he turned to her and said, "Emma, is there anything I can do to help?"

When she said nothing, he continued, "It grieves me that you have joined our family and you are unhappy. I would certainly like to help. I know you cannot speak of it now, but at a more appropriate time and place, will you tell me about it?" He sounded anxious and concerned.

Looking directly at him, but unwilling to speak lest the nurse or one of the children should hear, she nodded and said, "Thank you, yes," in a voice that was hardly audible.

Darkness had fallen as they reached the outskirts of London. The streets were busier and noisier. James returned to his place beside the window opposite Emma, but before he moved, placed his hand on hers to reassure her. Without understanding why, Emma felt she was not as alone as she had been before. While nothing had happened to relieve her situation in any way, the merest glimmer of hope, which had resulted from their brief conversation, seemed to lift a weight from her heart as the carriage pulled up before the house in Mayfair.

They had travelled as expeditiously as possible, breaking journey only for a meal and to rest the horses, arriving around dinner time.

Mrs Wilson, who was entertaining a couple of old friends from Bath— a Colonel and Mrs Barclay—welcomed them home. She was happy to see them, especially Victoria and Stephanie, who were her particular favourites.

She informed them that David had not yet returned, having gone out directly after tea with another Member of Parliament. "I assume he will be back for dinner. We shall wait half an hour for him, no more," she said for the benefit of the hovering servants.

Emma was genuinely pleased, and the relief she felt lightened her manner as she greeted her mother-in-law. James Wilson noted that she had lost the look of apprehension that he had seen on her face as they approached the house. There was no doubt in his mind that she was relieved at not having to face her husband upon arrival, grateful to have time to prepare herself for their meeting. Clearly, she feared his disapproval.

James could only guess at the reasons for her trepidation. Neither his brother nor their mother had ever spoken of any problems between David and his wife. But, having observed his sister-in-law's demeanour, her happy, relaxed manner when she was at Pemberley with her family and friends, and her reluctant confession of unhappiness as they journeyed home, James Wilson was convinced that something was wrong, and he was quite determined to discover what it was.

Since the death of his father earlier that year, he had inherited not just his father's legal firm and the house in which his mother and his brother's family continued to live at his invitation, but he had also acquired the status of the head of a professional family, with an enviable reputation for probity and public service.

Recent reports of some of his brother's social activities had given him cause for concern, and he had intended to talk to David about it. The realisation that Emma was unhappy made it obligatory that he should do something about it.

Stephanie and Victoria were so tired from travelling that they had to be taken upstairs, bathed, fed, and put to bed at once.

Emma took some time to refresh herself and change before returning to join the others. As she had expected, James had been persuaded by his mother to stay to dinner. There was still no sign of her husband, and Mrs Wilson, becoming rather impatient, ordered that the meal be served.

When they went in to dinner, James, having taken his mother in and helped her into her seat, returned to escort Emma and then sat between her and Colonel Barclay's wife. The colonel applied himself to entertaining Mrs Wilson with tales of mutual friends in Bath.

When Mrs Barclay was also drawn into conversation with his mother, James Wilson took the opportunity to remind Emma of her promise to talk to him about her present problems. When she fell silent, he pressed her for an acknowledgement, "My dear Emma, I cannot help you unless I know what makes you unhappy. It is not just for your sake, but for Victoria and Stephanie, too; they should not grow up in an atmosphere of mistrust."

She was immediately defensive. "I have said nothing of mistrust! You must not assume things."

Chastened by the swiftness of her rebuke, he apologised. "I am sorry, but there you see it. Unless I know the cause of the problem, I am more likely to make inaccurate assumptions."

The servants were clearing away the dishes before placing platters of fruit and cheese on the table. Taking advantage of the movement around them, he appealed to her, "Will you at least agree to talk to me about it? You can decide how much you want to tell me."

Emma could not avoid his eyes, and his sincerity was so compelling that she gave in. "Yes, yes of course, but I shall need a little time."

"Good, you can have all the time you want, Emma. I shall make some arrangements next week," he said, clearly pleased.

After dinner, Emma asked to be excused, pleading tiredness, and Mrs Wilson was sympathetic. "Of course you may Emma, my dear. Indeed, it is most inconsiderate of David to be so late. I cannot imagine what he is about."

She was about to go upstairs when a light carriage was heard in the street. It stopped at their door, and presently David walked in. He appeared slightly unsteady, but cheerful enough.

He greeted them all, kissed his mother and went to help himself to the port. Unhappy with the bottle on the tray, he sent the footman off to fetch one of his favourites from the cellar.

Meanwhile, addressing both James and Emma, he demanded to know if they had enjoyed their journey to Pemberley. "Is Mr Darcy still as proud and arrogant as ever?" he asked. "And did you meet Colonel Fitzwilliam? He has an uncommonly beautiful wife. God only knows what she sees in him."

Seeing Emma's look of panic, for she knew this was his way of starting an argument—one that only he could win—James Wilson intervened to say that Darcy had seemed not in the least arrogant. "He was the perfect host, and indeed the evening turned out to be most interesting and pleasant. Pemberley is one of those great houses that implies pride and arrogance in its owners, but I did not find it so. Both Mr and Mrs Darcy were most hospitable, and I have been invited back to dine with them soon."

David's raised eyebrows expressed his opinion. "Have you indeed? They must prefer you to myself."

Emma could not remain silent at this suggestion, "That is not fair David, we have been asked many times, but recently, you have been too busy to accept."

Mrs Wilson, tired of the bickering, interrupted, "David, you work too hard. You should get away from the city more often. Colonel Barclay has a splendid place in Bath; I am sure he would love to have you both, wouldn't you, Colonel?"

This led to a further discussion on the attractions of Bath, which held no interest for Emma, who slipped out of the room and went quietly upstairs while her husband continued to argue. Soon afterwards, she heard the front door close and James's carriage proceeding down the road. He had an apartment in Brunswick Square conveniently situated close to the Inns of Court, where he worked when Parliament was not sitting.

Emma had been there once or twice with her mother-in-law, who was always giving her son items of household linen and other equipment to ensure the comfort of his bachelor existence.

She recalled a linen press and a chest of drawers, which Mrs Wilson had insisted he needed to have installed in his dressing room, despite his protestations that it would only clutter up the place.

"My mother insists that I need all these things when, in fact, all I need is a good butler, a cook, and a manservant. I am fortunate that I have all three. In fact, I inherited my man, Watson, from my father; he is so good, I scarcely need give any instructions at all—he anticipates everything!" James had claimed when they had met a few days later and she had teased him, asking if he was finding the linen press useful.

Even in those early days, she had wondered at her ability to engage in light-hearted banter with her husband's elder brother in a manner that she could never contemplate with David. His capacity to turn every conversation into an argument, one he had to win, whatever the cost, had soon crushed her enthusiasm for trivial chat or playful teasing.

The week after their journey to Pemberley, Mrs Wilson surprised her daughter-in-law at breakfast one morning with the news that they were to make a visit to the family property in Kent. "There are some things of Mr Wilson's which James thinks I should have moved to London before we close the place for the Winter. I agree with him, and I should be very glad of your company, Emma," she said and added, "David is busy, as usual, but James will accompany us. He has promised to let me know this evening if we can travel on Friday."

Emma knew at once that James had "arranged," as he had promised, an "appropriate time and place." Knowing the old house in Kent well, he could not have chosen better. She agreed immediately to accompany Mrs Wilson, adding that she hoped the weather would remain fine.

Later that day, when his mother was resting upstairs and Emma was reading to her daughters, James Wilson arrived unexpectedly, only staying long enough to take a cup of tea with them before rushing away. He did, however, leave a message for his mother. "Please tell my mother that everything has been arranged for Friday's journey to Kent—it is best that we return on Sunday afternoon. We shall have to take her carriage—mine is not big enough."

Emma asked, "How many shall we be?"

"Just the three of us and mother's maid, of course. She goes nowhere without her," he said as he apologised and flew out the door on his way to a meeting in the city, leaving her smiling at his enthusiasm.

After he had gone, Emma contemplated her situation. Once again, she felt as if her isolation was being opened up and her unhappiness was relieved, just a little.

She had deliberately held back from her parents the true state of her ten-year marriage. It was not only because she had not wanted to break their hearts—she knew what the truth would do to her father. There was some of her pride involved, as well.

The decision to marry David Wilson had been hers alone. She had consulted no one, not even her brother Jonathan.

David was the good-looking, ambitious one of the two Wilson brothers. She had known him first as a boy, when their families became acquainted; he had been at Winchester and only came home for holidays. Then he had gone away to Cambridge and had spent some time in Europe before returning to London. It was not long after the deaths of William and Edward had devastated their family.

David had just entered Parliament and when Emma and he met again in London; he was the most sought after young man in town.

Emma Bingley's beauty had been universally admired. Like her mother, she was a rather reserved young woman, with a reputation for graciousness and gentility. David Wilson had courted her assiduously throughout the season with extravagant compliments, saying on one memorable occasion, when they had met at a ball, at which he had monopolised her, "My God, Emma, you were always pretty, but now, you are beautiful!"

They had met often during the months they had spent in London and had a good deal of fun together. His parents seemed to like her and had invited her to stay at their country house in Kent. When he proposed, she had had no reservations about accepting him.

James Wilson, who was some seven years older than David, had occasionally been present, but had seemed more interested in the company of her parents, she recalled. David used to think him dull and given to good works. "He takes his position as the eldest in the family very seriously indeed," he had said.

That there was some truth in his description, Emma could not deny. James did take his position in the family seriously, especially after his father's death. As for being dull, there was no more truth in that accusation than in several others her husband was wont to throw around, as she was to learn later.

More recently, she had realised how utterly unfair David had been to his brother.

At Pemberley, in the days after Julian's party, much discussion centred around Mr James Wilson, their unexpected guest.

Not many people had paid much attention to David Wilson's quiet, serious-minded brother, whose legal and Parliamentary work kept him occupied for most of the year. When he could get away from London, he was known to prefer Standish Park—his family property in Kent—which accounted for his unfamiliarity with the Pemberley families, who had seen him rarely since Emma's wedding.

His sudden appearance at Pemberley with Emma had ignited their interest. Apart from his generosity in conveying Emma and her daughters to the party, for which he was universally praised, Elizabeth was inclined to agree with Jane's original judgement, which was now supported by several of the gentlemen.

Fitzwilliam recalled meeting him as a much younger, new member of Parliament, during the heady days of the passage of the Reform Bills. "I remember him as intelligent and thoughtful even in those days; he made a quite remarkable speech on the need for wider representation in Parliament as part of Britain's claim to be a democracy. Many of the older Tories were horrified."

"And so were a few old Whigs, I bet," quipped Anthony Tate. "I was most impressed by his arguments against excessive protection. I hope he will not object if I borrow some of his ideas for my next editorial on the subject."

Darcy, who gave approbation rarely, and then not in a fulsome way, was generous with his praise. "In the short time he spent at Pemberley, I found him to be a man of sound principles and good judgement. Even better, he was not opinionated and arrogant—and having once suffered from that condition myself, I am quick to diagnose the contagion in others. Mr James Wilson is, happily, free of such folly. He is certainly the kind of man with whom I would be happy to be better acquainted."

"Darcy, this is high praise indeed," said Fitzwilliam.

"Indeed, it is," said Mr Gardiner, "and I am inclined to agree with Mr Darcy. I shall certainly look forward to our next meeting."

Listening to the gentlemen, Elizabeth was amazed at the general approval that James had received, but her sister was not surprised. "I have said all along, Lizzie, that while he could not boast of the good looks and popularity of his brother, James Wilson is by far the better man. I have not changed my mind."

It was something she had said to Bingley on one occasion, but it gave her no joy to know that she was right.

A week later, a letter from Emma reached her mother just as she was setting out to visit her Aunt Gardiner. Elizabeth was also expected to join them, and Jane decided she would take the letter along and read it with her sister.

She was reluctant to open it in the presence of her aunt, who was not as yet privy to Emma's troubles. However, she need have had no fears on that score, for the letter contained not a single word of complaint. It was filled with Emma's delightful memories of her visit to Pemberley.

Reading it together, Elizabeth and Jane marvelled at the lightness of its tone. There was never a hint of her present unhappiness or a twinge of self-pity. Instead, she revelled in the pleasure, unexpected as it had been until the day before, of being able to visit Pemberley and see them all.

Dearest mama, she wrote:

> *There is nothing I wanted more than to see all of you, especially you and papa, but also Aunt Lizzie and Cassy and Richard, and all the others. I have missed them all so much.*
>
> *If there is one thing that I dislike about living in London, it is that it is so distant from the places where so much of my heart is held hostage by my dear, dear family.*
>
> *I should have been truly miserable at missing Julian's party and little Elizabeth Jane's christening, and I would have done, were it not for the kindness of Mr James Wilson and my dear mother-in-law.*
>
> *It was she who had whispered to him that we were very disappointed about not going to Pemberley, on account of David's work, and so brought about his offer to convey us himself.*
>
> *Dear Mama, you will, I am sure, be very pleased to hear that Mr Wilson was very happy that he had been treated with such friendliness and shown so much hospitality at Pemberley.*
>
> *On our return journey, which was accomplished in remarkable time, he quizzed me about everyone he had met at Pemberley—not, I hasten to add, in a prying or inquisitive way, but simply because, as he said, "They were all such interesting people."*
>
> *He says he is looking forward to visiting Derbyshire again—he has had so many invitations, I am sure it will not be long before you see him."*
>
> *As for myself, I cannot say often enough how happy I was to be back with you and be a part of the Pemberley clan again. I do miss you all so.*
>
> *We are to go to Kent next week with Mrs Wilson. I shall write again when we return.*
>
> *Your loving daughter,*
> *Emma.*

Elizabeth and Jane were quite astonished at the letter. "Emma is clearly so happy at having been able to come to Pemberley," said Jane, "she is able, at least for a while, to put her troubles aside."

"She is certainly fortunate in her in-laws," said Elizabeth, pointing out that Mrs Wilson's kindness to Emma matched that of her eldest son. "I wonder, Jane, do they know of the pain Emma has suffered and continues to suffer in her marriage?" she asked.

Jane was unsure; Emma had not mentioned speaking of it to anyone. "I do not think she has told them. She might be afraid that they would take David's part against her, as in-laws often do," she said.

"His mother might—mothers are forgiven if they are partial to their sons," said Elizabeth, "but I cannot believe that a man as fair and sensible as James Wilson seems to be would let his judgement be similarly distorted."

Elizabeth was sure that if James Wilson discovered how his brother was treating Emma, he would not stand idly by. Jane agreed, but her own qualms for her child overwhelmed her. As she tried to put her letter away, tears spilled down her cheeks, and she had to be comforted by her sister.

Jane was taking her daughter's unhappiness very hard. Her own almost idyllic marriage, in which, after some thirty years, husband and wife still considered themselves particularly blessed to be wedded to one another, had not prepared her for coping with the type of continuing misery that Emma's situation implied.

The weather on Friday was cold, but fortunately, it was also fine. The journey to Kent was, therefore, not as trying as it could have been had it been wet. They travelled the road from London to Canterbury, stopping for a meal at Dartford. As they travelled on, Mrs Wilson tended to fall asleep, leaving James and Emma to maintain a conversation.

He was surprised to learn that, having spent only a small part of her life before marriage in London, Emma had done very little travelling in these parts. She had, for instance, only once visited the historic town of Canterbury, and then just for a few hours, during which she'd had only time enough to see the exterior of the great Cathedral.

"That will not do at all, Emma," said James, who confessed that Kent was his "most favourite county." He had travelled all over it since he was a boy, but never had he grown tired of its beauty and variety. Their family had lived in Kent for two centuries.

"Next Summer, we shall make sure that you visit Canterbury and Chilham, perhaps Ramsgate as well," he promised. "I cannot believe that you have not been to Ramsgate—David and I spent many Summers there when we were boys. We have been most remiss."

It was late afternoon when they reached Standish Park. The house, standing amidst woods and parkland not far from Maidstone, was older and larger than her home in Leicestershire. It had been in the family for well over a hundred years, having been built in the middle of the last century of a russet red brick that seemed to glow in the late afternoon sun, making the house stand out from the green meadows and dark woods behind it.

Emma liked the house very much—more than the one they occupied in Mayfair, in spite of its fashionable style. It was a comfortable and welcoming place, with large airy rooms and beautiful landscaped grounds. She had spent most of the early years of her marriage here, and it brought back many memories of her daughters' early childhood.

That evening, after dinner, they spent some time in the library—a fine, well-proportioned room which held an excellent collection of books.

Amidst the family portraits on the walls was a painting by a little known French artist which Emma had always liked. Since they were selecting things to take back to London, Emma asked if she might borrow the painting for her room.

Mrs Wilson was delighted. "Emma, of course you may. It would look very well in your sitting room." It was immediately taken down, cleaned, and packed for transport. When Mrs Wilson was ready to go to bed, Emma followed her upstairs while James remained downstairs, reading in front of the fire.

Saturday was one of those remarkable late Autumn days when the season appears to move back into Summer. The morning had been cold but clear, and by midday, it was almost warm enough to deceive one into believing it was not November at all.

Having spent the day with Mrs Wilson, Emma took some time in the afternoon to visit the Conservatory, which was full of Winter blooms. Attracted by the warmth of the last hours of sunlight, she stepped out onto the terrace, where James found her looking out at the view, which fell away from the terraced gardens to the meadows and river valley below.

He joined her, apologising as he did so for startling her. "Mother has gone upstairs to rest before dinner; I wondered where you had got to."

Emma smiled. "I wanted to see the Conservatory—the flowers are always beautiful—but I could not resist coming out here," she said.

"When we first came to live at Standish Park, this used to be my favourite spot." He agreed that it was the best view from the house, and took some time pointing out familiar landmarks and his favourite woodland walks, which he recommended to her.

Emma confessed she was not much of a walker. "Perhaps in Spring," she said laughing, "I might be persuaded."

"Well, I shall try again in Spring," he said, with a smile. "Kent is a very special county, you know, Emma. William the Conqueror believed that being nearest to France, its men were less ferocious and more cultured than those inhabiting the rest of England."

She laughed and wondered aloud what Mr Darcy might have to say to that, to which James replied, "Oh, the men of Derbyshire have always been strong, Emma. Even the Romans feared them and left them alone, for the most part!"

Even as they talked, Emma realised that David had not shown an interest in the house or its grounds, and certainly had never made the effort to talk to her about it. His brother clearly loved the place.

A sudden gust of wind caused her to shiver and draw her wrap more closely around her. James suggested that they return indoors.

In the Conservatory, which was pleasantly warm, she sat down facing the terrace, and James took a chair across from her.

When he spoke, his voice was serious, though his manner was gentle. "Emma, I cannot make you tell me. I will not even attempt to persuade you to tell me why you are unhappy, but if you want to talk to me, I am ready to listen and if I can help in any way, I shall," he said.

For a while it seemed as if she would not respond at all and then, quite suddenly, when he leaned across and touched her hand and said, "You have nothing to fear Emma. Whatever you tell me will be in the strictest confidence, and I will do nothing without your permission. You have my word," her resistance seemed to crumble and it all poured out, as though she no longer had the will to hold it back.

For James Wilson, it was a revelation that left him appalled and grieved. He had asked the cause of her unhappiness and when the problems had manifested themselves. He had not for a moment anticipated the answer he received.

Within a very few months of their marriage, while they were still on their wedding tour of Europe, Emma had realised that David Wilson had not married her because he wanted a wife, as her mother had been to her father, or a partner, as Caroline was to Fitzwilliam.

"It was soon clear to me that while my husband enjoyed taking me out and introducing me to his friends as his new bride, it was the role of a doll or a pet that I was expected to fill, not a partner." Her voice, diffident at first, strengthened as she spoke. "David's friends were permitted to dance with me or compliment me on my looks or my clothes, but I was not permitted to engage them in anything but the most superficial conversation. When we visited art galleries or museums, David would ask the questions—I was supposed only to smile and drink it all in. One memorable evening in Paris, we had been asked to a soiree at which two of the most celebrated opera singers had been invited to sing. It was a great privilege to be there and hear them. But, when Madame Lemercier, our hostess, invited me to join a small group of ladies and sing a chorus or two, together with her famous guests, David was so annoyed, he walked out into the night and did not return for several hours. I was so mortified. I had thought he would be proud of me. I had spent many years learning under a very famous teacher, and I enjoyed singing. After we returned to England, he forbade me to spend any more time on singing lessons. He thought they were a foolish indulgence."

James's countenance betrayed his astonishment. He had often heard Emma sing and could not understand his brother's objections. "Do you mean he stopped your singing lessons?"

Emma nodded, "And he has since refused to let me have Victoria and Stephanie taught as well. He says he will not have them turned into performing monkeys."

James shook his head, aghast that she had lived with such harassment and neither he nor his mother had known of it.

Emma explained how much it had meant to her mother, who had never had much of a voice, when it turned out that Emma could sing. She had been encouraged to have lessons and had developed a good singing voice, but David wanted none of it.

"Do you mean you no longer sing?" James asked, incredulous.

"When I am alone or with the children, but not in company. I have no wish to annoy him," she said.

James was almost speechless, but there was more to be heard.

Emma revealed that she had had to fight for the right to care for her babies; David had demanded that they be handed over to their nurses day and night, and it was only the intervention of his mother that had led him to give ground and let her stay at Standish Park with the children.

"If David had had his way, they would have been banished to a nursery in the South Wing—out of sight and out of earshot. He wanted to take me back to London with him, but when I was there, he had no use for me, or very little. Unlike Caroline, who used to accompany Fitzwilliam to all the parliamentary functions, I was only expected to grace the ladies' tea parties, and then I was to smile and say very little. David made it clear that he was the Member of Parliament. I was not to have or express opinions on any significant subject. He was quite adamant about that."

James, quite unable to comprehend the reasons for his brother's behaviour, could only express sympathy. "Have you attempted to remonstrate with him or to persuade him to a different way of thinking?" he asked.

She answered with a degree of hopelessness that saddened him, "Indeed I have, particularly at the start of our marriage, but it did me no good at all. I soon learnt that crossing my husband or even pleading for a change in his attitude would only make matters worse. It irritated and made him even more stubborn."

"And the situation has never improved?"

Emma explained things had got much worse since they had gone to live in London after his father's death. "Now, I do not get told where he is going or whom he is going with. He has also started to drink quite heavily, and I dare not object. He can get very angry indeed."

James, looking anxious, stood up and came around to her, "Emma, tell me, has he ever threatened you or has he…" His face was dark with anger, but she was quick to deny the implication of his question.

"No, never; he has been rude and surly, I admit, but never has he laid hands upon me in anger." As tears filled her eyes, she added, "There have been times when I have been afraid, I confess, but it has never come to such a pass."

James was clearly appalled. At first, he said nothing, walking away from her to the end of the Conservatory, his face gloomy, his brow furrowed. He wanted to alleviate her distress in some way, but had no means to do so. He was mortified and revolted by her account of his brother's behaviour, yet knew there was little he could do to change it. When he came back to her, it was to apologise. "Emma, I am sorry, profoundly sorry. I had no idea, and yet, I should have known. Why have you not told us, my mother or myself? Why have you endured this torment alone for so long?"

She admitted then that she had only very recently confided in her mother, pleading with her that it should go no further. "I had no wish to anger David or bring dishonour upon your family by taking such a step," she replied.

James was astounded. "Dishonour! Emma, how can you speak of bringing dishonour upon our family? It is David, my brother, who has dishonoured us all with his appalling behaviour and his vile treatment of you! I can only apologise for him on behalf of my family, and I give you my word, Emma, that I shall do all I can to set things right." Though he spoke with restraint, there was no doubting his anger nor, indeed, the compassion he felt for her.

Emma begged him not to tell his mother. "She is not in good health, and I will not have her hurt on my account. And should you approach David, he will, in all probability, deny everything and blame me. He will surely refuse permission for me to go out with any of my friends and may even forbid me to see my parents."

James's consternation could not be concealed. "Emma, if I am to say nothing to my mother or David, how then I can help you?"

Emma shook her head. Her distress was obvious as she pleaded with him. "Please, James, I know what I ask may seem unreasonable, and I thank you for wanting to help me, but for all our sakes, David must not know that I have spoken of these matters to you. It will infuriate him and I will suffer the consequences."

This time, realising the depth of her distress, he assured her of his secrecy. He felt the frustration of his situation keenly. He wanted to help, to relieve the pain and suffering to which she was being subjected, yet he could also understand her fears. His brother could be moody and stubborn. He knew now he could also be irrational and cruel, and Emma and her children had to be protected from the consequences of any action he might take. He decided to consult a very close friend in London before taking any steps in the matter.

Meanwhile, he gave Emma his word that he would say nothing to David or their mother.

She seemed much calmer since they had spoken, and he presumed that the telling of it had helped. Indeed, she almost smiled as she declared that she would like to go upstairs now and rest awhile before changing for dinner. For his part, James had never felt more wretched and helpless than he did at that moment.

After dinner, at which Mrs Wilson remarked that Emma looked rather pale, they withdrew to the drawing room. James opened up the pianoforte and sat down to play. It was a most superior instrument with a beautiful tone, and Emma knew her brother-in-law played very well. Having worked through a couple of simple compositions, he turned to her, inviting her to sing and offering to play for her.

Before Emma could protest or beg to be excused, Mrs Wilson intervened. "Now that is just what I would like, above anything. Emma has a charming voice, yet, except to sing to the children, she rarely lets us hear it."

James needed no further encouragement. Coming over to Emma as she sat beside his mother, he offered her his arm. "Come now, Emma, you cannot disappoint my mother," he said.

Emma did not require much persuasion. She began with a couple of popular English airs and, soon finding it more enjoyable than she had imagined, continued with some of Mrs Wilson's favourites.

Her sweet, clear voice delighted James and his mother, who said quite firmly when Emma had finished singing, "When we return to London, Emma, you shall sing for me every evening. You have the most pleasing voice of anyone I know. What's more, I think it is about time that Victoria and Stephanie started music lessons, don't you agree, James?"

James could not agree more and added that he would look forward to hearing Emma sing whenever he dined at the house in Mayfair.

"Perhaps we may soon hear my nieces too," he added, and Mrs Wilson agreed.

"Certainly, there is no reason why they should not be as talented as their mother, now is there?"

Emma looked across at James and smiled. He was glad to see how her general demeanour had improved. She smiled more easily and her eyes were bright. The singing had certainly lifted her spirits. The evening, he decided, was a great improvement on the afternoon.

Returning to London on the Sunday, Emma noted that of all the things being taken to Mayfair, James had chosen only one for himself.

When they broke journey, she made a comment, at which he smiled and said, "Yes, it was my father's writing desk, and I have a sentimental attachment to it. For the rest, since I hope to return to live at Standish Park next year, it did not seem sensible to move too many things."

When Emma expressed some surprise, he explained, "It is the area I represent in Parliament; I ought to spend more time there."

"Does that mean we shall not see you as often as we do now?" she asked, a note of regret creeping into her voice. There had developed between them a close and friendly relationship over the years. James, unfailingly courteous and considerate, had been for Emma relief from her moody, demanding husband.

She had been frequently grateful for his company, especially at family gatherings, when her husband often neglected her to spend time with his friends. James had always found her good company. More reserved than the society ladies of London, but more talented and certainly more beautiful than most of the women of his acquaintance, and blessed with a sweetness of disposition unmatched in their circles, Emma was a natural favourite.

Though he had never suspected the extent of her unhappiness, he had occasionally detected in her a melancholy strain. He recalled her saying, after a grand family gathering, "These occasions seem calculated to make one miserable." And when pressed for a reason, she had added, "I cannot explain it, but I often find I am less happy after than before. Perhaps the anticipation of enjoyment is always better than the fulfilment of it."

He had teased her then, saying, "This is a very grave, philosophic comment from you, Emma."

On this occasion, however, with his deeper understanding of her situation, he sympathised with her apprehension and hastened to reassure her. "You will see me at my mother's house very often, Emma. I am hoping to transfer a lot of my routine legal work to my cousin, Hugh, who has recently joined the firm. That will leave me with more time for my Parliamentary work, and I shall certainly not be neglecting my family. Indeed, the way I see it, when Parliament is sitting, I may spend more time at the house, not less—Mayfair is a lot closer to Westminster."

Seeing the relief on her face, he continued, "Emma, you need never worry that I will not be there to help you. If David continues to harass you and you are unable to reach me, you must go to my mother and seek her protection. You are entitled, as her daughter-in-law, to do that. You cannot let him keep you like some latter day prisoner in the castle."

Emma laughed. They had all read the much talked of novel by one Currer Bell in which a young woman, Jane Eyre, discovers the dark secrets of Mr Rochester's life, locked away in a room at the top of the house. "I cannot believe that even David will attempt to lock me up, and fortunately, there are no Gothic castles in Mayfair," she said lightly, and he was happy to hear the laughter in her voice. Soon she was serious again as she thanked him for the opportunity he had afforded her to speak frankly of her situation. "It was very kind of you. I cannot tell you how good it feels to have spoken."

The arrival of Mrs Wilson, ready and eager to be gone, ended their conversation, and James assisted first his mother and then Emma into the carriage.

While there was little he could do that would materially change her circumstances, the very act of speaking openly with him and having his concern and sympathy had given her a good deal of comfort.

At Pemberley, they were preparing for Christmas.

Elizabeth and Jenny were drawing up the lists that always preceded such occasions when Julian came in to announce that Jonathan had arrived.

Elizabeth went out to greet her nephew and, thinking he was there to see her husband, informed him that Darcy was away on business in Liverpool with Mr Gardiner and was not expected back until that evening.

Jonathan expressed some regret at missing Mr Darcy, but he said, "I am really only here as a messenger, Aunt Lizzie. Colonel Fitzwilliam and Caroline wondered if you and Mr Darcy would dine with them tomorrow."

"Tomorrow? This is rather sudden, Jonathan." Elizabeth was puzzled and asked if he knew of any special reason for this invitation. "Are we celebrating anything?" she asked.

Jonathan looked a little uncomfortable. "I would not call it a celebration, but, yes, there is something particular happening. It concerns David Wilson, Emma's husband."

Surprise turned to astonishment at this news. "David Wilson? Is he invited too?"

"Oh no, he is not," said Jonathan quickly, looking more confused and awkward as he tried to fend off her inquiries.

Elizabeth, realising there was more to this visit than met the eye, decided it was time to ask some serious questions. "Jonathan, I think we need to have some tea," she said, and having rung the bell for a servant and ordered tea, she took Jonathan into the morning room.

Sitting him down, Elizabeth faced her nephew and said firmly, "Now Jonathan, tell me, what is this all about?"

After some initial reluctance, he told her of information he had recently received from a very reliable source. It concerned David Wilson and his activities.

"Do you mean his political activities?" asked Elizabeth.

"Yes, and also his … I suppose you might call them his social activities," said Jonathan, more ill at ease than ever.

"And what were these activities?" asked Elizabeth.

Jonathan shook his head, "Oh Aunt Lizzie, I don't know how much I should tell you. You see, I have not said a word to Mama and Papa. I have spoken with Colonel Fitzwilliam because of his contacts in Westminster and Whitehall. I really did not know what else to do. It was Caroline's idea that we meet and discuss it with you and Mr Darcy before my parents are told."

Elizabeth was completely bewildered, "Jonathan, what is it you have heard about David Wilson that you cannot reveal to your mother and father? What has he done?"

Jonathan was silent for several minutes, during which time a servant brought in the tea, and Elizabeth rose and went over to the window, looking out on the west lawn.

There was some weak sunlight but very little warmth out there, and Elizabeth shivered involuntarily. Jonathan rose and followed her. "Aunt Lizzie, you must give me your word that nothing I say will reach my mother or Emma—at least not until we have decided on some plan," he said, and it seemed to her there was a new serious tone to his voice.

Elizabeth agreed, and they returned to their tea.

Jonathan related as briefly and precisely as possible a tale of deceit and betrayal that left Elizabeth incredulous. When she had urged her nephew to speak openly, she had certainly no expectation of hearing the kind of information that Jonathan was to place before her. First, regarding his brother-in-law's political activities, it seemed he had defected to the Conservatives and was now actively working against the Reformist cause. "When he did not contribute to the debates on Factory Inspections and the Ten-Hour Day, we had our suspicions. He had been remiss about certain votes in the House and was often seen fraternising with some of the old Tories," Jonathan explained.

"Is that unusual for him?" Elizabeth asked.

"No, no it is not, which is why I for one did not take the rumours seriously."

"What rumours?"

"The rumours that he was going over to the Tories," he replied.

"And has he?" asked Elizabeth.

Jonathan nodded, "Yes, he has. He deliberately absented himself from the vital vote for the Ten-Hour Day and has declared that he will not support the Public Health Act."

Elizabeth was amazed but wondered at the level of Jonathan's outrage.

"Surely the government does not need his vote?"

"That, my dear aunt, is not the point at issue," he explained patiently. "Wilson has been nurtured and given his chance to enter Parliament by the Reform Group and the Whigs. To betray them now and remain in the Parliament is odious and totally dishonourable."

Elizabeth agreed. "Yes, but why must this information be kept from Bingley and Jane? I have no doubt your father would be outraged, but David Wilson would not be the first member to change sides and he certainly will not be the last," she said.

"There is more, Aunt Lizzie and I do not believe you will be as sanguine about the rest of it," said Jonathan, putting down his cup and rising as the servant returned to stoke up the fire.

It was clear to Elizabeth that Jonathan was seeking some privacy, and, waiting until the footman had left with the tea tray, she closed the door.

Her nephew had by now begun to look a good deal more serious. "The rest concerns David's private activities," he said and still seemed to speak reluctantly, when a carriage was heard coming up the drive.

Elizabeth went to the window and he followed her. The carriage belonged to the Gardiners, but the occupant was not one of them.

"Good God, it's Amelia-Jane," he exclaimed. "I thought she was with Aunt Gardiner," he said as they went out into the hall.

Amelia-Jane had alighted and was quickly ushered indoors. Seeing her husband with Elizabeth, she was clearly pleased. "Jonathan, I am so glad you are here. I've come directly from Matlock, where Becky Tate has told me all about David Wilson's disgraceful behaviour, and I was determined that Aunt Lizzie should know…"

She was hushed and almost dragged into the morning room by her husband, "Amelia, dearest, you must not talk about it so openly."

"Why ever not?" she asked, "I believe everyone in London knows about it except poor Emma."

Elizabeth had by now realised that something much worse than she had anticipated was about to be revealed, and she experienced a cold, unpleasant feeling totally unrelated to the wintry weather.

This time it was Amelia who related the story, in far more colourful terms than her husband would have used accompanied by a high degree of indignation.

Since his defection to the Tories, David Wilson had been the subject of investigation by two journalists employed by Anthony Tate's newspapers. Ordered to discover the motivation or at least the reason for his defection, they had spent a good deal of time in London and their inquiries had turned up some quite startling information. Amelia-Jane did not mince her words when she gave her aunt the news. "Aunt Lizzie, David Wilson has not only betrayed his colleagues in Parliament; he has consistently deceived his family and betrayed his wife," she went on.

As she related the information that she had gained from Rebecca Tate, who now managed the newspaper empire that her husband was building, Amelia-Jane added her own comments.

"I have never liked David Wilson; earlier in our acquaintance he did try to insinuate himself into the good graces of my family, and I would have none of it," she declared, having explained that the information uncovered by the Tate's investigators was sufficient to destroy the man's political career and his marriage. "He is not only a turncoat and an adulterer, but he has got himself so deep in debt through gambling and high living that he seems beholden to a group of villains who could ruin him if he does not do as they demand. He is corrupt and disreputable, Aunt Lizzie. Clearly, neither his mother nor Emma would be aware of his conduct or they would not tolerate him."

"I am astonished that his brother, James, who we met here a few weeks ago, has not discovered this," said Elizabeth, but Jonathan intervened to suggest that it was quite likely James, whose integrity and honour were unquestioned, may have been spared the knowledge because most of his colleagues were reluctant to embarrass him with gossip about his dissolute younger brother.

"I know of no one who has a bad word to say of James Wilson, and I would venture to suggest that most members would have deliberately avoided the subject of David's profligacy rather than cause him pain and embarrassment," he said.

Amelia agreed with her husband. "Becky tells me that the two men who investigated David's activities heard not a single accusation against his brother or any other member of the family. His father and uncle were highly respected, and it seems Mr James Wilson is not only well regarded at Westminster; he has, since taking over management of his father's affairs, acquired a reputation as a fair and decent businessman. I cannot believe that he will tolerate the type of impropriety and wild behaviour that David has indulged in, should he be told of it."

Elizabeth realised that they had now reached the very nub of the problem. "Is he to be told?" she asked. "Is this what the dinner at Fitzwilliams' is about?"

Jonathan and Amelia admitted that they needed Mr Darcy's advice. "Fitzwilliam will not move without consulting Mr Darcy—especially because of the particular closeness and affection that exists between him and my father," said Jonathan, adding, "I cannot imagine how they will take this news. Papa will be most upset—it was through his long association with the Wilson family that Emma came to know David Wilson. I know he will blame himself."

Elizabeth was outraged. "That would be utterly unfair," she protested. "Your father could never have imagined that David Wilson, the son of respectable parents, the brother of an honourable man, could turn out this way."

But Jonathan knew how hard his father would take the news of David Wilson's despicable behaviour—especially the effect it would have on Emma and her two daughters.

The dinner at Fitzwilliam's house was to provide an opportunity for them to discuss the situation and plan some action with the benefit of Mr Darcy's wise counsel. Darcy, more than any other member of the family, had become their source of reasoned and sensible advice. They looked to him whenever they were unsure of their own judgement.

Elizabeth agreed to acquaint him with the information they had given her and promised that, unless some more pressing problem emerged to demand their attention, they would meet at the Fitzwilliams' the following evening.

After they had gone, Elizabeth sat alone, unable to leave her chair for quite a while, so acutely painful were her reactions to the news she had received. She was grateful to Jane for having at least given her some hint of Emma's unhappiness, but nothing her sister had said could have prepared her for the appalling tale of betrayal that she had just heard. Jenny came in search of her mistress and was surprised to find her sitting before a dying fire. When she offered to bring her more tea and stoke up the fire, Elizabeth thanked her but preferred to retire upstairs.

Her depression worsened as she thought not only of Emma's situation, now made considerably worse by the new revelations, but of her sister and brother-in-law. Jane's tender heart would surely be devastated, and

Bingley—whose devotion to his wife was matched only by his love of his daughters—how, she wondered, would he cope with Emma's sorrow as well as the public disgrace that must surely follow?

The fact that the investigation had been carried out by two journalists only served to increase the threat of exposure and added to her unease. Almost sick with worry, Elizabeth asked for a pot of tea to be brought up and stayed in her room, where Darcy, returning earlier than expected, found her in a state of some anxiety.

Aware that something was amiss, he was at her side instantly. "Elizabeth, what is it? Jenny says Jonathan and Amelia were here this morning. What did they want? Is someone ill?" He was most concerned to discover the cause of her distress.

Elizabeth would have liked to pour out the whole sorry story, but realising her husband was tired from his journey, she tried to reassure him and said it could wait until after dinner.

Only after Julian had gone to bed and they were alone did she tell him everything—including the early hints she had had from Jane.

Darcy listened like a man who had been turned to stone. Except to ask occasional questions, he let her tell the tale uninterrupted. Only the darkening expression on his face betrayed his feelings of consternation and outrage. Elizabeth was reminded of his reaction on hearing the awful news of Lydia's elopement with Wickham. She recalled his grim countenance as he had heard the wretched story.

For his part, Darcy had never felt really easy about David Wilson and, despite the obvious attractions of the match and the links it provided with an established, professional family, he had tried to warn Bingley when the news of Emma's engagement had taken them all by surprise.

His contacts in London had not given him very encouraging reports of young Wilson, though they had spoken very highly of his father and brother James. Stories of high living and big spending were legion, and no one would vouch for his credit. It had been all too reminiscent of another young man of his acquaintance, one whose handsome face and pleasing manner had helped him win the hearts and confidence of an inordinate number of people, resulting in much heartache and unpleasantness.

He had hoped that Bingley with his long association with the Wilsons would be better placed to counsel Emma against a hasty marriage. But Charles Bingley, it seemed, was not of a mind to cross his dearest daughter, who was very much in love. The marriage had gone ahead, and since he had heard nothing untoward from either his friend or his wife, Darcy had begun to hope that perhaps marriage to the beautiful Emma Bingley might have put an end to Mr Wilson's transgressions.

Elizabeth had expected him to be reluctant to believe the story she related, demanding evidence of the supposed misdemeanours. But in fact, it seemed almost as if he half expected it.

"Darcy, have you known of this?" she asked, wishing to discover the extent of his knowledge.

"No, I had no idea things were this bad, though I confess that before they were married, I did hear tales of gambling and high living, which concerned me sufficiently to warrant a word in Bingley's ear."

"And how did he respond? Was he concerned?" asked Elizabeth.

"Not as much as I had hoped he would be. He was unwilling to upset Emma, who you will recall was deeply in love at the time. It was generally regarded as an excellent match and with my previous experience in these matters, I don't think Bingley took me seriously," he replied, acknowledging his failure to influence his friend.

Elizabeth sighed, "Poor Emma. If only someone had warned her, it might have spared her a good deal of heartache."

Darcy disagreed, "Lizzie, is it likely that Emma, at nineteen, with her head full of dreams, would listen to some gossip about the man she was in love with? Quite obviously, her father did not think so. I offered him the names of my informants, but he would have no truck with them. He was not about to break his daughter's heart with some wild rumour."

"Was that why you did not tell me about your reservations?" she asked. "Did you fear that I would tell Jane, when you knew that Bingley had already dismissed them?"

He admitted that he had not thought it would do any good at all. "Besides, my dear," he explained, "You and I had rather more than we could cope with at the time. We had just returned from Italy with Emily still grieving for Paul; we were struggling to endure our own loss of

William. It was no time to burden you with gossip that may or may not have been true."

❦

The following day, the party that gathered at the Fitzwilliams' was sober and cheerless. Christmas was a mere four weeks away, but no one even mentioned it. Not even the good news from Jonathan that the government was confident of getting the numbers for the passage of the Public Health Bill in the New Year raised their spirits.

The Tates arrived shortly afterwards, and Rebecca was bursting to give them news of the big literary sensation of the year—that the author of *Jane Eyre*, Currer Bell, was in fact a young woman from Yorkshire, Charlotte Brontë. Even this brought only a brief respite from the general gloom.

Initially, everyone seemed reluctant to bring up the subject until Rebecca Tate decided it was about time and spoke up. Perhaps she felt some responsibility, since the information had been uncovered by their investigation of Mr David Wilson.

"Mrs Darcy, is it your opinion that Mr and Mrs Bingley should be told of this information? The reason I ask is that, next to Jonathan, you are Emma's closest relation here, and none of us would wish to do anything without your advice and Mr Darcy's, of course. Do you suppose we would be acting correctly were we to expose Mr Wilson's activities, or would that be too harsh?" she asked.

As if in a dream, Elizabeth heard Rebecca's words and recalled her own conversation with Jane many years ago, when, having been told by Mr Darcy of Wickham's infamous conduct, she and her sister had decided that 'twere best to say nothing about it to their family and friends. It was a decision they had made after much thought and only with the best of intentions, yet how much had it been regretted when news broke of Lydia's elopement with Wickham.

Only two people in the world knew the extent of her own sorrow at that lapse—Mr Darcy and Jane. Darcy had blamed himself for not speaking out to expose Wickham, who alone had profited from the concealment afforded him.

Now, with Darcy beside her, she steeled herself and, even though she knew how much it would hurt her sister, said, "There is no question that Jane and Bingley must be told. They have a right to know. So has Emma, but I believe her parents will have to make that decision. Our clear duty is to inform them without delay."

Jonathan agreed immediately.

Darcy intervened to ask how reliable the information was. Did the journalists have any evidence?

Anthony Tate, who had hitherto remained silent, asserted that they were two of his best men. They had not been satisfied with the gossip, of which there was plenty, but had followed up the stories, and their investigations had led them to the house in Chelsea where the woman, who was supposedly David Wilson's mistress, kept an illegal gaming house that was patronised by several so-called "gentlemen" of London society. They had seen Wilson arrive and leave quite openly on many occasions. Indeed, they had been amazed at how brazen he seemed about it. The address of this establishment, said Mr Tate, was available, confidentially, to anyone who wished to verify their story. The shocked silence around the room was proof of the outrage felt by them all.

Finally, Fitzwilliam spoke. "Darcy, if you agree, I intend to go to London and contact an old friend—a Parliamentary colleague from the old days—and if I can confirm that Wilson has, in fact, defected to the Tories, Anthony is prepared to publish this information. We believe he deserves to be exposed."

Elizabeth gasped at the thought of what it would do to Emma, but she had to agree with Caroline, who said, "He is a member of Parliament, who is immoral in both his private and public life. He is a law-maker who is breaking the law with impunity. He has betrayed his party and the people who elected him. I can see no alternative."

"Unless we were to give him an ultimatum, warn him of imminent exposure," said Jonathan, who thought it might be fairer to do so.

After some discussion it was decided that Darcy and Elizabeth would tell the Bingleys of their son-in-law's predicament while Jonathan, Anthony Tate, and Fitzwilliam would travel to London to confront Wilson himself and hear his story, prior to any further action.

Elizabeth was concerned for Emma. She worried that in London, Emma would have to bear the brunt of the exposure, when it came, as well as David's anger.

Jonathan was more confident. "Aunt Lizzie, I am quite certain that as soon as Mama knows, she will want to go to London to be with Emma. She will not be alone—both James Wilson and his mother will protect her once the truth is known."

Darcy wondered whether they did not owe Mr James Wilson and his mother some consideration too. "Should they not be advised? After all, neither of them is responsible in any way for David Wilson's actions, but they will have to face the consequences of this wretched business."

"Sage counsel, Darcy. How right you are," said Fitzwilliam. "I will see James Wilson first and acquaint him with the facts. He has the right to know, and no doubt he will want to advise his mother."

Anthony Tate gave his word that nothing would be published that would damage the rest of the Wilson family—nor would he publish any of the material relating to David's activities—until after Fitzwilliam had spoken with James Wilson and Emma had been advised.

Returning to Pemberley that night, Darcy and Elizabeth retired to their apartments. They had not discussed the matter in the carriage, and Elizabeth waited until her maid had withdrawn before saying, "Would it not be akin to blackmail?"

Darcy knew exactly what she meant. "No, Fitzwilliam and Jonathan would never be involved in that. However, Wilson may feel that he is being threatened with exposure. Unfortunately for him, there is very little he can do about it. Tate can use his newspapers to unleash an attack upon him and since Wilson has probably antagonised so many people in Parliament, he will have very few friends willing to defend him."

"Poor Emma, I wonder how many friends will she have to support her," Elizabeth sighed as she prepared for bed.

Several hours later, unable to sleep, she crept out of bed and, lighting a candle, moved to a sofa at the other end of the room, so as not to disturb her husband. Her mind was constantly turning over ideas and images—images of Jane, Emma, and her two daughters, for whom she had the greatest love—and yet, she could do nothing to protect them from the disaster that was about to overwhelm their lives.

She lay awake for several hours until fatigue finally brought fitful sleep.

When Darcy awoke, it was not yet dawn. Missing his wife from their bed, he came in search of her. "Lizzie, what are you doing here?" he asked. "You are very cold and will make yourself ill."

He wrapped her in a warm shawl and took her back to bed.

"I could not sleep—I kept thinking of Jane and Emma," she confessed as he pulled the bedclothes up around her.

He was sympathetic but very firm. "Come now, dearest, we shall be going to Ashford Park later today. I intend to acquaint Bingley with everything I know, and you will have an opportunity to talk to Jane and decide what should be done to help Emma cope with the shock of this thing. There really is nothing we can possibly do at this hour," he said reasonably.

Elizabeth, who had been turning a thought over in her mind, asked, "Do you recall a letter, some time ago, in which Jane expressed doubts that she deserved all the happiness she had in life?"

Darcy nodded, "Yes, but that was many years ago."

"Well, when we lost William, I wondered, too, how one of us could remain untouched by tragedy while the other could be so desolated. I was almost envious of Jane and her comfortable, happy family. I never dreamed that something as dreadful as this would befall them. I feel so mean." She was tearful and sad, illogically blaming herself. It was a long while before she was comforted and finally fell asleep.

The following morning was cold and grey. They had hardly finished breakfast when a man arrived from Ashford Park bearing a letter from Jane. Elizabeth, anxious, opened it hurriedly.

Jane had written in great haste, her writing almost illegible in parts. Elizabeth raced through it and then, with Darcy at her side, read it again.

My dearest Lizzie, wrote Jane:

I know that I may be asking too much, especially in this dreadful weather—but can I prevail upon you and Mr Darcy to come over this afternoon? You should be prepared to stay overnight, Bingley says the roads may be icy and unsafe at night.

Dear Lizzie, a very grave matter has arisen with regard to Emma and David.

We have had a letter from Emma which suggests that some sort of crisis is imminent. I am wild to go to her, but Bingley insists that I must talk it over with you and Mr Darcy before doing anything at all.

Please do come. I need your clear head and brave heart, my dearest sister, as well as your husband's wise counsel.

Your loving sister etc…

A reply was dispatched forthwith, stating that Elizabeth and Darcy would be at Ashford Park that evening.

They had not, as yet, decided how much should be revealed to Jane and Bingley. Darcy expressed a preference for frankness. "I cannot believe that it will be possible to keep much of the information from them once the story breaks in London," said Darcy.

"We are not even aware how much Emma knows already. No doubt her letter to Jane will reveal some of that, but I do not think she could possibly know very much about David Wilson's other activities. He seems very secretive."

Darcy declared that he thought it would be important to warn the Bingleys of the storms that might be brewing but not necessary to go into too much detail about Wilson's private life at this stage.

When they arrived at Ashford, they were soon ushered from the cold into a warm sitting room replete with food, drink, and a comforting fire.

After the tea things were removed and the servants had withdrawn, Jane brought out her daughter's letter. Elizabeth read it first. Emma had obviously been under great strain when it was written, for her hand had been unsteady and her writing, usually perfectly rounded and neat, was all shaky and difficult to read.

Dearest Mama and Papa, she wrote:

Something rather awful has happened and I don't quite know how to tell you.

Strange as it may seem, David, my husband, has disappeared, and we do not know what has happened to him.

He has not been seen since last Sunday.

I know that this sounds childish and silly, but please believe me: it is serious. His mother is very upset because no one has been able to tell us where he might be. James is doing all he can to find him, but so far with very little success.

I have to be careful not to upset Victoria and Stephanie, for they may be frightened, and if the servants find out, there will be all sorts of gossip.

Dear Mama, I may need you to take the children for a few days until we have some news.

Please let me know if you are able to help. I do hope I am not interfering with any other plans you might have had.

Mama, I wish with all my heart that I was with you and Papa at Ashford Park, but for the moment, I think I must stay with Mrs Wilson.

I shall write again as soon as we have any news, though we are fearful of what we may hear!

Your loving daughter,

Emma.

So bewildering were its contents, Elizabeth could not take it all in. She handed it to Darcy, who read it with Bingley standing beside him.

Watching them, Elizabeth thought she had never seen Bingley look so unhappy. He hovered around until Darcy had finished reading, and when he looked up and shook his head in complete confusion, Bingley said, "Can you understand it Darcy? Why has David Wilson disappeared?"

It was a question to which they all wanted an answer. Darcy certainly had no idea. It had thrown a completely unforeseen ingredient into an already confused situation. The mystery cast a shadow of doubt over their deliberations, creating more suspicion.

Darcy was cautious when he spoke. "I cannot imagine why he has disappeared, unless he has already got wind of something that was about to happen to him," he said.

"Do you think he could have gone into hiding?" Elizabeth asked.

Jane was confounded. "Why would he do that? I know he has not been very good to Emma, but that is not a reason to go into hiding, is it?" she asked.

Elizabeth glanced at her husband. It was time for her to take Jane upstairs and talk to her about some of the problems David Wilson and his family were likely to face. Darcy would probably sit down with her brother-in-law in the library and tell him all he knew. It would not be easy. Neither of them felt comfortable about telling two people they loved dearly the worst news they were likely to hear in their lives.

As Elizabeth told her the facts as she had them from Jonathan, Amelia, Rebecca, and Anthony Tate, Jane, at first quiet and even disbelieving, became extremely agitated and finally wept bitterly. Elizabeth held her sister, comforting her. Their thoughts were all of Emma.

"My poor, dear Emma! Oh, Lizzie, how is it possible for her, for all of us to have been mistaken and so badly deceived? I know I have said that I preferred his brother James, but that had nothing to do with his character— it was merely my own preference for the disposition and manners of his brother," she said, unable to accept that the world had treated her beautiful, gentle daughter so unfairly.

Elizabeth was searching her mind for some words of comfort when the sound of a carriage drew them to the window. "Who could that be? We are not expecting anyone else," said Jane.

Looking out, they were just able to see Emma being helped out by James Wilson, who then picked up young Victoria and Stephanie and set them down. As they disappeared indoors, their nurse alighted, weighed under with coats and bags.

By this time, Jane and Elizabeth, speechless with surprise at first, looked at one another in bewilderment, then rushed out of the room and down the stairs. When they reached the sitting room, Emma was in her father's arms, while the two little girls were already helping themselves to cakes, oblivious of the adults around them.

As they entered, Mr Wilson, who was speaking earnestly to Darcy, turned and came forward to greet them, his face grave.

"Mrs Bingley, Mrs Darcy, forgive me for this untimely arrival, but as I was explaining to Mr Darcy, we are in the midst of a most unsettling situation. I do beg your pardon for not giving you any warning..." But Jane, delighted to have her daughter right there in front of her, simply dismissed his apologies as she enfolded Emma in her arms.

James Wilson approached Elizabeth and Darcy, standing a little apart from the Bingleys' tearful reunion. "Mrs Darcy, I have had some extraordinary news today concerning my brother David, and I had to make a hurried decision in the interests of Emma and the children: to get them out of London," he explained.

While Jane took Emma and her daughters upstairs, James Wilson briefly related the events that had led to his decision.

David had mysteriously disappeared, and after several days of enquiries, James had discovered that he was concealed at a friend's house in Richmond. It transpired that he, having defected from his party and being deeply in debt through gambling, had been threatened with exposure in the press.

"Regrettably, I have to inform you, Mr Bingley, that David's conduct has been thoroughly dishonourable. I will not burden you with what I have discovered at this stage, but suffice it to say that he has proved himself quite unworthy of your daughter as well as the trust of his colleagues. He has also caused untold distress to my poor mother and myself. I am well aware that Emma has borne a great deal of privation and harassment with saint-like patience, and it was in her interest, chiefly, that my mother and I felt that she and the children should come to you."

He was at pains to make his own attitude clear. "Should there be some kind of scandal, a public or Parliamentary excoriation of David, which he may well deserve in the light of his behaviour, it would not have been fair that Emma and her children should be at the centre of it all in London, innocent victims of his dishonour and disgrace."

Darcy and Elizabeth agreed at once that James had done the right thing, and Bingley was so appreciative of the fact that James had brought his beloved Emma home that he needed to hear no more. "I cannot say how grateful we are to you, Mr Wilson. You could not have done anything that would have pleased us more," he said. "Now, do sit down by the fire and let me get you a drink, for I am sure you are chilled to the bone."

Afterwards, they were determined that he stay to dinner, and when James rose to leave, Bingley intervened once more to persuade him that it would be most unwise to venture out at such a late hour.

It was of no use to declare that he had reserved rooms at the inn—at Ashfordby—Bingley would not hear of his travelling in this weather.

Emma, who had changed and joined them at dinner, looking a little weary but obviously happy to be home, added her voice to her father's. "Papa is quite right, James, you must not go—not in this weather. Should you have an accident, whom would we turn to then? What is more, it is surely far kinder to your driver and the horses, too."

She was so persuasive that James Wilson simply shrugged his shoulders and gave in, saying, "I cannot deny that the prospect of a warm bed at

Ashford Park is far more enticing than the thought of another journey of some ten miles to Ashfordby. I thank you very much indeed, and I hope I have not put you to too much trouble, Mrs Bingley."

Having been assured that he had not, he was, however, determined to be up and ready to leave very early the following day.

Therefore, he took his leave of the ladies before they retired, remarking that he did not expect to see them at such an early hour.

Jane and Elizabeth could not fail to be impressed by the remarkable dignity and sincerity of James Wilson, who continued to be distinguished from his brother by his unimpeachable conduct. Emma had already regaled her mother and aunt with tales of his kindness and concern for her and the children.

Before Emma retired for the evening, she thanked him with great sweetness, sending compliments to his mother and wishing him a safe journey on the morrow.

James promised to return as soon as he had some better news. "I know you are going to be safe and happy here," he said. "God bless you, Emma, and keep you well."

Meanwhile, Fitzwilliam, Anthony Tate, and Jonathan had spent three days in London, before they discovered that David Wilson had gone into hiding and was unlikely to see them. Fitzwilliam had confirmed through his source in Parliament that the Whigs no longer relied upon him for his vote, which they regarded as having been sold to their opponents. He had heard from contacts in the city that David Wilson had been abandoned by most of his friends.

Only when he met James Wilson, to acquaint him with their intention to confront his brother, did he discover that the Wilson family had already dealt with their black sheep in their own way. All that was left now was for him to bear the public disgrace. James was certainly not about to protect him from it.

❧

At Ashford Park, Emma and her daughters settled in as if they were never going back. Her parents were delighted to have her home in time for Christmas. Other members of the family who called to see her were happy to find her looking so well, for indeed, Emma had recovered her spirits remarkably since her return to Leicestershire.

Apart from the few who were aware of the crisis she had been through, none guessed the true reason for her flight from London.

Despite her continuing anxiety, Emma found it easy to immerse herself in the traditional preparations for Christmas at her parents' home, where the warmth and affection that surrounded them gave her a welcome sense of security. Like her mother, she seemed content to enjoy her present situation.

Unfortunately, reality could not be denied.

It was less than a month to Christmas when Jonathan arrived bearing the news. David Wilson was dead. He had shot himself.

The shocking news had taken some time to reach them because Parliament was not sitting and the weather had been dreadful, making communication difficult, he said. It seemed Wilson had been unable or unwilling to face the scandal of exposure that was certain to engulf him as soon as Parliament returned.

A short note to his mother asking her forgiveness and apologising to his wife, his brother, and his daughters for "letting them down" was all he had left, apart from a load of debt to be discharged by his unhappy family.

Jonathan, as his brother-in-law, had accompanied James Wilson to the formal inquiry into the death and was able to report that there had been no suspicion whatsoever of foul play. "He had taken dinner and retired to his room with a bottle of wine, around midnight. He did not usually rise early, so there was no alarm raised when he did not appear at breakfast.

"However, when the chamber maid had drawn the housekeeper's attention to the fact that she had not been able to clean the room all day, suspicions were aroused and the door forced open," he explained.

Jane and Elizabeth were amazed at the calmness with which Emma received the news.

No one who had not known the extent of her suffering, in what had become a loveless and often frightening marriage, would have understood her response. She appeared to feel nothing but relief, saying little except to express her sympathy for Mrs Wilson and James, who she knew would bear the brunt of public exposure. Her own feelings had been numbed by years of abuse and indifference.

There were no tears, except when she had to tell the children of their papa's death, and no deep mourning except as a formality and in deference to her mother-in-law.

Conscious, however, of her duty, she set out immediately, with her parents and Jonathan for London, where she went directly to the house in Mayfair.

She conducted herself with grace and decorum at the funeral and afterwards was determined to repay the kindness of her mother-in-law by being there to support her at what was surely a time of great distress. In all this, she was assisted by her brother Jonathan and by James Wilson, who could not help but admire her courage and sensitivity.

His mother, to whom he had explained in painful detail that her son had treated his wife very ill indeed, had been horrified to learn of her problems. When Emma had arrived at the house to prepare for the funeral, Mrs Wilson had wept as she apologised for David's behaviour, but the generosity of Emma's response had surprised them both.

She stayed with them a fortnight, helped James sort out David's personal papers, and sat with his mother when she had the inevitable callers, who were not always as sensitive as one might have hoped.

Mrs Wilson was most grateful for her support, and James greatly appreciated her kindness to his mother. "I cannot thank you enough, Emma, for your concern and care for my mother. It was not expected of you, considering the circumstances," he said as they sat together after dinner on her last evening.

Her reply was charity itself. "What injury have I to complain of from any action of my mother-in-law? She has been kind and generous at all times to me and the children. That she had no knowledge of our difficulties was my choice—I had not wished to cause further discord in our family than already existed. I had accepted David in good faith and discovered too late that it was a terrible mistake; what justice would there be in attaching blame to his mother? None, surely."

While he could not argue with what she said, he marvelled at her magnanimity. It was a rare quality and a precious one.

When it was time to return to Ashford Park, James Wilson insisted upon taking her home himself. The journey turned out to be pleasanter than either of them had expected. With only her personal maid, Sally, for company, it could have been dull indeed. But in fact, it was quite the reverse.

They broke journey at Cambridge, where he proudly showed her around his old college, and they rose early on the morrow in order to make good time.

Free of bitterness and awkwardness, no longer hobbled by guilt through association, James was an excellent companion. They talked of many shared interests, chief among them reading and music, which they both loved.

"I suppose you will resume your singing lessons soon," said James, to which she replied with a smile that she would need a great deal of practice to master the lessons she had already learnt before venturing into fresh fields.

"I shall, however, be sending Victoria and Stephanie for singing lessons in the New Year," she declared with a smile.

"I'm very glad to hear it. Mother will be especially pleased. Shall we hear them sing when you are next with us?" he asked.

"You certainly shall," she promised, knowing Mrs Wilson would hope to see the children again soon, "but not in London, I hope."

He was quick to respond, "We expect to move to Kent, very soon."

"That is excellent news," she said and her smile confirmed she was delighted to hear it.

They reached Ashford Park by early afternoon.

"I felt I had to bring her home to you myself," he said as he left her with her parents, promising once again to keep in touch but knowing that it would be a while before Emma would visit them again.

The Bingleys, in their usual hospitable way, urged him to stay; but this time, James wanted to return as soon as possible to his mother, whose health had worsened since David's death.

That he was a dutiful and considerate son had been noted and only served to enhance James Wilson's reputation among the Bingleys and their friends.

As Emma said her farewells, she reminded James of his promise of a visit to Canterbury in the Spring.

"Indeed, I have not forgotten, Emma," he said, plainly pleased that she had remembered. "It is not at all far from Standish Park, and Canterbury is at its best in May."

"Then I shall certainly look forward to seeing it," she said as she smiled and gave him her hand.

With the kindest wishes, greetings, and salutations from them all, he was gone, leaving only the best of impressions upon a family that a few weeks earlier had been devastated by the news of his brother's infamy.

Christmas was, of necessity, a quiet one at Ashford Park this year.

Except to attend church with the family, Emma did little more than help her mother with traditional household activities and keep her daughters occupied. Her younger sisters were very excited about attending the usual Christmas Eve celebrations for the children of the Pemberley estate, and so were Victoria and Stephanie.

Emma had asked to be excused, but she was happy to attend a quiet family gathering at the Gardiners, where she met with her cousin Cassandra and her husband Richard Gardiner for the first time since her own husband's death.

Richard and Cassy had been away in Europe when it had happened, but being well informed of the circumstances by their respective parents and sufficiently aware of the pain it may have caused Emma and her children, they showed admirable sensitivity. Cassandra embraced her cousin and whispered her sympathy and understanding. As girls together, they had been close, though not perhaps as intimate as their mothers, Jane and Elizabeth, had been.

Cassandra, happily married for several years, had always regarded her beautiful cousin Emma as an extraordinarily fortunate young woman. Learning the truth about her wretched marriage and the catastrophic events of the last month had shocked and saddened her. Unable to do more than offer sympathy, Cassy was glad when her husband spoke more seriously to their cousin.

Emma knew Richard less well—with his studies and busy working life, they had not met often, especially since their marriages had taken them into very different circles.

She had, however, heard nothing but excellent reports of his character and professional skills. She was not surprised when he approached her and, while making no attempt to pry, asked gently if she and her children were well—offering his help, if there was anything he could do.

"You must feel free to call on me, Emma," he said and exploded in a great laugh when she responded gratefully, calling him Doctor Gardiner and thanking him for his kind offer of help.

"And my very first piece of advice to you would be to call me Richard. Come Emma, we are cousins, and I certainly do not stand on ceremony, so you must not. I should like to think that you would call on me without hesitation."

Emma smiled and assured him that she would.

Later, at dinner, Richard was serious again, telling the family of the chaotic situation in Europe. "We were exceedingly glad to be leaving. There is no knowing when the whole place will erupt in rebellion," he said, his countenance darkening. "In the low countries, crops have failed, food is scarce, and many villages are close to famine, while in the towns, there is so little work that skilled craftsmen beg for odd jobs so they may feed their families. Everywhere, everyone predicts revolution because governments seem incapable of doing anything to alleviate the misery of their people. If the famine spreads, there is no doubt at all that there will be civil unrest," he warned.

"Speaking of famine," Mr Darcy intervened, "we have had letters from Huw Jenkins and Kitty, who have been in Ireland working to help the poor. They speak of dreadful poverty and suffering as a result of the failure of the Irish potato crop."

"What is worse," added Mr Gardiner, "successive British governments have done very little to help the poor farmers. Starvation is rife, and women and children are dying while men are wandering the lands in search of work or food."

Emma had heard nothing of this, being closeted away in Kent or Mayfair, where Ireland had barely received any attention.

"Is this true?" she asked Emily, who was sitting next to her, and the reply shocked her deeply.

"Indeed it is," said Emily, and reaching into her reticule, she produced a letter received just two days ago from Kitty, in which she begged them to keep her two children for a few more days, for she could not possibly leave the work she was doing.

Dearest Emily, she wrote:

It is not possible for me to leave, to turn away from the pleading eyes of starving children and the begging hands of women wanting food not for themselves, emaciated though they are, but for their dying children.

Driven by compassion, Kitty wrote to ask that her family's share of Christmas food and gifts be donated to the same charity.

Mr Darcy and Lizzie always send us a generous hamper for Christmas. Huw and I feel we would like to donate it, together with our gifts to the Irish poor. It is the very least we can do.

I am so ashamed to think that we lived our lives so comfortably, unaware of the misery and suffering of our neighbours across a narrow stretch of water.

Reading Kitty's letter, Emma felt tears flood her eyes.

Emily was explaining how Kitty and her husband had gone to Ireland with their two elder children, Anne and Maria, to work with a charitable church group, leaving their two boys with the Courtneys.

"They have set up two soup kitchens, a crèche for orphans, and are trying to provide some basic medical care for the sick. But they are being overwhelmed and just cannot cope."

Returning Kitty's letter, Emma pleaded, "I want to do something to help, Emily, anything useful. I feel as if I have spent so much of my life in ignorance. Please let me help."

There was no doubting her sincerity, and Emily accepted her offer with alacrity, inviting her to join their group. Caroline Fitzwilliam, Becky Tate, Cassy Gardiner, and Emily Courtney had started working to help the poor many years ago, when the farm folk of the Midlands had been thrown onto the streets by the bailiffs as landlords enclosed their small farms and took over their cottages.

They had continued their good work with the active assistance of the Darcys, Sir Thomas Camden, and the Gardiners, whose help had been invaluable in collecting and distributing food and clothing to the needy.

Emma was enthusiastic; she wanted to start immediately, promising to get her parents to help as well. "I know Mama will want to help," she declared, "and Papa knows many businessmen, who may be persuaded to donate money."

Emily was delighted. "Well Emma, if you will come along to our meeting at the Kympton Church Hall on Friday, I promise we shall have plenty for you to do."

Emma had always admired Emily Gardiner, an intelligent and independent young woman who had shown extraordinary courage in the face of sorrow when she had lost her first husband—courage that had proved an inspiration to others in the family.

Since her own marriage to David Wilson had taken her to London, Emma had had less contact with many of those she had known at Pemberley. She had missed both Caroline and Emily. Now, life had brought them together again, and she rejoiced at the chance to help Emily and her group of friends in the work they were doing for the victims of the Irish famine.

Back at the rectory in Kympton, Emily mentioned her cousin's enthusiasm to her husband, James Courtney.

He had, as usual, a simple and clear explanation. "I am not surprised, my dear. Often in great sorrow, we are faced with two choices: to turn inward in bitter recrimination, blaming the world for our misfortune or turn outward and do whatever we can to help others less fortunate than ourselves. Clearly, Mrs Wilson has chosen the latter path; it is far more likely to bring her satisfaction and peace."

Emily smiled as he added, "And I know you will help and inspire her."

His recognition of Emily's greatness of heart and her appreciation of his simple goodness had led to their unexpected but happy union. She had surprised her family when, after losing her beloved Paul and immersing herself in charitable work for years—during which she had showed no interest in marriage—she had suddenly accepted the popular Rector of Kympton. Since poverty posed no problem for Emily, who was very well provided for by her father and her first husband, it was clearly his sense of moral purpose that she appreciated.

On the journey home, as her parents and sisters chatted together, Emma was quiet, wrapped in her own thoughts. It seemed to Emma that her cousin Emily had never been as contented as she was now. Her mother, sensitive to her daughter's reflective mood, left her alone.

Over the next few weeks, they worked incessantly, collecting donations of food, clothing, and money from households, shops, and textile mills, all of which were sent over to Ireland for distribution by Kitty's group of charitable friends.

Emma, who had never worked so hard in her life, found it extremely rewarding—keeping her from dwelling inordinately on her own situation.

While she knew she was welcome to stay with her parents at Ashford Park, she was well aware that her younger sisters were growing up. She had wondered whether she should seek employment as a teacher at the Kympton parish school. Her own excellent education would surely stand her in good stead. Her opinions on the subject were far from settled however, and she determined to seek Emily's advice.

Returning to Ashford Park on a wet Saturday afternoon, she had changed and was coming downstairs when the door bell rang.

As she reached the front hall, she was surprised to see James Wilson surrendering his coat and hat to the servant. Emma was delighted and greeted him warmly.

He in turn expressed great pleasure at seeing her looking so well. "I can see that you are well, and I have no doubt you are also happy," he said as they went into the sitting room, where afternoon tea would soon be served.

Victoria and Stephanie were highly excited to see their uncle. He was always a favourite with them, now even more so when a servant followed him bearing a large box of toys and books.

"Christmas gifts," said James, "from my mother and myself. Alas, delivered too late, I do apologise," and while the girls fell upon the unexpected treasure trove with glee, he produced a small package for Emma, adding quietly, "This is also from my mother and myself, for you, Emma."

Urged by Louisa and Sophie, Emma opened it to reveal an elegant brooch of gold with tiny pearls. She was overwhelmed. That it was a piece of family jewellery, there was no doubt.

Though her mother and sisters were full of praise for its beauty, Emma could not speak for a while, so surprised and delighted was she by the unexpected gesture. Later, she thanked him profusely, promising to write a note which he must take to his mother—a task he agreed to carry out with the greatest pleasure.

"My mother has long wanted to give you some of her jewellery, but she said it never seemed to be the right time. Well, it seems this was just the right time. I am delighted that you are pleased with it," he said.

Emma tried to discover whether he had any part in choosing the particular piece, but she was disappointed by his reticence and the lack of an opportunity to pursue the matter by subtle means. Despite the ease of their companionship, she was unwilling to question him directly.

By the time the children had opened up their gifts and exclaimed with pleasure at each and every one, it was late evening and quite dark.

Jane had assumed that James would be staying to dinner, an assumption confirmed by her husband, who insisted that of course he was staying and not just to dinner but for whatever period he wished to stay in the district. Bingley had already ordered that his trunk and bag be brought indoors.

"Really James, you cannot want to go back and forth in sleet and rain," he declared, and so it was settled without argument that he should stay.

James was not averse to the idea. The family was clearly happy to see him and so was Emma. He found their company congenial, and the liveliness and warmth of the Bingleys' home was especially comforting after long, depressing days in London arranging the disposal and settlement of his brother's affairs.

When they went in to dinner, Jane naturally assumed that James would sit beside Emma. As they talked, he told her that since he had last seen her, they had all moved to Standish Park in Kent, where he expected his mother would remain permanently.

"What will you do with the house in Mayfair?" Emma asked.

James admitted he had not decided but added it was too large for him, "I shall probably use it far too infrequently to warrant maintaining a complete household there. If I receive a good offer, I may sell; if not, it will be leased. There are many affluent businessmen who could find it suitable—more so than I would."

Turning to Emma, he said, "You would not miss it, would you Emma? I gather you never liked the place."

Surprised that he knew of her aversion to the house, she confessed that she did not really care for it. "But where would you live in London?" she asked.

James confessed that he had not made any arrangements yet but would probably lease a smaller place closer to Westminster. "Since I intend to spend most of my time in Kent when Parliament is not sitting, I do not think I shall miss it either," he said.

Changing the subject, he was keen to remind her of their plans to visit Canterbury and extract from her a promise to come down to Kent in Spring.

Emma was equally determined to tell him of her concerns about the Irish famine. "When you arrived today, I had just returned from Kympton, having spent some time with my cousin, Emily Courtney, the rector's wife," she said. "We have been working very hard collecting donations of food, clothing, and money for the victims of the Irish famine. I am sorry that our government has done very little or nothing to help."

James, touched by her intensity of purpose and concerned at the stories she related was very surprised. "Emma, I cannot believe that the government has done nothing, I shall make enquiries when I am back in London and write to you," he said earnestly. It was the first time he had seen her so deeply concerned and ready to be involved in anything outside of her immediate family.

Sunday, being cold, was spent mostly indoors, where they made music and played card games with the children to keep themselves occupied after walking briskly to church and back.

Emma took the opportunity to acquaint James with more tragic tales from Ireland, using Kitty's letters as evidence, leaving him greatly disturbed. Before leaving, James promised again to send news of the government's work in Ireland.

The Bingleys bade him farewell, at the same time inviting him to return and stay with them whenever he was in the area. "You must not wait for an invitation, Mr Wilson," said Jane. "As you can see, we have plenty of room—and you are always welcome."

He thanked them profusely and, before he went, bade farewell to Emma and the children, reminding them that they were expected at Standish Park in Spring.

The following day, Emily and Caroline called to take Emma on another round of what Sophie had called "begging visits."

Aided by Rebecca Tate's articles in *The Review* and *The Courier*, a good deal of attention had been drawn to the cause of the suffering poor of

Ireland. Church congregations and workers' clubs had started to collect food and clothing, while some businessmen were even willing to donate money. So successful were they that a further consignment of goods and donations of money were ready to go within the month.

Returning from visiting the Courtneys some days later, Emma was greeted by her sisters with the news that an express had come for her from London. It was from James Wilson.

He thanked her and her parents for their generous hospitality and sent regards from his mother. But chiefly, the letter contained information on the topic that had troubled her so much.

He wrote:

I have made several discreet enquiries of some of the men who are most likely to know the truth of these matters, and I am told that because of the peculiar nature of the Irish economy, having little or no industry to provide employment and thereby relying almost solely on farm labour, many people at Westminster had barely realised the extent of the problem until it became desperate.

However, in the course of last year, churches and private charities, having provided as much help as they could muster, had begun to clamour for action from the government, especially to alleviate the dreadful consequences of the rapacious practices of certain landlords—many of them English, I am ashamed to admit. This year, I am reliably informed, the government has begun to provide some direct help, opening food distribution centres and soup kitchens.

Inadequate though this may be, it is at least a start, and I promise I shall personally lobby those responsible to ensure that more is done.

Dear Emma, your concern does you great credit, and the work done by all those who have been engaged in providing help to these unhappy people will surely receive God's blessing as well as their gratitude.

Alas, we may never know the whole truth—how many unfortunate souls perished and how many more are even now fleeing their homeland and emigrating to America.

I do apologise that this letter is almost wholly taken up with depressing news, but there is at least one thing which I know will bring a smile to your face.

My mother was so deeply affected by what I have told her of the terrible circumstances in Ireland and your concern to help the unfortunate victims that she has asked me to send you a substantial donation of money to be forwarded to the charity whose work your group supports.

I shall arrange for it to be sent to you as soon as possible.

For the moment, I shall take my leave of you, conveying our kind regards and every good wish to your self, your parents, and sisters—and to Victoria and Stephanie, of course.

God bless you, Emma,

Yours sincerely,

James Wilson.

The letter's contents, especially its last paragraph, filled Emma with delight. She could not wait to tell Emily of the donation from Mrs Wilson. It was such a wonderful surprise.

An opportunity arose when her mother suggested a visit to the Gardiners, and it was eagerly taken.

A note was dispatched to Emily, and the following day, when they arrived at the Gardiners' house at Lambton, Emily was already there.

The two women had struck up a close friendship, even though Emily was almost thirty-nine, while Emma was barely thirty years old. They had both suffered harrowing experiences and emerged with their spirits unscathed and their resilience enhanced.

Emily, now a mature woman with very strong convictions, was the ideal person to provide Emma, whose tragic marriage had only recently become known to her, with inspiration. As she had done many years ago for her cousin Elizabeth, whose life had been devastated by the death of her son, Emily gave Emma both comfort and counsel. They shared also a love of music and seemed to imbue their children with the same enthusiasm.

Emily's three children were all talented. Elizabeth, her eldest, was a bright and industrious scholar, while young William was already receiving accolades from his teacher for his performance on the pianoforte. As for little Jessica, it seemed she could hardly wait to be tall enough to play upon the same instrument.

The same teachers were now engaged to teach Victoria and Stephanie, and the two mothers had a great deal to discuss. Bingley and Jane were delighted to see Emma engaged in a variety of pursuits and seemingly so contented. Darcy and Elizabeth, who were dining with them, were likewise amazed at the change in her since her return to Ashford Park.

"I cannot believe that this is the same rather timid, young Emma we used to meet in London, or on the rare occasion when she could get away to visit us," said Elizabeth.

Jane shook her head, still unable to comprehend the terrible circumstances of her daughter's ill-fated marriage. "I can only thank God that things have turned out this way. A year or two more and Emma might well have been driven to desperation or become very ill," she said.

"I cannot tell you how grateful we are to Mr James Wilson and his mother for having the foresight and good sense to remove her and the children from London and send them to us," said Bingley.

Darcy agreed that it was certainly an act of great good sense on their part, but even more was it evidence of the good judgement and character of Mr Wilson. "That he should have made such a clear-sighted decision, while setting aside any feelings he may have had for his brother, distinguishes him as a man of high principles," said Darcy, adding, "Everything I have heard and seen of him and his conduct towards Emma and her children only serves to confirm my view."

Joining them at dinner, having put her daughters to bed, Emma told them of the donation from James and his mother for the famine victims and how it had come about. The pleasure she took in detailing the news she had received from James and her obvious appreciation of his efforts did not go unnoticed by Elizabeth.

Earlier reports of the gift of a beautiful piece of jewellery had also excited her interest, especially when Emma gladly produced the item for their admiration. There was no doubting her response; she was clearly delighted to be treated with so much affection after years of indifference or worse.

It was inevitable that the matter would come up for discussion as Elizabeth and Darcy returned to Pemberley.

Darcy had a simple and logical explanation, "Plainly, both Mrs Wilson and James wish to make amends for the suffering Emma endured at the hands of her husband, and her own generous nature lets her accept their kindness without rancour."

Elizabeth wondered if perhaps there was more than mere gestures of kindness and concern involved.

"Could it not be that James Wilson is a little bit in love with our beautiful Emma? From all I have heard and observed, he appears to display some of the signs of a man in love or very close to it. Jane will not say more than that he shows a marked partiality for Emma's company, but whenever he visits, she is the centre of his attention, even though he professes an interest in his nieces," she declared, prompting her husband to smile and warn her yet again against matchmaking.

Elizabeth protested that she was not matchmaking at all, merely observing a couple of persons who might be falling in love. "Surely you must agree that, were it to happen, it would be no bad thing. Or do you see any strong objections to such a union?" she asked, challenging him to produce a contrary view.

Darcy knew her far too well to be drawn into the game. "My dear Lizzie, I doubt if there is anything that I might say which will change your mind on this subject—but if there were some impediment to their mutual happiness, I am quite certain Emma and James will discover it for themselves. If there is not, and they are continually in each other's company, they will probably marry. They certainly appear well suited," he conceded.

"There you are," she said, triumphantly, "so you do not deny that my original notion was a reasonable one."

Darcy, realising that he had almost lost the round, decided that surrender was inevitable. "Of course not, I cannot possibly accuse you of being unreasonable in this, as in most other matters. No doubt we shall discover before very long whether you are right about James and Emma. For my part, I can see no objection, providing it is what they both desire. It is their happiness that matters."

In the first week of May, Emma and her daughters, accompanied by her maid Sally and their nurse, Mrs Elliot, left Ashford Park for London, whence they were to proceed to Standish Park.

As Jane told it to her sister Elizabeth and her Aunt Gardiner, a letter had arrived for Emma from the Wilsons' lawyers, acquainting her with the terms of her husband's will, under which she inherited his share of the Wilsons' property in Kent. There had also been a letter from her mother-in-law inviting her most cordially to make Standish Park her permanent home.

"I have to say, however, that it was the letter from James that seemed to make her mind up," said Jane, smiling as she explained. "He added his voice to Mrs Wilson's invitation and detailed the arrangements for their journey. He will be meeting them in London and accompanying them to Kent. Well, within an hour of receiving it, Emma had announced that they would be leaving for London on the morrow and an express was dispatched to advise Mr Wilson."

Mrs Gardiner expressed surprise, but Elizabeth seemed to expect it. "After all, as you can see, Spring has not reached us yet, it's still rather cold and it has not stopped raining across the Midlands. In Kent, I am informed, the daffodils are out in the woods around Rosings; no doubt they will be out at Standish Park, and who can blame Emma for wanting a change of scene? Especially when such a warm welcome awaits her."

Mrs Gardiner remarked that she had noticed Jane's smile and the twinkle in Lizzie's eye. "Are you both teasing me?" she asked. "I have been busy recently, but from the tenor of your remarks, I feel I have missed something."

Both Jane and Elizabeth laughed and assured their aunt that they would tell her everything in the course of the afternoon, a remark which she took to mean that they had no wish to discuss the matter while the servants were in the room.

The arrival of an express from London interrupted their conversation.

Opening it hurriedly, Jane revealed that it was from Emma. "It seems she is already at Standish Park," she said, and sat down to read the letter to them. Emma wrote:

Dearest Mama,

I know you would want to be assured that we have concluded our journey successfully and safely.

As you know, we were to go first to London. The coach made good time even after breaking journey at Cambridge and Hertford. Mr Wilson met us and conveyed us to the house in Mayfair, where we dined and stayed the night. Since the children were very tired, we thought it best to wait until the morrow, when we left for Kent soon after breakfast.

At Rochester, where we broke journey, the daffodils were out in the meadows, and along the way we could see the Spring blossoms coming out everywhere. It was truly pretty, but nowhere was it prettier than in the great cherry and apple orchards of Standish Park, which we could see blooming profusely as we approached.

Mrs Wilson greeted us very warmly. She declares she has been pining for her granddaughters, and both Victoria and Stephanie seem happy to be back. Victoria loves the house and remembers every nook and cranny of the place.

Speaking of the house, dear Mama, there has been a great deal of work done on the house since I was last here. James has had an architect refurbish the suites in the east wing and, Mama, they are quite beautiful.

I could not believe my eyes; they all look so new and different, with pretty pastel colours and tasteful furnishings. Everything we need for our comfort is here. Nothing has been forgotten.

The school room is a picture—light and airy, not at all forbidding like the old one used to be. Even Mrs Elliot has a bright, new room, just next door to the girls. The children were overjoyed. They could not make up their minds which room they preferred.

I had no such difficulty. I had a choice, but took only a moment to decide that the suite which afforded a view of the downs and woodlands reaching as far as the eye could see was to be mine.

Mrs Wilson had feared we would not like the new rooms—we used to have apartments on the other side of the house when we lived here—but James was confident we would enjoy the change.

I have assured them both that we, all of us, love our new rooms and expect to be very happy here.

Dear Mama, I have written this before going down to dinner, which is always at eight. James has promised it shall be sent express, so I expect it will reach you tomorrow.

Do give my love to Papa, Louisa, and Sophie, and my dear uncles and aunts.

Your loving daughter,

Emma.

By the time Jane had finished reading Emma's letter, both Elizabeth and Mrs Gardiner had exchanged so many glances, it was plain they had drawn some new conclusions.

It was quite clear that the Wilsons intended to make Emma feel as welcome and as much at home as possible at Standish Park. They had spared neither effort nor expense.

What was equally clear was that Emma needed very little persuasion indeed. When Darcy called to take her home, Elizabeth was full of the news in Emma's letter and talked about it all the way back to Pemberley.

Darcy waited until they were in their apartments before responding. He knew she expected him to comment and did not disappoint her.

"I know you are excited about Emma's letter, my dear, and I concede that it looks very much like your vision of Emma's future is likely to come true. But I have even more important news for you."

Looking at his face, which was, by now, creasing into a broad smile, Elizabeth was suddenly aware that she was being teased by the husband she had introduced to the art.

"What news?" she demanded, feigning outrage at the ploy he had used.

"If you will let me tell you, I can guarantee that you will be both surprised and pleased," he said continuing to tantalise her, knowing she was dying to hear it all at once.

Elizabeth pleaded with him not to be so vexing, and he finally took pity upon her. "Well, as you know I've been with Bingley all day. He asked to see me about a family matter."

Elizabeth could not suppress a smile. Even today, a man married some thirty years, Bingley still unfailingly sought his friend's advice.

"Bingley has recently received a communication from James Wilson proposing the setting up of a trust to administer the interests of Emma and her daughters," Darcy explained. "He was very surprised. Knowing the circumstances of David Wilson's death, he had not expected that there would be very much at all for Emma and the girls to inherit. But, contrary to his belief, Bingley found that James was proposing to put in trust a substantial sum of money, to which would be added the one-third share of the proceeds of the sale or lease of the property in Mayfair. He has asked that either Bingley or Jonathan be appointed as a trustee along with himself, to administer it. Now, Lizzie, what do you think of that?"

Darcy enjoyed seeing his wife's expression change as she went from mild surprise to complete amazement. "Darcy, what does this mean?" she demanded.

"James Wilson obviously wishes to establish some method by which Emma and her children will be fully supported and provided for in the future," he replied, reasonably and logically.

"And he clearly intends to play some part in that future, would you not agree?" she asked, and when he said nothing, Elizabeth could not resist throwing her arms around him. "Darcy, you must not tease me, please. I suspect you do know something more than you have revealed, do you not?"

After a suitably tantalising pause, he nodded. "Yes, but you are to tell no one because, until Bingley replies, it is a confidence and must be respected."

She was so keen to hear everything; he sat her down on the sofa before he continued.

"James Wilson has asked Bingley's permission to propose marriage to Emma. There, 'tis out now. Are you happy?"

Elizabeth was ecstatic. "Happy! My dear, it is surely the best news for Emma."

Darcy had to agree that it certainly was that, but advised her again not to speak of it even to Jane, until matters had been settled between Bingley and James Wilson.

Elizabeth wanted to know more. She was impatient for information. "Have you seen the letter? How does he write?" she asked.

Darcy, holding the better hand, for once, played with her. "Yes I have; he writes exceedingly well. There is no doubting his sincerity." Seeing the look of sheer frustration upon her face, he relented and proceeded to explain, "James has asked only to be allowed to approach Emma. If she accepts him, he has promised they will wait until the formal year of mourning is over before they marry."

"And?" she prompted eagerly.

"He has also declared in the warmest terms his deep love for Emma and her children, and claims that he has reason to hope that his addresses may not be unwelcome," Darcy added.

Having considered this, Elizabeth persevered, "Tell me, what is Bingley's response? Will he consent?" she asked.

Darcy chose his words with care, "In truth, James does not have to ask Bingley's permission—Emma is a woman of independent means and can marry whom she pleases. But I think Wilson is simply attempting to do everything right."

"A sensible course, certainly, but I still do not know how Bingley intends to respond," she complained.

Darcy indicated that Bingley had only praise for James Wilson, and if Emma wished to accept him, he could see no objection to the match. He imagined the reply to Wilson would be in similar vein.

"I cannot believe that either Bingley or Jane would wish to thwart Emma's wishes if she wants to marry him, not after what she has endured."

"Nor can I. But, from a purely practical standpoint, too, it would be an excellent thing for Emma and the girls, would it not?" Elizabeth asked.

Darcy agreed, "Certainly, especially since it is unlikely that there would have been much left for Emma and the children after all David Wilson's debts and liabilities were cleared."

Darcy further pointed out the generosity of Mrs Wilson and her elder son in offering to share a substantial part of their own inheritance in order to make provision for Emma and her daughters. "It indicates that they take their duty to her and the children seriously and are unwilling to let her fall back on her parents for support."

His tone indicated his approval, and Elizabeth was sure he would have said as much to Bingley.

"Do you know when Bingley will reply?" she asked.

Darcy had no idea but said he imagined it would be soon. "I am sure he realises that Emma's happiness and the future of her daughters depend upon it. He is unlikely to delay longer than is necessary to acquaint your sister of the content of James's letter."

Elizabeth asserted with confidence that Jane was unlikely to lodge any objection, having always expressed a preference for James over his brother David.

"Jane indicated to me at least six months before Emma's wedding that it was James, not David, who was the better of the two Wilsons. She went so far as to declare that he was the best man she had met since Bingley first came to Netherfield all those years ago!" she explained. "It made me wonder whether Emma was marrying the wrong man, which, clearly, she was."

Darcy's face was grave again. "It is such a pity that Emma had to endure so much unhappiness before it was put right. Worse still, she suffered mostly alone. I know Bingley knew very little of the parlous state of Emma's marriage until it was all revealed at the end. He still feels guilty about it. It is, without doubt, a terrible situation for a parent to face!" he declared.

Elizabeth sighed. "Poor Emma," she said. "Have we not been very fortunate with Cassy and Richard?"

Darcy agreed. He had never doubted that Richard would be a good husband to his daughter; it had been an added joy to discover that they appeared to have found true happiness together. "Yes, you are quite right, Lizzie," he said, "they are indeed blessed. We can only pray that Emma's second chance at happiness will be as good. James is a thoroughly decent and honourable man, and I am sure if she accepts him, she will do so because she loves and trusts him."

❧

Spring had well and truly arrived in the Weald of Kent, with its rich pastures, orchards, woodlands, and many splendid country estates, when Emma wrote to Emily Courtney.

Dear Emily, she wrote:

I gather from Sophie's letter, which arrived last week, that Spring has not quite reached the Midlands.

In Kent, we have been blessed with truly perfect Spring weather—of the kind that makes one's spirit soar!

Except for the threat of an occasional seasonal downpour, for which one must always go well prepared, it is ideal for walking, being uniformly soft and subtle, without the heat of Summer or the chill of Winter to complain about.

I have taken to indulging in my favourite pastime of reading out of doors rather than in the library or the living room. The girls and I have been walking all over the park and occasionally down to the village, which lies at the bottom of the valley. There are always plenty of excellent spots in the woods, which are beautiful now, and in the meadows beside the many streams, where we enjoy a quiet rest and read.

Last Saturday, we had gone out on just such a venture, enjoying the fresh air and exercise, when the sound of horses alerted us to the arrival of visitors, who turned out to be none other than Jonathan who had come down from London with James.

So enamoured were they of the pretty spot we had chosen for our "reading place" that they were loathe to leave and stayed with us until it was time to return to the house.

Victoria and Stephanie were a little weary and wanted to be lifted onto the horses, which the gentlemen then carefully guided home while I walked with them. We walked along the lanes and across the meadows, strewn with wild flowers, all in soft sunshine and a gentle breeze.

Can you not imagine, dear Emily, what a happy afternoon it made— for all of us and especially for my dear daughters?

Emily could certainly see that it would have made a very pleasant afternoon, but reading between and betwixt the lines, she could also sense the delight in her cousin's words.

They had spent several hours during the last few months, sharing their experience and understanding of the sorrows that life had dealt them. Here for the first time, Emily was being given a glimpse of the effect that a healthy dose of happiness could have on Emma's life.

She read on to learn that preparations were afoot at Standish Park for their journey to Canterbury, which was to be undertaken over a period of a week, for there was much to be seen both in the ancient cathedral city and on the way. It was natural that they would all be very excited.

Emma wrote that Mrs Wilson had asked to be excused:

Her health has improved somewhat since we have been here, but she has been advised not to risk its deterioration by undertaking a journey at this time. I was concerned about leaving her behind, but she assures me that with her maid and the two excellent nurses, who care for her day and night, she will be well looked after.

Our party will therefore consist of Mrs Elliot, myself and the two girls, James, his manservant, and my maid Sally—apart from the coachman and groom, of course. We are all looking forward to it very much, indeed. Stephanie and Victoria can hardly sleep for the excitement, and try as I might to remain calm, I am being drawn into the whirlpool, too.

When I next write I promise I shall tell you all about Canterbury,
Chilham, and the other interesting places I am assured we are going to see.
God bless you.
Your loving cousin,
Emma.

On the morning on which they were to leave, the post brought several letters for James and one for Emma. Seeing it was from her mother, she tucked it into her pocket book, while James took his into the study, where he spent but a short time before emerging, apparently pleased with his correspondence, smiling and eager to set off for Canterbury.

The children were agog with excitement, and everything they would need on their journey had already been packed; all that remained was to take their leave of Mrs Wilson and be gone.

It was a fair distance to Canterbury, and they broke journey twice on the way. They visited the great estate and mansion at Godmersham and the neighbouring village of Chilham, some five miles from Canterbury, where a unique castle had been built in Jacobean times on a spot where Julius Caesar was supposed to have camped when he invaded England.

Its present owners had obtained the services of "Capability Brown," England's most celebrated landscape gardener, to create a romantic retreat. James was full of information about its history, and while Emma could appreciate the design and artistry of the place, Chilham did not really appeal to her.

She reluctantly admitted that, except for the lovely vistas of the gardens, she was not greatly attracted to Chilham. James pretended at first to be very disappointed, but when she was immediately contrite he laughed and confessed that he was teasing her. "It would not distress me unduly if you were not to like Chilham, Emma, but Canterbury, now that would be quite another matter."

Emma promised to make every effort to like Canterbury, asking to be guided on its most remarkable features so she could properly appreciate them. James, thereafter, spent the rest of their journey telling them all there was to know about the ancient cathedral city.

Emma and Mrs Elliot had asked many questions and were both quite amazed at the depth of his knowledge until he confessed to having spent several years of his boyhood at the home of his uncle, a former warden at the cathedral, from whom he had learnt most of the history of this great medieval place of pilgrimage.

Emma was familiar with the story of Thomas à Becket, but both her daughters were wide eyed as James told the terrible tale of his murder in the cathedral.

On reaching the town, they went first to their lodgings, which were not far from the cathedral precinct. Later, they would walk about the town and savour its historic atmosphere as well as its fine Georgian architecture. They planned to spend the following day at the cathedral.

That night, Emma and her daughters, despite being weary from travelling, sat down before going to bed and wrote in her diary an account of their journey and the many things they had learned.

Later, in a letter to Emily, she recounted the experience:

I am continually astonished at his knowledge and interest in so many subjects. I could scarcely have conducted a conversation of the most trivial nature on any of these topics with David, so little interest did he display in them, yet with James, there is no end of matters to talk about.

Furthermore, he surprises me daily with his kindness and consideration—not just to me and the children but to Mrs Elliot and Sally, as well.

Nothing seems to be too much trouble if it will enhance our comfort or improve our conditions. Unaccustomed as I am to all this attention, I have to confess that it is exceedingly pleasurable and I certainly do not complain of it.

Emma had become increasingly aware in the past few days of the particular attention that James paid to her—his customary consideration seemed to be enhanced by a degree of tender concern.

Whether it was in a look or a touch of his hand upon her arm, or a particular expression on his face as she caught him watching her in an unguarded moment, she could not exactly tell. She was certain, however, that their relationship had deepened almost imperceptibly from a general warm friendliness to a level that had struck a new chord in her heart.

She did not stop to question whether her own feelings were deeply involved. There was no need to do so, she told herself—James was her brother-in-law and she had always loved him for his kindness to her and her children.

Now, however, a new emotion was confronting her and demanding attention. She was not uncomfortable with it, but wished she had someone, a sister or a friend, to confide in. She longed for Emily, sure that from her she would receive both understanding and wise counsel.

Emma, unlike her mother at an earlier age, was neither naïve nor unsophisticated in her understanding of social relationships. Spending most of her ten years of marriage to David Wilson in London had considerably sharpened her perceptive faculties.

Each night after dinner, James would inquire after their comfort and well-being, before planning the program for the morrow. Were they tired of ancient historical sites? Would they prefer a drive up into the downs where there were several pretty villages to be seen? "There is nowhere else in England quite like Kent," he said, as they planned another excursion. "Almost every fold of the downs holds a hidden piece of history or some beautiful old village."

Mrs Elliot had a strong constitution and appeared to suffer not at all from all the exertion, and the girls seemed quite tireless and were eager to set off on yet another expedition. Emma, however, had wearied after days of sight-seeing and asked if she could stay in and write her letters—all of which were overdue—while the others went into town.

Resting in the cool parlour, where their host had provided her with tea, she had been working industriously when James returned in the middle of the morning, having left the others visiting the ancient abbey of St Augustine.

She was reading again the letter from her mother, which she had received on the day they had set out on their journey. She put it aside when James walked in, apologising for interrupting her.

He sat down beside her and, remarking that she looked rather pale, asked if he could bring her some refreshment.

Emma protested that she was quite well. "It is just that I was a little tired from too much walking yesterday, and I thought I should rest today and write my letters," she said.

"Of course, you must," he said and then, seeing the letter lying on the table, asked in a tone that was meant to sound light-hearted, "No doubt your parents are missing you and wanting you back?"

Emma smiled and James seemed to believe that it implied confirmation of his remark. Yet, when she spoke, her reply was ambivalent. "Mother has her days full with my two sisters and Jonathan's little ones whenever he and Amelia are in London. I do not believe she has had time to miss me—yet. In a month or two, perhaps…"

"Does that mean we shall have the pleasure of your company for a while longer?" he asked, and when she replied that she had not decided when they would be going home, he was unable to contain his anguish.

"Emma, but Standish Park is your home. You must not speak as if you are mere visitors there."

There was something in the altered tone of his voice that prompted her to look up at him, and she saw in his countenance, and particularly in the expression of his eyes, what she recognised as the change in the relationship between them. While nothing had been said, she could not fail to be aware of a distinct deepening of their feelings towards one another. It was clear to her that James was aware of it, also.

Emma had already acknowledged to herself a subtle change in her own attitude towards him. It had altered her view of life as she realised that she was no longer looking forward to going "home" to her parents. Instead, she found herself anticipating the evenings they spent together at Standish Park, which was—as James had pointed out—her home and that of her children.

During the weeks since she had returned to Kent, she had become more involved with running the household on account of Mrs Wilson's ill health. She had known several of the staff for many years, and they accepted her as the mistress of Standish Park with ease. James had begun to consult her on decisions concerning the house and grounds. It gave her a new dignity, which she was enjoying very much.

There had been days on which they spent many pleasant hours discussing the changes that were being made at Standish Park, changes that were to improve the property or the lives of the people who lived and worked on the estate.

While James did not press her further, she felt obliged to make it clear to him that she had, at this time, no plans to return to Ashford Park.

The smile that lit up his face was sufficient to express his feelings, but he had to say, "I am very happy to hear it, Emma. No one wants you to leave here—we would all miss you very much, and the children, of course. I know my mother would be particularly sad and so, indeed, would I."

The sounds of the others returning interrupted their conversation, but Emma was very glad they had spoken.

Returning to Standish Park the following night, they were very tired, but wanted to talk about their wonderful week at Canterbury.

Victoria and Stephanie had so much to tell their grandmother, Emma was afraid they would weary her. But Mrs Wilson enjoyed it all. "It is so good having you all home again," she said at breakfast the next morning as she looked around the table at her family, "I missed you very much, especially you, Emma—no one can sing for me as you do."

Emma looked across at James and, catching his eye, she smiled, remembering their conversation. He had been quite sincere when he had said how sad they would all be had she decided to return to Leicestershire.

Some days later, the post brought some sad news. Mrs Elliot had an urgent letter from her sister in London. Her mother was ill and was asking to see her.

She was anxious to go to her. "Of course, you must go," said Emma, and she went immediately to find James and arrange for transport to take her to meet the coach.

She left soon afterwards to get the coach to Rochester, where she would change for London. The girls were tearful, pleading with her to write soon. They would miss her terribly. Emma and Sally made sure they were bathed and in bed early.

Later, Emma came downstairs to find James alone in the sitting room. He was standing at the end of the room, looking out of the big bay windows and turned as she entered. It was a truly perfect late Spring evening.

When he spoke, she responded naturally, almost without thinking. "It is such a beautiful evening Emma, will you take a turn in the garden with me?" he asked.

There was no need for words. She smiled and took his arm as they went out onto the terrace and down the steps.

They walked along a familiar path, between the rose garden and the shrubbery. Very little of any substance was said by either, as they watched the birds fly in from the distant fields to rest in the trees around the grounds, and yet they were clearly in harmony as they walked together, turning away from the house towards the grove of fine old oaks that shaded its western face from the afternoon sun.

Hearing church bells in the distance, James broke the silence, reminding her that the bell ringers were practising for the wedding of Claire Greenacre, the daughter of a neighbouring family.

"Tomorrow she will marry her childhood sweetheart; I have known them both all our lives. We played together as children," he said.

"Do you think they will be happy, James?" Emma asked. She knew Claire very slightly but had no knowledge of her bridegroom.

He smiled and nodded, but he did not exactly answer her question. Instead, he turned and, looking directly at her with a very purposeful expression, said, "Emma, forgive me. I know I have not said anything to prepare you for this, but please, let me tell you now how much you are appreciated and loved, and how happy you would make me if you stayed on with us at Standish Park permanently."

She was at once surprised and flattered, but she seemed also a little puzzled, not quite comprehending his meaning.

"Thank you, James, you are very kind. I have no intention of leaving, at least not in the near future. Do you mean…?"

He interrupted her, realising that he had to speak clearly now, lest his words were completely misconstrued and the opportunity lost. "I mean, my dearest Emma, that I love you dearly and would be honoured if you would agree to be my wife," he said and, seeing her eyes widen with astonishment, he went on very quickly, "Please, do not say no at once. Take some time to think about it. But I do ask you, most earnestly, to believe that it will make me the happiest of men, and I would do everything in my power to look after you and the girls and make you truly happy."

She looked at him and was surprised at what seemed to be a look of genuine apprehension upon his face.

He was about to tell her of his affection for Victoria and Stephanie when she gently took his hand in hers and said quietly, "James, thank you. I am truly honoured, but…"

But he interrupted her again, afraid she was about to refuse him. "Emma, please, there is no hurry; you can take all the time you want."

"I don't need any more time, James—and you are right, I was unprepared for this, so I have not got a pretty speech ready for you, but may I say...would it be acceptable if I just said thank you and yes?"

She was watching his face as his expression changed from slight bewilderment to alarm and then to complete heartfelt delight as he embraced her and thanked her from the bottom of his heart.

"My darling Emma," he began, but neither of them would remember how he ended as he told her in many sincere and loving words how deeply he cared and how much joy she had given him.

He had dared, he said, to hope, but he had been afraid to ask too soon. "I was terrified you would refuse my love," he confessed, and Emma smiled and set his heart at rest.

"Dear James, there was never any danger of that; because, you see, I already knew I loved you. You have been so good to me..."

But he would not let her continue. "Hush, my love, please do not speak of that, for I have done little more than I—my whole family—owed you for the intolerable mistreatment you endured at the hands of my brother for years. My love for you, which has grown upon me gradually, has taken over all my waking hours. Emma, my dearest, I give you my word; you will never regret your decision today," he said with so much warmth and sincerity that she was overwhelmed.

Her certainty not only of his love but of her own deep feelings, which had come rushing to the surface as he spoke, prevented her from saying very much more. Yet, her face was suffused with an expression of such sweetness as left James in no doubt of her state of mind. There was surely, in their case, the happiest coincidence of feelings.

As they went indoors, the candles were being lit, and James suggested that it would be best to tell his mother their news tonight and the children tomorrow. Emma said she would write to her parents immediately. "I do not need their permission, but I would like to have their blessing," she said.

"You have that already, Emma," said James, taking her father's letter from his pocket. "This arrived on the morning we left for Canterbury; I have been carrying it around like a talisman all this time, waiting for the right moment to approach you."

She read it quickly. Bingley's letter was brief but quite clear. He thanked James for his letter, pointed out that his daughter was certainly entitled to marry whomever she chose, but that he and Mrs Bingley would be delighted to give them their blessing if she accepted his proposal of marriage. He added that if he was accepted, James should consider himself the most fortunate of men.

"Of that there is no question," said James.

"Dear Papa," she sighed, "he believes that the entire world shares his high opinion of his daughters."

"Well, I have not met a single soul who thought differently," James countered, and Emma smiled as she also noted the reference by her father to the trust arrangements for herself and her daughters, suggested by James. She asked him what they were meant to accomplish.

"That, my dearest, was signed and sealed before our attorneys more than two weeks ago," he said, reminding her of Jonathan's visit.

"That was when it was arranged," he explained. "The reason it was put in place was simply this—we felt, Mother and I, that the trust would give you independence. It was the right thing to do because, had you decided against me, it would have been unthinkable that you should remain financially dependent upon my mother and myself. As it is, the arrangement stands; whatever happens to us, your income and the children's future can be assured."

Emma was so touched by the generosity of this gesture that she pulled him closer and hugged him affectionately, careless of who might see them.

"Dear, dear James, how much kinder or more generous can you be? I am seriously concerned that I shall never be able to match your goodness." And when he tried to hush her, for his natural modesty was outraged, she turned to him with tears in her eyes and said, "No, James, let me say it, now that I have a right to do so. I have not known such kindness outside of my own dear family. I shall not only be happy but proud, indeed, to be your wife."

Later she would write to Emily in similar vein:

He is, in truth, such a genuinely good man, Emily, that I am concerned that I shall never attain a similar level of virtue.

It is impossible to believe that he is of the same blood family as David, for how could one brother be so morally reprehensible and the other so imbued with goodness? I can honestly say that in all of my life, I have met no one who has inspired similar feelings in me.

Forgive me for being so free with the superlatives. It is not my usual way, but what I say is true—believe me, Emily. When you know him better, I have no doubt at all that you will agree with me.

Mrs Wilson was so pleased when they told her that she enfolded Emma in her arms, declaring that she was certain James would make her very happy.

After dinner, she produced a ring, a family heirloom, which she asked James to present to Emma, causing even more happiness—if that was possible on such a day filled with so much joy.

Later in the week, James asked Emma when she would like to visit her family. "I know they must be impatient to see you," he said.

Emma was overjoyed; she longed to see her parents.

Since Mrs Elliot had returned, there was no reason why they should not go forthwith. Having first sent an express to announce their plans to the Bingleys, they set off for Leicestershire.

Victoria and Stephanie had been told gently by their mother that "Uncle James was going to marry Mama" and look after all of them. It was clearly a proposition that held no fears for them, for they were more anxious to have permission to attend the Spring Fair in the village, which promised much fun and games, complete with clowns and dancing bears.

Consequently, the newly engaged pair were left mostly to themselves, and, as if this were insufficient deprivation, it seemed they were to have only each other's company on the journey north. Strangely, this appeared to cause them no unhappiness at all.

The Bingleys, on receiving Emma's letter, followed by the express advising of their visit, were so overjoyed that they had to share their good news with the rest of their family and friends.

So it was that after the first day, during which they kept Emma and James to themselves, Bingley and Jane gave a dinner party, at which the couple were the centre of attention. Not everyone had anticipated the engagement—apart from their closest relations and friends—but seeing them together, noting especially Emma's almost ineffable happiness, no one could be other than delighted.

Emma and her mother were inseparable as they shared their joy.

"Oh dear Mama, I am too happy, I know it," she said. "James loves me and I do not know if I deserve him; he is such a good man."

"Hush, Emma. There is no one in the whole world who deserves a better husband than you do," said Jane.

Elizabeth and her sister embraced before they parted. "Lizzie, I cannot tell you how much it means to me to know that my Emma is happy at last," said Jane, who had for years shared the strain of her daughter's unhappy marriage.

Elizabeth could only concur. At last, it seemed Emma—gentle, kind Emma—had found the happiness she so richly deserved.

It was agreed that the wedding would take place in October, at the church in Ashford Park. Sophie and Louisa were bridesmaids.

Despite her affectionate heart, which would have liked to have her daughter settled closer to her family, Jane was pleased to see Emma as mistress of Standish Park, presiding over such an elegant home.

Of her husband's devotion to her, there was never a question, and his care of her children was exemplary.

Emma herself maintained the closest connections with her immediate family, but her most intimate friendship continued to be with Emily Courtney, to whom she felt she owed a debt of gratitude for her friendship during unbearably painful times.

Her letter to Emily some months after her marriage provided the clearest insight into her present frame of mind. Written shortly after Christmas—spent at Standish Park, where her parents and sisters had joined them—Emma's letter reached Emily on a cold, January morning. Yet the warmth and happiness her words conveyed seemed to flow from the closely written pages and envelop Emily as she read it.

Dearest Emily,

Thank you for your kind letter and Christmas greetings.

You have wished us happiness. I wish I were cleverer with words. I would have given anything to be able express my deepest feelings as felicitously as a writer like Charlotte Brontë would. But I am not Miss Brontë, so you must bear with me as I try to find the words to tell you how remarkably, utterly, and unbelievably my life has changed.

Emily, if anyone had told me a year or more ago that I could be in such a situation, I think I would have laughed them to scorn. I had reached the very nadir of existence, with little or no hope of liberation from a life steeped, for the most part, in deep despair.

Yet today, by the intervention of Fate and the love of my dear husband, my position is totally reversed. From a situation fraught with fear and shame, I have been transported to a state of happiness that I could not have imagined before.

As you, who have been twice blessed, will acknowledge, marriage with a loving partner is a blissful state. For me, this time, with a husband whose love is of the deepest and most devoted kind, it is indeed the happiest experience of my life.

With him it is possible to share the deepest and most passionate feelings, knowing that esteem and honesty are the bedrock upon which they rise.

Dear Emily, I thank God each day for my present happiness and thank you for your prayers.

We both look forward to seeing you in the Spring when we have been invited to Pemberley for the Festival of Music, where I know your William will be playing for us.

James sends his love and asks to be remembered to your James (is this not the most charming coincidence?), and the children both send love and kisses.

Thank you again, my dearest friend.

Your loving cousin,

Emma Wilson.

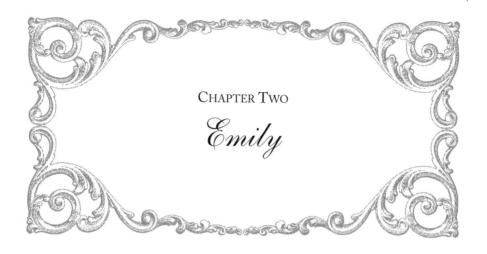

CHAPTER TWO

Emily

EMILY COURTNEY PUT DOWN her letter and smiled.

Her husband, James, looking up from his breakfast, noted that it was a particularly happy smile and said, "My dear, you have quite clearly had some very pleasing news from your cousin."

Emily confirmed that it was indeed pleasing to learn that her cousin Emma was so happy in her marriage. "She writes of being transported from a situation fraught with fear and shame to a state of genuine happiness. It is truly amazing that she could have been through so much and remain unembittered," said Emily, handing the letter to her husband while she poured out another cup of tea. Persuading her son, William, to finish his breakfast, she picked up little Jessica and took her upstairs.

Emily had no difficulty understanding her cousin's feelings. The comfortable domesticity of her own life, as the wife of the rector of Kympton, was in stark contrast to the years that had preceded her marriage to James Courtney. She was no stranger to suffering, having nursed her first husband, Paul Antoine, through his illness. Following his untimely death from tuberculosis, Emily had devoted her life almost entirely to the study of music and service to the community.

While she lived at Pemberley with the family she loved as dearly as her own, she had gradually come to terms with her own loss and, in doing so, helped Elizabeth and Darcy bear the dreadful sorrow of the death of their son, William. It was at Pemberley that she had met James Courtney, first as a young theology scholar, using the vast resources of the Pemberley library, and later when he returned as rector to the living of Kympton.

Their association had continued for many years, during which they had worked together on the hospital, school, and parish councils and on many charitable projects, helping the growing numbers of destitute families in the area. Sharing a passionate commitment to the poor and dispossessed, both James Courtney and Emily were determined to do more than pay lip service to the concept of charity preached in church. They had initiated several schemes to help, especially the children of the rural poor, who, bereft of their homes and land, mostly begged or stole for a living.

With the willing and generous support of Mr and Mrs Darcy, her own parents, and the help of a bevy of young cousins and friends, they ran community cottages and soup kitchens, providing shelter and food to many who would otherwise have starved or been incarcerated in the poor house.

Drawn together by their shared commitment and genuine sense of Christian charity, they had quite naturally reached a point when James, who had concealed his feelings for some time, finally proposed, and Emily was happy to accept him.

In James Courtney, Emily recognised the same goodness of heart that had endeared Paul Antoine to her. Though he had neither the good looks nor the style of her young Frenchman, the Reverend Courtney had a sense of humour which lightened her life considerably.

Their marriage had delighted her family. Mr Darcy immediately increased the stipend of the Rector of Kympton to acknowledge his elevation to the married state, while Mr and Mrs Gardiner spared no expense to redecorate and furnish the modest house that came with the living.

Emily, accustomed to gracious living at both Pemberley and Oakleigh, made no complaint about the proportions or style of the Kympton rectory; indeed, she set about making it as comfortable and pleasing a home as was possible.

Childless in her first marriage, Emily then went on to have three children—Elizabeth, William, and Jessica—and seemed remarkably content with her situation in life.

Writing to her sister Jane, Elizabeth had observed of Emily:

I have never ceased to be astounded at her energy and determination.

Her ability to undertake more and more work in the community while continuing to be a most devoted and loving mother is quite amazing.

Visit Kympton rectory at any time and you will find the place is spotless, even with less than half the domestic help one would normally expect to have. Call at any hour and the children are clean and contented—Elizabeth engaged in study or drawing or some such activity, while young William practises his piano constantly and with so little prompting that he puts the rest of us to shame.

Just last Sunday, we called in on our way to the Gardiners and there, in the middle of the kitchen, was Emily with two young ones from the parish whose unhappy, deserted mother had left them at the church while she went to work at the inn as a scullery maid!

Emily had no idea when the mother would return, except that the poor woman had left the little ones a scrap or two of stale bread and cheese tied up in a handkerchief for their dinner. Needless to say, Emily had flung out the pathetic little crumbs and was feeding them a hot meal of soup, pota-toes, and freshly baked bread.

It is an example, dearest Jane, of the kind of thing she does as a matter of course, a sign of her willingness to travel that extra mile to help someone who needs her. Some may call it Christian charity, but I am inclined to believe there is more to Emily's compassionate heart than charity.

She is, of all the women I know, the most selfless. I am sure you agree.

Elizabeth had concluded her letter with the hope that Emily's service to the community would be appreciated and recognised, even though it was the last thing Emily herself would have sought.

Returning to the dining room with Jessica, Emily explained to her husband that she was expected at Pemberley. "I am to meet Lizzie and Jane at Pemberley to decide on arrangements for the music festival. Papa is to call for me—he has business with Mr Darcy. I thought I should take Emma's letter along. I am sure it will please cousin Jane…"

She was interrupted by a great commotion in the kitchen, which caused her to rush out of the room.

When she returned, having settled satisfactorily some minor domestic drama involving the cook and a couple of runaway chickens, Emily found her husband folding up her letter, which he handed to her saying philosophically, "Your cousin appears to have a found a great degree of felicity in her marriage. I believe her character, which is both generous and affectionate, has enabled her to deal with disappointment and sorrow better than most. You are quite right to take it along to your meeting. I am sure Mrs Bingley will appreciate it very much, especially if it is true that she always preferred the elder Mr Wilson," he added with a twinkle in his eye. Emily smiled as she picked up the letter, "Well, yes it does seem as if she was right from the start. Pity poor Emma made the wrong choice the first time around."

"Well, I am for Derby," he said, standing up and moving into the hall. "We are trying to persuade the council to let us have the old almshouse in Bridge Street for a soup kitchen and shelter for the street children. It is draughty and old, but it would be a vast improvement on serving soup from a cart under the bridge! It's often a struggle to keep the cats and dogs at bay until we have fed the children."

Emily sighed, "I do hope you have more success than Caroline. When she wanted to use an old wool store for a schoolroom, the council was quite intransigent. It was Father's intervention that finally got them to agree."

James was about to suggest that he might need Mr Gardiner's help, too, when the sound of a carriage approaching drew them both to the window. The children had already seen the visitor from the windows upstairs and were calling out to him when Emily and James went to the door.

It was her brother, Robert. "Robert, what a nice surprise. We had no idea you were home."

Her youngest brother had spent so much time away—first overseas, in the colonies and then, more recently, in Liverpool, where he was in charge of a large trading house—they saw him rarely.

As he walked up the path to the house, Emily noticed how much more mature he looked—"quite a distinguished citizen, in fact," she remarked later to her husband.

"I am invited to Pemberley, too, on a different mission than yours, Emily," he said. "I am to discuss some business with Mr Darcy on Father's behalf; he is feeling rather poorly today."

Emily was immediately concerned for her father's health and had to be reassured by Robert that it was only a head cold. "He would have come himself, but Mother was determined that he should stay home and not risk catching a chill." Robert was smiling. "So here I am. Are we ready to leave?"

Emily, having taken a little time to ensure that Elizabeth and William knew what was expected of them while their mother was away for the day, put on her bonnet, scooped up little Jessica in her arms, kissed her husband and set out with her brother for Pemberley.

"I do wish you would come and live in Derbyshire, Robert," she said as they proceeded towards Pemberley. "It would mean so much to Mama, and you could help Papa with the business."

Robert could not keep the laughter out of his voice. "You will persist until you convince me, will you not, Emmy? Well, I have to say, the prospect of living in comfort at home with my parents, rather than in rented rooms in Liverpool, attracts me vastly. There is no comparison between the food I have served up to me by Mrs Brown and dishes that grace the table at home."

"Well, then?" His sister expressed her annoyance that he, in spite of so many obvious advantages, would not do the right thing.

Robert was evasive. "Emmy, it is not that I am unwilling to assist my father with the business; indeed, I am truly interested in the work to the extent that I have far more knowledge of it than I had before. But, apart from my family, whom I would visit anyway, there is little to hold me here."

Emily understood his concerns—she had some sympathy for her brother. Robert, the youngest and plainest of four children, had grown up in the shadow of a handsome, highly successful brother, two active and popular sisters, and several accomplished cousins.

Quiet and rather isolated from the rest of them, he had suffered a series of unfortunate problems which had culminated in his departure for the colony of Ceylon some fifteen years ago, where he had worked successfully for a large British trading firm for many years.

The experience had not only helped sharpen his commercial under-standing and skills, but it had forced him to be more independent and deci-sive than he had been as a young man. In fact, Robert Gardiner, now almost forty years old, was a good deal more eligible and attractive a proposition than he had been at twenty-five.

Looking at him, Emily smiled and said, "Robert, perhaps you just need a wife. That would give you a good reason to stay."

Robert threw back his head and laughed out loud. "Emmy, not you too! It's been Mother's obsession ever since I returned last year."

"Well, is it such an unattractive proposition?" she demanded.

"Certainly not, provided it is with the right person," he replied.

Emily was of a mind to pursue the matter. "And what might such a person be like?" she asked, only to have him challenge her.

"Someone I could love, of course. Emily, I know how deeply you feel about such matters. Surely you would not have me make a loveless marriage of convenience, just so I could remain in Derbyshire?"

"Robert, of course not! Would I ever suggest such a thing? All I meant was that the prospect of a happy marriage may well persuade you to stay."

They seemed to take an inordinate amount of time negotiating a deep bend in the road, which brought the house into view and, knowing it would not be long before they reached it, Emily did not pursue the subject.

On reaching Pemberley House, they were met by Elizabeth and Darcy as well as Jane and Mr Bingley, who had stayed over from the previous evening.

Bingley and Darcy, aware that Robert was there to represent his father, took him away to talk business while Emily and little Jessica were whisked upstairs.

Jessica was a calm, undemanding child who gave very little trouble, content to draw or play by herself for seemingly hours on end. Having settled her down in the old nursery with one of Elizabeth's maids for company, Emily joined her cousins in Elizabeth's sitting room.

Plans for the third music festival to be held at Pemberley were well advanced. The first, universally judged to be a success, had been held in 1843, when James and Emily Courtney, assisted by Georgiana Grantley, had persuaded a reluctant Elizabeth to approach Mr Darcy with a proposition. Surprisingly, he had not been at all averse to the idea, and the program had soon grown from a modest soiree to an outdoor festival.

The elegance and graciousness of Pemberley soon invested the occasion with its own magnificence, and a second festival in 1846 had seen an increase in the number of performers wanting to appear at such a celebrated venue.

Three years later, appropriately celebrating the end of a year of turmoil across Europe, the festival was planned to provide a special program for mainly young performers, including several of Georgiana's pupils.

A group of young Irish singers, as well a French choral ensemble, were expected. Georgiana herself had decided to play a recently published work by the Irish composer John Field, and the Matlock Chamber group was practising assiduously for their debut with young William Courtney. There was already an air of excitement around.

Elizabeth still felt a cold sadness in her heart each time she gazed out at the crowds gathering in the beautiful grounds, remembering her young son William, who, had he lived, would surely have been an accomplished pianist.

It was ironic that their son Julian, born some two years after William's death, had no musical talent at all, but Emily's boy, whom she had named William with Elizabeth's permission, had a prodigious talent, even though his mother sensibly refused to let him be treated like some precocious child prodigy. He had already had two teachers who had decided that they were insufficiently qualified to develop his remarkable gifts, and the third, a maestro who came to them every week from Coventry, had warned them that they had in William a young person who was likely to achieve great things in music.

"He must not be persecuted with Algebra and Latin," he had declared, "they will be of no use to him. Let him spend as much time as he likes with his music. In that, he may go far, for he has talent but he must work hard."

The Courtneys, with their modest means, were determined to do their best. However, when Elizabeth and Darcy heard of it through Mrs Gardiner, a plan was hatched: all of William's expenses in the teaching and learning of music would be borne by the Pemberley Trust, which had been set up in memory of William Darcy to provide for talented children.

Naturally, Emily and James Courtney were grateful but somewhat reluctant to accept such a generous and long-term gift—but Elizabeth and Darcy had insisted. It was a gift that would be repaid hundredfold as young William developed his skills and his love of music. He was to perform in public, alone, for the very first time at the Pemberley festival.

When the day arrived, Elizabeth and Emily were far more nervous than the young performer. Amazingly unperturbed and at ease, he was a complete contrast to his anxious mother, aunts, and grandparents, who hung upon every note he played until it was over in a great burst of applause from an audience enchanted by his performance.

When Elizabeth and Emily embraced, each understood why the other was weeping on this happiest of occasions. They had shared both the sorrow and the joy. Emma and James Wilson had attended, accompanied by a friend from London. A composer himself, the visitor, who had stayed discreetly in the background during the performance, was enthusiastic about young William Courtney and, at the supper afterwards, predicted that he had the talent to become a remarkable musician.

His modest parents, wanting only that their son should be happy, discounted a great deal of the praise but did not neglect to tell William how well he had done. Mrs Gardiner made them all smile when she declared that, wisely, "Emily and James were making quite certain that William received sufficient praise and encouragement to please his little heart but not too much to swell his little head!"

Since his return to England, Robert Gardiner had been making friends anew with the members of his family, and the Bingleys had been most hospitable. Their daughter, Sophie, though less of a beauty than her elder sister Emma, was, he had noticed, a particularly pleasant young woman and did not appear to be spoken for.

With his sister's words still in his mind, Robert accepted their invitation to dine with them on the following Saturday. It might, he thought, be an opportunity to spend some time getting to know Miss Sophie Bingley better. He had always liked her parents immensely, and Sophie appeared to share many of their qualities. If, as Emily suggested, a good wife and a happy marriage might encourage him to settle in Derbyshire, Robert was not averse to giving the matter some serious thought—although, he told himself, he was in no hurry at all.

He had not counted, however, on the Bingleys also inviting to the same dinner party the Darcys and their cousins, James and Rosamund Fitzwilliam, together with their daughter, Rose, a startlingly beautiful young woman of about twenty-seven.

Having been introduced to Robert and hearing of his long sojourn overseas, Miss Fitzwilliam evinced such a deep interest in his travels and work in the exotic east that in answering all her queries, he found he had no time at all left for Miss Bingley.

Robert found that conversation with Rose was an unexpected pleasure; she was open and frank with no airs or pretensions. She also played and sang, when invited to do so, with the same insouciance, which he found quite disarming.

Frequently, in London, Robert had been disconcerted by the affectations and silliness of many vain and ignorant young women whose prominence in society owed more to an accident of birth than to their intelligence or character. Being a shy young man of a somewhat serious disposition, he had not found it easy to converse with them. On the rare occasion when he had met a young woman with whom he had enjoyed a pleasant conversation, it was only to discover that she was as good as engaged to a friend of his.

Miss Fitzwilliam was different. By the end of the evening, Robert was sufficiently intrigued by Rose to accept an invitation to call on the Fitzwilliams and dine with them the very next week. Indeed, he had hesitated but a few seconds when asked, and when Rose had turned and looked at him, he had accepted without delay.

He determined to ask his mother, before he went to dinner with the Fitzwilliams, how it was that such a self-possessed and handsome young woman could have remained unwed.

Mrs Gardiner was a mine of information on the subject.

Rose, she told him, should have been wed some four years ago, except for the dreadful misfortune that had cost the life of the young surgeon to whom she had been engaged. "He was John Greaves, from Derby, a friend of Richard's and of her brother, Thomas, who is at Cambridge," she said. "They were a very handsome couple, very much in love and set to be married when he returned from South Africa, where he had gone with a team of surveyors.

"But, tragically, he never came back. He died, they said, of some dreaded tropical fever. Rose was devastated. For months she hardly spoke to anyone or went anywhere. Her mother was afraid they would lose her. She would ride for hours, alone, through the woods and across the moors. Frequently, her father had to go out in search of her and would find her weeping, unwilling to come home to the reality that John Greaves was dead."

Robert listened, shocked and sympathetic, as his mother continued. "Recently, she has been coming out more; she accepts invitations with her parents and has attended functions in Derby and Birmingham. She is an excellent pianist and sings very well. In the last few months, she has joined Caroline and her children in the Matlock Chamber music group. I am sure James and Rosamund are very pleased."

Robert was thoughtful but said little. He decided to observe Rose more closely when they next met. He had, at their first meeting, detected no sign of bitterness or self-pity, which one might well have expected in the circumstances. While she had neither the sparkling brightness of his sister Caroline nor the vivacity of his sister-in-law Cassandra, Rose Fitzwilliam had attracted his attention by her intelligence and quiet charm, as well as her beauty.

The following Saturday turned out to be an unusually warm Spring day, and quite a large party had assembled at the Fitzwilliams'.

Anthony and Rebecca Tate, and their daughter, Josie, were just back from Kent, where they had attended the wedding of Rebecca's elder sister, Catherine. Sir Thomas Camden, his wife, and their two daughters were there, as well as young Julian Darcy, who was a friend of Rose's brother, Stephen. Julian's parents had been invited but, having attended Catherine Collins's wedding themselves, had stayed on at Rosings.

As the evening grew cooler, most of the party moved indoors, and Rose Fitzwilliam disappeared upstairs. Robert had been prevented from spending much time with her by the sheer persistence of Sir Thomas Camden, who had demanded to be told all about the price of tea. Robert discovered later that he had shares in tea.

Escaping from the commercial concerns of Sir Thomas, Robert found himself involved in a political discussion with the Tates. Anthony, whose newspapers supported the Prince Consort's initiative for an international exhibition to be held in Hyde Park despite the derision of *The Times*, sought Robert's opinion on the project. Did he not see it as a great opportunity for British Industry? they asked.

The Tates' enthusiasm, though commendable, held very little interest for Robert at this time. His attention was engaged elsewhere. He had hoped that the occasion would afford him an opportunity to get to know Rose Fitzwilliam rather better. But, apart from a few pleasantries exchanged as he arrived, the opportunity had not arisen. Rose had been busy with the other guests, and when she vanished upstairs, he almost gave up hope altogether.

As the candles were lit and the curtains drawn, however, she returned, and Robert had to exercise great restraint to stop himself staring at her.

Rose had changed for dinner from the simple muslin day dress she had been wearing into a striking gown of blue silk, whose flowing lines resembled the costume of Greek maidens in a play he had seen in London.

It was a complete contrast to the rather unbecoming fashion of wearing several petticoats, which was popular among the younger women. Both Camden girls, who were thus attired, exchanged glances as Rose joined them. Quite clearly, they, too, were struck by her elegant appearance and neither could stop gazing at her as she moved around the room.

Robert could not take his eyes off her either, remaining quite oblivious to everything else around him until it was time to go in to dinner.

As the ladies moved forward, Rose hung back, allowing the guests to go through into the dining room first. The hesitation gave Robert time to reach her side and offer her his arm, which she readily accepted, thanking him with a smile.

When they were seated, thankfully at some distance from Sir Thomas Camden, Robert found he was totally incapable of making small talk. All intelligent conversation seemed to have dried up—his mind was a blank, and he feared the meal might be spent in silence.

The animated conversation at the top of the table, which was all about Italy's struggle for unification, helped to mask some of his embarrassment until Rose, with a level of ease and friendliness for which he was truly grateful, picked up where they had left off the last time they had met.

As if acknowledging that it was her duty to put him at ease, she said, "Mr Gardiner, I have been trying to discover more about your island of gems. I believe it is known as the Pearl of the East. Is this true?"

"Indeed, it is," said Robert. She had thrown him a lifeline, and he was most appreciative. "So it has been known for many centuries and to several ancient travellers. It is, today, a most valuable part of the British Empire, and we know it as Ceylon, but the Greeks called it Taprobane, while the Arab traders spoke of Serendip," he said, happy to be back on a familiar subject—one in which she had confessed an interest.

"Is it the same Serendip as the one in the fairy tale?" she asked, and when he looked puzzled, she told him of the story of "The Three Princes of Serendip," which she had read as a little girl.

"I had no notion then that Serendip was a real country," she declared, giving him the opportunity to expand on the theme of its exotic beauty.

For the rest of the evening, Robert was as a man bewitched. Though the food was excellent, he ate little, so engrossed was he in their conversation as his companion plied him with questions. He was glad to explain and elucidate, even to spend the rest of the evening satisfying her interest.

When they retired to the drawing room, where a great fire burned and the pianoforte stood open, Rosamund Fitzwilliam invited the young ladies to entertain the company.

The two misses Camden obliged. They sang sweetly but were not in the same class as Rose, thought Robert, who was torn between the desire to hear her sing and his reluctance to let her leave his side, fearing she might not return.

Finally, urged by her cousins, Rose obliged with a charming English lyric by the poet Ben Jonson, which so enchanted Robert that it immediately became his favourite song. He could not believe he had not heard it sung before; but if he had, it could not have been rendered better.

Poor Robert had never been seriously in love before, and it seemed that, this time, he had been stricken pretty hard. Almost the last guest to depart, clearly reluctant to tear himself away, he thanked his hosts and was about to leave when James Fitzwilliam asked if he enjoyed horse riding.

Robert, who enjoyed riding, claimed immediately that it was his favourite pastime.

"Well, we are all riding over to Rushmore Farm, and thence to Dove Dale, tomorrow," said Fitzwilliam, to which Rose added, "and if this weather holds, we may take a picnic."

When Robert looked interested and eager, Rose's mother said, "Well, Julian Darcy and Josie Tate are coming too and you are very welcome to join us, Mr Gardiner."

Even before she had finished speaking, he had accepted, thanking them for the invitation. They arranged to meet at the cross roads between their property and the Gardiners.

Meeting her eyes as he said goodnight, Robert was certain that Rose looked pleased. Himself, he had never enjoyed an evening more—nor had he looked forward to a Sunday morning with greater anticipation of pleasure.

~❦~

The following morning, having excused himself from a family dinner and asked his mother to apologise on his behalf to his sisters, Robert rode out to meet the Fitzwilliams' party.

They rode first to Rushmore—the old Camden family farm, overlooked by a rugged ridge of hills that comprised the boundary of the property—where they were joined by some of the younger members of the party before proceeding along the river's edge to the breathtakingly lovely Dove Dale.

Rose was familiar with the wooded dales of Derbyshire, having spent most of her life in the district. Robert, however, had been away overseas for much of the time, since his family had moved to Derbyshire from London. He was enchanted by the beauty that surrounded them, and when, after lunch, the younger members of the party decided to take a walk along the path beside the river, he waited only to ensure that Rose was agreeable before jumping up to join them.

As the others walked briskly beside the water's edge, Robert and his companion lagged behind them a little, lingering while Rose chose to point out her favourite features of the landscape, and he to admire them with her. At each bend in the river, a new and lovelier prospect greeted them, and nothing would suffice but that they should stop awhile and absorb its beauty. They both expressed the wish that they had had an artist's skill to sketch or paint and lamented the fact that neither possessed such a talent.

As they walked on together, he fell silent and was surprised again when she asked, "Tell me, what heinous deed did you commit that warranted your banishment to the colonies? Or was it something I should not ask about?"

Robert was horrified for a moment, fearing she was serious; but, soon realising that she had spoken in jest, he answered honestly and without embarrassment. "Ceylon is not a penal colony, Miss Fitzwilliam," he explained with a smile. "Had I done something seriously wrong, I would have been bound for Australia," adding that he had gone voluntarily, not in chains, and had never regretted it.

Rose was immediately contrite, thinking she had offended him, but Robert laughed and assured her he was only teasing, too.

He did, however, tell her how he had tried, foolishly, to help a friend pay a gambling debt and overcommitted himself.

"My father and Mr Darcy were most helpful in extricating me from that rather uncomfortable situation, and, feeling I had made a fool of myself, I decided to take a position with a commercial firm in Ceylon. Your uncle, Colonel Fitzwilliam, was instrumental in getting me accepted; I was most grateful. It was a fresh start, and as you can see, it has done me no harm at all. My mother was upset at first—it seemed to her like I was being banished to the ends of the earth—but even she agrees now that it was for the best."

"Did you make a fortune?" she asked, smiling.

Robert answered lightly, "A small one, but I made the most of my time and learned everything I could so I have come home with much more knowledge and skill than I had when I left England."

Rose had listened, laughing gently at first but, as he told the tale, with increasing sympathy. "Mr Gardiner, I am sorry. I did not mean to make fun of you or pry into your past. I was just curious. Were you dreadfully lonely?" she asked.

"I was, at first," he confessed, "but there are many English people out there—there is so much work going on. I stayed, at first, with Charles Bingley's cousin, Frank, and he certainly helped me settle in. So it was not as bad as it might have been."

Rose was generous in her admiration. Never having left England, the thought of travelling to a far country and living there among strangers for several years left her amazed. She looked at him and smiled, as if reassessing him in her own mind.

Robert decided it was his turn to ask some questions—with the advantage of knowing more about her than she knew of him. "And, having confessed to the reason for my being banished to the colonies, may I ask how you occupied your time since escaping from that lady's seminary?" he asked.

Rose was genuinely surprised and her eyes widened, as she was about to ask how he knew where she had acquired her education, when he informed her that his cousins Emma and Sophie Bingley had attended the same excellent institution.

"Ah, yes, of course, the Bingley girls. They were two of the prettiest pupils in the school, and so accomplished, too," she said, remembering days past.

Soon, however, she grew quiet and rather solemn. A melancholy expression settled upon her countenance, and Robert was afraid he had upset her by his questions.

"Miss Fitzwilliam, I see I may have upset you. I apologise, I had no right to question you," he said gently, but she turned to him with a smile and reassured him.

"You have done no such thing, please do not apologise. In truth, while you were working in your exotic paradise, I was engaged to be married to a gentleman from Derby—a surgeon. John Greaves was perhaps the best man I have ever known … he was clever, generous, and compassionate, and I loved him, but it was not to be." Her voice was suddenly soft and barely audible.

Robert, sensing rather than seeing her grief, intervened. "Rose, please do not distress yourself. My mother did tell me about John Greaves, so I do know, and I do not want you to go through it all again. Please, believe me, I would hate to cause you more grief."

She accepted his handkerchief, blew her nose, and grew silent again as they turned to walk back towards the main party. A chill wind from the hills made her stop and button up her coat. As they resumed their walk, she spoke quietly and deliberately, without looking at him, "Since John's death four years ago, I have paid little attention to any other man. Nor have I sought the company of anyone other than my family."

Robert made some inconsequential remark, as if to indicate that he understood exactly what she meant.

She continued as though she had not heard his words. "Until the other day, I had not met a man with whom I even felt the need to make the effort to carry on a conversation. It was different with you. I was surprised that I had really enjoyed the evening. I thought, perhaps, we could be friends," she said looking up at him, her words spoken quietly and casually, as though she were inviting him to afternoon tea.

Robert's expression changed in seconds from gravity to delight.

She spoke again, "Could we?"

Surprised, he hastened to agree. "Of course we could; why, nothing would give me greater pleasure." His words tumbled out; he was eager to accept her offer of friendship.

She stopped and gave him her hand. "Good, we shall be friends, then. I am glad," she said and smiled as he kissed her hand, which he was then reluctant to release. She, perhaps encouraged by the unevenness of the path, permitted him to keep hold of it for the rest of their walk.

When they reached the rest of the party, they were packing up to leave.

Rose's mother pointed to the clouds scudding across the sky to the north: "It looks like rain on the hills," she said. "It may be coming this way." She urged them to hurry lest they should be caught in a downpour.

As far as Robert was concerned, however, there was not a cloud in the sky.

❧

The following morning being Monday, Emily was sitting alone in the parlour, writing to Emma Wilson, when she was interrupted by a knock at the front door. She had heard no sound of a carriage, so she assumed that the caller had come on foot or horseback, probably on parish business. When she went out into the hall, however, she found her brother Robert in the doorway.

She was very surprised to see him, believing that he had already returned to Liverpool that morning. "Why, Robert, I had thought you had left for Liverpool already," she said as he greeted her.

He seemed anxious and appeared uncertain as she led the way into the sitting room, where he sat down beside her and said, quickly, "I have something quite serious to discuss with you." Then, seeing the look of apprehension that crossed her face, he hastened to reassure her, even before she spoke. "No Emmy, I am not in any kind of trouble; I can see your seriously worried expression, but you need not worry this time. I simply need your advice on a personal matter."

Emily sighed with relief. Although she was the younger of the two girls in their family, the fact that Caroline had married very young had left Emily with the responsibilities of an elder sister. While Richard had seemed well able to cope with the vicissitudes of life, such as they were, Robert had always turned to her for counsel.

Having once hurt and upset his mother and disappointed his father by a foolish lapse of judgement, he had, since his return to England, sought his sister's advice on many occasions. Emily had applauded his decision to remain in England and take the job in Liverpool; she was hoping she could persuade him to take the next step and join his father's business.

Mr Gardiner, though still active and interested in his business, was not in the best of health. Mrs Gardiner often wished aloud that Robert would offer to relieve his father of some of the burdens of his work, but he had shown no inclination to do so. Emily had hoped that the inconvenience of travelling to and from Liverpool as well as the unappetising food he had to put up with at his lodgings would soon make Robert change his mind.

This time however, it was plainly not a matter concerning his work that had brought him to see his sister. She could tell from his demeanour that this was no mundane problem of draughty rooms and dreary food.

"What is it, Robert?" she asked, seeing he was eager to tell her.

Still he appeared reluctant and uneasy; only when she had shut the door did he relax. Robert was plainly anxious that the matter he was going to talk about was to be kept confidential. Once she had promised that no one, not even her husband, would be privy to their conversation, he told her everything.

Robert was in love with Rose Fitzwilliam. He wanted reassurance from Emily that it was not some vain hope; he needed to know more about her parents, and their expectations for her, particularly her father, who was Mr Darcy's cousin. While he knew that Mr and Mrs Darcy had welcomed his brother Richard's marriage to Cassandra and were his parents' dearest friends, he was concerned that Rose's father might not be as well disposed towards him.

"I am not sure how much they know of the reason for my long exile in the East. Nor do I know anything of their attitude to the fact that my living is made entirely through commerce, as is my father's," he said with a wry smile. Robert had felt the sting of social snobbery before, when friends who were sons of the landed gentry had appeared to dismiss his father's fortune because it was made entirely through trade.

Emily smiled. "But Robert, on both these counts, Rose knows the truth, does she not?" she asked gently.

He nodded, "Of course she does. I have told her exactly what occurred all those years ago, and she did not appear to be concerned at all."

"Well, then?"

"Oh, Emmy, it's just that I have never done this before, and she is so beautiful; I feel most unworthy of her."

Emily was instantly up in arms, assuring him that he had no reason to feel unworthy at all. Rose, she said, was indeed a beautiful young woman, but if she had indicated her own feelings, Emily believed passionately that her parents would have no grounds for objecting to Robert.

"As for the matter of making your living in commerce, Robert, it is a perfectly respectable career, and as I have heard Mr Darcy say on more than one occasion, it is the lifeblood of England today," she declared. "Where would this nation be if it were not for the great trading firms? Much of our prosperity depends upon the work of men like Papa. You have nothing to apologise for on that score, Robert. Indeed, were you to become a partner in the business, as I have suggested you should, you would be in the illustrious company of their own kinsmen, like Mr Darcy and Colonel Fitzwilliam."

So persuasive was she that Robert seemed satisfied with her assurances. However, his next problem was more difficult to solve. While he was almost sure that the lady regarded him as a friend, he was afraid her affections might not, as yet, be deeply engaged.

"I am in a quandary as to what I should do. A premature approach may well scare her away, yet, were I to say nothing at all, she may suppose that I am totally indifferent to her," he said, appealing to Emily for guidance.

Emily responded with the affectionate smile of a tolerant and understanding sister. "Robert, my dear, if Rose has told you she would like to be friends, believe me, she must have some expectation that, before long, friendship may turn to something deeper. It is a perfectly natural progression, which any woman of reasonable sensibility will anticipate.

"If you have some concerns about the effect your advances may have upon her, then take care that you do not appear to take her affections for granted or demand too quick a response to your own. A soft approach is always appreciated—more so, I would think, in the case of Rose, who has, after all, loved and lost in the most tragic way."

Robert hastened to assure his sister that in no way would he be precipitate or demanding; indeed, he was so overwhelmed, he feared he might not say anything at all.

"You may not believe me Emily, but I get tongue-tied. I lack the eloquence of these young men about town who seem to have no trouble expressing their most ardent feelings quite openly," he said.

Emily smiled. She was reproving, but gentle. "Robert, you are an old-fashioned gentleman. Rose is an intelligent young woman who is twenty-seven years old. If she has invited you to be her friend, a privilege she has not extended to many others, she is unlikely to take fright if, after some time, you let her see that your feelings for her have deepened. Indeed, were I in her place, Robert, I would be singularly disappointed if that was not the case," she said.

Robert was not easily convinced. "Do you really believe that, Emmy? I know so little about the way young women think, I would be afraid to appear presumptuous," he said.

Emily sought to reassure her brother, "Robert I cannot believe that anyone could ever consider you presumptuous. I have to admit, I do not know Rose as well as I do Cassy, but from my limited knowledge of her, I think I could confidently say that a gentlemanly and sensitive approach is unlikely to cause alarm and may even be welcomed by a young woman in her situation."

Robert sighed, "I do hope you are right, Emmy."

Emily promised that she would observe Rose when they met. "I shall have an opportunity when she joins me next week to teach Sunday school. She is one of our volunteers," she explained. "If she is missing you, I shall know, and if she wants to talk to me about you, I shall be available."

Robert was grateful. "My dear sister, I know I was right to come to you. Just for now, however, we must keep this to ourselves. When I return from Liverpool, we shall talk again and if there is anything to tell mother and father, it will be done."

Emily agreed, promising to protect his secret.

Robert, buoyed by his sister's sound advice and optimism, was preparing to leave when a knock at the door heralded a visitor. Going to the door together, they found Rose, who had driven over in a curricle. She seemed a little confused, and Robert reddened as they greeted one another.

He was just leaving, he said, but Emily persuaded him to stay and take tea with them. Robert accepted, and they returned to the sitting room, where Emily left them together while she went to get the tea.

She seemed to take an inordinate amount of time, and Rose, who had seated herself by the bay window, while Robert remained standing beside the fireplace, became rather restless.

After she had answered all his concerns about the health of her parents and brother—all of whom he had seen in the pink of health just yesterday—she stood up and went over to the window, attracted by the profusion of blossoms on an old lilac leaning up against the garden wall. Robert joined her, and they were standing close together admiring the garden when Emily returned with a maid bearing the tea tray.

She noticed that neither of them seemed to feel the need to move quickly away from each other as she entered. Rose simply returned to her seat on the sofa while Robert went back to standing in front of the fire.

Emily poured out the tea, observing the couple with a degree of indulgent fondness. It was clear to her that, while Rose was probably not ready to reveal the depth of her own feelings, she was unlikely to resent a confession of love from her suitor.

The warmth with which she had greeted him lingered in their conversation, and when she heard he was taking the evening coach to Liverpool, Rose was very solicitous indeed, asking how many hours the journey would take and were the roads safe after dark?

Robert tried to allay her concerns, pointing out that there was very little to worry about, since the coachmen were experienced drivers and had few accidents, but Rose recalled a very nasty one on the Matlock road some years ago.

Emily remembered it too, but for different reasons. She recalled especially the efforts of her brother, Richard, and his friend, Paul Antoine, which had saved the lives of many people.

Rose seemed anxious, and Robert promised that he would write as soon as he reached Liverpool.

"I could send an express," he said a little tentatively and was rewarded with a delighted smile.

"Would you? I am sure we would be happy to know that your journey had been safely accomplished. Do you not think so, Mrs Courtney?"

Emily agreed, but she was vastly amused by the fuss, remembering how Paul and Richard had travelled regularly to Birmingham. Robert was only going to Liverpool, yet she felt sympathy for the anxious Rose. She, too, had once suffered a great loss.

Strangely, she thought, there seemed never any need to worry about her present husband, James. He seemed self-contained, almost protected.

Dragging herself back to her guests, who had finished their tea, Emily found them discussing a song Rose had sung recently, which Robert claimed was the prettiest he had heard in many years. She was promising to give him the words, while he was hoping to hear her sing it again, soon.

Looking at his watch, Robert said he really must leave and Rose, who had wanted to talk about the Sunday school, stayed behind.

Later, after they had both left, Emily returned to her letter:

Dearest Emma, she wrote:

Your letter was most welcome.

You have no need to covet the skills of Miss Brontë at all—your letters express your feelings with such warmth and sincerity that I am scarcely able to read them without shedding a tear.

Now, I have so many little pieces of news for you that I do not quite know where to begin.

After several pieces of domestic and local information, and the happy news that young William's performance at the Pemberley Music festival had attracted a very appreciative comment in the *Matlock Review*, Emily proceeded to give her cousin an account of the developments in the life of her brother, Robert:

Dear Emma, it is understandable that, in the midst of a somewhat tumultuous period last year, we did not get the opportunity to speak of my brother Robert's decision not to return to the colonies but to take up an appointment in Liverpool with the same commercial firm.

Well, it may be just as well that we did not, for as it happens, the circumstances have so altered that it is likely that Robert may not be remaining long in their employ.

Now, I know you will want to know exactly what I mean and how and why the changes have come about. Unfortunately, my dear cousin, I am unable to satisfy your curiosity until at least next week. The information has been placed in my hands in confidence and, until I have permission to divulge it, my lips are sealed.

This is not to say that we may not speculate, dear Emma, and I will give you a hint or two and then let your imagination roam at will.

Consider that Robert, who has never been seriously in love, appears to have been deeply smitten.

Consider that the young lady in question is from an excellent family and lives in Derbyshire, no more than an hour's journey from Oakleigh.

Consider also that if it were to come to anything, Robert will probably resign from his present position and become a partner in Papa's business.

I do not know if I have given you enough clues to help you solve our little mystery, but I am sure it will keep you busy speculating, when you can spare some time from your devoted husband and beautiful daughters.

When I am able, which I hope will be soon, I shall write you all the answers.

For myself, I intend to spend a few days next week helping to settle some of the children of the Irish immigrant families in our school at Kympton. The poor little things have no proper English and find it difficult to get on at school. They are usually teased and bullied because they are so poor and ill educated. They are frequently neglected but only because their parents needs must work to keep body and soul together.

Caroline and Colonel Fitzwilliam are also helping by providing a barn on their property to accommodate donations of food, clothing, and furniture, which are to be distributed to the Irish families.

Unfortunately, there is a certain amount of resentment against these unhappy people, among those of our own poor and unemployed folk, who feel some envy and fear that, like the Flemish weavers in the past, these Irish peasants may take their jobs or their land from them. It seems so unfair that the poor souls who have nothing, not even their country any more, are resented and reviled because we choose to help them.

Papa remembers a similar sentiment in London when the survivors of the French Revolution were escaping the Terror and arriving penniless in Britain. While many generous people helped them, mainly because they were members of the aristocracy, there were apparently several voices raised against them being given refuge in England.

Fortunately for them, the King himself supported their cause and praised those who gave the French émigrés protection. The poor Irish have no such highly placed advocates and, being poor and unprotected, seem to suffer an unconscionable level of harassment and abuse.

Dear Emma, I fear there is little evidence of the meek being permitted to inherit even a small portion of the earth!

James has spoken of it in his Sunday sermons, and all of us try to spread the word, but there are those who do not wish to hear. There have been rumblings in the villages and a few incidents. We can only pray that they will not prevail over the basic decency and Christian charity of ordinary English people.

You must come with me when you are next here and visit some of the families. They work so hard and are mostly good citizens; I cannot believe they would be resented.

Do give my love to James and the girls. We look forward to seeing you again soon. Meanwhile, I know you will write when you can.

Your loving cousin,

Emily.

The following day, Emily was as good as her word, going with her maid and her niece, Isabella, to the little village on the edge of the moorland where a few Irish immigrant families had settled.

In cottages that had been tumbledown shacks on abandoned land they had made their homes, working hard to scrape a living from the poor soil. Most of the men had gone to Birmingham to look for work in the mills.

The women stayed to work the land, scouring the moors for food and firewood and minding the children, who'd had no schooling since their families had fled the famine in Ireland. Because of their inability to read and write English, they were treated with contempt and even suspicion. Their spirits crushed, their bodies weakened by malnutrition, their communities decimated by social dislocation and disease, they were an uninspiring lot.

Yet Emily was determined to do whatever she could to change their circumstances and touch the conscience of the people among whom they had settled. To this end she worked tirelessly, collecting donations of food and clothing, while taking every opportunity to press for local government to assist them. Unfortunately, the resentful atmosphere generated by the anti-Irish element in rural areas was proving very difficult to overcome. Emily could not believe that ordinary English people, who had themselves known hardship, could be so hard-hearted.

⁓

Meanwhile, at Pemberley on a fine Spring afternoon, Darcy and Elizabeth, who were sitting on the west lawn after tea, had unexpected visitors—James and Rosamund Fitzwilliam arrived unheralded, though they were certainly not unwelcome.

After the usual greetings, they went indoors, where a fire had been lit in the sitting room. James and Darcy were cousins, but the families were not intimate in the way they were with Colonel Fitzwilliam and Caroline.

Having accepted some refreshment and waited for the maid and the footman to depart, they proceeded to reveal the reason for their visit. Their concern was for Rose, who had apparently begun to take an interest in Mr Robert Gardiner, whom she had met recently at the Bingleys'.

"We invited him to dine with us, and later he joined us on an excursion to Dove Dale, where we spent the afternoon together. Since then, Rose has hardly stopped speaking of him," said Rosamund.

Elizabeth and Darcy were not entirely surprised, but they wondered what the Fitzwilliams thought they could do about it.

James, who was not very articulate at the best of times, let his wife explain.

"We know very little of Mr Gardiner," Rosamund admitted, "and knowing the intimate relationship that exists between your family and the Gardiners, we thought you might advise us."

While Rosamund was reluctant to ask very personal questions, James who was very protective of his daughter, was more direct. He left no doubt as to the reason for their visit: he wanted to quiz Darcy about Robert.

Mr Darcy, whose loyalty to the Gardiners was absolute, made his position quite clear, explaining that Robert came from a family with an exemplary record in personal integrity and public service.

Placing his own business partnership with Mr Gardiner and the marriage of their daughter Cassandra with Robert's brother Richard at the very centre of his case, Darcy spoke very highly of the Gardiners.

Elizabeth, whose love of her husband was inextricably bound up with his warm regard for her favourite aunt and uncle, was proud to hear him speak of them in such terms.

Left in no doubt of Darcy's opinion, James Fitzwilliam hastened to assure them that he had no personal objection to Robert Gardiner. "Indeed," he said, "I have found him to be a pleasant and gentlemanly fellow, but, you will surely agree, Darcy, that that is not the same thing as saying that I would be happy to see him wed my daughter."

Darcy agreed that it certainly was not the same, but reminded his cousin that the person whose wishes were most important was surely Rose herself.

"Should Robert propose to Rose, has she indicated to either of you that she will accept such a proposal?" Elizabeth asked.

Rosamund denied that there had been any such indication, but James was far more assertive. "It is Rose that I am thinking of," he said stoutly. "You will recall how badly hurt she was when John Greaves died; we had great fears for her then. Now, I have no more important purpose in life than ensuring her happiness," he declared.

Darcy rose and went to the fireplace, over which a portrait of Cassandra and her sons had pride of place, and said quietly, "If that is what you want for Rose, I would advise you to let her tell you why she prefers Robert, if she does. I have no doubt they are both mature and sensible enough to have only the best possible reasons for making such a decision.

"Rose is twenty-seven; Cassandra was not yet twenty when she declared that she loved Richard Gardiner and could not live without him! It was necessary then to ensure that both of them were certain of their feelings and were not simply carried away by emotion; for my part, I found it was best to talk to them. They were, of course, absolutely certain, as one is in youth, and as you can see, they are as happily married as anyone could wish to be."

Rosamund said they had indeed been fortunate because Richard Gardiner was well known and esteemed throughout the county.

Darcy nodded and went on, "Well, I have known the Gardiners for almost as long as I have known Lizzie, and there is no family of my acquaintance I would place above them. Mr and Mrs Gardiner are well respected, and their children have been raised in an exemplary manner. James, you could have applied to your brother and I am confident that he would have supported me," he said, as Elizabeth listened, scarcely believing her ears, so passionate was Darcy in the commendation he bestowed upon the Gardiners.

James Fitzwilliam was apologetic. "Darcy, I did not intend to reflect upon any member of the Gardiner family," he said. "I did have some concerns about the fact that Robert Gardiner had been away in the eastern colonies for a very long time. One does hear strange stories about those places."

Elizabeth, unable to contain herself any longer, intervened. "Perhaps I might be able to set your heart at rest on that score. My cousin Robert obtained the position with Mathesons—a leading commercial firm—through Colonel Fitzwilliam, who had also worked for them when he was overseas.

"Robert was not getting very far with his study of the law, and his father felt a stint overseas would do him good. As you can see, he was right; Robert did well at Mathesons and when he returned to England, they offered him his present position in Liverpool. My aunt, Mrs Gardiner, is delighted to have him home, but even she admits that Robert is a far more confident and capable young man for his experience in the colonies."

Darcy sensed, from the rising inflection of her voice, that Lizzie's feelings had been hurt by what she had deemed to be a slight upon her cousin and his family. He decided to speak out on a subject that he was sure would interest his cousin James.

"Robert has certainly acquired sufficient skill and commercial experience to become a partner in his father's business," he said. "Mr Gardiner has spoken to me of his intention to offer him a partnership, and as partners in the business, Bingley, Fitzwilliam, and I have agreed. It will mean, of course, that Robert will relinquish his position with Mathesons and take over some of his father's responsibilities in the Company."

It was easy to see that both Fitzwilliams were impressed. Husband and wife looked at one another and though they smiled, they were plainly embarrassed.

Rosamund spoke quietly. "Mr Darcy, I should be most unhappy if I thought that you had misunderstood our intentions regarding Robert Gardiner. We have no wish to slight the Gardiners or suggest that Robert is in some way unsuitable. That was the very reason why we did not go to Colonel Fitzwilliam—we did not wish to embarrass Caroline by our enquiries about her brother.

"We came to you because we knew of your long and intimate association with the Gardiners and because we were certain that you would speak plainly with us, which is exactly what you have done today, and we thank you for it. I shall certainly take your advice and speak with Rose, so we may discover exactly how she feels."

Both Elizabeth and Darcy smiled and agreed that Rose would be the best person to tell her parents how matters lay between herself and Robert.

As they rose to leave, Darcy grasped his cousin's hand and said, "There is no substitute for trust, James. Rose must feel she can trust her parents to accept the man she has chosen—if that is what she has done—and likewise, Robert will want to know that you trust him with your daughter. We have been fortunate indeed, for there is no one above Richard to whom we would have entrusted Cassandra. We can only wish you the same good fortune."

Elizabeth felt sure that if there was one thing the Fitzwilliams would be absolutely certain of, it was Darcy's high regard for the entire Gardiner family.

That night, as they prepared for bed, Elizabeth asked her husband why he had spoken out so strongly in support of Robert. Darcy seemed surprised at her question, "Because I believed it was necessary, Lizzie; and furthermore, everything I said is true. I believe that Robert is now a mature young man, with a much greater grasp on reality than he had ten years ago. He is a perfectly eligible suitor for Rose, if she will have him."

"And you did not deem it necessary to mention the reason for his sojourn in Ceylon?" she asked.

"No," he replied, "because, viewed from where we stand today, Robert's lapse, which was no more than an error of judgement, seems quite insignificant. I could see no reason at all to burden James and Rosamund with the details. It was all so long ago, had no lasting impact on anyone we know, and has certainly not diminished Robert in any way at all. Should he choose to tell Rose, that will be a matter between them."

Elizabeth asked in what Darcy recognised as a characteristic teasing tone, "If it had been Robert who was courting Cassy, how would you have responded?"

He smiled as he realised she was not really testing him, simply playing a game with him. "That, dearest Lizzie, is an unfair question; but, since you have asked it, I shall answer you honestly. Had Cassy chosen Robert above Richard, I confess I would have been disappointed, but only because

Richard is my personal favourite. There is no other young man for whom I have greater respect, no one for whom I have more affection than Richard—except our son. So, as you can see, taking only my preference into account, I would have had some regrets. However, if Cassy had loved him and accepted him, I could not have refused her my blessing."

Elizabeth put her arms around him and hugged him to her.

His unyielding goodness had been his greatest strength, the source of her lasting comfort and delight. With Darcy she might disagree, she might even, occasionally, dispute; but never had she been disappointed in him.

Some weeks later, Robert returned from Liverpool and went directly to see Emily at Kympton Rectory. She was alone and very happy to see him, though she was surprised to hear that he had not, as yet, been home.

"I wanted you to be the first to know, Emmy," he explained. "I have decided to resign my position in Liverpool. Indeed, I have already written to Mathesons, and I hope to discuss the question of joining my father's business when we meet."

Emily was overjoyed. "Robert, I cannot tell you how happy I am to hear this news. I have prayed ever since you returned to England that you would come back into the business, and so has Mama. I know Papa would welcome you."

She could not hide her relief, but was keen to discover what had prompted his decision. Robert was frank in his explanation. "I shall be honest with you, Emmy. I am hopeful, very hopeful, that Rose Fitzwilliam will look favourably upon me. As soon as I have settled my business affairs, I intend to ask her to marry me. In view of my feelings, I cannot continue to live at such a distance from her. What is more, my work suffers from lack of concentration; it is unfair to everyone, including my employer," he said.

Emily sincerely wished her brother success and happiness, while reminding him to be mindful of the fact that Rose had been wounded and may be circumspect about letting her feelings become deeply engaged again. "I am confident that, were you to be accepted, it will be because she truly loves you and you will be very happy," she said as she saw him to the door.

~~❦~~

After they had dined that night, Robert told his parents of his decision to return home and work in his father's business.

Mrs Gardiner was speechless with delight, and it was quite a while before she could take it all in. So unexpected was the news that she determined to share it with her favourite niece and arranged to visit Pemberley on the morrow.

Aunt and niece were still very close. Many events in their lives over the last twenty years had drawn them into an increasingly intimate relationship. Elizabeth could share in her aunt's happiness, but even more, she could enhance it by revealing, having first extracted a promise of secrecy, those parts of their conversation with Rose Fitzwilliam's parents that would allow Mrs Gardiner to understand more fully the reason behind Robert's decision.

While she was not entirely surprised, for she did admit that Robert had seemed to spend a great deal of time with the Fitzwilliams recently, Mrs Gardiner had no notion of the extent of the understanding between Robert and Rose, or if indeed there was any.

"Would it please you to discover that there was?" asked her niece.

"Certainly. Rose seems a lovely girl with a gentle nature; who could possibly have any objection to her?" she replied, but added with a little sigh, "But, Lizzie, I do hope that Robert is sensible of the responsibilities such a marriage would entail."

"More than any other marriage?" Elizabeth queried, a little puzzled.

Her aunt nodded and proceeded to explain, "Indeed, yes, because to care for and love someone who has been previously deeply hurt is a very special responsibility. Her parents dote upon her and Robert is a kind man, so I have no doubt that if he married Rose, he would care for her with devotion. I would only counsel some caution."

Elizabeth, who never failed to be amazed at the understanding and integrity of her aunt, had to agree and admitted she had not thought of it herself. It was generally known that the Fitzwilliams refused their only daughter nothing, particularly not since the tragic death of John Greaves.

Nonetheless, she reassured her aunt, "I am quite certain, my dear Aunt, that Robert will heed your advice. But if they are in love, as I suspect they are, I am also sure they will find happiness together because they are both intelligent people."

As Mrs Gardiner was leaving, Darcy, who had been visiting the parish school, returned. He greeted Mrs Gardiner affectionately and was told the good news regarding Robert's return to the business.

"Mr Gardiner is so very pleased, Mr Darcy, as I am too," she said.

Mr Darcy was delighted and, to his wife's surprise, suggested that he would throw a party at Pemberley to welcome Robert home.

"We must show that we appreciate his return," he declared, "and you shall pick the date, Mrs Gardiner."

Later, writing to Jane, Elizabeth detailed her surprise and pleasure at the news.

> *My dearest Jane,*
>
> *I have such good news; if it were not such a wet morning I would have made the journey to Ashford Park to tell you all about it. I may still do that later, but for the moment, this letter will have to do.*
>
> *There is so much news, you shall have it in little doses.*
>
> *First, Robert has resigned his position with Mathesons and is returning to Derbyshire, to the delight of our dear aunt and uncle. Even better, he will be going back into his father's business. Darcy says that Uncle Gardiner intends to offer Robert a partnership.*
>
> *My second piece of news also concerns Robert; we believe that his decision is linked to his desire to be near a certain lady—Rose Fitzwilliam.*
>
> *They have been together at several functions, and we have it on the authority of her mother that Rose speaks of him incessantly.*
>
> *Julian tells me that Robert seems very attracted to Rose. Indeed, at a recent picnic, Julian noted that Robert and Rose were inseparable!*
>
> *The Fitzwilliams, James and Rosamund, called on us a few days ago, eager to quiz Darcy about Robert—a certain sign, you will agree, that something is afoot. They were given such a good account of Robert's prospects that they went away quite pleased.*
>
> *Just think, Jane, would it not be an excellent thing if Robert were to settle in Derbyshire? Our dear aunt has been praying for the day when he would show an interest in the business and take some of the burden off our*

Uncle Gardiner's shoulders, for though he is still very keen and active, his health is not what it used to be and Aunt Gardiner fears that he is working far too hard.

With this, Darcy also agrees and because he loves them both dearly, he is very pleased with Robert's decision. So delighted, in fact, that he has declared that we shall have a party at Pemberley to celebrate Robert's return, to which you are all invited!

The letter was concluded and dispatched without further ado, and Elizabeth made the most of a rainy afternoon sorting through some of her father's books, which Mary had sent over from Longbourn.

Some of them were valuable volumes, which could be placed in the Pemberley collection, but many were more likely to be at home in the new circulating library established at Kympton.

Coming upon her in the library, Darcy found her tearful, remembering her father, who had left several characteristic little notes and comments in many of his books, all of which brought back fond memories.

He had also missed Mr Bennet, whom he had grown to respect and whose wit and sarcastic humour had entertained them on many occasions. Darcy knew that Elizabeth had been her father's favourite and had mourned his death for a long while. He persuaded her to leave her labour of love for awhile and keep him company. He had something to discuss with her.

"Lizzie, my love, I have just come from visiting the new community hall and library that we are setting up at Kympton, and I have an idea which I hope will appeal to you." Elizabeth listened as he explained, "How would you like to have the library dedicated to your late father?"

Elizabeth did not know quite what to say. She had never considered such a possibility. "The library dedicated to Papa—how is it to be done?" she asked, a little bewildered.

"Quite easily," said Darcy, pointing out that since the building was situated on a part of the Pemberley estate and most of the money for its refurbishment had come from the Pemberley trust fund, the family would be entitled to dedicate it to whomever they chose.

"Since the main intention is to provide a library and reading rooms for the community, I cannot think of a more appropriate person to whom we should dedicate the building than Mr Bennet, whose love of books and reading was legendary," he said, adding quickly, "But only if it would please you, of course, my dear."

Elizabeth loved his generosity and greatness of heart, but most of all she loved his kindness; she had discovered and treasured it through the years of their marriage and it often brought her close to tears.

Occasionally, in rare moments of melancholy, she had dared to think of the awful prospect of life without him and when she did, a dreadful depression would engulf her. So deeply did they love one another, so completely had she come to esteem and enjoy everything about him and their life together, that she was quite incapable of envisaging life without him, except to know it would be totally insupportable.

Just thinking of it brought tears and Darcy, believing that his mention of her father was the cause of her grief, was immediately sorry and tried to comfort her, "Lizzie dearest, had I known it would upset you, I would never have suggested it. Forgive me, it was only an idea…"

But she would not let him continue. "Darcy, there is nothing to forgive. I am sorry to be so silly as to let my feelings get the better of me. Why, I think it is an excellent idea," she declared and, very quickly recovering her composure, dried her tears and smiled as she said, "Perhaps, my dear, you should, in future, give me fair warning of your good intentions, so that I do not make a fool of myself."

They had walked together to the end of the library and stood looking out over the prettiest prospect, from the alcove, which had been Mr Bennet's favourite reading spot.

"Then you have no objection?" Darcy asked.

"None at all. Indeed, I shall be honoured and so will my sisters—Kitty, Jane, and Mary, at least, I can vouch for," she said, and Darcy was clearly very pleased.

As they went downstairs, she told him she had written to Jane and was hoping to see her soon, when she would acquaint her sister with his plan for the library. "I am quite certain Jane will feel as I do," she said. "Papa was such a keen reader and always raged against the 'forces of ignorance' that kept poor folk and women uneducated and uninformed; it will truly be a great tribute to him. Many of Papa's books that Mary has sent up from Longbourn could be included in the collection."

Darcy was gratified by her response. He had spared neither effort nor expense to have the community hall and its library completed, in the hope that Elizabeth might be persuaded to open it.

When he asked her, she agreed with the greatest pleasure. "Of course, it will be an honour to do so."

"I am very glad to hear it. I had hoped to please you," he said, and he kissed her before going out to the stables, leaving Elizabeth contemplating the beauty of a huge rainbow whose arch of evanescent colours spanned the park.

Jane's response to her sister's letter came sooner than expected, in the form of a visit. Having called on Mr and Mrs Gardiner on her way to Pemberley, she was able to confirm that Robert was indeed intending to propose to Rose Fitzwilliam and had already written to her father.

"Oh, Lizzie, you were so right. Aunt Gardiner is very happy," said Jane, once the sisters were ensconced in their favourite room. "I believe that while all the rest of us had given up on Robert ever marrying, he seemed too serious and too shy, our dear aunt had always hoped he would find someone suitable."

"Well, Rose is more than suitable. She is an accomplished and hand-some young woman with excellent connections; now that Robert's own prospects are more settled, if they truly love each other, their happiness should be assured," said Elizabeth.

Jane's visit to her aunt had elicited more interesting details. "Lizzie, I believe our cousin Emily has been Robert's confidante and counsellor on this matter."

Elizabeth was not entirely surprised. "Emily? Well, she certainly kept her counsel; why, I was with her at the meeting of the hospital board only last Sunday and she said not a word."

"I understand that Robert had sworn her to secrecy until he had every-thing worked out right. She did not even tell her mother or James, but now it can be told, since Robert is to dine with the Fitzwilliams tomorrow," Jane explained, adding that if everything went well—that is, if Rose accepted him—they would announce their engagement immediately.

The sisters were naturally happy for their cousin. He, unlike Richard—who had always been a popular favourite with friends and family—had been a quiet, unassuming young man, and, having spent many years overseas, he had returned a stranger to most of them.

But Jane had some news of her own, which she was sure would excite her sister's interest. Young Sophie, the Bingleys' lovely daughter who had recently celebrated her seventeenth birthday, had been invited to spend the Summer in Kent with her sister Emma Wilson and her family.

"Emma is expecting a child and would like to have Sophie stay with her," Jane revealed to Elizabeth's great delight.

"Oh Jane, that is excellent news! It will surely complete Emma's happiness," she said, and Jane agreed.

"It should be very nice for Sophie too, I know the Wilsons lead a rather quiet life, but they are so close to London, I am sure she will have the opportunity to attend a ball or two and perhaps take in an opera," Jane said, adding that she hoped it would also give young Louisa a chance to come out of Sophie's shadow.

"Emily has offered to involve her in her charity work, and Bingley thinks that is an excellent idea. We are keen for her to develop her own interests; it can be difficult for a younger sister to make her own way, but we shall give her every encouragement," she said.

The sisters spent the rest of the day so happily that by the time Bingley arrived to take his wife home, they were scarcely aware that some six hours had passed.

Robert Gardiner went to dinner with the Fitzwilliams to find that his sister, Caroline, her husband Colonel Fitzwilliam, and their eldest daughter, Isabella, had been invited too. They had heard of his decision to return to Derbyshire and his father's business, and both Fitzwilliam and Caroline applauded his judgement warmly.

Rose, looking cool and beautiful in a simple silk gown, greeted Robert with a radiant smile and gave him her hand. Robert said he hoped he would have some time to speak privately with her.

Surprising him, she said, "Of course you may. There are some beautiful roses out in the conservatory; I should love to show them to you, but I do believe my father wishes to see you first, Robert."

Once again, he was astonished by the ease with which she dealt with the situation. Indeed whenever he seemed awkward, she intervened to put him at ease and smooth things over for him. Having already written to his prospective father-in-law, Robert was not expecting to have a meeting with him so promptly.

Sensing that he was somewhat nervous, Rose accompanied him to her father's study, reassuring him that her father was "by no means an ogre" before leaving him to return to their other guests.

As the evening proceeded, Caroline, seeking to ease her brother's path, suggested they take a look at the much-vaunted roses in the conservatory. Rose and Robert accompanied her and Isabella to view the famous blooms.

Caroline's plan became clear when she took a quick look, dutifully praised the roses, and then stepped out into the garden, taking Isabella with her to admire the view.

Robert, realising that she was obviously trying to give him some time alone with Rose, turned to find the lady standing beside him.

With as much courage as he could muster, he declared his feelings, expressing the depth and warmth of his love for her, and asked if she would marry him and so make him the happiest of men.

Rose, whose ability to surprise him continued unabated, listened with great attention and when he had finished, thanked him sincerely and accepted him without pretence or fuss.

Robert, his face reflecting his heartfelt delight, took her in his arms and told her in even more ardent terms how much he loved and admired her.

So engrossed were the couple in establishing the extent of their mutual admiration and happiness that the return of Caroline and Isabella went unnoticed until Isabella tripped over a plant stand and the lovers broke apart to accept their congratulations.

Caroline, whose own marriage was the source of great felicity, was overjoyed that her brother was to be similarly blessed, and so indeed was Colonel Fitzwilliam, who was swiftly told the news by his wife.

Thereafter, the evening became a celebration, for James Fitzwilliam had already privately assured Robert of his blessing, and Rosamund welcomed him with affection and hope that he would make her beloved daughter happy.

Following this auspicious event, the dinner party at Pemberley had grown into something approaching a ball, since it was no longer a party to welcome Robert home, but an occasion celebrating his engagement to Rose.

The younger members of the families were eager for a ball. Darcy was easily persuaded to overcome his lack of enthusiasm for dancing and a fine group of musicians was hired.

Preparations were afoot to accommodate a very much larger number of guests than had first been anticipated, and Jenny Grantham and her staff were working hard to ensure that all was in readiness.

⚜

On a warm Summer evening, with only a gentle breeze coming in the open doorway, James Courtney decided to take his two older children along with him on his usual Saturday evening parish visits. Emily and Caroline had agreed to meet and plan their own contribution to the Pemberley Ball.

The sisters had the house to themselves. Sitting around the dining table at the Rectory, they had plans and lists spread out all over when Isabella, who had been out in the garden with little Jessica, came racing into the room.

"Mama, there's a little boy running up the lane, he looks very frightened and quite exhausted..." And as Caroline and Emily rose to go to the door, she added, "I think he is one of the Irish children from the camp on the moors."

Believing the child was either lost or come for help (the Irish preferred to ask at the Rectory for assistance, rather than risk rejection or ridicule in the village), Emily went out into the lane to meet him. She recognised him as Tom, whose mother she had helped with food and clothes a few days ago.

To her astonishment, the child had stopped in the road and was calling to her to come at once. "Please ma'am," he cried, "the men are breakin' up the cottages on the moor ... they are comin' back when it's dark and they are goin' to burn our things..."

"What?" Emily was aghast.

Caroline, who had caught up with her, could barely comprehend the boy's words, unused as she was to the Irish accents.

But Emily, who had been helping the immigrant families and was familiar with their speech, understood him exactly. She had already been warned by some of the locals that there was a good deal of resentment towards the "Paddys," as they were called in the village, but never, not in her worst nightmares, had she expected anything like this. Despite that, it took her but a moment to understand the seriousness of the situation.

Quick to respond, she amazed Caroline with her instructions. "Caroline, you must go directly to Littleford and alert Richard and the others at the hospital. They must send some men from Pemberley to help the families on the moor. I shall take Isabella and go at once with Tom to see what can be done."

She took little Jessica indoors to her nurse and sent a man to find the Rector and tell him what had occurred.

Spending barely ten minutes to get her wrap and bonnet, and giving brief instructions to her maid, Emily was ready to depart, taking Isabella with her. Caroline, unable to do other than follow her sister's directions, had got back in her carriage and was looking out anxiously.

"Emily, are you sure you will be safe? What will you do if the men come back?" she asked.

Emily was quite calm. "Don't worry Caroline, no one will harm us. We are going to see how we can help Tom and his mother and the other women up on the moors. They are alone, with most of the men away working. I hope we are in time. You must get as fast as you can to Littleford and tell Richard what is afoot. He will know what to do. They must get help as soon as possible."

As she drove away, Caroline could not help wondering at her intrepid young sister's courage. Her admiration was, however, tempered with some apprehension. Unfamiliar with the Irish immigrants, although aware of the work Emily and James were doing to help them, Caroline was afraid for both her sister and her daughter.

Arriving at the camp on the moor, where some half dozen families were trying to eke out a living under exceedingly difficult conditions, Emily saw a scene of utter devastation and misery—the evicted women and their children were sitting in the dirt surrounded by their pathetic belongings tied up in bundles or strewn around them in the mud. Smashed furniture, pieces of wooden palings and makeshift roofing lay all around them. It was plain that the women and children were terrified, powerless to do anything, not knowing how to escape the wrath of the men who had threatened to return at nightfall to burn their belongings.

Most of their husbands were gone either to Liverpool, Manchester, or Birmingham to look for work. Some had not been back in weeks, leaving the women to struggle on, depending for the most part on charity and the hard-won produce of thankless toil.

Some of the children were crying, and their mothers, with no men to protect them, were preparing to run away into the wild moorland, where they could quite easily perish from exposure.

Young Isabella Fitzwilliam, who had never seen anything like it in her life, was wide-eyed and apprehensive herself; but in the face of her aunt's remarkable courage, she was determined to show no fear.

"What are we going to do, Aunt Emily?" she asked with not a little trepidation. "How will we help them?"

Emily spoke quite firmly, her words expressing her determination. "We shall stay with them until help arrives, Isabella; we should hear from Littleford, quite soon. We cannot leave them to the mercy of a gang of ruffians." She added more gently, "Have no fear, Isabella. Even if they return, they will not harm us. Everyone in the village knows Mr Courtney." So saying, she set about trying to comfort the fearful women around her.

Meanwhile, Caroline had barely driven half a mile up the road when she encountered Robert, who, with Rose, was returning to the Fitzwilliams' for dinner, having spent the afternoon with his parents at Oakleigh.

They were all smiles when they greeted her, but soon realised from her grave countenance that something was seriously amiss. "Caroline, what has happened? Where is Emily?" Robert asked.

Caroline explained, breathless and afraid for her sister and Isabella, and begged Robert to ride to Littleford and alert Richard while she followed with Rose.

Robert agreed and went immediately, waiting only to get sufficient information for Richard. "Caroline, you had best return to the Rectory with Rose and wait for James. When he arrives, tell him I have gone to get help and will be going directly to the camp on the moor with Richard," he said, taking fond leave of Rose, who pleaded to be allowed to go with him. Robert would not hear of it.

On returning to the Rectory at Kympton, Caroline and Rose found James Courtney preparing to start out on foot. Very relieved to see them, he was too preoccupied to protest when they declared their intention to go with him and climbed quickly into the carriage, plainly concerned for the safety of his wife.

James Courtney knew how strongly Emily felt about the suffering of the Irish immigrant families; only a week ago she had returned from the camp, extremely upset by the condition of the children.

"They cannot possibly survive a Winter on the moor; they have neither the clothing nor the shelter to protect them from the weather. If nothing is done for them, they will die of chills and pneumonia," she had said, and he had promised to talk to Mr Darcy about the problem.

"Perhaps he will agree to let them use some of the old vacant farm buildings on the estate," he had said at the time, but there had not been an opportunity to broach the subject with Mr Darcy.

By the time they reached the edge of the moor, where they had to alight and walk, it was almost dark.

In the distance, in the lee of a hill, they could see the light of flaring torches, and several huddled forms were silhouetted against the darkening sky. As they hurried forward, James, realising suddenly the danger in which the two young women accompanying him might be placed, stopped abruptly. "Wait here, you cannot go on, there is no knowing what might happen," he said.

They protested. "Surely, they will never harm any of us, they know all our families," said Caroline, but James was not so sanguine.

"I cannot see their faces, they may not be men from the village at all," he said, determined not to expose them to any further risk.

Rose and Caroline, anxious though they were to go to Emily's side, could not defy James. They concealed themselves behind a clump of trees as James went on without them. He moved forward cautiously; he could hear a low rumble like angry voices grumbling in unison.

As he got closer to the camp, he was aghast to see his wife standing, with young Isabella Fitzwilliam beside her and several bedraggled and frightened women and children crouched on the ground, confronting a group of men. Some carried torches, while others had short, thick sticks they had obviously used to smash the houses and furniture, which lay around them in the dirt. One big man had a vicious looking dog on a lead, which he looked ready to loose onto anyone that moved.

James Courtney could not hear what they were saying, and he felt as if his feet had turned to lead as he tried desperately to move over the claggy ground. "Please, God, let them not do anything rash," he prayed.

Suddenly, clear as a bell, he heard Emily's voice. "What do you want with these people? They have done you no harm."

Several voices were raised in argument—they were grumbling about the Irishmen taking their jobs, working for less money ... squatting on the commons ... poaching game ... taking the food from the mouths of the poor, and they were all papists, to boot!

It was a litany of complaint.

"And do you mean to punish the women and children by smashing up their belongings, burning their houses, and turning them out on the moor?" Emily's voice shook with emotion.

"What would you have them do? Have they not as much right to eat as your wives and children? They do not steal or beg. Are they not entitled to our compassion as much as the people who have come here from Scotland or Yorkshire?" she asked, knowing full well she had helped many such families over the years of depression.

Taking advantage of their silence, the result of some confusion among the men, she demanded to know how many of them were settlers from other parts of England? There were a couple of unfamiliar faces she did not recognise from Kympton or its surrounding areas. She was determined to drive home the point, as a few hands went up, albeit reluctantly.

"And how did our community treat you when you first arrived among us? Did we smash your houses and turn your wives and children out into the cold to starve? Or did we, perhaps, show you some Christian charity? Did we put food on your tables and clothes on your children's backs? Mr Courtney and I have helped many families from Scotland and Tyneside or the West Riding. Some of you have found work and decided to stay on here; your children come to our school. Yet, you would not have us do the same for these people. Why do they deserve less than you do?

"Their men are gone to find work; how brave is it to attack women and children while their husbands and fathers are out working? What would you do to men who attacked your wives and children and burned down your houses? Would you stand idly by or would you be calling for revenge? Then, why would you do it to these poor helpless people?"

Her voice shaking, her eyes filled with tears, Emily stood her ground as, one by one, the men began to turn away. James Courtney rushed to her side just as Robert, Richard, and several men who had ridden over from Pemberley arrived and confronted the thugs, taking many of them into custody.

To Robert's horror, one of the men skulking away was Morris, a game-keeper on his father's property, whose family had often benefited from the Gardiners' generosity. Seeing the expression of disgust and anger on Robert's face, he retreated quickly into the darkness, while Robert made a mental note to tell his parents about Morris and his role in this outrage.

As the men either made off into the night or were arrested and taken away to be brought before the magistrate on the morrow, everyone crowded around Emily and Isabella, ensuring they were unhurt. Caroline and Rose, who had crept up behind the contingent from Pemberley, rushed to embrace them, while Emily's brothers were speechless with amazement at what they had just witnessed.

The Irish women were loud in their praise of Emily, claiming she had saved them all from death or worse. Even allowing for exaggeration and a colourful turn of phrase, she had clearly averted a very ugly incident.

For Emily, however, the work was not yet done. "Something has to be arranged for the women and children; they cannot be left out on the moors without shelter or protection," she insisted.

Apart from the moorland weather, which could be quite bitter, she feared the men would return. It was plain that the women shared her fears.

But Darcy's steward said he had instructions from his master to remove all of the women and children to the Kympton church hall, provide them with food and shelter, and then, in a day or two, a way might be found to help them settle somewhere safer than the moors.

When everyone had been moved to the church hall, fed, and bedded down, the family gathered at the Rectory. Richard was to go on to Pemberley and report to Darcy, while Robert and Rose returned belatedly to the Fitzwilliams.

Neither could relate the story of that night without emotion. That Emily had put herself at risk to protect the poor Irish women and their chil-dren astonished everyone, but no one who knew her was surprised at the tenacity and courage she had shown, certainly not Darcy and Elizabeth, who had heard Richard's account with alarm.

That night, after everyone had returned to their homes, Elizabeth and Darcy discussed the day's events and spoke of Emily with great pride. "She never ceases to amaze; her integrity and strength are phenomenal," said Darcy, still shocked by the details of the story.

There had been several rumours of purported attacks on Irishmen and their families, but none had been as serious or as frightening as this one.

Elizabeth could not believe the savagery of the gang who had gone up to the camp on the moor. "How could anyone plan, in cold blood, to do such a thing to unprotected women and innocent children?" she asked, not really expecting an answer.

But Darcy did respond, pointing out the nature of the offence. "It is the kind of irrational brutality that takes over when men, especially ill-educated and powerless men, can find no solution to their problems. Without work, without money—now that the Poor Law prevents them receiving help unless they enter the workhouse—they will strike out at anyone. The Irish immigrants are convenient scapegoats," he explained. "Their situation is worse than most because, in addition to being destitute, they are treated as outcasts in England because they are different. To ignorant people, this justifies their persecution."

Elizabeth could not accept it. She had tears in her eyes as she spoke. "But they are as powerless and downtrodden as any of our own poor—even more so, having not even a piece of ground of their own!" she cried.

Seeing her distress, Darcy tried to explain, "Poverty is an ugly condition, my love. It may bring out the goodness in some, but mostly, it takes away the power to reason and lets us do terrible things. It is easy to be generous and caring when one has the means to live well while helping others, but grinding, hopeless poverty takes away the inclination and the means."

Elizabeth sighed, understanding his explanation but not reassured by it. "What is to become of them?" she asked anxiously.

He wanted to allay her fears and comfort her. "Tomorrow, Sir Thomas and I will meet to see what can be done to accommodate them in a safer place. There is some land within our two estates which may be suitable—chiefly abandoned farmland on the edge of the common. I have asked John Grantham to join me when I meet Sir Thomas; he would know best what can be done for them."

He was careful not to promise too much, unwilling to raise her expectations and disappoint her if a practical solution could not be found.

Elizabeth pressed for an answer. "Would you let them stay?" she asked.

He smiled. "You would like me to, would you not, my love?" When she nodded, he added, "We shall see tomorrow. I must get Sir Thomas to agree, but if it is at all possible, they shall stay."

Her arms tightened around him, loving him, willing him to do what was right. If a way could be found to help the Irish families, who had so narrowly escaped a dreadful fate just a few miles from Pemberley, she knew he would find it.

Darcy knew she was shaken and unhappy. Holding her close, he comforted her, hoping that on the morrow, he could bring her better news.

※

A few days later, writing to Jane, Elizabeth gave an account of Emily's "adventure," making no attempt to hide her own feelings.

Dearest Jane, she wrote:

> *I have given you the details exactly as they were related to us by Richard and later by both Caroline and Isabella. Emily has not spoken a great deal of these matters, being more concerned to see that the unhappy families and their children are safe.*
>
> *Words cannot describe my feelings of horror and revulsion, and I know you would feel the same.*
>
> *How it is possible for ordinary people to become so desperate as to behave more like beasts, I cannot imagine. Poor Isabella, she has neither Emily's courage nor her maturity of experience, and was therefore most frightened by the whole event.*
>
> *Yet, I am told, she stood bravely with Emily, clutching her hand until the fingernails bit into the flesh of her palms. Richard recalls seeing them in the light of the flaming torches with which the wretched brutes plainly intended to set fire to the battered cottages and furniture they had earlier destroyed.*
>
> *He says he felt rooted to the spot, unable to move or speak, while he watched Emily confront the villains and shame them into turning away from their foul intentions. Richard, Robert, and the men they had taken with them were afraid to rush in, lest they make matters worse. They stood*

in the shadows, ready to intervene at the first sign of danger. But Emily was completely unafraid, Richard said, and had the men looking ashamed and downcast.

Finally, the ruffians began to retreat. Only then did they approach and soon apprehended most of the culprits, who have since been brought before Sir Thomas Camden, the magistrate for this area. We can at least be sure that he will deal very harshly with them for their heinous deeds and make an example of them.

Meanwhile, we have been most concerned to ensure that the poor Irish families have a safer place to live than the moors. They have neither shelter nor furniture and are truly in a parlous state. Emily will not rest until they are settled somewhere safe.

Darcy and Sir Thomas are considering allowing them the use of a part of Lower Litton Common, which lies between the two estates. It used to be a grazing meadow but has not been used for many years, since the herds were moved to higher ground. There are a couple of vacant cottages and a barn which they may use, and the river is at hand, too.

Nothing has been decided yet, but we hope it will soon be settled for the sake of the poor children, at least, and to satisfy Emily, who will not be content until it is done and she can get the children into school.

Elizabeth could not say enough in praise of their cousin:

Dear Jane,
  Emily is surely an angel. Her selflessness is a rare jewel.
  Your loving sister,
  Lizzie.

⁓❦⁓

The ball at Pemberley, where Robert and Rose confirmed what everyone knew—that they were engaged and planned to marry in the Autumn—was a great success.

Emily was particularly pleased because, just that morning, she had seen the last of her poor Irish families moved from their temporary shelter in the Kympton parish hall to Lower Litton Common where, with the help of workmen from the Camden and Pemberley estates, a few cottages and a barn had been repaired and made ready for them.

Furniture, blankets, and clothes had been garnered from around the parish; many families, horrified by the news of the attack upon the Irish women and children, now gave generously. A rousing sermon from their Rector had helped, too. James Courtney did not mince his words. The entire incident had shocked and frightened the people of Kympton, who had never expected their grumbling about the Irish to have such dreadful consequences.

That evening, when everyone was gathered at Pemberley, Emily took the opportunity to approach Mr Darcy as he stood with Elizabeth, the Bingleys, and Mr and Mrs Gardiner, and, before the entire gathering, she thanked him warmly for his generosity and compassion. "Many people have helped us in lots of little ways, but there are only a few who have the ability to do something really important for these unfortunate people. You have done that, and may God bless you, Mr Darcy, for your greatness of heart," she said simply, and while he was a little embarrassed and reddened visibly, Darcy was also very touched by her words.

Julian declared that he was quite sure that "Papa was prodigiously pleased."

Elizabeth was immensely proud of him.

Not all the Irish families stayed on permanently. Several left when their menfolk found work, moving to Liverpool and Birmingham, where larger groups of Irish settlers afforded them some safety in numbers and formed large communities in those cities.

But some of them remained behind, working the land, helping on the farms and in the stables—they were excellent with horses—while their children attended the parish school at Kympton.

To this day, a small Irish community remains in this corner of Derbyshire; and among them, the tale of the plucky young wife of the Rector of Kympton, who saved a group of women and children from marauding thugs, is still told—with appropriate embellishment, of course!

❧

Robert Gardiner and Rose Fitzwilliam were married in the Autumn.

If universal good wishes can guarantee marital bliss, their felicity should have been assured. As well as their obvious affection and regard for each other, there was an impression that this union combined good sense with deep affection; a blessed combination indeed.

Shortly afterwards, the family received the happy news of the birth of a son to Emma and James Wilson.

They called him Charles after his grandfather, and Bingley was so proud, he went directly to Kent to bestow a small fortune on his beloved daughter's son, ensuring he would be well provided for when he grew up. With the birth of this little boy, the happiness of his parents, never in doubt, was now complete.

Jane, who had stayed on with her daughter, wrote to Elizabeth:

I know you will understand, dearest Lizzie, how much we appreciate what marriage to James has meant to Emma. She is so totally transformed, so fulfilled and content, I can hardly believe that a few years ago I had almost given up hope of her ever being happy again. God has truly blessed her and our family.

Elizabeth knew how deeply her sister had been hurt by Emma's unhappy first marriage and shared her relief.

～✢～

That Christmas, the families gathered again at Pemberley. They were celebrating also the end of a very full year.

Standing together at the entrance to the ballroom, Mr Darcy and Mr Bingley watched as their wives descended the great staircase, which was only used on occasions such as this, when Pemberley was in festive mood. Both men agreed as the sisters—unaware that they were being observed—came slowly downstairs that the years had only enhanced the beauty of their wives.

Jane, after four children, was still acknowledged as a woman of exceptional beauty, with a tranquillity of disposition that set her apart. Bingley, who had begun by insisting she was "an angel," still loved her to distraction.

Lizzie, on the other hand, had started out without finding favour with the man who had claimed to be indifferent to her beauty, but who had then fallen so deeply in love with her that he could not find the right words to propose to her. Thanks to a variety of circumstances and the timely, though unwitting, intervention of Lady Catherine de Bourgh, Darcy had been given a second chance to find the words that would secure the happiness they had both desired. Lizzie's slender figure had softened and filled out somewhat, but she was still elegant and lovely and remained, as her husband had once described her, "one of the handsomest women of my acquaintance."

As they welcomed the Gardiners, who remained their dearest friends, Elizabeth noticed that her aunt seemed more than usually happy about something and determined to find a moment alone with her.

This proved to be unnecessary, for Mrs Gardiner soon sought out her nieces and broke the news that Emily had received a letter from the Queen's secretary, recognising and commending her work with the poor and especially with needy children. Mrs Gardiner was convinced that Emily would soon be honoured by the Queen.

Mr Gardiner was what Julian would have called "prodigiously pleased," but Emily, arriving shortly afterwards, seemed very calm about it all. She was far more excited by the fact that two of her young Irish protégés were actually singing in the children's choir that night.

Emily had learned from their mother that the boys used to sing in the church choir back in Ireland and persuaded Dr Jenkins to try them out for the Christmas Carols. Impressed with their voices, he had put a good deal of time and effort into training them.

"Their voices are just beautiful, Lizzie, and I cannot think of a better Christmas present than having them sing for us, truly I cannot," said Emily, her eyes lighting up with pleasure.

Elizabeth had to agree. "What is more, Emily, they are even smiling for you," she declared.

Emily laughed. "Considering what they have been through, Lizzie, that has to be a considerable achievement," she said as they went in together to hear the children sing.

CHAPTER THREE

Cassandra

C ASSANDRA GARDINER HEARD THE carriage, put away the letter she was reading, and moved to the window. She watched, with a rush of tenderness, as her husband Richard alighted and helped their little daughter Elizabeth out, while young Edward and Darcy, who had already leapt from the vehicle, came running up the drive towards the house.

The children were back from Lambton, where they had stayed with Richard's parents while she and her husband had gone to Standish Park to attend the christening of Charles, the son of her cousin Emma and James Wilson.

By the time Cassy had reached the foot of the stairs, her two boys— now twelve and ten—had burst through the hall and enveloped their mother in an enormous embrace, leaving Richard to follow with little Lizzie, who had to wait in line to kiss her mother. Little Lizzie, as she was known to everyone except Nurse Marsh, who insisted upon calling her Miss Elizabeth, finally reached her mother, protesting that she had missed her most of all.

All the children wanted to tell her how they had spent their time at Oakleigh, apart from being spoilt by their doting grandparents, but Cassy, being rather tired herself after the long drive from Banbury, where they had spent the previous night, agreed to hear it all, but later.

Richard, sensitive to her needs, persuaded the boys to let their mother rest awhile before regaling her with their adventures. Being very active children, they needed little persuasion and went directly out of doors again.

"You are not going to Littleford today, are you dearest?" Cassandra asked anxiously as her husband accompanied her upstairs.

Richard knew she would be pleased if he said he was not. He worked hard at his practice in Derby and at the hospital in Littleford, which provided the only medical services for the poor for miles around. Cassy supported his work totally, but he knew that she often missed him around the house and was keen to reassure her.

"Not today, Henry Forrester is working in my place until Sunday. I met the Fitzwilliams' visiting mother and Isabella assured me that all is well, so, my darling, I'm afraid you have me all to yourself for the rest of today and tomorrow."

His wife's smile was proof that the news was welcome. "I am quite amazed at my good fortune, to have my husband at home for two whole days!" Cassandra feigned astonishment, "Whatever shall I do with him?" He responded in seconds, declaring that he would have no trouble at all finding ways to spend the time with her—all equally pleasurable.

She blushed, but made no effort to discourage him. Several years of marriage had done nothing to dull their passion.

There was no doubting their devotion to each other, but simultaneously, they had always had a strong sense of public duty, and were involved in everything from local charities to political campaigns promoting councils to provide health services for the district.

Ever since his return from Paris to start work as a physician, first in Birmingham and then in Derby, Richard had campaigned actively for better health services for the poor. He had been affronted by the ability of the wealthy to obtain the best medical care, while the poor, if they were fortunate, depended upon an apothecary or, worse, on backyard practitioners of so-called folk medicine.

There were so few hospitals that hardly anyone received proper nursing care, unless they were wealthy enough to afford a nurse at home as well as a visiting physician, which was why the hospital at Littleford, established with donations of land and materials from Mr Darcy and his neighbour Sir

Thomas Camden, and equipped with the generous bequest from his sister Emily's late husband, was so important to Richard. From modest beginnings it had grown over the years into a well-run, well-endowed institution dedicated to the provision of health services to the people of the area. For the rural families, especially those too poor to afford a doctor from Derby, it had proved to be, quite literally, a lifesaver.

After her marriage, Cassandra had joined Emily in managing the hospital, and, more recently, young Isabella Fitzwilliam had begun to take an active interest in the nursing work—helping especially with the children, with whom she seemed to have a special gift.

Cassy was proud of her husband's work. Not only did he dedicate himself to healing the sick, but also he campaigned untiringly for special programs to prevent disease—simple measures in sanitation and hygiene—which would surely save lives, especially those of young children. He had fought the municipal bureaucracy for the right to demand that they provide better public services that would improve the health of the community, using, wherever possible, the influence of his father, Mr Gardiner, or the local Member of Parliament to assist his cause.

In all these worthy campaigns, Cassy supported him unstintingly, and he appreciated the time she gave him. But she was frequently alone when he was working and longed for days like these, when she could have him to herself.

Theirs was a strong marriage based upon mutual esteem and the very deepest love, for neither would have been content with a marriage of convenience or worse, one that admitted only an exchange of shallow, lukewarm affections. Like her mother, Cassandra had been determined never to marry other than for love, and among the many young men she had met in society, none had inspired more than a passing interest.

At first, she had been very much in awe of her cousin Richard, who was not only several years older than her, but a distinguished medical scholar as well. Gradually, however, she had allowed herself to fall deeply in love with him; but as she discovered her own feelings, had been afraid to let him see them, lest they be unwelcome. Happily, as it turned out, far from being unrequited, they were passionately engaged and returned. Since then, there had never been any question of their mutual love.

Proud as she was of his valuable work in the community, she longed for more of his time for herself and their children. Richard was not unaware of her feelings, and though he did not speak of it as often as he might, he felt just as strongly about it, for he loved her deeply and, whenever the opportunity arose, lost no time in reassuring her. Such was their devotion that complete strangers, meeting them for the first time, would become aware of the depth of their feelings.

Emma Wilson had told them how James, meeting them at Pemberley, had remarked to her that theirs must have been a great love story. It was a story that encompassed their children, who were so dearly loved and well cared for that there existed between them the closest of filial bonds.

Cassandra, whose own ambitions had neither outgrown her circumstances nor ever been circumscribed by them, was quite content with her position in life. Married to a physician, she craved neither higher rank nor greater wealth, perfectly happy to enjoy the warmth of the love with which her husband and family surrounded her.

On this warm, soporific afternoon, when the languid atmosphere of late Summer was not conducive to energetic activity, Cassy was agreeably occupied. Lying in Richard's arms, she was about to tell him the news contained in a letter she had received that morning from Amelia-Jane when there was a loud knocking on the front door. Unwilling to spoil the moment, neither made any effort to rise. No visitors were expected that afternoon; even the sound of voices, grave and serious as they seemed, did not disturb them unduly. Richard merely raised a quizzical eyebrow.

"It's probably a tradesman or a neighbour—Mrs Morris will send them away," Cassy whispered, turning over as she spoke and closing her eyes.

Moments later, Edward was heard running up the stairs calling out, "Papa, Papa, it's Toby—George has fallen off his horse," and as he burst into the room, Richard sprang out of bed in time to hear that young George, the son of their groom, had probably broken a leg.

Throwing on some clothes, he rushed downstairs, while Cassy rose and put on a wrap before following him to the top of the stairs.

In the front hall, with Mrs Morris the housekeeper, was Toby.

No sooner had Richard heard the details of the accident then he prepared to leave, gathering his things and picking up his bag as he gave instructions.

With Cassy he was gentle, apologising for leaving her so suddenly, "Will you send a message to Henry Forrester at Littleford, my love? Tell him I will be bringing the boy in. He may need surgery and will certainly have to stay overnight at the hospital."

As Cassandra nodded and bent over the desk to write a note, he put his arms around her from behind, pulled her gently against him, kissed her cheek, and was gone.

Cassy spent the rest of the afternoon with her children. The warmth of her husband's love always left her feeling more loving towards them, as if, fulfilled and content, she had more to share with them. They were full of tales of the fun they had had at Oakleigh; even little Lizzie, who could rarely keep up with the excitement and energy generated by her brothers, was keen to impress her mother with her stories. The boys had fished and explored the woods, riding everyday with their Uncle Robert and his wife Rose, who were staying with the Gardiners. Rose was an excellent horsewoman.

"She rides superbly, Mama; she is much faster than Uncle Robert," said Edward, and Darcy agreed that Robert was no match for his wife when it came to taking her horse over the hedgerows. Rose had plainly made a great impression on the lads.

Cassy, recalling Rose—grief-stricken at the death of the man she was to marry—riding alone for hours across fields, woods, and moorland, was glad to hear that she was happy in her marriage to Robert.

When they had tired of talking and were ready for baths and dinner, she went upstairs to her room and lay on her bed awhile. She fell asleep and did not wake until Lucy brought her tea and prepared her bath. She was ready to dress for dinner when Richard returned.

As he went directly to his dressing room and scrupulously performed the ablutions he always followed when he returned from the hospital—so particular was he to protect his family from any contagion—she laid out his clothes. It was a task she performed as a matter of course. Richard disliked the intrusive presence of a manservant in their private apartments, which, on this occasion, was just as well.

Fresh from his bath, he seemed to remember that they had some unfinished business, which he was in a mood to complete. Cassy seemed to have had a similar notion; she had sent Lucy away, leaving her hair down and lingering over her toilette.

Much later, she asked him about Toby's son. "How is George? Was it a bad fall?" Her voice betrayed the apprehension she felt. Falls from horses had killed her beloved brother William and their cousin Edward on one night, some years ago.

His answer reassured her. "No, not at all. He was exceedingly lucky; the horse stumbled but did not fall. George was thrown, fortuitously, into a great pile of new mown hay. Apart from a sprained ankle and some minor bruising, he seems to have suffered little damage. I have asked Henry Forrester to keep a watch on him overnight, but I expect him to be home in a day or two."

Cassandra could not help herself. Her expression betrayed her feelings. Her eyes filled with tears as the questions returned to haunt her. Why had it been different for William and Edward on that night many years ago? It was a night she would never forget—the night of her engagement to Richard—when, after a weekend of pleasure and a day of unalloyed joy, the families had had to face the loss of two of their dearest children. Death had come like the proverbial thief in the night to snatch them away. Why? She had asked herself the question often enough, recalling the suffering of her parents, especially the prolonged anguish of her mother and her sister-in-law Caroline Fitzwilliam, as well as her own misery from which Richard alone had been able to rescue her. Wondering at the cruel and arbitrary nature of Fate, Cassy was unable to hold back the tears.

Sensible of her feelings and aware of her need for consolation after all these years, her husband put his arms around her, as he had done many times before, and held her until she was done with weeping. He had no answers for her, nobody had, but he loved her deeply and would do everything he could to comfort her.

As they prepared to go down to dinner, she told him Amelia-Jane's news. "They are expecting another child, and she hopes it will be a girl because Amelia wants to call her Catherine," she said.

Richard was puzzled. "Why Catherine, particularly?" he asked.

She laughed, teasing him, "You will never guess."

He tried, "She wants her sister to be godmother?"

"Oh, Richard, you are so innocent. It is not that simple. They have been spending some time at Hunsford with Catherine and Mr Harrison, and, of course, they have been invited to Rosings on many occasions."

"Of course, and no doubt Amelia-Jane is very respectful towards Lady Catherine de Bourgh!" said Richard with a mischievous smile.

His wife agreed, and he continued, "Let me guess; she wants Lady Catherine to be godmother, in the fond hope that she will make the child a beneficiary in her will!" He looked to her for confirmation.

Cassy was laughing, but had to acknowledge he was right. "Mama always said the Collins girls knew how to make the best of every opportunity," she said with a smile, "but even she will be surprised at Amelia-Jane's plans for her unborn daughter."

Richard wondered whether there was an even more devious plan.

"Remember Lady Catherine is quite old now, and her only child, Anne, is, I am told, an invalid. Perhaps Amelia-Jane hopes to gain more than a bequest. Could it be that she hopes for some position of influence for her husband with Lady Catherine?"

Cassy shrugged her shoulders, "It is certainly possible. She is very ambitious for Jonathan, and I do believe Lady Catherine approves of him. You must agree he is a very proper gentleman."

Richard did agree. "Indeed, he is, but, whatever their plans, they will have very little to do with our lives, my darling. I am very glad that you have no intentions of laying claim to any part of your father's estate, apart from whatever may naturally accrue to you as his daughter, for, while I regard Pemberley as the most handsome house I have seen, I think we are far happier making our own way in the world, rather than inheriting the problems of grand houses and great estates. Do you not agree with me, Cassy?"

"With all my heart," said Cassandra, who had never wanted to be the mistress of a great estate. "Stately homes do not attract me either; much as I love Pemberley, I am glad it will be Julian's to care for. I am so happy here that I cannot imagine what I would do in a place the size of Rosings—quite apart from Lady Catherine's stuffy formality, which would not suit me at all."

For a young woman who had spent her life at Pemberley, she had been surprisingly unimpressed with the prospect of becoming its mistress—a prospect that had loomed large after the death of her brother William. She had made it clear to her father at the time that she had her own life to lead, with Richard, and she had felt enormous relief when Julian was born some two years later.

Her own home was a modest but elegant Georgian house on a property of moderate size beside the River Wye, situated halfway between the historic village of Bakewell and the dales of Matlock. A wedding present from Richard's parents, it had been for them an exceptionally happy home. Ever since she had first walked through the front door, Cassy had loved the house.

The property, which included a small home farm, dairy, and orchard, occupied one of the prettiest sites on the river, where a happy combination of trees, rocks, and tumbling water created a prospect that both captivated the eye and soothed the spirit. They had been very happy here.

Now, several years later, she could not imagine living anywhere else.

❧

The engagement of Sophie Bingley to a Mr Daniel Lambert—youngest son of Sir Tristram Lambert of Derby, lawyer, aspiring Member of Parliament, and close friend of her brother Jonathan—was the occasion for a lavish dinner and ball at Ashford House.

Unlike Mr Darcy, who took little enjoyment from dancing and gave a ball more as a duty to provide for the diversion and entertainment of others, Mr Bingley always entered into the proceedings with great enthusiasm. Friends and relations from miles around were invited and preparations had been in train for weeks before the day arrived, when an army of servants would provide for the tastes of their master's guests. Perfect in every particular, the Bingleys' hospitality was legendary. The evening proceeded without a single slip, and as the guests left, they marvelled at the generosity of Mr Bingley and the good fortune of his lovely daughter. The Bingleys were universally liked, attracting much praise and little envy from acquaintances and neighbours alike.

Talking together afterwards, Richard found in Daniel Lambert a sympathetic listener when he complained of the procrastination he had endured from local government in matters of education and public health. It was certainly an appropriate issue for the attention of an aspiring young politician. He was keenly interested in Richard's professional comments.

Speaking of the Great Exhibition in Hyde Park, Mr Lambert asked Richard's opinion of the pavilion designed by Paxton, whose work for the Duke of Devonshire at Chatsworth had attracted the attention of Prince Albert himself. "Is it not a remarkable building, Dr Gardiner?" he asked. "I believe the French and German visitors have been mightily impressed."

Richard agreed that Mr Paxton had indeed designed a breathtakingly light structure of metal and glass, a "crystal palace" which was much admired by the general populace, but he railed against the hypocrisy of those who had commissioned it.

"I cannot believe that we are content to display to the world our wealth and trumpet our progress whilst we deny the majority of our people the basic necessities of a healthy life—decent housing, clean water, and sanitation. It is absolutely disgraceful that the men and women whose toil produces the wealth we boast of, as well as their innocent children, have neither basic education nor a public health service," he complained.

Mr Lambert was taken aback by the strength of his grievance. He listened attentively as Colonel Fitzwilliam, who had joined their circle, expressed his own disappointment. Fitzwilliam and Caroline had worked tirelessly to promote the ideas of the Reform Group. "The abolition of the rotten boroughs, as part of the Parliamentary Reforms of the 1830s, for which we fought, was followed by a similar liberation of municipalities from corruption," he explained. "The Reform Act of 1835 opened the way for local government to improve the lives of all people in English towns and villages. We worked very hard for it and regarded it as a triumph. We believed that the needs of working people could now be provided for, but things have not changed as we had expected." There was no mistaking the disillusionment in his voice.

"Richard has been trying for years to make them see the need for another hospital, or even a clinic for children of the poor in the area, with no success," said Cassandra.

Caroline Fitzwilliam added her voice. "And the Tates—Rebecca and Anthony—have campaigned through their newspapers for a village school for the children of working people who cannot afford the big public schools and seminaries, all to no avail."

"Why are they unwilling to attend to these matters?" asked Lambert, who was clearly surprised at the level of dissatisfaction. "Since they are no longer the puppets of the landlords, one might have expected better from them."

Fitzwilliam and Richard spoke as one. "Indeed."

"One might; but the 'ordinary men' who run the local councils now are most often land developers, mill owners, and shop keepers, with no interest in improving the lot of the poor," said Richard.

"And they are not anxious to spend the rates they collect on drains or sewers," added Fitzwilliam. "They would rather build monuments."

Daniel Lambert listened, bewildered and shocked as Richard explained that the cholera epidemic that had killed thousands in 1848 had led directly to the passage of the Public Health Act, but even this did not compel local government to provide sanitation and housing.

Outraged, Lambert wanted to help. "Doctor Gardiner, I would very much like you to meet my father. He has several friends on the council and in the government. I am sure he would help, if he could."

Richard was pleased to have his complaints fall on other than deaf ears and agreed to meet Sir Tristram whenever an appointment could be arranged.

"Do you believe Mr Lambert is genuine in his interest in your hospital project?" asked Cassandra when they were on their way home, "or is he more interested in his Parliamentary ambitions?"

Richard, who had suffered many disappointments, was not unduly optimistic, but he was prepared to credit Daniel Lambert with some sincerity of purpose.

"If he can persuade his father to use whatever influence he has on the council to help us get our hospital, I shall be forever in his debt. But, my love, I am no more hopeful this time around, so let us wait and see what follows."

"And meanwhile, people will continue to live in squalor, and children will die without proper care," said Cassy, her voice rising with frustration.

❦

Some weeks later, having met with Daniel and Sir Tristram Lambert for several hours, Richard returned, a good deal more hopeful.

Cassandra was pleasantly surprised to hear that Sir Tristram, having listened to him, had requested a tour of the hospital at Littleford and the parish schools at Kympton and Pemberley. "It does mean he is seriously interested, Richard," she said.

"Perhaps it does. I have agreed to seek permission for him to visit next week, and I am sure your parents would like to invite him to Pemberley," said her husband sagely, well aware of the value and prestige of his connection with the Darcy family in the eyes of businessmen like Sir Tristram.

The following week, Sir Tristram and Daniel Lambert were invited to visit the schools and hospital and dine afterwards at Pemberley together with Richard and Cassandra, Colonel Fitzwilliam and Caroline, and James and Emily Courtney.

Whether it was the hospitality of Mr and Mrs Darcy or the excellent impression created by the schools and hospital as well as the busy community hall with its popular library, they would never know; but Sir Tristram left very much impressed and, shortly afterwards, the council invited Dr Richard Gardiner in to discuss his proposal for a hospital.

Richard, accustomed to the snail-like pace of council deliberations, was astonished at their conversion. With Daniel Lambert at his elbow to reinforce his father's influence and a sheaf of plans and papers, he had expected to spend days persuading them to his way of thinking. The alacrity with which they accepted not just the need for a new hospital, but agreed to bear much of the cost of establishing it, was quite amazing. It left Richard in no doubt of the influence that a powerful industrialist and landowner like Sir Tristram could wield over a council.

Returning home he told Cassandra of their success. "Truthfully, I have to say, I was astonished. I could scarcely believe that their attitude had been completely reversed. Sir Tristram and his family have huge investments in the Staffordshire potteries and the railways in the Midlands. They must have enormous influence over council officials. Clearly, his interest in a project is the best way to ensure its acceptance."

Cassy was incredulous. "Does that mean our problems are at an end, then?" she asked.

Her husband was cautious in his reply. "One set of problems may be over, but another, related to managing the project and establishing the hospital, for which I have accepted responsibility, may be just beginning." Richard confessed that he could have left the new hospital project entirely to the council, but he had been reluctant to do so. "I shall talk to Emily and your mother before approaching Henry Forrester, but I am hopeful he will accept a position at Littleford."

"Where is the new hospital to be?" Cassandra asked.

"There are two possible sites—one in the north near Maclesfield and another closer to home, not much more than a mile or two southeast of Matlock," he replied, adding that he had expressed a preference for the latter site, which had a further advantage in that it lay within the area young Daniel Lambert hoped to represent in the next parliament.

Cassy smiled. "Ah, well, that should certainly improve its chances of selection," she said, "and perhaps, if I am fortunate, I might get to see my husband occasionally, then?"

Richard, aware that his involvement would surely mean his family would see less of him for a while, promised solemnly he would not get totally absorbed into the project. "But think, my darling, what a fine thing it will be for the entire district; you know how many years I have spent trying to get the council to agree to my plan. Once this is done, I shall feel I have achieved something worthwhile."

Cassandra understood completely; she would not dream of standing in the way of the goals he had set for himself.

The untimely death in 1849 of the composer Frederic Chopin had caused a frisson of sorrow across Europe. Nowhere was this greater or felt with more poignancy than in Paris, his adopted home. Two years later, amidst a festival celebrating the work of Chopin, a competition was held in Paris to which performers young and old were invited.

William Courtney's music master, maestro Louis Lecomte, an émigré who had fled the revolution as a boy and built an enviable reputation in England, urged his parents to let the boy participate.

Emily required little persuasion, especially when she discovered that Richard and Cassandra would be travelling to Paris at the same time. Richard was to attend an important medical conference, and Cassy assured Emily that William would be quite safe with them. "Besides," she said, "Maestro Lecomte will be there, too; so you need have no concerns at all."

Cassandra was proved right. Not only did William acquit himself very creditably, winning a prize—to the delight of his family and the satisfaction of his teacher—but his rendition of a short Chopin composition had been rated the most sensitive interpretation by any competitor of his age group, receiving special praise from the distinguished judges.

Cassy, who accompanied William and Monsieur Lecomte to the soiree at which the prizes were awarded, told Emily of their joy. "No one was surprised when William was awarded a prize after we had all sat spellbound during the beautiful *Berceuse*," she said.

"Of course, one is always afraid to be too hopeful, but Monsieur Lecomte was brimming with confidence. No sooner was the result announced then he turned to me with a triumphant look upon his face, as if to say, 'There you are, did I not tell you so?'

"He was, however the very soul of gallantry when we spoke. He is full of praise for William's success. Oh, Emily, I cannot tell you how very proud I was of William." She confessed it had reminded her of her own brother, William, who would have surely excelled had he lived to pursue a career in music.

"Would you permit William to make music his career?" she asked.

"Of course," replied Emily, "if that was what he wanted. But William is still very young, and it will be a few more years before he can decide."

James Courtney agreed. "If it happens that he is really talented, then it is God's gift and we would be wrong to stand in his way. But, as Emily has said, we shall have to wait awhile and be guided by Maestro Lecomte."

The simplicity of their faith and the gentleness with which they dealt with William touched Cassandra deeply. She wished more parents would be like them.

Later that week, Cassy, who was spending the day at Pemberley, told Elizabeth about William's success. She listened and expressed her heartfelt joy at William's award, but Cassy could not help noticing the tears in her eyes. She rose from her chair, went over to her mother and silently put her arms around her, knowing she had never recovered from the death of her son.

Later, as she was preparing to leave, "When do you expect Richard home?" her father asked.

"Very soon, Papa; he has been invited to look at the work of Louis Pasteur. He is so determined to drag English medical practice into the modern world," she said, laughing as she got into her carriage.

Darcy smiled but said seriously, "He is a dedicated physician, Cassy, and a brave one. We need more such men."

When Cassandra reached home, she had the usual warm welcome from her three elder children, but, on going upstairs, found Nurse Marsh putting her youngest, little Laura Ann, to bed, although it was still early evening.

The nurse explained she had been fretting all day, refused her food and by afternoon seemed to have developed a fever.

Thanks to the presence of a doctor in the house, Cassandra had never taken her children's illnesses very seriously. They had mostly remained fit and well, but even when they suffered the usual childhood complaints, Richard had been there to reassure her and look after them. On this occasion, however, without his comforting presence, she was anxious.

Laura Ann seemed listless and fractious. She had a headache as well as a fever.

"I think I shall send for Mr Forrester, Nurse," Cassandra said, preparing to go downstairs. "Oh, I do wish Dr Gardiner was here." Cassy hurried downstairs and dispatched a servant to the hospital at Littleford with a note for Henry Forrester.

In the hour it took him to arrive, Cassy, unused to being alone in a crisis, wondered if she should send for Caroline or Emily. Realising that Kympton was closer, she sent the carriage to fetch her sister-in-law.

Henry Forrester, when he arrived, examined little Laura Ann and, unable to diagnose her condition immediately, prescribed a mild medicine, which seemed to calm her somewhat.

When Emily arrived, the child was quieter and seemed more comfortable, but Emily, who had, by her experience at the hospital, acquired some knowledge of these matters, warned Cassandra not to be too much at ease—rather, to watch over the child constantly, lest the fever return with redoubled vigour. Emily had come prepared to stay the night. Her gentle strength was a great source of comfort to her troubled sister-in-law. She understood her fears, and Cassy was grateful for her company.

"I do wish Richard was home," she said again.

Richard Gardiner, meanwhile, having taken time to observe the work of Pasteur and attend many learned discussions on bacteriology, decided he had had enough of the conference and returned to London two days earlier than expected.

At a favourite bookshop he happened upon James Wilson, who invited him to lunch at his club. After the meal, during which they exchanged all the news that could be of interest to both men, James took Richard along to the new House of Commons, which was soon to be opened, and they later returned to his apartment in Grosvenor Street, where Richard was persuaded to stay the night. "I hope you will come down to Kent with me tomorrow, Richard. Emma will not forgive me if I arrive without you. It is quite some time since we have all met."

Richard declared he was happy to travel to Standish Park, so long as he could send a message to Cassandra, advising her of his imminent return. "Cassy does not know I am back in England," he explained.

James Wilson assured him that it would be a simple matter to send a message by the new electric telegraph.

On the following morning, which turned out to be fine and ideally suited to driving out to the country, they left for Standish Park.

Emma, who had not seen Richard and his family since Christmas, was delighted to welcome him and wanted to know everything about everybody. She was disappointed when James informed her that Richard would only be staying overnight, having arranged to return to Derbyshire the following day.

"Can you not stay a day or two?" she pleaded. "There is so much I wish to know. I cannot imagine we shall get through it all tonight. Tell me, how are all our cousins and the children? Are your two boys enrolled at Eton?"

"No, Emma, their mother will not have them so far away from her. They are to be enrolled at a school in Oxford, which has been highly recommended to us by Dr Grantley and Georgiana. Cassy likes having them no further than a short day's journey from home," he explained, adding that they both missed the children when they were from home.

After dinner, they had retired to the drawing room, where Emma had been persuaded to entertain them with a song or two, when a carriage was heard coming up the drive and drawing up at the front door.

James and Emma took little notice at first; Emma stopped playing to explain that it must be a caller for her husband. "Members of Parliament have many callers, some at the strangest of times," she said and Richard replied that it was not very different for physicians.

However, the sound of their visitor's voice was so familiar that James rose from his chair and went out into the hall, where they heard him exclaim, "Mr Darcy, please do come in."

Hearing his father-in-law's name, Richard wondered what had brought him to Standish Park at such a late hour. Could there be some problem at Pemberley? When he saw Mr Darcy's face as he walked into the room, Richard was certain of it. He looked tired and drawn, his expression grave.

It was quite plain that it was not just the effect of a long journey. Clearly, Darcy was under severe emotional strain. Richard knew him too well to doubt it; something was very wrong.

Mr Darcy was astonished to find Richard there. "Richard! How long have you been here?" he asked abruptly.

"I travelled down with James this evening, sir," Richard replied, adding that he had arrived in London from Paris only yesterday and had met up with James by chance. He had no doubt now that his father-in-law was preoccupied with something very serious. His first thought was for the Bingleys and Emma. Could it be some bad news about Mr Bingley?

The same thought must have struck Emma as she watched Darcy, still standing in the middle of the room as if he did not intend to stay long, his countenance grave and serious. Could it be he had bad news for her?

She thought, at once, of her father. Turning to Darcy, she asked, "Is it Papa? Oh, please tell me, Mr Darcy, has something happened to Papa?" she begged, obviously distressed.

Darcy shook his head, "No, no, there is nothing the matter with Bingley. Emma, pray do not upset yourself, your parents and sisters are all perfectly well. No, indeed my journey's purpose has already been achieved. I came here to ask Mr Wilson to help me find Richard, who I believed to be in France. Richard, we have been trying to contact you these last few days without success."

Richard was instantly concerned. "Why, sir, is there something amiss at home? Is it Cassy? Is she ill?" His voice betrayed his anxiety.

Again, Darcy was reassuring, denying that Cassy was ill, but he stopped in mid-sentence and, looking directly at Richard, spoke very quietly. "Richard, it's little Laura Ann; she has been unwell, with a fever. Henry Forrester has been attending her, but he has not been able to discover the cause of her illness. He thinks it could be quinsy or diphtheria, but he cannot be certain. We dispatched two messages to your hotel in Paris, and when there was no reply, I decided to come to London and ask Mr Wilson for his help."

Turning to James, he explained, "I was confident that, with your contacts at the Foreign Office, you would soon locate him. I had no indication that he was back in England. Cassy has been desperate to find him."

Meanwhile, Richard had leapt up and was scarcely able to wait until Darcy had finished speaking before declaring that they must leave at once.

James and Emma urged Mr Darcy to take some refreshment and let the coachmen partake of some food before they made their return journey. Richard was frantic with anxiety; so keen was he to be gone.

Finally, they were on their way. The Wilsons wished them Godspeed and Darcy expressed his profound thanks. "If it were not for your kindness in inviting Richard down here, I might still have supposed him to be in France. I thank you very much, James."

They left with no further delay, meaning to travel through the night, stopping only to change horses and take whatever refreshment they could on the road.

At first, the two men hardly spoke at all. Then, suddenly, Richard wanted to know everything. It was as if he could not bear to spend another second in ignorance. But just as abruptly, having exhausted all the questions that Darcy could possibly answer, he lapsed into silence again.

Both men realised the seriousness of the situation. The death of young children from croup or diphtheria was common, and they knew many families who had suffered such a blow. Richard could not believe it possible; he had left his family fit and well. Admittedly, little Laura Ann was rather more delicate than the others, but he could not comprehend how she could have been infected with quinsy or, worse, diphtheria.

"There have been no similar cases at the hospital in Derby, nor has Henry Forrester reported any from Littleford. I am at a loss to understand how she could have contracted it. Cassy is exceedingly careful to protect the children from infection, and so is Nurse Marsh." He shook his head, bewildered and distressed.

Mr Darcy tried to offer some comfort, "Pray, do not upset yourself, Richard. Henry Forrester has been very good indeed. Emily and Caroline, who have been with Cassy throughout, say he is at Laura's bedside all night. He will not leave her."

Stunned, Richard asked, "Has Laura Ann been removed to the hospital?"

Darcy nodded, "Yes, indeed she has. I believe she became ill and her condition worsened so rapidly that they had no alternative but to remove her to Littleford, where she could be watched over closely. Emily tells me Henry Forrester has insisted that she is never alone. He keeps a close watch on her condition and personally administers her medication. He seems a very dedicated young man."

Richard agreed that Henry was certainly an exemplary medical practitioner, but at this moment, his anxiety was for his daughter. How he wished that, on returning to London, he had gone directly home to Derbyshire. He was feeling wretched, and it took all Darcy's powers of persuasion to stop him sinking into guilt-ridden depression. "Cassy will be looking forward to our return, Richard. James Wilson promised to send a message by telegram so she will know you are on your way home. She will need you to help her through this crisis," he said, indicating to Richard, without preaching at him, that his family would need his strength, whatever fate held in store for them. "You know you can depend on my support, whatever happens."

It was an indication of the strength of their regard and affection for each other that Darcy was able to offer such counsel and Richard to accept it. Richard loved his father, but he had never felt as close to him as he did at that moment to Mr Darcy. Shared experience and the consequences of shared sorrow had added depth to their relationship. There was both understanding and trust.

They were silent for a long time afterwards, remembering, perhaps, another time when they had been together at a terrible moment in their lives: the moment of William's death. Richard had been much younger then—indeed, it was the night of his engagement to Cassandra—but being together on that dreadful occasion had wrought between them a lasting bond.

They broke journey, very briefly, for Richard was impatient to be on the road as soon as possible. An hour or so before dawn, as the sky in the east was reddening with the first hint of the rising sun, they drove into Matlock and, taking the road leading to the Pemberley Estate, approached Littleford.

By the time they reached the hospital, it was near dawn.

Richard leapt out of the carriage and ran into the dark, silent building. Striding down a corridor, he walked past a waiting room, where he found Emily, Isabella, and Elizabeth waiting anxiously for news. Not seeing Cassy with them, Richard feared the worst and rushed to his sister. "Emmy, how is she? Where is Cassy?" he demanded.

Emily implored him to be calm. She knew that Laura had been through a crisis during the night just past. Dr Forrester had come in a few minutes ago and taken Cassy into the child's room. Emily's husband, James, had also spent the last hour at the child's bedside.

Mr Darcy entered the room and went directly to Elizabeth, seeking information. He was exhausted but would not leave until there was some news of Laura Ann's condition.

Some minutes later, Henry Forrester came in and, placing a finger on his lips to caution them, called Richard to follow him. Emily went with them.

As they entered the room, Cassy looked up, saw her husband, and went to him at once. His arms around her, he asked, "How is she?"

Cassy did not speak, but led him quietly to the bed. The little girl looked very pale, and her forehead was damp with sweat, but her body, which had been hot with fever for days, was cool to the touch. Henry Forrester stood on the other side of the child's bed. "We have just been through the longest night of my life, Richard. I think little Laura is breathing easier now, and her fever is abating."

"Is she out of danger?" Richard asked anxiously.

"Not entirely, not yet. She is still very weak, but I think the worst is over." Richard and Cassandra embraced, and their tears fell freely.

Once the good news had been conveyed to the rest of the family, Elizabeth insisted that Cassy must rest. She had had neither food nor sleep.

Richard agreed, and it was decided that they would go with Darcy and Elizabeth to Pemberley while Isabella and Emily took over the vigil at Laura's bedside.

Richard spoke to Henry Forrester, his words inadequate to thank him for his devoted care for their daughter. "I can never thank you enough, Henry. We shall be forever in your debt," he said, while Cassy, unable to speak, simply threw her arms around his neck and embraced him warmly.

Later, back at Pemberley, in what used to be Cassandra's own room, Richard apologised to his wife. "My darling, I am sorry. I should have been with you. If I had known, nothing would have kept me away."

Cassandra wept with relief but refused to let him take any blame. "How could you have known, Richard? But I did miss you, oh, how I longed for you to be home. I was so afraid, and I felt so alone, but you were not to blame, dearest. Thank God Papa was able to discover you, and thank God for the hospital at Littleford and for dear Henry Forrester. Believe me, Richard, he is an angel—our little Laura owes her life to him alone. He has been so good and kind through it all."

He let her finish, and held her while she spoke, before telling her how he had happened to be at the Wilsons' when Darcy arrived.

She listened but seemed to hear little. The shock of almost losing her child, of being alone without him, feeling bereft and frightened, in spite of the support she had been given by her parents and the rest of the family, had deadened her feelings. It was as if she had been drowned in emotion and cast ashore. She was worn out. It would be many days before she would feel normal again.

A week later, with Henry Forrester's permission, Laura Ann was taken home by her parents, whose gratitude more than matched their joy. Having come through the darkness and survived, she would always be a treasured child.

The following year, a month after the wedding of Sophie Bingley and Daniel Lambert, the new hospital in the Derwent valley, a few miles from Matlock, was opened with great ceremony and many splendid speeches from local government officials keen to associate themselves with a popular project.

Mr Lambert and his influential father were the chief guests, and Sir Tristram made it very clear that he had supported the council in its decision to build the hospital.

Daniel Lambert, who was now the Member of Parliament for the area, pleased everyone by declaring that he would seek support for the hospital from the government when Parliament resumed. But it was his bride Sophie who stole the show when she opened the building, expressing the hope that this was only the beginning and the council would now look at building a school for the children of the valley, concluding by handing over a generous donation from her father, Mr Bingley, towards special equipment for the children's ward of the hospital.

Richard and Cassandra were praised for their support—particularly Richard, who had given so much of his time to its successful completion that his family had seen very little of him and his wife had worried for his health.

Now it was done, and the people of the valley could enjoy the benefits.

Afterwards, Richard and Cassandra journeyed to Buxton, where they had been invited to join the Lamberts, who had taken an elegant Georgian house very near the celebrated spa in the centre of the town. They enjoyed more than the health-giving waters—famous since Roman times—using the opportunity to rest their bodies and restore their spirits after a difficult Summer.

While there was less social life than in Bath, which they had both visited once and disliked intensely, Buxton had a delightful elegance with the additional attraction of its situation in the heart of the Peak District. It was a perfect example of the blend of nature and artifice that was particularly agreeable to them. The time spent touring these salubrious surroundings helped heal their hearts, especially now that Laura Ann was fully recovered, due in no small measure to the care of Henry Forrester, who continued to keep a close watch over her.

On returning from Buxton, they went directly to the Gardiners' to collect their children and found Fitzwilliam and Caroline there, enjoying the mild Autumn weather with afternoon tea on the lawn. They were there to invite the rest of the family to a party.

Much teasing ensued when it was discovered, through some discreet questioning, that the celebration was in honour of Fitzwilliam's birthday, but Caroline hinted that there was another reason, but it was, for the moment, a secret. "I can assure you, all will be revealed very soon," she promised, but Cassy was not satisfied until she had discovered that they would also be celebrating the engagement of their daughter, Isabella, to Doctor Henry Forrester. A large party of relations and friends were expected, some from as far away as London.

Unlike Pemberley, whose grand proportions accommodated such occasions comfortably, the modest size and style of the Fitzwilliams' house necessitated the hire of a big marquee to be erected on the lawn.

The Wilsons and the Bingleys were expected to stay at Pemberley for a few days, and Elizabeth particularly looked forward to having Jane to herself again. Jonathan and Amelia-Jane were travelling from Rosings, where Jonathan was now the manager of Lady Catherine de Bourgh's estate. Cassy had heard her mother and her Aunt Jane describe how this amazing circumstance had come about and related the story to Richard as they dressed for the party.

"Mama says my father recommended Jonathan to Lady Catherine," she said as she pinned up her hair.

"Mr Darcy?" Richard was sceptical. "Why would he do such a thing?"

"As Mama tells it, Amelia-Jane has been quite a favourite at Rosings and since little Cathy was born and baptised at Hunsford, Lady Catherine has taken a great interest in their welfare. No doubt Amelia had hopes of some preferment for her husband or herself, but unbeknownst to them, Lady Catherine, who is almost eighty, had spoken to Papa about a manager for Rosings—not just the sort of person who will ensure that the bailiffs and stewards do their jobs, but someone with sufficient understanding and taste to supervise the place after her Ladyship and her daughter move to Bath. It is not generally known, but I understand that on the death of Lady Catherine, Rosings Park will become part of the national estate. There will need to be a good manager to run the place."

Richard was genuinely surprised. "And you say your father recommended Jonathan for this position?"

"Indeed, I believe he has been very impressed with Jonathan's management of Longbourn, which is now run a good deal better than when grandfather was alive," she replied, explaining that Darcy had advised his aunt that Jonathan Bingley was just the right man for the job, especially since he had decided not to contest the next election and would no longer be spending a great deal of time at Westminster.

"No doubt Amelia-Jane is exceedingly pleased," said Richard. "Well, I can only wish them well. I am sure the fact that Lady Catherine will be in Bath rather than in residence at Rosings will make Jonathan's position much more congenial, especially if they are to live on the property."

Cassy agreed. "They will have the dower house; Aunt Jane told Mama. Amelia-Jane wants her to advise on what needs to be done to get the place ready for them. They will, however, keep Jonathan's town house, where they will mostly live when they are in London."

And there the conversation ended, since it was time to leave, and Cassy went to kiss her children goodnight.

When they reached the Fitzwilliams' place, the sight of a splendid equipage taking up a great deal of room in the street reminded them that Jonathan and Amelia-Jane had acquired a remarkable patron indeed. Lady Catherine's customary generosity towards those she approved of and who, in their turn, were adequately deferential towards her, was once again apparent. Mr and Mrs Jonathan Bingley and their older children had arrived in one of her liveried carriages, which now stood to one side, leaving barely enough room for the lesser vehicles of other guests to pass.

If the range and level of conversation was an indication of the success of a party, then this party was a certain success. Every conceivable topic, from the design of the new houses of Parliament to the cunning strategy of Louis Napoleon, who, by a coup d'état, had made himself emperor of France, was discussed with vigour. The presence of several of Fitzwilliam's Reformist friends from his days at Westminster and younger colleagues of Jonathan Bingley and James Wilson meant there was inevitably a great deal of politics in the air.

Fitzwilliam, a great admirer of Palmerston, railed against the inaction of the present Prime Minister, Lord Aberdeen, and urged his friends who were still in Parliament to move to install Palmerston in his place. "He alone will restore Britain's influence in Europe," he declared, resolutely condemning the Peelites, for whom he had no time at all.

Although 1851 had been a year of peace in Britain, culminating in the success of the Great Exhibition, the years that followed were a good deal less so, especially in Europe, where there were several points of tension, any or all of which were likely to explode into conflict at any time.

Efforts to bring about agreements through negotiation were not proving successful, and ineffective diplomacy had become the butt of jokes. "Look at the Treaty of London," scoffed one of the guests. "Half of Europe will not accept it, and the rest could not care less."

Amid much laughter, Fitzwilliam, supported by Jonathan, was in full flight on the subject of ineffectual governments when Richard and Cassandra arrived.

James and Emma Wilson, who had only recently returned from France, were both concerned that there was, in Europe, much talk of war between France and Russia. "There is much more belligerent rhetoric now than I have heard in many a year," said James, and when Richard asked if there was a reason for this heightened temperature, he replied, "I am sorry to have to say this, but the ineptitude of our leaders is gradually pushing us into a situation where we will be at war before we even know why we are there."

The whiff of war in the air set the conversation alight, and it was only doused when the musicians struck up a familiar quadrille and the newly engaged couple led the company into the first dance.

Cassandra and Richard had not been surprised by the news of their engagement, having noticed the increasing warmth of the friendship that had grown up between them since Isabella had begun to assist at the hospital in Littleford. Emily, too, having been her niece's confidante for the last few months, had seen their relationship deepen during the fearful week when little Laura Ann's life had hung in the balance.

Unlike many of her cousins and friends, Isabella had not fallen in love in the first flush of youth. Quiet and unassuming to a fault, her gentle beauty was often overlooked among her more striking companions. Clearly, one man, at least, had known better. His compassion and gentlemanly charm had captured her heart, and her choice was universally applauded. Like Richard Gardiner, Henry Forrester was gaining a reputation for both professional skill and dedication.

Elizabeth found herself seated next to her niece Emma Wilson at dinner. The gloomy prognostications about war in Europe had been overwhelmed by the happy prospect of a wedding in the family. Indeed, Elizabeth told how upon hearing the good news, she and Mr Darcy had offered to host the wedding at Pemberley. "Isabella will be married at the church, of course," said Elizabeth, explaining that it would therefore be convenient, as well as appropriate, that the wedding breakfast be at Pemberley House.

Emma was delighted for Isabella. "I have always thought that she had intended to remain unwed, else I could not understand how such a lovely, gentle young woman would not have been married earlier," she remarked, adding that too many young men today were not looking beyond the powder and paint.

"It is gratifying to discover that goodness can yet be appreciated, though if I had been a man, I cannot believe I would not have noticed her sweetness of disposition and fine features even before I learnt to appreciate her goodness," said Elizabeth.

Emma agreed. Isabella had been a favourite cousin; they shared an evenness of temper that had made for an easy friendship as girls, but since Emma's first, unhappy marriage, and her more or less permanent residence in Kent, the cousins had seen much less of each other. Emma's own second marriage and Isabella's involvement with the management of the Littleford hospital had left both young women little time for anything above the usual affectionate greetings at birthdays.

She was, therefore, surprised to be singled out by her cousin, who brought Henry Forrester over to be introduced to "my beautiful cousin, Emma, and her husband, the distinguished Mr James Wilson, MP."

Not having met Mr Forrester before, James Wilson was happy to find him an intelligent young man with a remarkable dedication to his work. Quite clearly, he was also devoted to young Isabella.

While Caroline and Fitzwilliam were busy accepting the congratulations of their friends at the success of the evening and their daughter's engagement, a storm had been brewing amongst the hills and crags to the north. Concerned for the comfort of their guests, the Fitzwilliams urged them to move indoors.

Richard and Cassy, familiar with the house, decided to watch the storm's progress from the vantage point of the music room, which ran the width of the house and afforded from its windows a splendid prospect across the river to the woods and the peaks beyond, rising to the summit of High Tor.

Upstairs, they found the younger children gathered in the schoolroom, clearly frightened by the sound and fury of the weather. Richard urged them to come into the music room and enjoy the show, trying to counter their fears by describing the gathering storm as "Nature's fireworks." The braver ones ventured in and were treated to a spectacular display.

Happily, the worst of the storm seemed to miss that part of the dales in which their house stood, and though the great bolts of lightning in the distance seemed fearsome when accompanied by rolling thunder, it was a relief to know that they were dancing mostly over the rugged hills and moorlands to the north.

The music room was Caroline's favourite room. Since the day she had first seen the house, well before they were engaged, she had admired the room and received from Fitzwilliam a promise, albeit unsolicited, that it would be a music room as she had suggested. True to his word, after they were engaged, he had it fitted up to suit her taste. Now, it was her personal retreat. She found Cassy and Richard and a few of the children enjoying the superb view the room afforded.

"Cassy, there you are. Jonathan and Amelia-Jane are ready to leave. They are to stay with the Tates tonight and wish to leave before the storm reaches the dales," she said as she accompanied them downstairs. "I thought I would send a little note about Isabella's engagement for next week's *Review*."

When they reached the hall, Amelia and Jonathan were ready to depart, their fine carriage waiting patiently for them to conclude their farewells.

Soon after they had left, the party began to break up. Most of Jonathan's friends had left, and a few stragglers were making their way out. Richard and Cassy followed not long afterwards.

As the carriage turned onto the main road leading to Matlock, light rain was falling and in the distance could be heard the sound of horses. Richard noticed that ahead, the carriage from Pemberley had been pulled over and Darcy's driver had decided to alight and investigate. Richard did likewise.

Within minutes, two men on horseback loomed up in the rain and fog ahead, visible in the light of the carriage lamps. They were from Pemberley; windblown and dishevelled, they looked as if they had ridden hard. Talking to Darcy's driver they explained that the storm that had missed the dales had hit the rest of the area very hard: several trees had been blown down and lay across the road. They had ridden over to warn their master not to risk making the journey to Pemberley that night. There was no alternative but to turn back.

The Fitzwilliams welcomed their returning guests and made arrangements to accommodate them for the night.

Rain fell throughout the night, making the prospect of the road being cleared unlikely.

Waking just before daybreak, Elizabeth found Darcy already dressed and looking out of the bedroom window. Joining him, she noted that the storm had cleared and the sky was reddening with the first rays of the sun.

"Red in the morning…" she whispered.

"Yes, there could be more bad weather about, and it looks like we might be here all day if the road has not been cleared of fallen trees," said her husband. "I am glad the rain has cleared. I shall borrow a pair of boots and get Fitzwilliam to show me around the home farm after breakfast. He has made a number of improvements in the last few years."

As they watched, the sun rose, chasing the shadows from the meadows and woods below. The workmen were taking down the marquee, and in the lower meadow they could see Fitzwilliam, who had clearly risen before dawn.

Elizabeth smiled. "He has become quite the gentleman farmer since leaving Parliament," she said.

"He certainly has, and I do believe Caroline and he have done very well here. You cannot help but feel the sense of satisfaction they enjoy in their life," said Darcy and even as he spoke, the three youngest Fitzwilliams ran out into the yard; Rachel, James, and Amy were all laughing as they raced out to the stables for their morning ride. Darcy and Elizabeth smiled as they watched the young, healthy children.

"The simple life they set out to lead, quite deliberately, seems to have nourished them and nurtured their children in the best possible way. They are so cheerful and happy," he observed.

"Except Isabella, who has never been the same since Edward's death," said Elizabeth quietly, and Darcy agreed.

"Yes, Fitzwilliam has been very concerned about her."

Elizabeth knew that Caroline had been anxious too. "She has been quite disinterested in any proposal of marriage. I believe there have been one or two, but she would have none of them. I am truly delighted to see her so happy," she said. "But Isabella is a restless soul and, unlike Cassy or Emma, she will not settle into quiet domesticity. I know she feels very strongly about the poor and the sick. Once she is married to a man of some character and dedication, she is likely to want to go out and do something to change the world."

Darcy pointed out that, in doing so, Isabella would only be following the excellent example of her parents, both of whom had spent many years in active public service and still continued their interest in the affairs of their community. "I have never ceased to be amazed at Caroline's ability to throw herself with great enthusiasm into campaigns for political and social causes. It was understandable when Fitzwilliam was in Parliament, but she has not reduced her efforts since he retired," he said.

"No, indeed, she has not," said Elizabeth, "and I understand they've had a great success recently. I am told Rebecca and Caroline have received a promise of assistance from the council for the extension of the Kympton parish school."

Darcy smiled. "Yes, indeed, that is a great achievement," he agreed, adding, "and I have been petitioned for permission to hold a fête for the benefit of the Irish families. Emily declares that the children need clothes and shoes for the Winter."

"You will have no objection, will you, dearest?" Elizabeth asked, a little anxiously.

Darcy shook his head and said, "Of course not, I am delighted we can help. I have said they can use the lower meadow and ask my staff for any assistance they may need. The fate of the Irish families, the way the government ignores them, is a stain upon this nation, and I shall be very happy if Pemberley can make a contribution to their welfare."

It had always been important to him that Pemberley, which stood at the very heart of this community, should assist its people in dealing with their problems. He saw the sick, the homeless, and the dispossessed as part of his responsibility, not as the inevitable detritus of change and progress. Having grown up in a comfortable and cohesive social environment, he was outraged by the fracturing of that society and strove to build a sense of harmony around Pemberley and its neighbouring estates. While there was still much to be done, they had achieved a great deal through the work of many dedicated men and women, but chiefly as a result of the inspiration and leadership of the Master of Pemberley.

Glancing up at him, Elizabeth caught a hint of regret—the merest shadow—cross his face. She wondered at the reason for it, but before she could say anything, he sighed and said, "Lizzie, my dear, I wish I had been more successful in interesting Julian in the work we do here. He's clever and popular; he could help us achieve a great deal, especially with the young people."

She knew, then, the cause of his disappointment. Their son, while he was an amiable and intelligent young man, had as yet shown little interest in his father's grand obsession. Pemberley was for him a comfortable home; he loved the place but did not appear to share Darcy's sense of vocation. There was no doubt his father was disappointed.

Elizabeth's heart went out to him. "Julian is only seventeen. I know he loves Pemberley. Give him time, I am sure he will not disappoint you," she said.

Gratefully, he held her close and said, "I expect you are right, Lizzie. I forget that he is still a boy."

Elizabeth steered him towards a happier subject. "I think you can be very proud of what we have achieved. Has Richard told you he intends to nominate himself for election to the hospital board?"

Darcy's countenance brightened. "Indeed, he has, and I have promised to speak to Sir Thomas and a couple of others about it. I hope he succeeds; he is very keen and will work hard for the hospital and the community. He is very impressed with the work of Joseph Lister, and I have offered to fund his pet research project on bacteria and antisepsis—that should help him get the board's attention."

Delighted, Elizabeth embraced him warmly before reminding him that the Fitzwilliams breakfasted earlier than they did at Pemberley and she had better attend to her toilette at once, lest they disrupt the entire household.

Sometime later, when they had finished breakfast and the mist had cleared, Elizabeth and Jane went out into the garden, where they found Cassy, anxious because they had not heard from home. "Richard has ridden down to discover if all is well," she said. "Papa and Mr Bingley are down in the lower meadow with Colonel Fitzwilliam."

Caroline had followed them out into the sunshine. "Emma and James have only just come downstairs," she said with a smile, adding mischievously, "They must be accustomed to the luxury of late breakfasts at Standish Park."

Everyone laughed, but it was an indulgent, affectionate laugh; no one grudged Emma even the smallest scrap of happiness.

"Caroline, where is Isabella? Is she enjoying a late morning, too?" asked Jane.

"No, not at all; she was up and about before any of us. She had promised Henry she would be at the hospital today. They are treating a number of the schoolchildren who have developed a nasty rash by playing in the hay. Their mothers are bringing them in and Isabella has prepared a lotion of witch hazel and camomile."

"But with the road blocked, how will she get there?" asked Elizabeth.

"On horseback, of course. She rides well and was quite determined that she would go. She would not let Henry down," said Caroline, and, seeing the smiles on the faces of her cousins, she added, "She is a mature young woman, Lizzie. I cannot forbid her."

"Of course not, Caroline, nor should you. As I said to Darcy this morning, Isabella will always want to be doing something to change the world."

Caroline laughed, "You are absolutely right, Lizzie. Just the other day she was telling me she envied her brother David because he could do so many exciting things. When I asked her what in particular, she said, quite seriously, 'Mama, would it not be wonderful to go to Africa, like Dr Livingston?'"

Jane was shocked. "Africa? Surely she cannot be serious?"

Caroline was quite sanguine. "She was, but that was before Henry proposed. I do not think Africa will be as attractive a proposition now, but I do believe Henry once wanted to go to India to work on the missions, so I shall not be too surprised if they decide to do something quite extraordinary."

Remembering her conversation with Darcy that morning, Elizabeth was quite sure that Isabella would surprise them all.

Minutes later, Richard returned and, to Cassy's great relief, declared that everyone at home was well. "Were they worried when we did not return last night?" she asked.

To their surprise, he said, "No, they were not, because on his way home last night, Henry Forrester rode all the way there to tell them what had happened, which is why Mrs Morris did not send one of the men over to investigate."

Elizabeth shook her head; she could hardly believe it. This was surely well beyond the call of duty. Cassandra assured her that it was exactly the kind of thing Henry would do. Indeed, Isabella would expect it of him.

~∗~

A few weeks later, Richard and Cassandra arrived at Pemberley with the good news. The governing board had appointed Richard to manage the hospital and conduct a research program into sanitation and antisepsis. On the basis of a paper he had presented to them, they were willing to let him put in place a program of hospital hygiene, which he had claimed would save patients' lives and protect their staff from infection.

Elizabeth and Darcy were delighted. "I always knew you would succeed, Richard," Elizabeth said when the initial excitement had subsided.

"No one who knows Richard's dedication to his work could have doubted that he would," said Darcy, but, he added, it would have been no easy task to convince the conservative members of the hospital board.

Richard admitted that he had had doubts himself. "But the evidence I presented was so overwhelming and, with your generous offer to fund the research program, sir, they had to agree that it was worth trying," he declared. "I did tell them that their hospital could become a leader in the Midlands, if we succeed." His eyes were bright with the eagerness of the enthusiast who is convinced he has the right solution to a problem.

It was a quality Mr Darcy admired and Cassandra loved. She was immensely proud of her husband. Elizabeth understood how much Darcy loved his son-in-law; he shared his conviction and willed him to succeed. He would gladly help him in any way possible.

Cassandra then informed them that they had to go away to London, where Richard was to attend the great teaching hospital, Barts, for a term in order to prepare himself for the position he was to hold at Matlock. "This is a great honour, Mama," she explained, "and we are indebted to Daniel Lambert's father, Sir Tristram. He arranged it through his cousin, who is on the board."

The rest of the evening was spent in discussing preparations for their departure, especially since Cassandra wished to accompany her husband and take her younger children with them.

Naturally, Darcy offered them the use of his town house in Portman Square, which would save them having to take all their servants along. Cassy was overjoyed and very grateful, "Oh, thank you, Papa. That means I need only take Nurse Marsh and Lucy," said Cassy, embracing both her parents and promising to write regularly.

As they were leaving, Julian, who had been out riding with friends, returned in time to wish them farewell and promise to visit them in London, where he expected to be with some friends fairly soon.

His mention of the name Henry Wickham in this context startled both Darcy and Elizabeth, but when he said no more, they asked no questions until they were at dinner and Julian returned to the topic. "This fellow Wickham, he has a house in London and has invited us up there."

Darcy's countenance grew dark as he said abruptly, "Julian, if you wish to go to London, you can stay at Portman Square with your sister. There is no need at all for you to stay with this ... this person."

Julian looked surprised, and his expression changed to one of astonishment when his father went on, "I absolutely forbid you to see this fellow."

Julian opened his mouth to speak, but before he could say anything, Elizabeth intervened, "Julian, I think you should talk to Papa after dinner about this; if this man is the same Wickham..."

"Of course it is the same Wickham—he has to be George Wickham's son," snapped Darcy, who was now so angry that he could barely speak. He had almost conquered what had been a quick temper, but when it came to the Wickhams intruding upon his family, he could not be sure of controlling it.

Elizabeth tried again, "Dearest, I think you should have a talk with Julian—after dinner. I know he will understand why you feel as you do, once he knows all the facts."

Realising that he was embarrassing her before the servants, Darcy agreed, and Julian, taking his cue from his mother, said no more.

Grateful that they had avoided an unseemly fuss, Elizabeth said nothing. When they repaired to the drawing room, she noted that father and son were soon deep in conversation at one end of the room while she sat at a side table and completed her letters. There was no further mention of Wickham.

Julian spent some time at the piano but grew bored with it, said good-night, and went upstairs.

Later, in their bedroom, Darcy suddenly apologized. "Lizzie, my dearest, I am sorry about this evening. I should have known better. I never meant to embarrass you. Will you forgive me?"

She smiled and took his hand. "What is there to forgive? We, all of us, and you most of all, have every reason to be angry with Wickham. I can understand that perfectly. I was only concerned that Julian did not know why you were displeased and was bewildered and confused by your anger and your order forbidding him to see this young man."

Darcy was contrite. "I know it was stupid of me to lose my temper. It is just that I could not bear to think of anybody connected to Wickham having anything to do with our son. Henry Wickham is apparently staying with friends in the Bakewell area; Julian has met him at the Camden's place. Aware of his father's example, I do not believe that the son will be a suitable companion for Julian."

She made it clear that she understood him completely and was further reassured when he explained that he had given Julian some, but not all, of the background of Mr Wickham's activities and obtained from him a promise he would not accept his son's invitation.

"He has given me his word; I know I can trust him," he said.

❦

Some weeks later, Elizabeth, returning from a visit to the Gardiners at Lambton, found a letter from Charlotte Collins awaiting her. It was always a pleasure to hear from Charlotte, who was one of her oldest and closest friends. On this occasion it was doubly so, for the letter not only brought news from her friend but announced her likely arrival at Pemberley for a short visit, if the dates were convenient to Elizabeth and Darcy.

Charlotte explained that she had been persuaded by her daughters to retire and sell her now very successful school for ladies.

I think you will understand, dear Eliza, that the girls feel I have worked long enough and are determined that I should spend however many years I have left in some comfort. For myself, I feel quite fit and healthy and, God willing, will remain so, but they will not let me continue working.

We have therefore negotiated a sale to a Mrs Peach of Mansfield, who will take over the lease and the school in November. I have the luxury of being invited to live for all or part of the year with any of my daughters, but, while I love them all dearly, I should prefer to retain some degree of independence. I have therefore decided to accept the invitation conveyed to me through Jonathan from your sister, Mary, to make my home with her at Longbourn.

Elizabeth was a little taken aback, but it was a consequence of surprise rather than disapproval of Charlotte's decision. Neither her sister Mary, who lived at Longbourn, nor her nephew Jonathan, who was in fact the ultimate inheritor and present manager of the Longbourn estate, had mentioned it to her.

She was surprised but not necessarily upset.

Charlotte continued:

Dear Eliza, I am not aware if Mary and Jonathan have discussed their kind invitation to me with you, but, for my part, I would like very much to see you and know that you and Jane have no objection to it.

I want to reassure you that I shall be taking up residence as a guest, invited by Mary and Jonathan. I believe Mary has been rather lonely of late, especially since the death of her friend, Mrs Langley, the organist at the church. She had indicated to Jonathan that she would very much appreciate my company. I am sure I shall feel the same.

I shall, of course, pay my share of the expenses and the wages of my maid.

The letter concluded with her usual greetings and good wishes.

Elizabeth hastened to reply, wishing both to reassure Charlotte that she had no objection at all to her accepting Mary's invitation to stay at Longbourn and to confirm the dates for her visit to Pemberley.

She was about to ring for some tea when her maid hurried in with a letter that had only just been delivered. Elizabeth could tell from the hand-writing that it was from Cassandra. Opening it at once, she settled down to enjoy what she expected to be an account of their first few weeks in London. She had missed her daughter and welcomed all the news.

Indeed, she was quite diverted by Cassandra's description of a visit to a dressmaker, where she had been confronted for the first time with the very latest in ladies' fashions—the hideous and unwieldy cage crinoline.

Cassy was horrified by it; she wrote:

> It must surely be the most inconvenient fashion ever—I am sure it would get in the way of everything. And how one would ever get into a carriage or a hansom cab, I cannot imagine!

But, just as Elizabeth was relaxing into her chair with a smile, the next page of Cassy's letter, which appeared to have been written a couple of days later, caused her to sit up in considerable agitation.

Cassandra's tone had changed altogether.

> Dear Mama, I do not know quite how to tell you, but there is something very disturbing going on, which I am sure will concern you and Papa.
>
> You will remember Sophie's sister-in-law, Frances—Daniel Lambert's youngest sister—who was one of the bridesmaids. Well, she has been in London staying with an aunt in Knightsbridge. I have met them briefly in the park and at the Robinsons', where we were invited to dinner last Saturday.
>
> Mama, you will not be pleased to hear that on both occasions Fanny Lambert was escorted by none other than Henry Wickham, Aunt Lydia's son, and his father arrived in the course of the evening to join the party. They appear to be friends of the Robinsons.
>
> At first, I thought I might have been mistaken, since I am not very familiar with Mr Wickham Senior; but I was introduced to him, so there

could be no mistake. Indeed, he rather cheekily asked to be remembered to you and Papa!

"Did he indeed?" cried Elizabeth, angrier than she had been in years. Turning over the page, she read on.

I have mentioned this to Richard, who thinks it may be much ado about nothing, since Fanny Lambert is not yet sixteen. But I am not so sure, for she seems very naïve and impressionable, and Henry Wickham is very handsome and has a smooth manner that could well take her in completely. I did manage to have a little chat with her and have invited her to take tea with me next week, when I shall attempt to discover more about this friendship with young Mr Wickham.

I do know that Papa and you are exceedingly wary of the entire Wickham clan, so I promise to keep you informed.

When Darcy returned that evening, Elizabeth did not wait long before she mentioned Cassy's letter. "I have had a letter from Cassy," she said, and he turned to her with a smile.

"Indeed, and is she enjoying London?" he asked, expecting her to hand him the letter or read it to him as she usually did.

When she did not, he seemed puzzled. "What is it, Lizzie? Is there some problem? Is it Richard or one of the children?" He sounded anxious, and she immediately tried to reassure him.

"Oh no, dearest, it's nothing like that. They are all perfectly well. But I'm afraid there is some unpleasant news. Fanny Lambert—Daniel's youngest sister—is in London and so, it seems, is Mr Henry Wickham. Cassy has seen them together twice and has gained the impression that he is courting her. On the last occasion, when they dined at the Robinsons', George Wickham himself was one of the party." She handed him the letter, which he scanned hurriedly.

Darcy was clearly appalled. "Lizzie, this is bad news indeed. Miss Lambert must be totally ignorant of his background. The Lamberts would be horrified if they knew the truth."

Elizabeth was at a loss. "What is to be done? She is little more than a child."

"That has never inhibited Wickham. He probably knows that her father is a wealthy man and, with her brother in Parliament, she is just the kind of young woman Wickham would seek to exploit. If Henry Wickham is anything like his father, and is determined to woo her, she is in grave danger indeed," he said, and Elizabeth could hear the suppressed anger in his voice.

Darcy had a very determined expression and even before he spoke, Elizabeth guessed what he intended. "There is only one thing to be done, Lizzie—what I did not do on the last occasion all those years ago, when so many people suffered as a result. This time, I shall do what I must. I shall speak first with Bingley and then see Sir Tristram Lambert.

"It is intolerable that Wickham and his son should be able to insinuate themselves into the society of those who have no knowledge of his true character and his past behaviour. Their ignorance makes them vulnerable.

"I shall lay the facts before Sir Tristram, and he can decide if he wishes to acquaint his daughter with all or part of the story. At least I shall have done my duty."

Elizabeth realised what it would cost him to do this thing—the mortification would be unbearable. She put her arms around him and told him that, if he preferred it, she could speak to her sister and let the Bingleys tell Sir Tristram. But he was quite determined. It was, he said, his responsibility, and he must carry it through.

"Bingley has no direct knowledge of Wickham and his misdeeds. I do, and I must speak up. There is no other way, Lizzie," he said.

Darcy made his plans with discretion and care, reporting later to Elizabeth that Bingley had agreed with him that the Lamberts had to be told. It was a matter of principle, and the fact that he would need to reveal information that was private and personal to his own family was something that had to be borne.

"I would not wish to have it on my conscience, Lizzie," he said with the kind of determination against which, Elizabeth knew, it was impossible to argue. On some issues he was implacable, but so strongly did she believe in his integrity and trust his judgement that she accepted his decision on this matter without question.

Elizabeth visited her aunt, Mrs Gardiner, to discuss the subject and found her in every way in agreement with Mr Darcy. "There is no question, Lizzie, your husband is absolutely right. The Lamberts have to be told—if only to allow them an opportunity to protect their daughter from what might be a most unfortunate association. Should the girl believe herself in love and, like our Lydia, do something foolish, it would be disastrous!" she warned.

"And Darcy would never forgive himself," added her niece grimly.

Elizabeth had already written to Cassandra urging her to keep as close a watch as possible on young Fanny Lambert:

> *It is imperative that you stay in touch with her and her aunt; be as friendly and amenable as you can, but do not let her discover that you have written to us. If she should confide in you, listen and advise caution, but do not say anything that may cause Mr Wickham to be suspicious of you. Dear Cassy, whatever you do, do not let Fanny elope with Henry Wickham!*
>
> *Meanwhile, Papa will attend to matters here; he hopes to warn Sir Tristram of George Wickham's past misdeeds.*

Elizabeth hoped desperately that nothing untoward would happen in the meantime. She knew Bingley would soon convey all of the matter to Jane, and she wondered what her sister's response would be. Would Jane, ever tender-hearted and scrupulously fair, consider that it was unfair and uncharitable to condemn young Henry Wickham on account of his father's sins and perhaps blight his reputation and prospects in the way that Darcy's revelations would? Could there be another way to deal with the situation? Try as she might, Elizabeth could not see one.

She was in a flutter of uncertainty when a letter was received from Jane revealing that her sister and Bingley were as one with Mr Darcy on the subject of the Wickhams and Fanny Lambert.

Anxious to avoid any embarrassment to the Lambert family resulting from an association with Henry Wickham and his father, Jane wrote:

> *In fact, Lizzie, Bingley was so concerned he offered to speak with Daniel Lambert himself, but Mr Darcy was quite determined that it was his responsibility.*
>
> *I suppose it must be done, if only to avoid any awkwardness should the Lamberts, in ignorance, permit him to court Fanny. She is, Sophie tells me,*

very young and innocent, and it would be dreadful if young Henry Wickham turns out to be as duplicitous as his father.

Of course, as I did say to Bingley, we cannot know for certain that this is the case. Henry Wickham may be a perfectly decent gentleman— although, with a father so lacking in principle and a mother as undisciplined as Lydia, it is very unlikely.

But Lizzie, we are all astonished at the remarkable forethought and sensibility Cassandra has shown in this matter. To have remembered young Wickham and observed Fanny's involvement with him is natural enough, but to go further and alert you and Mr Darcy shows a keen awareness of her responsibility to her family. I know we are very grateful to her, and I am sure the Lambert family will be too, once the truth is known.

Elizabeth smiled as she read Jane's words; her sister had certainly come a long way since the days when she had been reluctant to make any judgement at all, fearing she would be too harsh upon one of her fellow human beings! She agreed wholeheartedly about Cassy, whose fine understanding and sensitivity set her apart. Elizabeth was very proud of her daughter.

Darcy returned later that evening and, to Elizabeth's relief, he was smiling as he came up the stairs. Seeing her puzzled expression, he stopped at the top of the stairs. "Why, Lizzie, my dear, you look rather surprised to see me," he said, to which she confessed that she had not expected to see him looking quite so cheerful after what must have been a difficult day.

At which, Darcy took her arm and guided her towards their sitting room, where he revealed that, far from being "difficult," it had turned out to be an excellent day.

Elizabeth was even more confused than ever. "Dearest, whatever are you talking about? Were you not seeing Sir Tristram today to tell him about Wickham?"

"Indeed, I was, and that is exactly what I did. But, my dear Lizzie, I had no need even to mention the name of Wickham," he declared.

"Why ever not?" Elizabeth asked, quite nonplussed.

"Because, my dear, Cassy and Jonathan Bingley had got there before me." Seeing the look of astonishment upon her face, he proceeded to explain, "Indeed, I understand Cassy spoke last week to Daniel Lambert and

Sophie, who in turn had warned Miss Fanny Lambert, while Jonathan and Daniel confronted young Wickham and warned him off. I believe he is just as feckless and wasteful as his father and spends a lot of time at the gaming tables in the clubs, and he is not very discreet about the company he keeps."

"How did you discover all this?" Elizabeth asked, still unable to understand how it had come about.

"I met Bingley in Derby this morning. Jonathan was at Ashford Park yesterday and Jane has a letter from Sophie."

"So you did not need to see Sir Tristram after all?"

Darcy had a mischievous smile when he replied, "No, but I did at the cricket to which Bingley insisted on taking me. We had a most satisfying day. Sir Tristram is very impressed with Richard and Cassy. He said to me, 'Mr Darcy, you must be very proud of that fine young couple.'"

"And of course, you agreed completely," said his wife.

"Of course," he replied, smiling as she rang to order tea.

As Elizabeth contemplated the quiet evening, watching the sky darken and a quarter moon emerge from the clouds, Darcy remembered that he had something for her. "Oh, I do apologise, my love. I had forgotten about this. Jonathan brought it. It's for you, from Cassy."

Elizabeth could hardly wait to take the wrappings off the little package he had handed her. When it was open, she gave a cry of delight. "Oh, look, is it not beautiful?" she cried as she showed him a small, carved elephant in shining ebony with little ivory tusks. Surprised and delighted, she admired the superb craftsmanship. "It is perfect in every detail," she said, marvelling at its tiny proportions.

Darcy agreed and suggested that the enclosed letter might explain where it came from.

Elizabeth wasted no time at all opening Cassandra's note, obviously penned in haste, which she proceeded to read aloud:

> Dearest Mama,
>
> We found this dear little elephant at an exhibition of crafts from the colonies and thought you would like to have it. I am sure he would look very nice on your dressing table.
>
> We are well settled at Portman Square now, and Richard works very hard at the hospital every day. He says there is a lot to learn. I think he

wants the new hospital at Matlock to be the best in England, so keen is he to get it all right.

Meanwhile, the children and I have already been to Hyde Park, the Museum, and the Tower of London, where the boys insisted on calling out "Off with his head"—much to my embarrassment!!

Now, Mama, regarding this distressing matter of Fanny Lambert and Mr Henry Wickham—you will be happy to hear it is all settled.

As I wrote you in my last letter, she was to have tea with me and I had hoped to pass on a few discreet words of advice, but suddenly, with no warning at all, things became very serious.

Fanny arrived looking nervous, which I could not understand, for she had been very much at ease when we last met. In less than an hour, she became restless and exceedingly keen to depart. She claimed her aunt was expecting her home before six o'clock.

I offered to convey her there if she could wait until Richard returned, but she seemed to become very desperate indeed and declared that she had arranged to be conveyed from Portman Square to Knightsbridge in a hansom cab.

At this, even my unsuspicious mind was alerted.

When the cab arrived sharp on five I escorted her to the door, and lo and behold if it was not Mr Wickham—Henry, that is—in the cab! Mama, I was absolutely determined she was not to leave my house with him and was about to chaperone them myself when Richard arrived home. We sent the cab away and went indoors again, this time including Mr Wickham. Richard, who had read your letter, was determined that Fanny was not leaving with Henry Wickham in a hansom cab!

Later, we drove them over to Knightsbridge and there, as luck would have it, we found Sophie and Daniel Lambert just arrived and waiting for Fanny.

Well, that was the last time we saw Henry Wickham because, as soon as he had left, I made sure that Sophie knew enough to convince Daniel and Fanny that the Wickhams were personae non gratae.

Sophie tells me that Fanny claimed she had liked him at first because he is awfully handsome, but she was rather bored with him because he talked only of horses and gaming! He had asked her aunt's permission to escort Fanny to a ball next week, and a picnic to Henley was being planned! I do believe Jonathan was called in to help Daniel tell Mr W he was not welcome.

So, Mama, you need have no fears; we have probably saved Fanny from a fate worse than death!!!

It is to be hoped the poor girl has not been put off beaux altogether. If she has, no doubt she will get over it in time. She is certainly young and pretty enough, and, fortunately, unlike our Aunt Lydia, she is not stupid.

To change the subject to something far pleasanter, we are invited to Standish Park on Saturday to spend a few days with Emma and James. Emma has been exceedingly helpful, for I know so little of London and would have been lost without her help.

She and James are so happy; it is a joy to be with them. Charles is a most adorable infant, and Victoria and Stephanie are quite grown up and look just beautiful. Emma is very protective of them, and as for James, you cannot believe what an excellent father he is to the girls.

Dearest Mama and Papa, London is crowded and exciting, but it is also cold and wet, and some of the streets are far from clean. The children do not much like it, either, except when they can ride in a hansom cab, which we all love. I am assured that the weather is a good deal nicer in Kent.

There is a lot of talk around about a war, which everyone seems to think is inevitable. James, who has many friends in the Foreign Office, says that France is eager to go to war with Russia to recover some lost prestige. Can you think of a more stupid reason to go to war?

Richard believes there may be war because everyone is very suspicious of the Tsar and they are spoiling for a fight with Russia.

This I do not like at all and do hope and pray it will not happen, or at least not until we are all safely back at home in Derbyshire.

We do miss you all very much. I trust you and Papa are well—and now that the problem of Mr W is settled, you need have no anxieties at all.

Your loving daughter,

Cassy.

P.S. Richard and the children all send their love. We think of you and miss you every day.

Darcy was smiling as Lizzie finished reading the letter. There was no doubting the pride he felt in his daughter. He was pleased and very grateful. Her excellent judgement and remarkable sense of responsibility had spared them all a great deal of aggravation and embarrassment.

Elizabeth folded the letter and carefully put it away in her pocket book, then took it out a few minutes later and read it through again. Cassandra had proved her intelligence and sound common sense once more. But for her mother, there was a much deeper satisfaction. The warmth of Cassandra's affectionate nature flowed through her letter. They had grown a good deal closer in the last few years, since Cassy had become a mother herself, and Elizabeth, who had never shared similar feelings with her own mother, cherished the relationship with her beloved daughter. She missed her keenly and looked forward to her return.

CHAPTER FOUR

Isabella

ISABELLA FITZWILLIAM WOULD NEVER forget the Autumn of 1834, the month of October in particular.

It had been a mild Autumn, and the families had gathered at Pemberley for a weekend of celebration—there had been the Harvest festival, which had proved a huge success. The well-being of the people of the district depended largely upon the prosperity of the Pemberley estate. In 1834, there was no doubt that this was a thriving, contented community.

Then, there had been the grand ball at Pemberley. Three young women—Cassandra Darcy, Emma Bingley, and Rebecca Collins—had turned seventeen that year, and Mr Darcy had given a ball in their honour. While Isabella had been too young to dance, she and several other little girls had been able to sit in the gallery above the ballroom and watch the dancers. She could still see the couples in her mind's eye. Emma, who was universally regarded as the most beautiful of them all, had danced mostly with her brother Jonathan, even though she had many potential partners, while Becky Collins and the handsome Mr Anthony Tate seemed to know all the newest European dances. But it was Cassy Darcy and Richard Gardiner who received the most compliments on the night. Isabella would always remember how they had looked, as if they were alone in the world and not another soul mattered.

Isabella recalled her mother's remark to her father as they drove home. "Fitzy, I cannot believe that Richard and Cassy are not as yet engaged; they clearly love each other very much."

Her father had smiled and replied, "Caroline, my dear, have you forgotten that I had to eat my heart out for half a year before I plucked up sufficient courage to approach your father?"

The story of her parents' romance was legendary among the members of the family, but even they acknowledged that Richard and Cassandra were a special couple. No one had been surprised when, on the following day, they were all together again at Pemberley to celebrate their engagement.

On a perfect Autumn day, when the skies were a startling blue and sunlight poured down, they had enjoyed a picnic beside the stream in one of the prettiest spots in the park at Pemberley. The entire family and several of their friends had joined to wish Richard and Cassy happiness, which, considering their present bliss, seemed almost superfluous. It had seemed to Isabella, as no doubt it would have seemed to many others present, that nothing could go wrong on such a day.

And yet, some few hours later, her own brother, Edward—who had been just fourteen years old—and their cousin, William Darcy, had both been killed in a terrible riding accident, and the joy that had filled their hearts on that bright day had turned to dust.

Isabella recalled the harrowing evening that had followed—the tears, the rage, and the bitter recriminations. Her mother, who saw the death of her son as the result of stupidity, had taken years to recover her brightness of spirit, while her Aunt Lizzie had seemed remote and lonely after the death of her beloved William. Even now, many years later, there were moments when the sadness in her eyes was almost too painful to bear.

In that same wretched month, the Houses of Parliament at Westminster had been destroyed by fire. Like the deaths of Edward and William, it had been the result of carelessness and stupidity. She remembered the news being received with disbelief by her parents. The conflagration had shocked the country; Isabella was quite sure it had hastened her father's decision to retire from public life. Colonel Fitzwilliam had been outraged and found that Parliamentary activities no longer gave him satisfaction, though he still retained an interest in politics.

Isabella recalled his comments, on returning from London the following year, when Turner was showing his amazing paintings of the fire at the Royal Academy; he was glad, he said bitterly, that someone had derived pleasure from the blaze, because he had felt as if much of his life's work had gone up in the flames.

Since the death of Edward, he had decided that his wife and children needed him at home, and Isabella had watched as he let go of many of his Parliamentary interests and turned increasingly to the work on the farm.

Edward and Isabella had been very close, and William had been like an older brother to both of them. She had missed them terribly. Unlike Edward, who had never wanted to leave home, her younger brother, David, had actually elected to go to boarding school. He seemed to have matured very quickly and was now, at twenty-one, almost a stranger to her. Isabella had grown up mostly alone, with only her grieving mother for company. The tragedy of losing Edward and William, and the burden of carrying her own sorrow as well as the agony of her parents, had left her exhausted.

For many years she sought only peace and quiet, preferring safety to excitement, not tempted by prospects of romance, fearful that love was short-lived and pain its inevitable companion. Her favourite authors, the melancholy Brontë sisters, served only to reinforce her view of life.

Twice in the last five years she had either fled from a situation that looked as if it might lead to romantic involvement or turned down a perfectly reasonable offer of marriage. Content to remain at home, she had nevertheless obtained great satisfaction from helping her Aunt Emily with charity work in the parish and working at the hospital at Littleford. She found particular pleasure in her work with the children.

"Nothing can compare with the joy of helping the children," she had declared when Elizabeth, hoping to draw her out, had asked whether she would not prefer to be assisting in the library at the community centre.

Richard and Emily had declared on many occasions that they could not run the children's ward without her, and Mr Forrester had been astonished to learn that she had no formal training in nursing. "Miss Fitzwilliam, forgive me, but I have to say I have never met anyone who was so good at nursing the sick as you are. I cannot believe that you have no formal training," he had said a few weeks after he had arrived to work as a locum for Richard. She had thanked him but had not paid much attention to his words, pointing out that she had learnt a great deal about nursing from her Aunt Emily. She had always taken it for granted that she, being fit and healthy, should feel compassion for the sick, especially the little ones. She was gradually to discover in Henry Forrester similar compassion and dedication, which made working with him a special pleasure.

When little Laura Ann's life had hung by a slender thread, he had found her in tears and comforted her, and Isabella, who had never stopped to think that she was in need of comfort, was profoundly grateful for his thoughtfulness. Over many months, she had noted that he could be as kind and thoughtful with all his patients, and especially with anxious or grieving parents of sick children. It was a quality that had endeared him to her.

Today, as she stood before a mirror in a charming room that had once been Georgiana Darcy's bedroom, preparing to step into her wedding gown, many of these vivid memories came to mind.

Sally, the young maid who attended her, could not take her eyes off Isabella in the flowing, silk gown specially made for her by the best seamstress in Derby.

"Oh, Miss Isabella, you look so lovely," she cried when she finished doing up the tiny buttons that went all the way up the back of her dress.

Caroline, arriving to do her daughter's hair, was taken aback by her calm, almost luminous beauty. Not since she had been a bridesmaid at Jane Bennet's wedding had Caroline seen a bride look as serenely happy as Isabella did.

When Isabella was ready to go downstairs, her father came into the room to escort her to the carriage that would take her to church. So overcome was he with the thought of giving this very special daughter in marriage that he struggled to hold back the tears. It was Isabella who comforted him as she kissed both her parents and thanked them.

"Dear Papa and Mama, thank you for all you have given me. Henry Forrester is the only man I have met for whom I felt I was willing to change my comfortable, happy life with you. He is indeed a good man and he loves me," she said simply.

Although the couple had said they had no wish for a big wedding, there was never any chance that they could escape one. Their own popularity with friends and family, the affection that so many felt for the Fitzwilliams, and the Darcys' generosity ensured there would be a large and appreciative gathering at Pemberley to help celebrate the happy event. Henry Forrester, whose parents were away in India, where his father was an administrator of one of the provinces, could only produce an aunt and two sisters, who had travelled from London to represent his family. Having no available male relatives, he asked his friend and colleague, Richard Gardiner, to be his best man, a role that Richard filled with pleasure. The excellent food and fine Spring weather contributed to make a memorable occasion for the large party assembled at Pemberley.

Perhaps the only thing that soured the perfect day was the news from Westminster. Once the wedded couple had been fêted, teased, and sent on their happy way to their honeymoon in Wales, the conversation turned to the topic that was dominating conversations around the nation—the possibility of war with Russia. James Wilson's friends in the Foreign Office were absolutely certain that war was imminent. "I cannot help feeling that there is more to this quarrel with Russia than meets the eye," he said.

Though a member of the governing party, James was quite critical of Fitzwillam's favourite Parliamentarian, Palmerston, who was using the press, or that section of it that he could persuade to do his bidding, to whip up anti-Russian sentiment in Britain in preparation for an alliance with France and an attack upon Russia.

It was perhaps because Fitzwilliam was in a benevolent mood on the day of his daughter's wedding that he did not respond more aggressively to James' claims, saying only that Palmerston was a true patriot and would not do anything that was not in the nation's interest.

But James was supported by Jonathan Bingley, himself a member of the Whig party, who declared, "Palmerston is using the popular press to push the British people into a war that is not in their interest. There is no justification for wrecking the forty years of peace and prosperity we have enjoyed to support the military ambitions of Louis Napoleon."

Others agreed but seemed to be even more fatalistic about the inevitability of war.

"I cannot see that we can avoid it. The way Palmerston has taken us down this path, there is a kind war fever in the community; all up and down the country men are joining up, often without any understanding of the reasons for this campaign," said William Camden.

James Wilson pointed out that most Britons were not particularly enthusiastic about a military alliance with France, which within living memory had been the implacable enemy.

Anthony Tate, whose newspapers had already published several editorials on the subject, and his wife Rebecca, who was perhaps the only woman more interested in the war than the wedding, were even more concerned about the state of the armed forces. "It is absolutely unconscionable to be pushing a nation into a war with the military in such an ill-prepared state, with so many poor leaders," said Anthony, echoing the sentiments of his editors, while Rebecca pointed out that the women and children who were going to be left widowed and fatherless were not likely to be as enthusiastic about Britain entering the war as Palmerston and his government.

The talk of war made Mrs Gardiner most unhappy. Having grown up through the nightmare of the Napoleonic wars, when attacks upon England were said to be imminent, she had often told her nieces of the bad memories she had of friends and brothers sent to fight the French, one of whom had been at Trafalgar but had never returned to savour the victory.

Hearing some of the younger lads getting quite excited about it, she spoke up. "You are all too young to go to war, and if you were old enough, you would not enjoy it. There are many courageous men who will tell you that they felt neither brave nor heroic on the battlefield."

Even Jane, who hardly ever became involved in political discussion, ventured the opinion that it was surely unnecessary for Britain to go to war unless Britain feared being attacked by Russia. She agreed with her son Jonathan that it was indeed a poor excuse to suggest that Britain had to go to war to defend Turkey, who had declared war in the first place.

Mr Darcy had said very little during the wedding festivities, conscious of his responsibilities as the host, but after the guests had left and they had retired upstairs, Elizabeth asked her husband the inevitable question. "Do you really think we will go to war?"

Darcy answered quickly, "I do. Unfortunately, I think our stupid, self-serving leaders have dragged us too far in to let us extricate ourselves now. They are heavily committed, and their rhetoric has us involved in Europe already."

Elizabeth could not fail to hear the anger in his voice. She spoke quietly. "Colonel Fitzwilliam does not seem to think so."

Darcy smiled, a funny, crooked, almost sarcastic smile. "Yes, I had no wish to engage Fitzwilliam in an argument, especially not on Isabella's wedding day, but the unhappy truth is quite clear—Palmerston is guilty of panicking the rest of the government and some sections of the press into a state of outrage and suspicion directed against Russia. He is also determined that we shall have an alliance with France, despite the fact we were enemies just thirty years ago and still carry the scars of our battles. Most Britons would be quite astonished at this enthusiasm for cosying up to Bonaparte's nephew, especially when he seems determined to pick a fight with the Tsar," he explained.

"Do you think it will be soon?" his wife asked.

"Yes, I do," he replied, adding, "James Wilson believes we are on the verge of a declaration of war, and his sources in the Foreign Office are usually impeccable."

Elizabeth looked very anxious and her voice trembled a little as she spoke. "I am worried about Julian. Do you think he will want to join up?"

He was quick to reassure her. "No, dearest, I do not. You have no need to fear, I am sure of it. Now he is at Cambridge and seriously interested in his science studies; I cannot imagine why he would want to get involved in a war. He certainly did not seem at all affected by the hysteria sweeping London."

"But what if all his friends join up? Is he strong enough not to be drawn in?" Elizabeth seemed uncertain.

But Darcy was quite confident. "Julian has never expressed any interest in a military career; though I do believe Isabella's brother David is attracted to the idea of holding an officer's commission in the Cavalry. I cannot imagine what Caroline will say to that. But, my dear, if it will set your heart at rest, I shall sound Julian out before he returns to Cambridge and discover his thinking on the matter."

Elizabeth was grateful for his understanding. The thought that their only son could risk his life in a useless war was sufficient to make her fearful. "Would you? Thank you, yes, I would like to know how he feels."

That she was apprehensive did not surprise Darcy, and he was determined to do everything he could to reassure her.

Some time later, Elizabeth wrote to her sister Jane, expressing her relief:

My dearest Jane,

I write with so much joy in my heart that you may be forgiven for thinking that some amazing good fortune has come my way. Indeed, in a manner of speaking, it has.

You will recall, when we were speaking with Aunt Gardiner at Isabella's wedding, with all the talk of war that swirled around us, we wondered whether any of our young men would be tempted to plunge into the madness that seems to be overtaking the nation.

I recall remarking that you were spared the anxiety, since Jonathan was in Parliament and the rest of your family consisted of young women!

Our aunt was concerned that her grandson David had remarked that a commission in the Cavalry might suit him well. It set me worrying about Julian and later that day, I pressed Darcy about it.

He was convinced that Julian would not be interested in the army, but realising how my thoughts were running, he spoke with him before he returned to Cambridge, and, dearest Jane, the news is all good. Not only is Julian completely uninterested in a military career, he has persuaded David to abandon his idea of a commission in the cavalry.

Indeed, so opposed is Julian to this war, he has declared his intention to speak in the University Union against it. I need not tell you how delighted we are. I have spent many anguished hours, and I am certain Caroline and Aunt Gardiner have done likewise, though it must be said that Darcy was very confident from the start that Julian had no interest in a military career.

Colonel Fitzwilliam, on the other hand, seems not to see anything wrong with the war fever generated by Palmerston. Darcy tells me that, having come through the entire campaign against Bonaparte unscathed, Fitzwilliam has not the same horror of war that we have.

Dear Jane, I have some other news, too, and this is not anywhere near as pleasant. Our sister Lydia has written again, this time after many months of silence. While I cannot pretend that I have missed her letters—they are all uniformly boring, being either requests for money or boastful accounts of the activities of her "boys"—I have wondered how they were getting on.

It now appears that they have acquired some money through a bequest that Wickham has received from an aunt. While not being very substantial, it is still enough to let Lydia boast that they are looking to lease a small house in the Meryton area, where she thinks Wickham and she would have friends. After the notoriety they acquired when last they were there, I cannot think they would have many friends, can you?

However, if they do find a suitable place and retire to Meryton, I must say I am most grateful to Jonathan for inviting Charlotte to live with Mary at Longbourn, for I have no doubt that they would have wasted no time at all exploiting her charitable nature.

Now, however, with Charlotte Collins in residence, they will not find it easy. I intend writing Charlotte to warn her, so they may be prepared for any invasion, but I shall not bother to advise Lydia of Charlotte's presence at Longbourn. Let it be a surprise!

Do you think I am being cruel? Indeed, if I am, it is only to be kind to Mary, who surely needs some protection from the Wickhams. Do you not agree?

Having dispatched her letter to Jane, Elizabeth proceeded to write to her friend Charlotte at Longbourn.

Her letter, though welcome for all the usual reasons, was not necessary to warn her of the Wickhams' imminent arrival in the area.

Mary Bennet had herself received a short note from her sister Lydia with similar news, and on passing the information to Charlotte, she, too, had alerted her to the same possibility that had concerned Elizabeth.

Charlotte Collins, being of a practical and thoroughly sensible nature, assured Mary that she need have no concerns at all, since if and when the Wickhams arrived, Charlotte would be quite capable of dealing with them.

What actually transpired—the extent to which Lydia was disconcerted by Charlotte's presence, and the annoyance that both she and Wickham had shown at having to make other arrangements—was described in minute detail in a letter from Charlotte, which so amused Elizabeth, she summoned her carriage and set off for Lambton to share her news with her Aunt and Uncle Gardiner. Darcy and Robert Gardiner were gone to London to finalise some legal matters for her uncle, who did not travel much now, owing to his advancing years.

They spent a lively afternoon enjoying the prospect of the Wickhams' discomfiture. Elizabeth was exceedingly amused by the thought of them finding Charlotte at Longbourn and discovering that, if they decided to stay there while they looked for a suitable house in Meryton, which had clearly been their intention, they would have to put up with what she called "The Order of Service" that Charlotte would impose upon the household.

The Gardiners remarked also upon the ironic twist of fate that had seen Charlotte finally settled at Longbourn not as mistress of the house but as a welcome guest.

"It would surely have had your poor mother in a fit, Lizzie," declared Mr Gardiner, recalling the days when the family had lived in fear of being turned out of their home by the Collinses.

Mrs Bennet had never ceased to rail against them, regarding Charlotte with abhorrence whenever she came to visit. But now, Elizabeth and her aunt agreed that things had turned out very much for the best.

"Charlotte is an excellent manager, and Mary has been sensible enough to let her manage the household at Longbourn, which will ensure that they will never be short of money or live beyond their income," she said.

Mrs Gardiner was quick to agree. "Apart from the fact that they will be good company for each other, there is an advantage in having more of the house occupied and the servants kept busy."

"Which I am sure Charlotte will do exceptionally well," said her niece, and all three laughed heartily, imagining the effect Charlotte Collins would have had upon the Wickhams.

"She says she has made it quite clear to them that Mary is the Mistress of Longbourn and Jonathan Bingley its manager. They cannot have liked that," said Lizzie, and the Gardiners agreed.

Mrs Gardiner had just ordered tea and they were still quite merry when the carriage bearing Darcy and Robert arrived. Elizabeth rose, went into the hall to greet them and was confounded by the expressions of imponderable gravity on their faces.

Robert greeted her quickly and went directly upstairs to where his wife Rose, who was close to being brought to bed with their first child, was resting. Darcy embraced his wife, followed her into the sitting room and greeted Mr and Mrs Gardiner before saying in a very matter of fact voice,

"We are at war with Russia; an alliance is in place with Emperor Louis Napoleon, the Baltic Fleet is to sail for Kronstadt and our armies are to join the Turks in an attack upon the Russian naval base at Sebastopol in the Crimea."

His words fell like stones into water, sinking deeply. Lizzie understood now why Robert had gone directly upstairs to Rose and Darcy looked so grave. Both Mr and Mrs Gardiner looked most unhappy. Having lived through the dreadful era of the Napoleonic campaigns, they had hoped to spend the latter part of their lives in a period of peace, but it seemed this was not to be.

Fitzwilliam alone seemed to continue to place his faith in the skill of Palmerston to bring Britain through this latest wholly unnecessary piece of adventurism.

Thankfully, no member of their families was likely to be directly involved in the coming conflict, but war was war and none of them had any doubt that hundreds, maybe thousands of men would die before this stupid campaign was over.

❧

The newly wedded Mr and Mrs Forrester spent two quite delightful weeks in Wales before the disturbing news of Britain's entry into the war in the Crimea reached them.

Since neither Isabella nor her husband had visited Wales previously, there was much to engage their interest. Travelling through Cheshire to the west coast via the historic city of Chester and the busy market town of Denbigh, they found ample sources of inspiration and enchantment in both the natural beauty of the rugged countryside and the large number of ancient forts and castles that lay in wait for the traveller in its midst.

It was at the little coastal town of Colwyn Bay, while they were trying to decide whether to follow the coast road or turn inland and travel along the valley of the Conway, that a railway engineer from Liverpool, who was staying at the inn, gave them the grim news.

Thereafter, they were both keen to return home. Neither had any experience of Britain at war, having been born during the forty years of peace and prosperity that had blessed the land since Waterloo.

Nor did they have sufficient information to understand the reason behind the declaration of war, and both had immediate fears for the suffering and loss of life that was bound to follow.

Abandoning plans to travel further, they made arrangements to return home as expeditiously as possible.

On reaching Littleford, they stopped at the hospital to discover if there was any more news and heard with alarm that several thousand men had already been shipped off to join the French in the attack that the Turks were planning upon Sebastopol.

Richard, who was at the hospital, introduced them to his new assistant, Matthew Ward, a young Cambridge graduate who was to work on the research projects planned for the new hospital at Matlock. With the generous grant from Mr Darcy, they were ready to begin the work, which, Richard had promised the board, would change hospital practice and save lives. Matthew had the advantage of being the son of a physician in the army, one whose skills and endurance were soon to be sorely tested in the war.

Some weeks later, Henry and Isabella were dining with Richard and Cassandra, and Matthew Ward, being a veritable mine of information, was easily the most sought-after person in the party. He was able to confirm what Anthony Tate's war correspondent had already reported—the ill-equipped and ill-prepared men Britain had sent to the war were already suffering from typhus and cholera.

Isabella was incredulous. "I cannot believe our government would send our soldiers to war without protection or training," she said, but she was soon listening to even more shocking stories of inept leadership and bad management in the army.

"Not many people would believe that the British army would send men away to war, without proper field hospital arrangements," said Richard, "yet Matthew has learned that there has been very little done to prepare for the inevitable casualties."

"How do you mean?" asked Henry Forrester.

Matthew explained, "Well, I believe there were no preparations for dealing with the typhus and cholera that has broken out among the men, amazingly little provision for transporting the injured from the battlefield to a field hospital, and very few qualified medical personnel to deal with the casualties."

Isabella could hardly believe her ears, and when she met her parents, she related the terrible tales she had heard and was pleased to find that not even her father's loyalty to Palmerston could prevent him from expressing his dissatisfaction at the way Britain had been thrust into this futile war. Fitzwilliam had long been unhappy about the direction in which the government, which he had loyally supported for many years, was moving.

His reservations had increased on hearing accounts of the shameful actions of the British Navy in Finland. Frustrated by their inability to make headway at Kronstadt, they had vented their wrath on a small Finnish ship-yard, burning several ships and large quantities of goods on the docks. The newspapers had carried stories comparing their behaviour to that of the plundering Vikings in the ninth century.

"We are not likely to be regarded as a civilising influence in our colonies if we behave like barbarians in Europe, in the middle of this, the most civilised century of the modern era," wrote the editor of *The Review*—a sentiment with which most of his readers, Fitzwilliam included, heartily agreed.

That Palmerston, from whom he had expected more important reform, was spending much time and resources on what Fitzwilliam considered to be an unnecessary overseas adventure, which could bring Britain no credit, was, in his opinion, quite inexcusable and deserved the severest censure.

"It is absolutely abhorrent to me that the British government should be prepared to pander to the military ambitions of the Emperor of France by sacrificing the lives of thousands of our soldiers. They are there not to defend Britain from attack but to impose a solution on Russia and Turkey. I cannot believe that the English people, who have enjoyed the fruits of peace for so long, are now ready to support this foolish adventure," he declared.

Isabella was saddened by the disillusionment her father had suffered, but happy that he had recognised that a wrong course was being followed. Settling into their home, which lay less than two miles from Littleford Hospital, she had less time to worry about the war, but a stream of distressing information was accumulating gradually from reports and anec-dotes, and one could not avoid the bad news.

Rebecca and Anthony Tate, whose newspapers now received reports from the front by electric telegraph, kept everyone well informed. Much of the news was bad, exposing lack of resources, poor preparation, and often total ineptitude on the part of the generals. Soon, they began to worry about the conduct of this strange war. But it was not until the first reports of deaths of young men from Derby and Birmingham began to reach them that the dreadful gravity of the situation came home to them. English soldiers were dying on foreign soil not to protect England but upon the whim of the government and its new allies.

Many men had gone, believing they would be home by Christmas; others had been swayed by patriotic fervour in the press; but none had expected the conditions to deteriorate to the point where the campaign would become an embarrassing debacle, costing thousands of lives and destroying the reputation of the British War Office.

War correspondents reported in fearful detail the bloody battles of Inkerman, the disasters of Balaclava, and the infamous blunder of the Charge of the Light Brigade against the Russian guns, the resulting carnage so terrible, not even Tennyson's patriotic verse could disguise the incompetence of those in command.

Both Mr Darcy and Richard Gardiner spoke out openly against the conduct of the war.

"We are losing lives and our country's reputation as a result of this foolish expedition to the Black Sea," said Darcy when the families were dining together at Pemberley.

Both Richard and his friend Matthew Ward agreed. "You are quite right, sir," said Ward, who had only recently received a letter from his mother detailing his father's outrage at the lack of facilities to treat the sick and wounded at the front. "There are no litters or carts to transport the wounded and dying from the field. Dying men must lie there, often in the path of the battle, until their comrades arrive to carry them away. It is a scandalous situation."

"I have to admit I am utterly ashamed of our government and our leaders—both political and military," Richard confessed, expressing the feelings of most of those at the table as well as his own frustration at his inability to do anything about the situation.

Bingley confirmed that Jonathan had told them the government seemed to have no solution to the problems. "It is as if they are faced with a situation they never expected to encounter," said Bingley, deploring the lack of organisation and preparedness. "I cannot imagine that any government would embark on such a campaign with so little planning."

There was not a dissenting voice in the room.

Throughout 1854, and into the following year, while the siege of Sebastopol dragged on, thanks mainly to the remarkable incompetence of the French and British High Command, horror stories of the suffering of the soldiers continued to reach Britain. Not only were there daily reports in the press, but anecdotal evidence in letters from the front written by soldiers, officers, and medical professionals was eagerly read and shared around, so that the news soon spread across the nation.

Henry Forrester and Isabella heard many distressing reports. Conditions were said to be appalling; the hot, unsanitary camps were rife with disease. Matthew Ward and others vouched for the truth of the dreadful tales of disease, starvation, and suffering in the camps. They learned of men who had little chance to serve their country, dying of pneumonia, typhus, and cholera well before they fired a shot in anger.

Anthony Tate used his newspapers to flay both the blundering men in the army and their political masters. Shocked readers discovered the ineptitude of England's leaders and the suffering of her soldiers in the field. The extent of the debacle was truly outrageous, and demands for something to be done were loud and unceasing.

Britain was not alone in this parlous state, but in Russia and France there appeared to have been an early realisation of the need for some action. In both countries, groups of women volunteers—usually aristocratic women of substance—had started to go into the disease-ridden camps and treat the sick and wounded. It was the first time, in any war, that women played an active role in helping the medical teams.

In Britain, however, the machinery moved rather more slowly. Following the public outcry that accompanied the revelations of the horrors of Inkerman and Balaclava, an approach was made on the initiative of the Secretary for War, Sidney Herbert, to Florence Nightingale, organiser of a group of women being trained to minister to "gentlewomen during illness."

She was invited to organise and manage a team of volunteer nurses and apparently accepted readily, going immediately to Scutari, to the army hospital, if such a name could even be attached to the appalling mess that she found there. Shocked beyond belief by the conditions, Florence Nightingale wrote to Sidney Herbert describing in horrifying detail the state of the hospital and the suffering of the men, demanding resources and personnel so she could carry on the task she had undertaken. The government had no alternative but to agree.

As news of Miss Nightingale's work filtered through, groups of women around the country began to offer their services to assist her. Some had taken an entire retinue along, while others, driven by compassion, asked only to be allowed to help in some way.

Emily and Isabella were having tea together on a Sunday afternoon when Louisa arrived, unannounced, at the Rectory. She was on her way home from the new hospital, where Richard had gratefully accepted her offer of regular help.

Her cousins welcomed her warmly, and Emily went immediately to fetch a fresh pot of tea. Louisa was very excited. She had recently received from her elder sister Emma a letter, which she had brought along.

"I had long been wondering how we could help Miss Nightingale's wonderful work at the front," she explained, adding that she had twice written to the war office offering her services and, having heard not a word, she had written to Emma Wilson, hoping her husband James would be more forthcoming.

"And was he?" asked Isabella, just as Emily returned with more tea and shortbread.

"Indeed, he was, as I expected he would be. Papa says James has very good connections within the government and knows a good deal more than most of us," Louisa replied, extracting her sister's letter from her pocket book.

Emily and Isabella were immediately interested. Louisa read quickly, omitting the purely personal paragraphs and proceeding to the heart of her sister's letter:

And now, to the main burden of your letter, my dear Louisa. You say you would like very much to help Miss Florence Nightingale in the wonderful work she is doing for our soldiers in the Crimea.

While this is a very praiseworthy intention and you are to be commended for your Christian compassion, I hope you will understand that there are certain limits to the numbers of us who can travel to the front at this time. I have met some of the ladies who have been there, and I have it on their very good authority that it is not a task that may be easily accomplished; indeed, some of them have returned because they could not cope with the horrifying conditions. Many of their ladies' maids are not happy to be there, either. The work is dirty and often dangerous, and Miss Nightingale works very long hours. Only the most dedicated survive the rigour of the work and conditions for longer than a few days.

James has also made enquiries and discovered that the government would not welcome too many more women going out to the front at this time.

I am not supposed to speak too openly of this, but James believes that since Lord Palmerston is now Prime Minister and the new Tsar Alexander II is more ready than Tsar Nicholas to consider peace, a settlement may be imminent…

Emily and Isabella were delighted at the prospect of peace and the cessation of what was for them, the first experience of a horrible war, but Louisa hushed them at once, her voice sinking to a conspiratorial whisper.

"Oh, dear! You must not say a word about it; remember, Emma warns us not to speak too openly," she cautioned, and Emily was reminded of a play she had seen in which a young woman is arrested for spying. She was amused by her young cousin's serious attitude, but not wishing to hurt her feelings, suppressed her desire to laugh.

Louisa resumed reading her letter:

However, much will depend on negotiations over the next few months. Both James and I think it is probably better for any of us who wish to help the soldiers to prepare for their return, remembering there will be many thousands of sick and wounded men who will need hospital care.

In London, there are already organisations preparing to assist the returning soldiers and their families. Perhaps you and Isabella may like to do something similar in the area. A few hospitals here have started to train volunteers in this kind of work. If you wish me to, I could discover more about this scheme. I do believe it is a more practical way of helping the men than going out to the Crimea at this time.

Furthermore, dearest Louisa, while you are single and without too many responsibilities, Bella is not, and it may suit her better to undertake some work in the area. It may be best to discuss the scheme with Emily and Richard, too, since they will know what preparations need to be made at the hospitals.

I know you are very concerned and eager to help. I hope you will not be too disappointed, but, dear sister, remember: whatever we do to alleviate the continuing suffering of the men who return will be blessed indeed.

"There, is that not exactly what you would expect dear Emma to say? She is so kind and yet so sensible, is she not?" said Louisa, putting her letter away.

Emily and Isabella agreed and pointed out that the prospect of peace bringing thousands of injured, disabled, and diseased men home was a grim one and there would certainly be plenty of work for trained volunteers to do. While Louisa seemed a little disappointed, she had to agree that Emma's suggestion was eminently practical. Emily, in her usual gentle way, revealed that it would not have been possible for Isabella to go anyway, for she was expecting her first child.

This announcement brought so many exclamations of congratulation and delight from Louisa that she was about to leave without imparting another piece of important news. "Oh, dear, I did mean to tell you about it, but with all this excitement, I almost forgot. Cassy and Richard are attending the Spring Ball in Derby, and I am invited to join them. I understand Mr Matthew Ward is to be one of the party, and I am told he has confessed that he enjoys a dance," she said, her voice back to a conspiratorial whisper again.

Isabella and Emily smiled and could not help noticing the sparkle in her eyes. As she left, they predicted that Mr Ward was a fortunate young man and would be assured of a very pleasant evening, indeed. "I do hope he can dance," said Isabella. "Louisa loves dancing and will be very disappointed if it turns out that he has leaden feet."

Later, Emily and Isabella revealed to their husbands most, if not all, of Louisa's communication from her sister Emma, making sure they did not break the diplomatic confidence, which Louisa had been very particular to protect.

Both James Courtney and Henry Forrester agreed that it was a sensible and useful idea. Neither of the men had any objection to their wives being part of such a group, which did not surprise, since they were both compassionate men. What was astonishing, however, was their absolute certainty that Palmerston would press the new Tsar for a peace settlement.

Neither Emily nor Isabella had said a word. Both were puzzled but reluctant to comment lest they break Louisa's confidence. When they were back at home, Isabella ventured to ask a question, making it seem as casual a query as possible. "Do you really believe we shall have an end to the war soon?" she asked, adding that it would make her much happier if Britain was at peace when their child was born.

Henry Forrester turned and put his arms around his wife. "Indeed, my dear, I think we shall all be much happier if this wretched war was at an end. Well, if Anthony Tate's sources in the Foreign Office are reliable, we should, at least, be well on the road to a settlement by Christmas."

"Did he tell you about it?" asked Isabella, surprised because Henry had not mentioned meeting Mr Tate.

"It is in all his newspapers, my love. I was reading it only yesterday, and then this morning Richard mentioned it, too. It has been in all the London papers, as well, and he is convinced that Anthony has had it from the same reliable source."

Isabella smiled. So much for poor young Louisa's great diplomatic secret!

As for the idea of forming a group of nursing volunteers, she had no doubt of the need for such a scheme. One of the most pressing problems in the community was the care of the sick. With no national commitment to a health program, the sick and the wounded, whether in war or peacetime, would largely be left to the care of their families and such medical attention as the few district hospitals and charitable institutions could provide.

Encouraged by their husbands, Isabella and Emily began the first volunteer group in the district, drawing in several keen young women, including Louisa Bingley, who soon overcame her initial distress and threw herself into the venture with enthusiasm. That young Mr Ward was almost always available to advise and answer their questions and often to commend them on the speed with which they mastered their tasks may well have helped alleviate her disappointment.

Isabella was convinced that this was the case, especially after she discovered from Cassandra that the party to the Spring Ball had been a great success, and indeed Mr Matthew Ward had proved himself a very satisfactory partner in the dances.

"Louisa enjoyed herself immensely," Cassy had said, "and I would venture to say that Mr Ward had a pretty entertaining evening, too. They certainly danced together very well, and when they were not, he showed little inclination to rush off in search of other young ladies to partner, though several were available. He seems a sensible young man, and Richard assures me he is very clever."

Isabella was amused and confided in Emily, who cautioned her not to indulge in matchmaking, but then declared, with a twinkle in her eye, that it would be a very good thing if young Matthew Ward were to fancy their cousin. "Just think, Bella, it would mean that Louisa would be living in Matlock or Kympton and not miles away in Leicestershire; she would be a good deal closer to the hospital and therefore able to be much more useful. Best of all, it would mean that the clever Mr Ward would continue to stay and work with us, instead of going off to London or Birmingham as these young men are wont to do."

Isabella could not keep serious, aware that Emily was not. "Even better, as Mr Ward is such a keen dancer, there will no objections to the match from Mr Bingley!" They laughed together, knowing that young Louisa's desire to volunteer for training to nurse the sick would surely increase with any sign of interest from Mr Matthew Ward.

In the Spring of 1856, Tsar Alexander signed the documents leading to the Congress of Paris, at which the Peace Settlement was to be negotiated. Close to half a million men had been lost, and despite several documented acts of heroism, the Crimean War continued to be regarded as an unnecessary adventure in which none of the participants gained any prestige or glory.

Perhaps the most important permanent consequence was the total re-organisation and improvement of medical services and the introduction of professional nursing through the intervention of Florence Nightingale—the Lady with the Lamp. The small but dedicated groups of women who undertook the difficult task of providing nursing care to the sick and dying drew their inspiration and much of their discipline from her.

In April, Kitty and her husband, Dr Jenkins, returned from a short holiday in Hertfordshire, where they had stayed with Maria Faulkner and her husband. Having been childhood friends, the two had kept in touch over the years, and since Maria and her family had moved to Haye Park following the departure of the Gouldings from the district, she claimed there was plenty of space to have all of them over to stay.

Kitty and her three children got on exceedingly well with Maria and her family, and their husbands found much to talk about, being both men of keen intellect and modest ambitions. Maria and Kitty had matured into sensible women, both more interested in their families and the neighbourhoods in which they lived than in the world at large. Each, in her own way, made a useful contribution to improving the lives of people, especially the children in the community.

Kitty's return to Pemberley coincided with the departure for Oxford of Georgiana and her husband Dr Grantley, who had spent a very pleasant fortnight with the Darcys. Shortly afterwards, they were to depart on a tour of Northern Europe which would extend over several months, since Dr Grantley had been invited to visit a number of universities during his sabbatical. Georgiana was always welcomed most warmly to her former home, and Elizabeth, whose relationship with her sister-in-law had grown into a strong, loving bond, was sorry to see them go.

"I shall miss you terribly, Georgiana. Will you promise to write?" she pleaded, and her pleas were immediately answered in the affirmative. Georgiana promised to give an account of all the interesting places they were to visit.

"I shall miss you too, dear Lizzie, and of course I shall write very often."

Elizabeth smiled and reminded her that there would be some very special pleasures in store for her in Europe.

"I can see you enjoying the feast of music that awaits you in Salzburg, Vienna, and Paris; you will probably find very little time to miss any of us. But I do not wish you to be depressed; rather I shall count on you to tell me how much you are enjoying it all."

"And so I shall, my dear sister," she promised as she took affectionate leave of her brother and sister-in-law.

Looking at her, a tall, handsome woman, elegantly dressed, Elizabeth could hardly believe this was the same, shy, nervous young girl she had first met at the inn at Lambton and later at Pemberley those many years ago. It was an occasion she would always recall with the greatest affection and pleasure. Darcy's desire to introduce his young sister to Elizabeth had given her the first inkling of his continuing interest in her. From that happy meeting had flowed a great many things.

Kitty came to tea shortly after Georgiana's departure. The two sisters had never been close in the intimate way that Lizzie and Jane had been. But, since her marriage to the Rector at Pemberley, Kitty had matured remarkably and, having developed a pleasing sense of humour, she was at least a more interesting companion to her sister. Though she would never be as deeply loved as Jane or Georgiana, Kitty was more than welcome at Pemberley.

The work that Kitty and her husband had undertaken with the children's choir, which was now a permanent feature of the community, and their dedication to the Parish school they ran for the children of the Pemberley and Camden estates had earned them a special place in Elizabeth's heart. On this occasion, Kitty brought much news from Hertfordshire and especially from Longbourn and Meryton.

Jane was spending the day at Pemberley with Elizabeth while their husbands were attending a cricket match in Derby. The sisters had much to talk about. Jane wanted to know how Maria and her family had settled in at Haye Park, while Lizzie was interested to hear of Charlotte and Mary, and of course everyone wanted to know if Kitty had seen anything of the Wickhams!

"Now Kitty, you must tell us everything," said Elizabeth.

As for Kitty, she was very keen to tell her sisters all she knew and more! Jane could hardly wait for the maid and footman to leave the room before demanding to know whether Kitty had been to the house in Meryton that Lydia and Wickham occupied.

"Amelia-Jane tells me it is a large and rambling place with an untidy garden. Surely this cannot be true?" she asked.

"Indeed, it is, and situated just a mile or so outside Meryton, down a very poor sort of road," replied Kitty. "We were asked to tea one afternoon, and Lydia had all this food prepared and laid out on tables on the lawn, but the surroundings were so unkempt that we were continually attacked by Summer gnats and midges, so that Maria and I had to retreat indoors. The children didn't seem to mind, though I was glad my girls had elected to stay at Longbourn with Mary and Charlotte. They would not have enjoyed it, I am sure." Kitty continued with an unflattering description of her sister's household, which she declared was "without doubt the most disorganised I have ever seen.

"I swear, Lizzie, if it were not for poor overworked Mrs Brown, who looks after anything and everything that needs looking after—including Lydia's youngest, the naughtiest little boy I have ever met—the household would be a complete muddle."

Neither Elizabeth nor Jane were surprised. Lydia had been so totally spoilt by their mother that she had never shown any interest in learning to run a household, much less to cook or sew. Having been married at a very young age, and before any of her sisters, she had continued to follow a path of self-indulgence and irresponsibility, letting her children grow up as they wished, making no attempt to influence their upbringing. A similar lack of interest appeared to prevail on the part of their father.

Kitty, accustomed to the care and concern of her own husband, found this to be quite reprehensible and said so. "Wickham just does not seem to have any interest in the children at all," she said, "and Lydia seems not to have made an effort to change him in any way. He is much as he was all those years ago."

Jane seemed exasperated, but Elizabeth showed little emotion. "Nothing you have said surprises me, Kitty. Lydia's mind was only ever fixed on fun, flirtation, and falling in love—whatever that meant to her silly way of thinking. As we all knew, Wickham had no thought of marriage when he eloped with her; it was only accomplished thanks to our dear Uncle Gardiner and Mr Darcy. Had they not been assiduous in their efforts to trace them and insist upon their marriage—to the extent of bribing Wickham to marry Lydia—there is no knowing to what depths she may have sunk when he abandoned her, as he surely would have done when he had tired of her."

The seriousness of Elizabeth's words reminded them of the dreadful circumstances they had lived through on their errant sister's account. None of them would forget, even though all three were perfectly happy and content today, how close Lydia had come to ruining all their lives. All three of them owed much of their present happiness and good fortune to the generosity and magnanimity of Mr Darcy.

They fell silent for a while, until Jane decided to lighten the conversation with a question about Mary and Charlotte at Longbourn. She knew Kitty had spent some time with them and was eager for news. "How do they get on?" she asked. "Jonathan seems to think they are very content together."

Kitty agreed. "Indeed, they are. I could see no sign of any trouble between them. Charlotte seems pleased to have a home at Longbourn, and in view of her sister-in-law's most uncharitable attitude, she is probably very happy with Mary. She certainly runs the household well. They have a very good cook, and since dear old Hill passed away, there has been only the one maid and Mrs Binns. Charlotte has her own maid, of course, a very proper young woman from Mansfield, who has been schooled to read and write. They seem to manage very well indeed."

"I am very glad for Mary's sake; Charlotte is interested in everything that goes on in the world, and she will keep Mary alert and informed, I am sure." Elizabeth was certain the association could only benefit Mary, who had overcome some, but not all, of her dullness of mind.

Kitty could only agree. "I am sure you are right, Lizzie. Mary seems very happy with her pupils. She has gained quite a reputation as a music teacher. Maria tells me she sent her own girls to her until they moved to Haye Park."

"And do they have a visiting tutor now?" asked Jane.

Kitty laughed, "Of course they do. They are both very proper young ladies and have different tutors for music, drawing, and French!" Seeing Jane's incredulous expression, she added, "Can you imagine us at Longbourn with tutors for everything and a dancing master?"

"A dancing master?" the sisters exclaimed, and all three dissolved into laughter at the idea, recalling the days when the five Bennet girls were all out, not a tutor or a governess in sight, much to the annoyance of some of their neighbours and the disapproval of no less a personage than Lady Catherine de Bourgh.

Lizzie, who was still an excellent mimic, provided her sisters with a perfect rendition of Her Ladyship's censorious comments, delivered at

Rosings. "What? Five daughters brought up without a governess? I never heard of such a thing! Who taught you? Who attended you? You must have been grievously neglected!"

"Oh Lizzie, you have her down to a T," said Jane, who had a vivid recollection of Elizabeth's original recital of Her Ladyship's outrage. Having subsequently met her at Pemberley on a few memorable occasions, Jane could vouch for its accuracy of tone and attitude.

They were still laughing when Jenny appeared at the door. The seriousness of her expression stopped their laughter. It was quite plain that something was amiss. "What is it, Jenny? What's happened?" asked Elizabeth, rising and going to her side.

"If you please ma'am, John's back, and there's a message from the master," Jenny replied. "There's been an accident at one of the mines near Whitfield and they need help. The master is taking some of the men from Kympton and Mr Forrester. John is to get some of our lads together, take some blankets, rugs, and things, and go out there. John says they may be there awhile, ma'am."

While she was speaking, Jane and Kitty had joined them, eager to discover what had happened and what was known about the accident. When Elizabeth went downstairs, they followed her.

John, who was in the kitchen having a cup of tea, sprang to his feet as Mrs Darcy and her two sisters came in with his wife, Jenny. He looked so tired and distressed that Elizabeth ordered him to sit down at once and finish his tea. Though determined to obtain more information, she decided she would wait until he had finished.

While they were waiting, a man from the Camden estate arrived to inform them that a roof cave-in had occurred in one of the older pits, and several miners were trapped underground. Mr William Camden and his son had already left, taking a couple of farm hands with them to help.

Elizabeth, Jane, and Kitty looked at each other. "There must be something we can do," said Jane. "We cannot just stay here while everyone is out there helping in some way."

John had joined them and added his voice to hers. "If you please, ma'am, I think the master hoped you and Mrs Bingley could get to the hospital and join the others who will be waiting to attend on the men and boys who are brought out. There is no county hospital anywhere near the mine; the nearest is over in Newcastle under Lyme," he explained, pointing out that at least some of the injured miners might have to be transported to Littleford or Matlock.

"Do you know whether Dr Gardiner is aware of what has happened?" Elizabeth asked.

"Yes, ma'am, we stopped at his house and the master went in and told him and Miss Cassandra. He was going at once with Mr Ward who was also at the house. They thought we might need more medical supplies at the mine. Mr Forrester has also taken some supplies with him."

"Has Mrs Forrester gone, too?" Elizabeth asked.

"Yes ma'am, and Mrs Courtney." It was plain that John was eager to be gone, and Elizabeth asked only that one of the smaller carriages be readied for them.

While they were preparing to leave, Kitty's husband, having heard rumours in the village, arrived and was distressed to discover that it was indeed true. He declared his intention to go with John to the mine in case his services were required.

Kitty agreed to go with her sisters to the hospital to prepare for the injured who may be brought in. Within the hour, they were ready and on their way to Littleford, where they found a number of volunteers waiting to be taken to the mine. Alighting from their carriage, Elizabeth, Jane, and Kitty urged them to use their vehicle, and to their surprise, two young women, who were waiting with medical kits at the ready, climbed in with alacrity and were gone in a trice. They were part of the enthusiastic group who, inspired by the work of Florence Nightingale in the war, had been training for several months with Miss Louisa Bingley, they said.

Elizabeth and her sisters went into the building to begin the long wait for the casualties, who would surely arrive sooner or later.

The mine was situated southeast of Whitfield on an old coalfield that straddled the border between the two counties. Over the last fifty years several new pits had been opened, as coal became the mainstay of the industries that had been established here. Like the potteries all over Staffordshire, these coalmines had spawned small towns with grimy rows of cottages accommodating hundreds of families, who had moved here in search of work. Many of the men and boys went down the pits while the pottery works employed others, including women and girls. Hundreds of the pottery works produced the crate loads of chinaware that Britain exported to the world. Accidents in the mines and factories were not rare, and most communities had taken their share of pain, but a pit collapse was quite another matter.

When they reached the site of the accident, Isabella was struck by the silence, for there was quite a large crowd present. A small knot of men stood close to the entrance to the pit. Further away, on a hill slope, a larger crowd waited quietly, concerned folk from the villages around the coalfield. A few old men, women, and children predominated. Some had obviously come direct from the pottery works or the warehouses—a fine greyish dust lay all over them, the dust that hung in the air around the potteries where the clay was pulverised, ground, sifted, mixed, and moulded into shape. The dust covered their clothes and hair, making even the young women seem old.

In spite of the seriousness of the situation, Isabella noticed that the miners, standing by the pit were similarly covered in dust, black coal dust, which seemed to be ingrained in their pale skin. Yet they hardly seemed to notice it, so accustomed had these men become to it; they must breathe it in and eat it with their food, she thought, grimacing slightly. Later, Henry would explain to her that many of them died of it, too, as it filled their lungs, causing a dreadful respiratory disease.

The miners who had managed to struggle out of the pit were already being helped—large mugs of soup, slabs of bread and cheese, and cups of tea were being handed around. It was plain that people had come quickly to do whatever they could to help. Even as they watched, more groups of people were arriving—from Newchapel, Tunstall, Burslem, and Hanley—even as far away as Stoke on Trent, where the news had spread earlier that day; they came eager to help.

Teams of men were digging out the rubble, clearing a path for rescuers to use to bring out those who had been trapped by the cave-in. Some of the miners, who had not been on the shift, had come back to dig their mates out. No one seemed to know how many were trapped underground.

A few boys, looking stunned and shaken, sat in the dirt by the side of the road. Isabella began to organise their removal to a more suitable place—the church in the meadow opposite was the only possibility. Dr Jenkins had obtained permission to use the small hall adjoining the church and helped her take the boys over.

The women had brought hot soup and bread for the rescue workers as well as the rescued, and others had supplies of a more potent brew for those who needed it. Indeed, as they waited, some, who could bear the suspense no longer, had imbibed already, and were a little the worse for wear.

As they started to bring them out, Richard and Henry went at once to the mouth of the pit. Some were only bruised and shaken, covered from head to foot in coal dust, while others, injured and obviously in pain, seemed unable to comprehend what had happened, surprised that they were alive. Richard began to examine them quickly, taking those who needed immediate treatment aside into a makeshift surgery, dispatching others to the church hall for further examination.

The women worked as hard as the men, fetching, carrying, and caring for the injured. Isabella worked with them, oblivious of the dirt and grime. Suddenly, after about an hour, during which about twenty men and boys had been brought out from the mine, there was silence.

No one spoke or moved. Isabella was cleaning the cuts and bruises on a lad who had been brought out earlier. "What is it?" she asked. "Why have they all gone quiet?"

The boy spoke in a whisper. "They're listening ma'am. They're trying to hear if anyone is still alive beyond the fall in the tunnel."

"You mean they could all be dead in there?" she asked, her eyes wide with alarm.

The boy nodded. "Unless they hear tapping or someone calling out," he said ominously.

Isabella ran across to where Henry stood with Richard. "Are there still men and boys trapped in there?" she asked desperately.

Henry Forrester put an arm around his wife; she was trembling. "Yes, dearest, we are trying to discover if they are still alive. Once we know they are, we shall have to try to get them out."

"How will you do that?" she asked, very quietly.

"We shall have to go in and dig them out," Henry replied in a very matter-of-fact voice.

Isabella said nothing. If she had understood him correctly, Henry was calmly proposing to go down the mine himself.

She felt cold and ill. As she stood with his arm still around her, two of the rescuers emerged from the cage, their faces pitch black with coal dust and streaked with sweat.

The others gathered around them, anxious, eager to hear what they had found. "It's not good news, sir," one of them said as the other, his face crumpling with emotion and weariness, turned away. "We think at least four of them are dead; one's just a lad. But there's two more a little distance from the main group—they seem to be injured and their voices are very feeble, but they are alive."

"Can they be moved?" asked Richard.

"No, sir, not until we dig around them and make room. We have to mind what we do, or we might bring the rest of the roof down as well," he warned.

While they pondered how they might rescue the two who were alive, a third man emerged to declare that five were definitely dead and two were injured but still alive.

"They're father and son, sir, Jack Higgins and his boy Johnny. They work together," he said. "Jack's trapped; a piece of the roof has fallen on his leg, he cannot move, he is cold and numb, lying there all this time, and the boy can move, but he won't leave his father."

Matthew Ward stepped up. "Let me go down to him, I'll take him some brandy and a blanket and stay with him until they dig him out," he said.

As Matthew prepared to go in, Henry turned to his wife. "Bella, I must go down with Matthew. If this man is trapped, he may need surgery, and I will have to do it. It may be the only way to save his life. I want you to wait here with Emily and Richard and have everything ready to transport him and his son to Littleford. If I have to amputate, we will need to get him to hospital at once." Seeing fear in her eyes as he spoke, he added quickly, "Bella, you will be strong for me, will you not?"

Isabella nodded as he left her to join the rest of the men. Matthew had prepared a bag and a litter to be taken down and two of the miners led the way with lamps.

There was still plenty of light in the sky, but it had started to rain very gently but ominously, because with rain came the danger of flooding in the pits. Emily held Isabella's hand as they waited. The women and children across the way seemed to press closer, anxious for news. None came for what seemed like an eternity.

The owners of the pits were largely unknown to the men and women who worked there. They were generally investors who lived in Birmingham or London, leaving the running of the mines to managers. Two of them had arrived and left early after an initial inspection, showing very little concern for the feelings of the anxious people waiting for news. It appeared their chief concern was the fact that the mine would be closed for some time, a fact they would need to report to their employers. Richard was appalled at their apparent callousness.

Meanwhile, Mr Darcy and William Camden had gone to Newcastle under Lyme and returned with an apothecary, who brought with him a variety of medicines, ointments, and potions for those who had only minor injuries, bruises, and sore heads. He set to work at once attending to those who were waiting.

The women stood around in groups, some holding their children close, drawing comfort from them as they waited for the news they dreaded. No one knew who was dead and who remained alive below. The three men who had seen them had not revealed their names to the crowd, lest they cause panic. It was the way things were done. Fear and ignorance isolated each family. Wives and daughters clung together in hope, some praying audibly.

Looking at them, seeing, feeling, sharing their anxiety, Isabella wondered how she could have remained ignorant of the agony of these people, living such unimaginably hard lives only a few miles from her comfortable home.

One woman stood alone, a shawl over her head, almost hiding her face. Unable to bear the suspense alone any more, she approached Isabella and, reaching out to her, grasped her hand and clung to it. Isabella drew her close sharing her fear. They stood together without speaking, waiting.

Suddenly there were sounds; a rattle of the cage opening, the tramp of boots, and heavy breathing as two men appeared bearing two bodies. A deep sigh and several cries went up as they moved forward; one was the limp body of a boy, who could not have been more than fourteen, and the other a middle-aged man.

The women surged forward to see whose child it was that had been brought out first. There was a frightening silence until suddenly a cry of pain from one of them identified him as her son. Emily went to her at once, holding her, trying to offer comfort.

Isabella clung to the woman standing beside her, whose hand felt like ice in hers, so great was her fear. Tears coursed down their cheeks as they watched more bodies brought out—three big, strong men in the prime of life—husbands, fathers, brothers, all part of this small community, struggling to make a living in this most perilous of industries.

A temporary morgue had been set up in a tent and the mine supervisors were marking names off on a list, as grieving relatives crowded round.

Almost an hour later, a dull roar was heard underground. Alarmed, Isabella asked those around her, "What was that noise? What is happening?"

But no one would answer. They were looking at the entrance to the pit, where two men had emerged carrying a litter on which a man lay unconscious. Behind them, a slim boy, his face black with dust and streaked with tears, and then as Isabella watched, her heart racing with apprehension, Henry and Matthew stepped out into the fading evening light.

The woman, who had stayed with her throughout the ordeal, cried out in relief and ran, stumbling, across to the litter and embraced the boy as he stood beside his father. She had said not a word, but they were her husband and her only son. Later, Isabella learned that she was Mary, the wife of the miner, Jack Higgins, and mother of Johnny. She followed her as a great cheer went up from the crowd. Amidst those who were grieving for their dead, others gave thanks for the lives that had been spared.

Richard had already taken the man on the litter aside and, using his stethoscope, checked his heart, for he had suffered severe shock lying in the dark for many hours, even before his foot had been amputated to free him. As Richard completed his examination, Matthew was moving to get the man, his wife, and their son into the vehicle that was to take them to Littleford. The patient needed to be treated in hospital, and Richard would go with them.

There was a sense of relief now it was all over, and some of the people were talking at last, relieved that the casualties were not as many as they had feared. Others sat or stood around, dazed with shock and grief. But Isabella saw only her husband, exhausted with the strain of the ordeal, stained with grime and coal dust, and she went to him at once. Henry, blinking against the light, cleaned his face with a cloth someone had thrust into his hand before he held her close.

At first he made light of his ordeal and the danger they had been in. There was still work to be done. Arrangements were made to transport those who needed further treatment to Littleford and Matlock, and deliver the dead into the care of their families.

James Courtney and Dr Jenkins were staying on to conduct a short service for the dead and comfort the living—a melancholy task, indeed, but an essential one.

When it was all over and they were at home after they had bathed and dined, only then did he tell her how close they had come to catastrophe. The dull roar they had heard above ground was the rest of the roof collapsing minutes after they had pulled Jack Higgins out. "Fortunately, Matthew had persuaded the lad to get out first, or there would have been more tragedy. I did not know then that he was their only son."

Isabella told him how Mary Higgins had clung to her hand, saying not a word, not even her name, while they waited. Henry smiled. "She probably knew you were the surgeon's wife and did not wish to alarm you," he said lightly.

Isabella was not deceived by the calmness of his voice. She knew how close she had been to losing him, as close as Mary Higgins had been to losing her husband and only son.

A week later, they dined at Pemberley with most of their family and friends. Mr Darcy took the opportunity to pay tribute to all the men and women who had helped during the mine disaster. He thanked especially the women whose voluntary work at the mine and in the hospitals had been invaluable. He had heard from the mine wardens that the pit was flooded and would remain closed. "I know it will come as a relief to all of you, as it did to me, that no more lives will be placed in jeopardy to extract coal from that old pit, which should have been abandoned years ago," he declared to cheers of approval from all those gathered around the table.

But the loudest cheers erupted when he turned to his son-in-law Richard and said, "Richard, I know that without your wonderful work, and the brave efforts of your excellent colleagues Henry Forrester and Matthew

Ward, many more lives would have been lost. All of us, the entire community is deeply grateful to you all. Thank you."

Isabella, sitting between her husband and Richard Gardiner, was very proud of them. Across the room, Matthew Ward looked very pleased indeed. A week ago, he had been unknown; today he was being listed among the heroes.

❧

Two days later, Isabella was resting in her room when her maid came in to say a woman had come to call on her. "I told her you were upstairs ma'am, but she insisted that she would take up very little of your time. She says her name is Mary Higgins."

Isabella rose at once and put on a loose wrap.

"Sarah, go down at once and ask Mrs Higgins to wait in the sitting room, I will be with her soon. Would you also bring us some tea, please?"

When she dressed and went downstairs, Isabella found Mary Higgins standing quietly in the corner of the room, looking out at the garden, which was filled with late Summer blooms. She went to her at once and took both her hands in hers. "Mrs Higgins, Mary, I am so happy to see you," she said, and the sincerity in her voice reassured the woman, who had been somewhat nervous while waiting for her.

"I was admiring your lovely garden, ma'am. I wish we had room for one."

She sat down almost reluctantly and then jumped up again to get a parcel she had left on a side table. "I brought you this, ma'am. We called at the hospital, and Mr Forrester said you were at home, and he said you would not mind if we called on you to say how grateful we are to you and Mr Forrester."

Isabella asked whether her son was with her and was told he was out in the pony cart they had borrowed for their journey. Immediately, Isabella sent for Sarah and instructed her to ask young Johnny Higgins in and make sure there was plenty of cake on the table for tea.

When she opened the brown paper parcel, she found within an exquisite bowl from the Wedgwood potteries, where Mary Higgins worked. Isabella exclaimed with delight but was tongue-tied at first, unable to express adequately her appreciation. Having put it down carefully on the table, she held Mary's hands in hers. "Mary, thank you, it is so beautiful; but you did not have to bring me anything," she began, but the woman stopped her.

"Mrs Forrester, it is we who must thank you and Mr Forrester, for all you did for us. Were it not for him and his great courage, I would surely have lost both my husband and my boy. No lady has been so kind to me as you were that day, I did not know then you were the surgeon's wife. You were so patient and so understanding, I shall not forget your goodness as long as I live."

Isabella tried to say first one thing and then another to stop her, but she would not be stopped. "And there is another matter, ma'am; when we visited Mr Higgins in the hospital, Mr Forrester asked my Johnny if he would like to work for him as an orderly, helping out, doing jobs around the hospital. So since the pit has closed, Johnny said he would, and he starts at the hospital next week. No more working down the mine. So you see, ma'am, we have a lot to be grateful for, and that little bowl is only a small token to show how we feel."

Isabella was delighted. She had wondered how the family would cope and whether they would have to go on letting the boy work in the mines. Henry had obviously given the matter some thought and had done something about it.

When they had finished their tea, Mary Higgins rose to leave. "Should you need any help around the garden, ma'am, or if you have any odd jobs that need doing, you ask our Johnny. And if there is anything you want me to do, you send me word through him and I'll be over as soon as I can," she promised.

Mary Higgins held Isabella's hands very tight and there were tears in the eyes of both women. They knew they had shared something very special on that terrible day, something that would make a bond between them forever. Isabella was immensely grateful for the experience.

She recalled asking her husband, on the night after the cave-in, whether Jack Higgins would live, and he had replied with a sigh, "Yes, if you call life without your right foot living. Remember Bella, he is only forty-two years old and in every other way a healthy, active man."

Isabella had wept then and said, "It seems so unfair that they should pay so high a price, just so they can earn a living. Each time I throw a piece of coal on the fire, I shall remember that.

"I have never known such fear, waiting for you, wondering if you were going to be able to save them and get out alive, I knew exactly how Mary Higgins felt. I shall never forget the look on her face when they were brought up out of that dreadful pit."

Isabella was glad she had something more by which to remember that awful day than the memory of the agony of a woman who had spent all day wondering whether she would see her husband and son alive again. Mary Higgins was clearly delighted to have her husband home, even if he would remain a cripple for the rest of his life. She was a strong woman. She could work. Isabella had felt a remarkable strength in her hands as she held them. She had no doubt they would survive this tragedy and was determined to help them as best as she could.

The Wedgwood china bowl, with its delicate classical design, had pride of place on the sideboard in their dining room. Each morning, when Isabella came downstairs and opened the window, it caught the rays of the morning sun. It was much admired by everyone who sat at their table, and its story would be told and re-told for years to come.

J OSEPHINE TATE WAS NOT happy, which was unusual, since she was generally of a sunny disposition. On this fine Autumn morning, however, she was standing before a mirror in her bedroom, holding up a gown, trying to decide what to wear to the ball at Pemberley. The occasion was the twenty-first birthday of Julian Darcy.

Josie could not decide which of her best gowns would suit. Two had already been tried and discarded as unbecoming or unsuitable, and the third—a pretty silk with a damask rose pattern—was about to join the rest when her mother entered the room.

"Ah, there you are, Josie darling," she said. "That is a most attractive gown. Have you decided to wear it tonight?"

Josie pulled a face and looked uncertain as her mother, glancing down at a letter, which had arrived that morning, announced, "Amelia-Jane is to have another baby."

Josie stood as if transfixed. "What? Another baby!" She was incredulous. "Mama, this must be her fourth, or fifth, if you count the little one they lost two years ago."

Her mother seemed quite unperturbed by the news. "Well, it is, and why ever not? Amelia-Jane seems to love having children. She has very little to do besides running her household and looking after Jonathan. The nurse looks after the children for her. I know you do not like the idea of having lots of children, Josie, but many women do. Jonathan and Amelia-Jane seem to enjoy their children, you must admit. Now," she said, briskly changing the conversation, "have you decided on that dress?"

Josie sighed, "It matters not what I wear, anyway, Mama. Louisa Bingley can wear a simple shift and look like a princess! So why should I bother?"

"Louisa? Why Josie, you are not jealous of her, are you? She is older than you are and besides, is she not as good as engaged to that Mr Ward who works at the hospital?" asked her mother, more amused than concerned.

Louisa, the youngest of Jane and Charles Bingley's famously lovely daughters, was admittedly a very attractive young woman with the added sophistication that a few years in society had given her. Since her sister Sophie's marriage, Louisa seemed effortlessly to outshine most of the young ladies in the district. Josie sounded rather petulant, "Mama, if you were my age and attending a ball at Pemberley, you would be jealous too. She is so pretty, she makes the rest of us look quite ordinary, and it does not signify at all if she is engaged or she is not. And then, there is always dear Anne-Marie, another famous Bingley beauty. Aunt Amelia always makes sure she shines, wherever she goes."

She was wickedly recalling Amelia-Jane Bingley's inclination to overdress her lovely daughter, a tendency generally agreed to be akin to gilding the lily and quite unnecessary.

"Oh, Josie, that is nonsense," chided her mother. "You are quite pretty yourself and have particularly fine eyes. I am sure if you had your hair styled differently, sort of swept up more, you would look very well. Now, come along and let us see what we can do about this gown. The colour is just right for you, and I think that if you wore my garnet earrings and necklace with it, it would be quite perfect."

"Thank you, Mama, but aren't they a teeny bit old fashioned?" said Josie as she followed her mother out of the room.

꙰

There was indeed a good deal of truth in Mrs Tate's words. Josie, the daughter of Anthony Tate and Rebecca Collins, was just nineteen years old. She was well educated, intelligent, and witty, and though not classically beautiful like the Bingley girls, she was endowed with fine features and a slender figure, more characteristic of the Tates than the somewhat sturdier build of the Collinses. Her appearance was enhanced by a bright smile and a happy, generous temperament, which endeared her to her many friends.

Her father, who owned a number of provincial newspapers, appreciated Josie's intelligence, and had always encouraged her to speak up for herself, which she did often, without giving offence to anyone, despite a degree of pertness usually attributed to her youth.

Mr Darcy had commented on more than one occasion that Josie Tate reminded him of his wife, Elizabeth, when he had first met her at Netherfield. "She has the same insouciance with which she contests, without reservation, a point of view or declaration with which she cannot or will not agree," he had said, causing a good deal of mirth among their children.

"Did Mama argue with you, Papa?" Julian had asked and was told, "She most certainly did, but mark you, not out of some perverse desire to be contrary, but because she genuinely believed I was wrong."

Elizabeth thanked him for his generous assessment of her conduct and did not bother to tell them that there had been times, especially in the company of Bingley's boring sisters, whose fawning acquiescence with his every word had irritated and goaded her, when she had been tempted to argue with very little cause.

That, however, was many years ago, he said, assuring Julian that today, after years of happy marriage, they were as one on so many topics, that he could not recall when they had last disagreed, much less had an argument. Elizabeth smiled and said nothing, but she was clearly pleased with this endorsement of their felicity.

Faced with this example of contentment, Julian pointed out that he rarely had an argument with Josie Tate; indeed, they agreed on most things. "Unlike many other girls of her age, Josie is not silly. She is well informed on most matters and has some strong opinions," he said.

"And if she does argue to defend them, she is entitled to do so," said his father.

Elizabeth added that, with parents like Anthony and Rebecca Tate, it was no surprise that Josie had strong opinions. "They are both well read and have independent views."

Julian agreed and said he was looking forward to meeting with her at the ball. "And have you asked her to reserve a dance or two for you?" asked his mother with a smile.

"I have not, but I intend to do so as soon as she arrives," replied Julian, who, unlike his father, genuinely enjoyed a dance.

The ball at Pemberley had been organised with all the usual efficiency and style that characterised similar celebrations at the great house. When the guests began to arrive, they were greeted by Mr Darcy, Elizabeth, and Julian—who was just as tall and handsome as his father with an additional measure of natural charm, inherited from his mother.

Where the young Fitzwilliam Darcy had been shy and reserved to the point where he had often given offence, Julian was amiable and friendly with the easy manners of a young man who enjoyed the acquaintance of many and hoped to find most of them agreeable. While undoubtedly clever and enjoying intelligent company, he had that happy knack of putting people at ease, a quality that ensured he was generally well liked. A keen intelligence and scientific discipline stood him in good stead. Though justifiably proud of Pemberley and his family's traditions, he never let them intrude into his general discourse, nor did he permit conceit based upon his heritage to cloud his judgement.

Jonathan and Amelia-Jane arrived early, and as Josie had predicted, their daughter Anne-Marie was so fashionably gowned and adorned with jewels that she looked much older than her seventeen years. While she was very much admired and did not lack for partners, Julian Darcy was not immediately one of them.

Indeed, when the dancers took the floor, Josie was proved right again, for it was his lovely cousin, Louisa Bingley, whom Julian led into the dance. Josie herself had been claimed by another gentleman and proceeded to enjoy herself, giving little thought to either Louisa or Julian.

She was, therefore, pleasantly surprised when he appeared beside her and applied for her hand for the next two dances. Though taken aback by his unexpected approach, so early in the evening, Josie accepted with pleasure and turned with a delighted smile to her partner.

Their debut on the floor did not go unnoticed. They made a handsome couple and danced well together. Jane, who was watching the dancers with

Darcy and Elizabeth, commented that they seemed to have no problem making conversation.

Soon afterwards, Bingley arrived to claim his wife for a dance and, left alone with Darcy, Lizzie mischievously reminded her husband of the difficulties they had experienced when she had attempted to engage him in conversation on the occasion of their first dance together at Netherfield.

It was not an occasion Darcy cared to recall, but he smiled, knowing she was teasing him, and could not resist indulging her. "I am afraid I remember very little of that dance, Lizzie, except how completely lost I was in admiration for my partner. Perhaps that might account for any difficulty we might have had in maintaining a conversation. After all, we have no such problem now."

Elizabeth laughed out loud. "Now, you are trying to tease me!" she declared and was about to take him to task when Cassandra and Richard joined them.

"Are you determined not to dance, Papa?" asked Cassandra, who knew that dancing was not her father's favourite pastime; indeed, he would only dance with her, her mother, or, on the very rare occasion, Aunt Jane.

Darcy immediately denied that he had made any such resolution. "Certainly not; indeed, we intend to take the floor very soon. We were indulging ourselves a little, observing your brother and Miss Tate, who are a pleasure to watch," he said, quite calmly.

"They certainly are," said Cassy. "Doesn't Julian look handsome? And Josie is delightful, so light on her feet!"

As they went down to the dance floor, Elizabeth took her husband's arm and said, "They certainly look very much at ease with each other."

Something in the tone of her voice caused Darcy to smile and say, "Lizzie, I do believe you are indulging in that very dangerous pastime again," and she protested immediately that she was not matchmaking!

"No, indeed, I am not. Pray do not misunderstand me, I do like young Josie but I do not know that she will suit Julian. She is very clever, independent, knows her own mind, and will not be led by him."

"And if all those qualities have not impaired our marriage, why do you suppose they may cause Julian any concern? Being a modern, self-assured young man, with far less baggage than I carried at the time we met, I cannot imagine why they would do so."

"Can you not?" she asked, softly, understanding the point he was making.

Darcy shrugged his shoulders. "Not if he loves her. All such associations involve something of a risk. But then, what human activity does not? And surely, the rewards are worth the effort. Do you not agree, Lizzie?" he asked.

Elizabeth, moving onto the floor and into the dance, smiled and said softly, "Oh, indeed I do, and I would not have it any different for the world."

Had Elizabeth and Darcy been able to hear the conversation between their son and Josie Tate, they may have been rather puzzled, for it was hardly the stuff of romance. Josie had long been what her mother used to call "an incorrigible scribbler:" as a little girl, she had produced little scraps of writing which her father had liked well enough to have printed on the end of a galley proof for her entertainment. Occasionally, when they were particularly good, he would have them typeset in a special font and printed on a separate sheet under the banner of *The Review*, her own special edition to pin up on the wall of her room.

As she had grown older, she had become increasingly interested in writing for the newspapers and every so often a short piece would appear in *The Pioneer* or *The Review* under the pen name of one Jane Collins. But what she dearly wanted was to be published in the metropolitan press.

"I know I can get articles into Papa's newspapers," she told Julian as they danced, "but that is not good enough. I must get accepted by one of the London dailies—*The Times*, *The Chronicle*, or *The Herald* or at the very least *The Guardian*. If I do not, no one will take me seriously."

Surprisingly, he neither laughed nor appeared astonished at her ambition—he was in fact the first person who had not advised her to temper her goals with some common sense. "Of course, that would be absolutely splendid, but while you keep that worthy goal, there is nothing wrong in trying for the journals or the provincial weeklies, is there?" he asked, quite reasonably.

Josie was taken aback. "Then you think I should keep trying?"

"Of course, there is no question of that. But, not having read any of your writing, Josie, I am at a disadvantage. Perhaps when I have seen some of it, I could speak with greater conviction," he said, a little tentatively, half expecting her to withdraw, as many young ladies would have done, and declare that she could not possibly let him read her work. He was pleasantly surprised when she agreed, and they arranged that some time would be found for him to read some of her work before he returned to Cambridge.

As the dance concluded, he escorted her to her seat and left, but not before extracting a promise of another dance later in the program.

～❦～

Two days later, Josie was upstairs, when her mother's maid appeared at the door of her room. "Miss Josie," she said, "Mr Julian Darcy is here to see you."

Josie brightened somewhat, but not even Julian's arrival could restore her spirits. She had received another rejection, this time from the editor of *The Times*, of London, returning what she regarded as the most worthwhile piece of writing she had yet undertaken. It was a piece on the mine collapse at Whitfield, and she had written of the consequences of the disaster for the miners' families and the small community in which they lived. Inspired by the courage and dedication of the volunteers from the Pemberley and Camden estates, who had turned out to help their neighbours in the Whitfield mining community, Josie had spent a good deal of time discovering all the facts and talking to several people, including some of the miners' wives, before putting pen to paper. She was clearly upset by the rejection, couched as it was in very bland terms.

When she went downstairs, taking her article and the offending letter with her, she found a patient Julian Darcy taking afternoon tea with her mother. "I have told Julian you've been fretting since *The Times* rejected your piece on the mine disaster," said Mrs Tate, by way of introduction.

Seeing dejection written upon her face, Julian was immediately sympathetic. "I am sorry Josie, what reason have they given?"

Josie's eyes filled with tears, as she said, "No reason at all. That's what hurts; it is not that my work is bad, they are just not interested in it," she said as she tossed the letter and article onto the table and sank into a sofa, looking truly miserable.

Julian picked them up and sat down to read them while Josie was persuaded to take a cup of tea. She watched him as he read, turning over the pages of her neatly written manuscript, and his expression changed from interest to concern and finally to exasperation. As he finished reading, he stood up, and walked away towards the window, standing silent, looking out across the river for several minutes, before returning to say, "Josie, I am at a complete loss to understand why this piece of writing has been rejected. It is an important subject, carefully researched, and well written. I cannot imagine what the editor could find wrong with it," he said, his voice betraying the frustration he felt.

"Would you like me to tell you?" she said, a touch of sarcasm sharpening her tone. When he turned and looked at her, she continued, "The writer is a woman. Jane Collins is not acceptable, but I can wager anything that if I had called myself John Collins, there would have been no rejection."

Julian, who had never had to confront such an issue before, seemed quite shocked at her blunt statement. "Do you really believe that to be true?" he asked, incredulous.

"I certainly do. A year ago, tired of being rejected, I sent in an article using Walter's name. It was accepted and what is more, I was invited—or rather, Walter was—to submit another piece in the same vein."

"And did you?" he asked, astonished at her revelation.

"No, I did not. Why should I? It's my work, why should I have to pretend it is not, in order to get published?"

Her mother had returned and, having overheard the exchange between them, she said gently, "Josie, Walter wouldn't mind."

Josie's eyes flashed. "I am sure he would not. But that is hardly the point, Mother. If they found my work acceptable, it should not matter if I am a man or a woman. Can you not see that?"

Julian understood and came to her rescue. "Mrs Tate, Josie is quite right. It should not matter who she is if the work is good enough to be published."

Rebecca Tate felt for her young daughter; she was a regular writer to the papers herself, but she had had the good fortune to marry her publisher, which had made her path a good deal smoother. Now she had a modest reputation as a writer, and she certainly did not mind that it was almost entirely sustained by publication in her husband's journals. "You know you will always find space in any of your father's newspapers, and if you want me to ask him about this article…"

Josie shook her head, "No, Mama, though it is very kind of you, and yes, I do know I can get it into *The Review* or *The Pioneer* or any of Papa's provincial papers; but that would not be the same."

Julian agreed, adding that the article on the mine disaster deserved to be more widely read. "I cannot believe that it is not in our interest to be better informed about these catastrophes and how they affect people in our towns and villages—what it does to a family to lose its breadwinner or its only son. If we are to understand what is happening to our society, we need to read the type of story that Josie has written."

Rebecca Tate pointed out that if Josie had been writing "real stories," by which she actually meant fiction, she would have much less difficulty finding a publisher. "The writing of novels and novellas has become quite a pastime with the ladies—of course, some prefer to use a gentleman's name—but the telling of stories is popular today," she explained.

Josie was adamant. "I don't need to concoct stories, Mama—there are a million stories to be told, true stories of ordinary people that I could tell, but no one wants to publish them. They are not interested in ordinary people, nor do they pay attention to matters like health, sanitation, and education for the poor. They would rather I wrote rubbish—romantic melodramas about desperate maidens in crumbling castles!"

Julian could hear the passion in her voice; he knew she would get little satisfaction from writing romantic "penny dreadfuls" for the circulating libraries. On an impulse, he asked, "Josie, may I take this copy with me?"

She agreed at once. "Certainly, I have two other copies, but what will you do with it?" she asked, intrigued and a little flattered by his interest.

"I should like to show it to a couple of friends of mine at Cambridge. They are not publishers, but I think they would be interested to read your article," he explained. Josie was clearly pleased and thanked him for his interest.

It was getting late, and as Julian prepared to leave, Mrs Tate invited him to return the following day and dine with them when Mr Tate would be home from Liverpool. He accepted with pleasure. As they walked to the door, Josie thanked him again. She was sensible enough to know that Julian could not influence the editors of newspapers, but that he had shown suffi-cient interest in her work to want to show it to his friends at Cambridge was a kindness and a compliment for which she was grateful.

At dinner on the morrow, he found himself talking mostly to Mrs Tate and Josie, while Josie's father was monopolised by another guest, a banker from Birmingham. He gathered enough from the conversation, however, to realise that Josie had probably inherited her strong opinions and deter-mination to succeed from her father. Anthony Tate was clearly a man of ideas and influence.

Before returning to Cambridge for the rest of Michaelmas term, Julian went to see his sister Cassandra.

She was sitting with her youngest child, Laura Ann, when he arrived; he had ridden over from Pemberley after breakfast.

Cassy was delighted to see him. He sat with her awhile until she sent for the nurse and surrendered her daughter. She was about to order some tea when he said, "Cassy, could we take a walk in your garden?"

She was surprised, but agreed at once, waiting only to get a light wrap before joining him and taking his arm as they walked down towards the sloping flower-filled garden beside the river. Well away from the house and anyone who could have overheard them, she did not have long to wait before he asked, "Cassy, how well do you know the Tates?" Seeing the puzzled expression on her face, he added quickly, "Oh, I don't mean Josie, but Mr Tate and Walter. I've never had a great deal to do with them. Do you know them well?"

His sister smiled. "Am I allowed to know the reason behind these inquiries?" she asked, a little archness creeping into her voice.

Julian seemed a little embarrassed. "I would certainly tell you if I knew myself, but right at this moment, there is not a great deal to tell," he said.

"Would this have anything to do with Josie Tate?" she asked.

He was quick to reply, "Yes, but not as you might imagine it."

"No? There, you have me completely confused now," she said. "Only a moment ago I thought I had an answer."

Julian laughed and, sitting down, leaned back with his hands behind his head and sighed, "This is such a perfect place, Cassy. I wish I did not have to return to Cambridge."

Cassandra laughed. "Oh, dear, it cannot be as bad as that already," she teased, but he would not let her continue.

"Cassy, be serious, please. I am not concealing anything from you; I am happy to tell you everything, but I cannot reveal what I do not know myself."

Cassandra apologised, feeling sorry for her brother, whom she, being close to twenty years older, had always regarded as a boy, until he had turned up at Sophie's wedding looking so grown up and grand that even his sister had to take him seriously. "I'm sorry Julian. I promise I will be serious. But you must tell me where this is leading, or I shall not know what I am to be serious about."

This time it was his turn to be contrite. "Forgive me, I did not mean to be difficult or deliberately obscure. You shall judge my predicament for yourself," he said and proceeded to explain, "While I have known Josie Tate quite well for a number of years, I have very little knowledge of the rest of the family. I have met both her parents but not enough to be at all familiar. As for her brother Walter, he has been away at boarding school and now at Oxford for most of the last few years. I have had little contact with him or Mr Tate, who is often away on business."

Cassandra was beginning to wonder where this was leading when quite suddenly he said, "I should like very much to know how you think they would respond were I to ask for Josie's hand in marriage."

Cassandra was so surprised that she was unable to say anything for several minutes, and, seeing her expression, Julian looked alarmed. "Cassy, this is terrible. Why do you appear so astonished? Is it such an improbable idea? If I cannot convince you that I am serious, how can I hope to persuade them, who know me far less well?"

He sounded depressed, and Cassy was immediately remorseful and spoke up quickly. "I am sorry, Julian, I was more surprised than I have the right to be. Indeed, I have noticed your interest in Josie, and the other night at the ball, it was quite clear to us that you were more than friends."

Julian shook his head and seemed confused. "That is just the problem. While I am certain of my feelings for her, I am not at all sure that she regards me as anything more than a friend whose company she enjoys. We have a lot in common and are attracted to similar pursuits and ideas, but we have never spoken of love. Josie is only nineteen, and I would be reluctant to say anything to her without being sure I had her parents' approval," he said by way of explanation.

Cassandra was smiling. "My dear brother, I am sure I can reassure you on both counts. While I do not know Josie's parents intimately, I do know them to be intelligent and sensible people, well regarded in the community. And, being intelligent and sensible, I cannot imagine that they will have any objection to you, the heir to the Pemberley Estate, applying to marry their daughter." Holding up a hand to stop his protest before he had expressed it, she continued, "I do not mean that in any mercenary sense, but it stands to reason, Julian you are a very good match for any young woman, quite apart from the fact you are my dear brother and the best looking gentleman in the district." She went on, ignoring his embarrassment, "As for Josie, I do know her better than I know her parents, and she is probably quite unaware of your interest in her. However, if she were to care for you, Julian, I know her well enough to tell you that she would not be ruled by her parents or anyone else. Josie, you will have noticed, is rather like Mama; she is open and forthright and will not be put upon. If you are unsure of her feelings, ask her first, but be advised she will tell you the truth, however painful."

Her brother seemed a little downcast as she went on, "Now, what I wish to ask you, my dear brother, is how confident are you of your own feelings? Are you certain of your intentions?"

At this, he brightened considerably. He reassured her in no uncertain terms that he knew his mind; indeed, he had carried the knowledge within him since Sophie's wedding when he had seen Josie after almost a year away at Cambridge and discovered that the rather awkward, young girl had been transformed into an attractive, intelligent young woman with a mind of her own. "We spent some time together during the weeks that followed, and I have been bewitched by her ever since. I admit I have been a bit of a coward about confessing it, but I have no doubt at all about my feelings now. She is the brightest, most engaging young woman, I know. I love her, Cassy."

Cassandra rose and embraced her brother warmly. "You poor thing, you do not deserve this. Go and see her, Julian, and ask her, and once she has said yes, then ask her father."

Julian left soon afterwards, having thanked his sister for her advice. Returning that evening to the Tates' place at Matlock, he expected to find the family at home and hoped for an opportunity to speak with Josie alone. To his great disappointment, he found the parlour full of Anthony Tate's business friends, who had been invited to celebrate his acquisition of another provincial journal. Josie, far from being available to listen to an ardent proposal, was virtually run off her feet assisting Mrs Tate with arrangements for the evening. Like her mother Charlotte, Rebecca Tate was a practical woman who insisted on her daughter learning to manage a household, whatever other interests or aspirations she might have.

While Julian was made welcome, he could never find the time or the opportunity to say more than a few words to the young lady he had come to woo. At the very end of the evening, when it was time to leave, he did get a moment during which he thought perhaps he could at least indicate his intentions and receive some hint of her response. As they waited in the sitting room for the hall to be clear of guests waiting for their vehicles, Julian reminded Josie that he would be back at Pemberley for Christmas. "I hope we can meet again, soon," he said, trying to keep the conversation light.

Josie smiled, but she was clearly not concentrating. "Oh yes, indeed," she said, but then added, "I do wish I could go to London and work there. All Papa's friends say it is where you have to be if you want to get anything into the big metropolitan papers. Mr Drummond, that's him over there with the big moustache, who has shares in the newspapers in Manchester and London, laughed when I told him I wanted to write for the metropolitan press. 'What would you write, my dear?' he said," and Josie mimicked his gruff throaty voice, "'they don't print recipes for jam or fairy stories, you know.' Recipes for jam indeed, hateful man!" She was furious and so was Julian, though he could see the funny side of it, but did not dare let her know.

"Have no fear, Josie. One of these days, Mr Drummond will have to eat his words when one of your pieces appears in *The Times*!"

"Oh, I do hope so, Julian. I would give anything to live and work in London," she said wistfully. "There is something interesting happening in London all the time. There would be hundreds of things to write about."

Julian agreed, but before he could say anything more, he was called out into the hall. The carriage from Pemberley was at the door. It was time to leave. He smiled and kissed her hand and had to race out and into his carriage to escape the gusts of wind and rain that had started to blow in from the north. The last he saw of Josie was her unhappy face through a rain-swept window. It had not been a very satisfactory evening.

Later that night, Josie wrote in her diary:

I wonder what brought Julian Darcy here this evening. I felt he had come with something particular on his mind. Perhaps he wanted to talk about my piece on the mine disaster; I do not know. He did not expect to see all Papa's business friends here, that was quite obvious. He was most discomfited. We spoke very little to each other all evening, except right at the end, when I told him about horrid Mr Drummond telling me the London dailies don't print recipes and fairy stories. Beastly, insufferable man. Julian was about to laugh, I know he was, but he saw my face and thought better of it. He promised that one day Mr D would eat his words! I would like that more than anything.

I do wish I knew what it was Julian came for. Perhaps I should not have chattered on so and he might have told me. It is very vexing indeed not to know, but there it is, there's nothing I can do about it now. I shall have to wait until Christmas to find out.

A postscript was added on the following day:

Mama is convinced that Julian Darcy came last evening either to propose to me or to see Papa and ask his permission to do so!

Mama must be dreaming. Julian, propose to me? Me, Mistress of Pemberley? Hardly! I told Mama that Julian had never given any indication that he was in the least interested in me in a romantic sort of way. He has been friendly and fun to dance with and talk to, and he was kind enough to say nice things about my writing, but no romance. I know he is passionate about science and talks incessantly about the need for more people to use scientific methods in agriculture. Boring? Maybe, maybe not. But definitely not romantic!

A few days later, Cassandra received a letter from her brother, confessing that he had failed miserably in the task she had set him:

My dear Cassy,

You will be ashamed of me, I am sure, but there was nothing I could do. Having left you, I returned home and, as soon as I was able, presented myself, suitably attired, to ask Josie if she would marry me prior to applying to her father for his blessing.

Alas, absolutely nothing was accomplished. Why, you ask? Well, I arrived, to discover the house bursting at the seams with the gentlemen who own and manage the provincial newspapers—Mr Tate's business associates.

Both Mr and Mrs Tate made me most welcome and, despite my protestations, insisted that I stay to dinner; but, sadly, there were acres of table between me and Josie. At no time did we get more than a few minutes together, and never were we alone.

Just as I was preparing to leave, I did get a few minutes with her, but all she wanted was to chatter on about her ambition to live and work in London. I cannot believe that a single thought of being married to me and living at Pemberley has ever entered her head.

I am pinning my hopes on the Christmas festivities at Pemberley, which I know the Tates will attend. I shall have to try again then.

I need not ask you, I know, even as I do, to keep this matter to yourself. I would not wish to trouble Mama until there is something worth telling.

Thank you again, my dear sister, and God bless you.

Your loving brother,

Julian.

Christmas brought more disappointment for young Mr Darcy. Having settled on courting Miss Tate during the festive season when they would surely meet frequently, he was devastated to find that Josie was compelled to spend most of the time between Christmas day and the New Year in bed with an appalling attack of quinsy, which her mother declared had caused the poor girl's throat to become so sore and painful she could not speak, and was permitted to eat nothing but soft jellies and junket.

Twice, Julian called, once with his mother, but on neither occasion were they able to see the patient, who was said to be asleep. They left flowers and fruit and two books, which Julian had bought for her in Cambridge, in one of which he had inscribed what he hoped was an affectionate message, wishing her a speedy recovery.

Early in the New Year, when he had almost given up hope of seeing her at all, a note arrived from Josie.

Dear Julian, she wrote:

I do apologise for not writing earlier to thank you and Mrs Darcy for the kind gifts you brought me when I was ill. The flowers cheered up my sickroom very well. I am sorry I was too sick to see you on both occasions.

Thank you most of all for the charming collection of vignettes; they have kept me entertained while I struggled to recover from this vile affliction.

Thank you also for The Pickwick Papers, *exactly what I needed at this time. I do so love Mr. Dickens. How does he conjure up all those delightful characters?*

Your kind inscription was much appreciated too. I awoke this morning feeling very much better and the sun is out as well. Mama and Dr Gardiner have both declared that I am now fit to see and be seen, so if you are still free to call, I shall be most happy to see you.

Yours very sincerely,

Josie Tate.

Julian could not recall when he had last been quite so excited at the prospect of seeing anyone, much less a young woman he had known all his life. He was dressed and out of the house so swiftly, there was barely enough time to tell his mother where he was going.

When he reached the Tates' place, he was most gratified to find no other carriages or horses in sight and hoped fervently that this meant there were no other visitors within. The servant who opened the door left him sitting in the parlour until Mrs Tate could be found, and only then was he taken upstairs to an informal sitting room, where Josie sat in front of a welcoming fire. The weather outside was quite cold, despite the sun being out, but the room was comfortably warm.

Apologising for not bringing more flowers because he had come as soon as he had received her note, he was soon reassured that no apologies were called for. Josie declared she was very glad of his company after what had been, for her, an exceedingly dull festive season.

Looking pale, but claiming to be feeling much better, she urged him to give her all the news. "Do tell me what exciting things have been happening in London."

Poor Julian, having come directly from Cambridge and spent most of the last three weeks in Derbyshire, had very little news from London. He did, however, have news of her aunt Amelia-Jane and her husband Jonathan Bingley, who had recently moved to their new residence at Rosings Park in Kent, where Jonathan—who had retired from the House of Commons—had been entrusted by Lady Catherine de Bourgh with the management of her estate. Julian had called on them before returning to Pemberley at Christmas. "I could not believe how much formality was maintained, even in the absence of Her Ladyship, who has moved with her invalid daughter to live out her retirement in Bath. Everyone carries on as if she were still in residence!" he declared, and Josie, who had always found the stiffness of Rosings rather ridiculous, was most amused.

"It is no wonder that my grandmother prefers to live at Longbourn. She must have grown tired of all that bowing and scraping," she said, and Julian agreed. He had heard his mother speak of the patience with which her friend Charlotte Collins had borne the interference of Lady Catherine over many years. While Elizabeth had found it diverting to relate, she knew it would have been intolerable to live with.

Having exhausted that topic, they returned to the books, which Josie said again and again had brought her so much cheer and comfort when she was ill. Julian offered to read to her, and she was especially fascinated by his ability to render the Dickensian prose to perfection. They talked more of books and travel, especially of places to visit in Europe—where he had been the previous year and she was very keen to see—and the hours passed so agreeably that they hardly noticed the time.

When Julian decided it was time to leave, fearing that Josie was getting overtired, she begged him to return soon. It was a promise he had no difficulty making and one he would keep with pleasure.

After a fortnight, during which Julian visited Josie almost every day and found that on each successive occasion, his enjoyment of her company increased upon the last; he felt sufficiently emboldened to bring up the matter that had lain hidden in his heart. Having decided upon a course of action, he arrived at the house on an unusually mild morning to find that Josie had come downstairs and was dressed as if to go out.

Since she had not mentioned any such plan, he took his cue from her attire and asked if she felt strong enough to take a ride in his carriage, seeing it was a fine morning. She declared that she was but had to be wrapped up warmly before she was permitted to leave the house, with Mrs Tate urging care and caution at every turn. When at last they drove away, Josie was delighted. "I have not been out of the house since Christmas; this is exactly what I needed above anything."

They drove on until they reached the outskirts of the town and turned down a lane that led to a piece of woodland on the edge of the Pemberley estate. Josie, encouraged by the mild weather, decided she wanted to get out and walk.

Julian was not sure this was a good idea, but Josie insisted. They alighted and walked but a short while, but it became clear that she was in no state to persevere far on foot. On a piece of rising ground, sheltered by an old yew tree, stood a gazebo, which had been specially designed for Lady Anne Darcy. "My grandmother used to come up here to enjoy the view across the river and read poetry. She used to write poetry, as well; Papa says there is a collection of her notebooks in the library at Pemberley," said Julian as he helped Josie up the path and into the mock classical edifice.

Josie did not need to be persuaded that she ought to rest awhile. Gratefully, she accepted his arm as he supported her, and as he did, Julian had decided that he had to speak now, as another such opportunity might never present itself.

Her face was flushed with the exercise, but her gloved hands were still cold. Julian kept hold of them as she sat down on the old stone seat and spoke simply but with great sincerity. "Josie, if you have not already guessed, then you must let me tell you how dear you are to me and how very happy you will make me if you consent to marry me. Dearest Josie, will you, please?"

Her face, small and rather pale from being ill, became suffused with a blush as she gazed at him wide-eyed, plainly astonished by his words. Quite clearly, she had had no expectation of his proposal and took a few minutes to respond. "Julian, I did not know—no, I must not pretend; I did know you were fond of me. I knew you were my friend, but to marry me?" She seemed genuinely perplexed.

"Of course, why not?" he asked, equally confused by her response. "Is it such a preposterous suggestion?"

She shook her head, keen not to hurt his feelings. "No, of course not, but can you see me as the Mistress of Pemberley?"

"Josie, why ever not?" He was outraged. "In any event, that would be years and years away; my father is perfectly fit and well. I would not inherit Pemberley for many years. You would just be my wife, plain Mrs Julian Darcy," he said, adding with a degree of apprehension, "Josie, do you not like Pemberley?"

"Of course, I do," she said, knowing how much Pemberley meant to him. "It is a splendid place—how could anyone think otherwise? But Julian, that is not the point. I am grateful indeed and honoured by your proposal, but there are so many other things I want to do; I want to write, as you know, and be published by a serious publisher; to do that I must go to London. I cannot spend the rest of my days here and then feel that I had never made a real effort to achieve anything."

Julian asked gravely, "Josie, are you saying that you cannot, could not ever, love me enough to marry me?"

Her eyes filled with tears. "Oh, Julian, that is not what I am saying at all. Of course I could love you and marry you, but can you not see that I will never be happy just being your wife, being Mistress of Pemberley one day, if I have achieved nothing in my own right? I would probably regret it for the rest of my life, and that would certainly make us both miserable. It isn't that I cannot love you—indeed, I am sure I already love you," she said, and as she spoke, her words tumbling out spontaneously, Julian was overwhelmed by a strange confusion of feelings.

What did she mean? Was she rejecting him, while saying she loved him?

When he spoke, his voice was anxious and uncertain. "Josie, then, you are not rejecting me altogether?"

She was contrite. "Dear Julian, you do not deserve this. I must be totally honest with you. I would love to be your wife. I am sure we will be happy together, but I need some time to be myself first. Will you let me have that time?"

"Of course, Josie, my dear, you can have all the time you want. I still have a year at Cambridge to complete. If your father agrees, we could be engaged and wait a year before we..."

She interrupted gently, "No, Julian, we cannot become engaged now— that will involve us in all the fuss that goes with it, and then my mother will never permit me to go to London. I must be free to write, and I won't be if we are engaged. But, I will make you a promise that at the end of a year, if we both feel the same as we do now, then yes, we shall become engaged."

Her smile belied the seriousness of her words and gave him cause for hope. When she had finished, he took her hands in his and said very simply, "I love you, Josie. Of course you can be free to do whatever you choose. I want you to succeed, too, and I shall do all I can to help."

Suddenly, impulsively, she leaned forward to kiss him, after which neither seemed to have any doubts about their feelings. Presently, she pulled away and, settling herself down, said, "There, do you believe me, now?"

He nodded, still holding her hand. "May I ask your father's permission?" Julian, conscious of his duty, was anxious to do the right thing.

At first she said no, pointing out that it would make her mother unduly concerned and might prevent her going to London.

"I have a plan to go to London and stay with my Aunt Beatrice, Papa's elder sister, who has a great old house near Regent's Park. I know she lets rooms to ladies, and I think I could work comfortably there. I shall ask father's permission to go as soon as I am recovered from this wretched illness and can travel."

Julian was firm. "Josie, dearest, let us not leap too far ahead. You must fully recover your health before going to London. Before I return to Cambridge, I must write in confidence to your father, asking only that I be permitted to visit you in London, at your aunt's house. There is no harm in that; indeed, it may make it easier for him to permit you to go to London knowing that you could call on me in any emergency," he argued.

Finally, she was persuaded to agree. "And in the meantime, I promise that I will not accept the advances of any other man," she said with a smile.

"That would make me prodigiously happy," he replied, a big, happy smile breaking out and transforming his serious countenance. "And a year later, I confidently predict, we shall announce our engagement to the world!" he declared, like a man who found a treasure but must keep it hidden for a while.

So overcome were they with their mutual happiness that they embraced one another warmly and promised that they would not only keep faith with each other but would write every possible day when they were apart, if not more often. These and other predictable promises being made, they returned to the carriage.

When they arrived at the house, after being longer away than they had anticipated, it was fortunate for both of them and their plan for secrecy that Mrs Tate had gone out. She had left a message that if Julian could come to dinner on the Saturday, he would be very welcome. The invitation was accepted with alacrity, of course. But Saturday was two whole days away; it was unthinkable that he could stay away that long. He would surely return tomorrow with another of Josie's favourite books.

The presence of the servants and their natural discretion held them apart as they said farewell, but neither could hide their joy. They had known one another since childhood, but had grown up as neighbours and friends do, with plenty of good fun and companionship and very little thought of romance. The discovery of their mutual affection and hope of future felicity had kindled feelings of uncommon delight that could not easily be hidden from any but the most disinterested or unobservant of persons.

As soon as Julian had gone, Josie escaped to the privacy of her bedroom to give her time to settle her thoughts and dwell upon the events of the morning undisturbed, while Julian went home to compose what he believed must surely be the most important letter he would ever write. Before returning to Cambridge, he went again to see his sister. He could not bear the burden of his happiness alone he said, and since she had been his confidante and counsellor, he felt he owed it to her to tell her everything.

That Josie had not merely accepted his love but confessed to hers and agreed that they would become engaged within a year had left him ecstatic. He had more good tidings to convey; he had written to Mr Anthony Tate, of whom he had always been in some awe, only to find him a most amiable gentleman.

"I was concerned because Josie had insisted that the entire matter be dealt with confidentially, which took some explaining. But he invited me to join him at his club, where he was most hospitable, and once we had spoken, he said he understood Josie's wish to go to London and confessed—just as I had predicted he would—that it would set his mind at rest to know I was around to protect her, as it were," Julian explained. "I do not believe that Josie really knew how much her father supported her in her ambition to be a writer."

Julian had obviously changed his mind about Mr Tate. "As for matters of trust, once I had made my own feelings and intentions clear, he assured me that he had no doubt that a son of Mr Darcy would be a gentleman of absolute integrity, to whom he could entrust his daughter with confidence. I was very honoured, Cassy."

"Of course you were, but it was no more than the truth," said his sister.

"We are indeed fortunate that both our parents are held in such esteem. Papa is without doubt the most widely respected person in the county, and there is no one I know who will raise a word of criticism against Mama."

Cassy had some happy childhood memories of her grandfather, Mr Bennet, visiting them at Pemberley and reading to her, but her recollections of Mrs Bennet were few and far between, while Julian had known none of his grandparents, being born after they had all passed away. Fortunately, neither of them had ever been encumbered with the memory of Mr and Mrs Bennet's unsuitable and frequently ludicrous marriage, which had for many years embarrassed and saddened their elder daughters.

Elizabeth and Darcy had been not merely the most loving of parents, but a matchless example of marital felicity.

Cassandra was delighted for her young brother. Seeing how the last few weeks had changed and lightened his rather serious demeanour, she was glad she had advised him as she had done.

Julian thanked his sister and begged her to keep his secret, lest any revelation of their situation should upset Josie's plans. "Should that occur, she will not forgive me," he warned.

"You can depend upon me, Julian, except I cannot keep a secret from Richard, so he will have to know. He is, however, so wedded to notions of ethics and privacy that you may rest assured your secret will be completely safe with him," she said.

Having said his farewells, Julian left for Cambridge still wrapped in a cloud of bliss, believing that he had successfully kept his present state of happiness and the reasons for it from his parents. He told Josie confidently that their secret was quite safe.

He was unaware that Elizabeth and Darcy had both noticed the change in their son and correctly attributed it to his being in love. As to the identity of the lady concerned, a simple process of elimination would have sufficed—but even this was not necessary, for it soon became apparent that Julian's interest in Josie Tate had been observed and was generally known around Matlock, and it was likely to become common knowledge on the Pemberley estate, as well.

Returning from a visit to the Fitzwilliams', Elizabeth waited only until they were upstairs and free of the servants before saying to her husband,

"Caroline asked about Julian and Josie; she had seen them together in Matlock shortly before he returned to Cambridge. She claims that they were so engrossed in each other that they did not see her as she drove past in her curricle. Needless to say, Caroline is quite convinced that they are in love."

Darcy, who had started to smile as she began her story, laughed as she completed it and added his own chapter to the narrative. "If that is her conviction, she is probably quite right, Lizzie. There are few people whose diagnosis of that condition I would trust more than the Fitzwilliams'. They both possess such excellent credentials; two more incorrigible romantics would be hard to find," he declared. "Indeed, I had hardly been five minutes with Fitzwilliam when he informed me, with the greatest delight, that while he was aware we had to be discreet, it was widely known that Julian was engaged to Miss Tate, and congratulations were in order."

Elizabeth, who had been mildly irritated by her cousin Caroline's tale, was astonished by Darcy's revelation. "What did you say?" she asked.

He merely shrugged his shoulders and said, "What could I say? I muttered something about young people not being very discreet, and he just carried on as if it was all a fait accompli—as far as they are concerned, Julian and Josie are as good as engaged."

Elizabeth realised there was little more he could have done.

"What did you say to Caroline?" Darcy asked, curious to know how she had dealt with the situation.

Elizabeth's voice was serious. "I urged her not to share her thoughts with her general acquaintance, since neither you nor I had been informed of any engagement. I counselled caution in jumping to conclusions because the pair have been friends since childhood, and there may be no more to it than casual affection. Caroline was suitably impressed I think, because she agreed that it would not be fair to either of them if an impression was put about, which if it were to be proved false, could place both their reputations in jeopardy."

Darcy chuckled. "Poor Caroline, she will probably suffer a severe bout of guilt. Now you have terrified her," he said, but his wife was not at all contrite.

"That was my purpose exactly," she declared. "I had no intention whatsoever of revealing Julian's secrets or permitting anyone, however close to us, to know that we are as ignorant of his plans as they are."

Hearing the regret, however slight, in her voice and knowing the depth of her affection for their son, Darcy rose and went to her, as she stood looking out of the window. "Have you been upset, Lizzie?" he asked gently.

She shook her head but did not look at him as she said, "No, but it would have been nice to hear it from him. I am sure there is an excellent reason why he was unable to tell us at this stage; perhaps it is not settled between them. But I wish he had given us some hint of his intentions."

Darcy knew she had been hurt. He had not been deceived by her jesting tone. She had not been able to keep the feeling out of her voice. He knew she would soon recover her spirits and be herself again, but while he said nothing more, he had already determined to see their daughter Cassandra and attempt to discover whether she knew anything that would help Elizabeth understand Julian's situation more clearly.

Meanwhile, Julian and Josie kept their promise to write often and thereby contributed regularly to the revenue of the Post Office. While their correspondence caused no problems for Julian at his college, Josie had set up an elaborate scheme involving the cooperation of the young parlour maid in order that her mother remain in ignorance.

One morning, when she was practising upon her pianoforte, the maid brought in a letter from Julian, followed not long after by Mrs Tate bearing another.

"I think it's from your Aunt Beatrice, Josie. I cannot think what she wants."

Josie, who had hastily tucked Julian's letter into her pocket, opened up the one from her aunt. To her surprise, it was an invitation to her niece to spend a few weeks in London at the beginning of the Spring season.

Josie had no idea how this had come about, but it was so fortuitous that she exclaimed with pleasure and turned immediately to ask her mother's permission. Mrs Tate was completely taken aback, but knowing her sister-in-law well, she could raise no objection. "You must ask your father, Josie, and if he agrees, I dare say it should be all right. Your Aunt Beatrice must be in need of company."

Josie had little doubt that her father would agree—indeed, the longer she thought about it the more she became convinced that he had probably arranged it all. When he returned and she faced him with the letter in her hand, he did confess that he had approached his sister on her behalf.

"Because, my dear, I thought you deserved to get away and enjoy yourself, having been so ill at Christmas and missing all the fun," he said as she hugged him and thanked him for his kindness.

Her father looked rather more serious, however, and said, "Josie, I have informed your Aunt Beatrice that Mr Julian Darcy has my permission to call on you at her house and escort you to places you may wish to visit; I had in mind the theatre, balls, and such like; but you will be sensible, will you not, my dear, and not do anything that may cause your aunt consternation. Remember, you are her guest. I am quite confident that Julian Darcy's behaviour will be correct in every way. He seems a very proper young man."

Proud of the confidence her father had expressed in them, Josie promised to be absolutely discreet and sensible. He then reminded her that she should acquaint her mother with the circumstances of her agreement with Julian Darcy. "I would not like your mama to hear from Aunt Beatrice or anyone else some gossip that may cause her anxiety, or worse, reflect badly upon young Darcy. He has made his intentions very clear to me, but I think you ought to tell your mother that it is your wish that an engagement be postponed for a while," he said, adding with a smile, "perhaps you could find some time to confide in her before you go to London. It will hurt her deeply to discover that you have not been honest with her."

Josie agreed, and later that day, finding her mother alone in the sitting room upstairs, she decided to break the news to her as gently as possible. Initially it seemed as if Mrs Tate had not heard her correctly, so indifferent did she seem. But then, as the significance of what Josie had said dawned upon her, she became quite excited. "Josie, do you mean to tell me that Mr Julian Darcy has proposed to you and you have said not a word to me for all of this time?"

When Josie did not answer, her mother, taking her silence to mean she was right, went on, "And am I to understand that you have rejected his offer without speaking to me or to your father?" She was incredulous.

Josie tried to explain. "No, Mama, I have not rejected him; I have only asked that we wait a year before we get engaged."

Rebecca Tate was outraged. "My dear child, are you out of your mind? Have you not realised who this young man is? He is the heir to the Pemberley Estate and all that implies!"

Josie protested that she was well aware of that, and in any event, that would have had no bearing on her decision, anyway. "Mama, if I did not love Julian, the size of his father's estate and the status of his family would never persuade me to marry him; but, indeed, I do love him, and he has agreed to wait," she explained. "What's more, Papa has agreed as well."

"Do you mean to say your father is a party to this extraordinary arrangement?" Mrs Tate asked, unable to believe that her usually sensible husband could have agreed to such a plan.

"Well, you can ask him yourself. Julian has spoken with him, and Papa is agreeable."

Mrs Tate was not convinced. "And what if young Mr Darcy changes his mind in the course of the year?" she asked, revealing her real fears.

Josie was unmoved; she just shrugged her shoulders and said, "Should he change his mind, I shall have been spared the humiliation of an unfortunate marriage. But, knowing him as I do, I cannot believe that is likely to happen, so do not upset yourself, Mama. He has said he loves me and wants to marry me. He is quite prepared to wait a year."

Her mother's outrage continued unabated. She regarded Josie's behaviour as capricious and foolhardy; it was not every day that the son of the county's most distinguished family proposed to one's daughter. She felt Josie had slighted the most eligible young man she was ever likely to meet. It took all her husband's powers of persuasion to reassure her that Josie was not squandering an excellent opportunity to secure her future. Only a verbatim report of his conversation with young Mr Darcy would allay her fears.

Later that night, Josie wrote to Julian informing him of her plans and promising to advise him very soon of the date of her arrival in London.

Meanwhile, Cassandra had an unexpected visit from her father, who claimed he was on his way to Bakewell and had called in to see her. As it happened, Richard was away at the hospital in Matlock, where he was demonstrating the efficacy of his hospital sanitation procedures to a group of surgeons visiting from Scotland.

Darcy appeared not to be put out by his absence, taking the opportunity to ask Cassandra how much she knew of her brother's feelings for Miss Josie

Tate and to tell her of her mother's distress at being kept in ignorance of his intentions. "It is not that she has set her mind against Josie; indeed, she is very fond of her, as I am. But she is hurt by the fact that everyone in the district seems to know more about her son's romance than she does," he said gravely.

Cassandra was truly shocked and grieved by her father's revelations. "Papa, I had no idea. Julian made me promise to keep it a secret until they were ready to announce it. He was concerned that Mama should not have the aggravation of these matters being talked of before they were quite settled. At the time he left for Cambridge, there would not have been more than two or three persons other than themselves who knew. Oh, poor Julian and poor Mama; I should have known better, I should have warned him that it would not be long before their secret became widely known. It is the kind of thing everyone wants to gossip about. I feel it is my fault. Julian will be most unhappy to think he has, however unwittingly, upset Mama."

Mr Darcy tried to reassure her. "You must not blame yourself, Cassy. Indeed, no one is to blame. There is no doubt some very good reason for all this secrecy."

"Whatever the reason," said Cassandra, "it is not worth making Mama miserable. I shall write to Julian today, by express, and I will suggest that he write to Mama at once, telling her exactly how things are between him and Josie."

Darcy was pleased. He had been certain that Cassandra, kind, loving, and responsible, would know what to do. Her affectionate relationship with her brother made it easier. There was just one more thing he wanted to ask. "Cassy, do you know if he has spoken to her father yet? Does Anthony Tate know?"

Cassy knew she had to tell him the truth. "Yes, I do believe they have spoken, and Papa, I know that Mr Tate has been extremely complimentary. Julian was very gratified, indeed."

Darcy prepared to leave, having learnt enough to set his own mind at ease and knowing that Cassy would write to her brother.

She urged him not to be anxious. "Papa, as soon as I have news from Julian or, indeed, from Josie, I shall send you word," she promised, and her father, grateful for her loyalty and good sense, thanked her and went on his way.

So troubled was Cassandra by what her father had told her, she wasted no time at all before writing to her brother. Surprisingly, she did not wait to consult Richard, so certain was she of what had to be done. Indeed, she could not bear to be in any way responsible for causing her mother such grief, even though she was not directly to blame.

Writing to Julian, she begged him:

> *Write directly to Mama and tell her of the nature of your understanding with Josie and her father. You need have no fear of their disapproval, for Papa assures me that they are both very fond of Josie. It is the unfortunate fact that the matter has unhappily become common talk, while they have been left in ignorance that has hurt their feelings.*
>
> *You could and should put all this to right with a single letter. I know that Josie was not very keen for it to be widely known too early, but I am sure she will understand that, whatever her reservations, Mama's feelings must be assuaged as soon as possible.*
>
> *Dear Julian, I know you will feel the same and act accordingly.*

When Richard returned home, she told him the day's news and was surprised that he expressed no great astonishment. Indeed, he completely endorsed her actions. She asked him if she had been too precipitate; could Julian feel she had no right to ask him to do one thing or another? But, he was entirely in agreement with her.

"No, my dearest, you have done exactly the right thing. I never did think all this secrecy was necessary, anyway, but since it was what they wanted, I know you had to respect their wishes. However, in these matters, it is far preferable to be open and direct rather than employ subterfuge and secrecy; they generally lead to confusion and create situations one cannot control. No doubt the servants of the Tate household, who would have had more than an inkling of the progress of this romance, have been gossiping in the village," he said, smiling.

Cassy nodded, her face grave. "Indeed, you are probably right. I believe Mrs Tate's housekeeper has two daughters employed as housemaids at Pemberley. It is also possible that Mrs Tate has been unable to resist the temptation to boast of her daughter's prospects of becoming the Mistress of

Pemberley at some future date to some of her friends. Whichever it was, it has caused poor Mama some grief. I feel I should have advised my brother to be more open with my parents."

Her husband laughed and put a comforting arm around her, reassuring her that she was not in any way responsible for her parents' distress. "You have done your part, Cassy. Your parents know you too well to lay any blame upon you. I agree with your father; there is no need to apportion blame, only to ensure the damage is undone quickly and the hurt will soon heal," he said. "Josie is an intelligent and agreeable young woman. I have no doubt this minor lapse will soon be forgotten."

He was confident everything would turn out well. Cassy was comforted, as she always was, by his strength and sound common sense.

One morning, not more than a week after Cassandra had written to her brother, Darcy and Elizabeth were discussing plans to travel to Ashford Park to join the Bingleys, who were celebrating the engagement of their daughter Louisa to Matthew Ward, when their conversation was interrupted by the arrival of an express addressed to Elizabeth. She recognised the hand immediately. "It's from Julian," she said, smiling, and Darcy knew even before she opened it that Cassandra had done as she had promised she would.

Opening the letter, Elizabeth ran her eyes over it very quickly, as she was wont to do, and, smiling happily, began to read it to her husband.

"He writes from Cambridge:

Dearest Mama,

Let me first apologise for the lateness of this letter and the delay in giving you the news it contains. However, since it is pleasant news, I hope there is no harm done.

I should have written you directly, but on arriving in Cambridge, I found my friend and colleague, Daniel Pearce, very sick with a fever he picked up in Africa. He is a good deal better now, but is still weak and needs medication and care.

However, I now have some time to myself and am writing to give you and Papa an important piece of personal news. I do not believe that you are going to be very surprised by what I have to say, as I am sure you have already anticipated my feelings in this matter.

Mama, the news is that I have, with her father's blessing, asked Miss Josie Tate to marry me. I have loved her for several months now and felt it was time to present my credentials, lest I be outwitted by some more assertive suitor.

Josie, who is keen to pursue a career as a writer—not a novelist, but a writer of serious prose—was at first reluctant to agree to an early engagement. She has now consented, and we are to be engaged soon—within a few months, at any rate.

Her father, whom I saw before I left Derbyshire for Cambridge, was exceedingly kind and complimentary, and has given me permission to call on Josie when she is in London with her Aunt Beatrice.

Josie assures me that Mrs Tate, whom she has informed, is very pleased, too, which is good also.

Mama, I would have told you all of this sooner, but for two reasons: The first being Josie's desire to keep it secret until she had obtained her mother's permission to come up to London, and the second, for which I sincerely hope you will forgive me, being my earnest desire to arrange my affairs in my own right, rather than as the heir to the Pemberley Estate.

Pray do not misunderstand me. I have nothing but pride in my heritage and love Pemberley, as you well know, but there are times when one needs must stand on one's own, and I felt this was just such an occasion.

Now that Josie has permission to come up to London, I am able to tell you about it, as I always wished to do. If this delay has in any way embarrassed you or hurt your feelings, I do apologise with all my heart. Mama, I know that on receiving this you will want to call on Josie. Please remember she is very young and is very much in awe of you and Papa. She may be nervous, and I hope you will overlook any awkwardness on her part. I do love her very much.

I look forward to our being together when I come down for the mid-Summer break.

Your loving son,

Julian.

Elizabeth's pleasure at receiving Julian's letter was so great it could not be easily contained. Nothing would satisfy her but that she go directly to call on Josie Tate and her parents. She felt she had to acknowledge her son's decision and demonstrate her acceptance of Josie as his choice.

"I cannot have Josie believing that we disapprove of Julian's choice for some unexplained reason, which can ultimately be based only upon prejudice," she said and, recalling Lady Catherine de Bourgh's discourteous and pompous visit to Longbourn all those years ago, Elizabeth was particular not to present herself in like manner to the Tates.

Thus, while the best carriage was being made ready for the journey to Ashford Park, Elizabeth drove over in a smaller vehicle, hoping to find at least Rebecca and Josie at home.

On arriving at the house, she was disappointed to hear that Mr and Mrs Tate were both gone to Derby and were likely to be away all day.

She was about to ask if Miss Josie Tate was at home when young Josie, having seen Mrs Darcy arrive, came running downstairs to greet her as she stood in the hall. "Mrs Darcy!" she exclaimed, in some confusion at having to entertain her future mother-in-law with no notice at all.

Not standing upon ceremony and conscious of the awkwardness of Josie's situation, Elizabeth went to her directly and greeted her with warmth and affection. "My dear Josie, I apologise for arriving without warning, but I was hoping to see your parents. I am sorry to have missed them, but I am very happy to find you at home."

Seeing Josie's apprehensive expression, she moved swiftly to reassure her and kissed her on the cheek before following her into the parlour. Josie invited Elizabeth to be seated and ordered tea, which they took beside a window that offered a view of the rose garden in bloom, which drew immediate admiration from Elizabeth.

"The rose garden was almost entirely my dear grandmother's work," Josie explained, and Elizabeth remembered that Anthony Tate's mother, Therese, had been famous for her prize-winning roses as well as her excellent management of his newspapers until her death a few years ago.

As they talked, Josie seemed more at ease. Elizabeth recalled vividly the indignation she had felt after Lady Catherine's visit to Longbourn, when she had criticised the room and ungraciously refused any refreshment before proceeding to quiz her about Mr Darcy. He had subsequently apologised for his aunt's discourteous conduct. Elizabeth had no desire to subject young

Josie to a similar ordeal. Her tone was gentle as she said, "Josie, I have only today received a letter from Julian informing us of your secret engagement, and I have come to tell you how very happy we are—Mr Darcy and I—for both of you."

Josie's expression changed in an instant to one of delight as a smile transformed her anxious expression. She had feared that the arrival of Mrs Darcy might have meant an inquisitorial interview. Nothing was further from the truth.

Writing later to Julian, she described the encounter:

My dearest Julian,

I was, this morning, sitting at my bedroom window looking out over the park when, to my great surprise, a carriage drew up and your dear mother alighted.

I was not merely surprised that she had condescended to call on me, but also at how cordial and kind she was. No, indeed, she was truly affectionate—cordial is too cold a word for the warmth and sincerity of her words and manner. Having only met Mrs Darcy along with others in my family before today, I was naturally a little apprehensive, especially since with Papa and Mama away, I had to entertain her myself.

Your mother is so elegant and handsome that I have always been in awe of her, but it seems I was needlessly anxious, for she was friendliness itself.

And so she proceeded for another two pages or more.

Elizabeth, having reassured her future daughter-in-law, left asking that her compliments be conveyed to Mr and Mrs Tate. She promised that, on Julian's return, they would all dine together at Pemberley.

There was just one thing she had asked Josie to consider. "Josie, my dear, if you are going to be staying in London for any length of time, and if you and Julian intend to meet and be seen around town, would it not be more seemly if you became formally engaged? While a secret engagement is undoubtedly romantic, there is sound common sense in the argument that a clear indication of your intentions will protect you from malicious gossip."

It was an argument whose validity Josie could not deny.

Later that day, as they journeyed at a leisurely pace to Ashford Park, Elizabeth told Darcy of her meeting with Josie, and the parallel with Lady Catherine de Bourgh's visit to Longbourn was irresistible. Though it had happened many years ago, it had remained a matter of much hilarity in their close circle of family and friends. Elizabeth had been often urged to provide a dramatic recital of the encounter between herself and Lady Catherine, and, having ascertained that her husband would not be offended, she would occasionally oblige.

Darcy had decided that on this occasion, she would be teased. "And Lizzie, do you think young Miss Tate was as puzzled by your arrival as you were by the appearance of Lady Catherine at Longbourn?" he asked so casually that she did not immediately suspect his intention.

"No, indeed," she answered. "She may have been slightly nervous, perhaps, but I believe she coped very well; if she was daunted, she did not show it, and it was certainly not my intention to alarm or intimidate her."

"As my aunt was trying to do to you?" he remarked lightly.

Catching the mischief in his tone, she retorted, "Oh, please, you are surely not suggesting that I was trying to browbeat young Josie? I have neither the desire nor the inclination to do such a thing."

She sounded quite put out; he relented and, smiling broadly, let her see that he was teasing her, when he said, "No more than I would suggest that Miss Tate would allow herself to be put upon. She appears to be a sensible young woman with a mind of her own, well able to look after herself, even at nineteen. Not unlike another woman of my acquaintance, who is the only person I know undaunted by Lady Catherine's sense of self-importance, who was able to tell her to mind her own business!"

This time they both laughed, enjoying the memory, before acknowledging that they did owe some of their happiness to Lady Catherine's interference. "Indeed, had she not driven directly to London, in high dudgeon, to confront me with your defiance, I may never have realised there was still hope for me," he said, reaching for her hand. "Dear Lizzie, I had not dreamed that I would ever be grateful to my aunt for any measure of my happiness."

"Nor I," said his wife. "When I first made her acquaintance at Rosings, it was the very last thing I would have anticipated; but, if the truth were told, she has contributed, however unwittingly, quite significantly to it."

This was sufficient to start them talking of times past—of the difficult and sad times, the many good times they had known and how their lives had changed over the years. It was a favourite pastime and kept them occupied until the carriage took the fork in the road to Ashford Park.

Jane and Charles Bingley remained, along with the Gardiners, their most favourite companions. The two sisters were as close as ever, and between Darcy and Charles there was a strong friendship based upon trust and regard, nurtured over many years. There was no place they visited with greater pleasure.

That evening, the family gathered for a celebratory dinner party on the occasion of the engagement of Louisa Bingley to Doctor Matthew Ward. A bigger function had at first been planned, but then had been abandoned upon the untimely death of Mr Ward's mother a month ago. Indeed, Louisa had asked him if he would prefer to postpone the engagement, but the bereft young man had said no, whereupon the Bingleys, with their usual good taste and discretion, suggested a modest family gathering. Not wishing to disappoint his daughter, her father had said, "You shall have a ball later, Louisa, before your wedding in the Spring."

But Louisa, who resembled her mother more in her nature than in looks, had replied gently, "Papa, it matters little to me if we have a ball or not. I am most anxious to ensure that Matthew and his father are made really welcome in our family. They both miss Mrs Ward terribly."

It was generally agreed that this could be best achieved at an intimate dinner party for their closest friends and family. On hearing this piece of information, Elizabeth had remarked that young women appeared to be growing more sensible by the day. The Bingley girls, like Josie Tate and Caroline Fitzwilliam's daughter, Amy, were a far cry from the feckless, silly creatures who had been the bane of Meryton society when they were growing up. Memories of the youthful follies of their own younger sisters, Kitty and Lydia, were quickly dispatched with a shudder as being too painful to contemplate.

After most of the guests had departed, Darcy and Bingley retired to the games room to renew their interest in a frame of billiards and discuss the current political situation, while Jane and Elizabeth went upstairs to enjoy a cup of tea together. It was their favourite way to end a long day.

Both sisters had plenty to talk about. Jane had good and bad news to give. Sophie was expecting her first child, and Amelia-Jane was soon to be delivered of her fourth. Elizabeth noted with a smile that nothing seemed to please her dear sister more than new additions to her growing family! "They are all such sweet, good children, for the most part, Lizzie," Jane declared, but Elizabeth was not altogether deceived. She had heard that an indulgent grandmother had rather ruined Jonathan and Amelia-Jane's little boy, but then, what were grandparents for, she argued, if, having raised their own children in an exemplary manner, they were not to be permitted to spoil their grandchildren!

The bad news came in the form of an unwelcome report from Lydia, who had informed Jane that her two eldest sons, Henry and Philip, had joined the Volunteers, which had replaced the Militia in which their father had served when he had first become acquainted with the Bennet family. "They are to be stationed just outside London, she says. Lizzie, I cannot imagine that they will do very much more than strut around in uniform. Lydia claims that there is some new threat from France, but Bingley and Jonathan are convinced it is a lot of nonsense," said Jane, dismissing the threat from France.

Elizabeth was less sanguine. "I am a good deal more concerned about the threat of the Wickhams loose in London society, Jane," she declared. "I must tell Darcy he should advise Julian to avoid them at all costs. The Wickhams have always been trouble, and I would much rather Julian had nothing to do with them. He is so amiable and unsuspicious and could quite easily be taken in."

Jane agreed, reminding her sister of the problems of their cousin, Robert Gardiner, who had been deceived by his fine friends in an episode that had caused a great deal of pain to his parents. "I am sure Julian will never be so deceived, Lizzie," said Jane, "but it will be well for him to be forewarned."

Speaking of Julian brought Elizabeth to the big news of the moment. Taking out the letter she had received from her son only that morning, she put it in Jane's hands without comment. Settling back to enjoy her tea, she expected to hear cries of astonishment, but, amazingly, Jane read it right through and handed it back with a smile, saying, "Such a sweet letter, Lizzie, so sincere and honest. You are truly fortunate in your son."

Elizabeth was bemused. This generous praise for his style was all very well, but was she not going to remark upon the content of the letter? Before she could say anything, however, Jane poured herself a cup of tea and said gently, "Bingley and I have wondered when you and Mr Darcy were going to tell us. We were afraid you may have disapproved of the match and were therefore unwilling to give the young couple your blessing."

Elizabeth was completely confounded by her sister's remark. "What do you mean? Now, Jane, tell me—have you known of this romance for all of this time?" she asked, her voice betraying her astonishment.

Jane smiled and nodded. She did not mean to gloat; it was not in her nature to do so. She was almost apologetic as she explained, "Dear Lizzie, you must not be angry. Remember only that Amelia-Jane is Josie's aunt. She spent a fortnight with the Tates in Spring, when Jonathan was in Europe on business, and noticed that Julian visited Josie almost every day. To her mind it had seemed they were already engaged, so openly were their affections expressed. Were you not aware of this at the time?"

"No, indeed," said her sister, understanding more fully now how the news of the couple's romance must have become common knowledge. That Jane and Bingley and Jonathan and Amelia-Jane had all known before Darcy and herself was perplexing, even hurtful. She was, however, even more grateful now for Julian's letter. It would have been humiliating to be in ignorance and have no word from their son.

When Darcy and Bingley came upstairs, and they retired to their rooms for the night, Elizabeth told her husband of Jane's remarks. Darcy's response was lighthearted. "There, you see, Lizzie, it is always good to be well armed with information when one travels from home, even if it is about one's own children. Now that's out of the way, we can concentrate on worrying about their future happiness."

As if on cue, she asked, "Can you be sure they will be happy? They are both still very young."

Darcy refused to be anxious, "Their youth need not preclude them from making sensible choices, especially since they have known one another all their lives."

Seeing some uncertainty in her eyes, he sought to reassure her. "Lizzie, my dear, they are both obviously in love. Julian will not have made a foolish choice. He has far too much good sense. And from a purely practical point of view, it is certainly not an imprudent match for either of them. As for Josie, I believe that she, even more than her mother, has inherited much of your friend Charlotte's sound common sense. We know, from Julian's letter, that she is keen to become a serious writer. This does not suggest that she is some frivolous young woman unworthy of our son, but rather a thoughtful and sensible one with a mind of her own. I think we can confidently leave their happiness in their own hands, do you not, my dear?"

Elizabeth was easily persuaded that he was right to have confidence in their son's ability to make the right choice of partner. There was no reason why he and Josie should not be happy together. Neither Pride nor Prejudice would have any part in it.

❧

A day or two later, Mr and Mrs Tate, having regard to the fact that Elizabeth had called on them and missed them, returned the courtesy and travelled to Pemberley to wait on Mr and Mrs Darcy.

This acknowledgement of the engagement of their children's affections was the first stage of the establishment of a closer connection between their families. Mr Darcy had known Anthony Tate all his life, first as the young son of a good neighbour and later as an influential publisher, while Becky Collins, as her friend Charlotte's daughter, had been no stranger to Elizabeth. Though the families had not been particularly close, there had been no lack of mutual respect, and their children had always been friends. Cassandra and Richard had been grateful for the Tates' support in their campaign to establish the hospital at Matlock and their support for a number of community causes.

The Tates were a good deal closer to Fitzwilliam and Caroline, whose political activities had brought them together, and Becky was Emily Courtney's trusted friend. Since they would in time be relations as well as friends, it was quite natural that Darcy and Elizabeth sought to establish a closer association between them.

Josie, who had by now heard from Julian that he had written to his mother explaining everything, accompanied them, but was singularly quiet, while her parents, having got the formalities out of the way, seemed quite at ease.

After tea, Elizabeth, concerned at Josie's reticence, offered to show her the new suite of rooms that had been recently redecorated for Julian.

"The rooms used to be Georgiana's. As you can see, they are in a quiet part of the house with a pretty view of the park and the woods beyond," she explained, adding that she had had them refurbished for Julian for his twenty-first birthday.

Josie was impressed, admiring the tasteful colours and elegant furniture, as well as the charming prospect across the park.

"It means he will have a new suite of rooms when he returns from Cambridge," said Elizabeth.

Josie, while admiring everything about the rooms, still seemed nervous. Elizabeth wondered what she could do or say to put her at ease. Suddenly, without any prompting or provocation, Josie spoke.

"Mrs Darcy," she said, still somewhat hesitant, "there is something I wish to say ... something I want you to know before I go to London ... please let me say how truly sorry I am that you were embarrassed by the delay in our telling you of our engagement ... Julian is not to blame; it was my fault. I wanted to keep it secret for a while only because I just was not certain it was really going to happen."

Elizabeth seemed perplexed. "Why, Josie? Were you unsure of your feelings? I cannot believe that you doubted Julian's intentions," she said.

"Oh, no, but I could not quite believe it was really happening. You see, I think I have been in love with Julian for a very long time, but I never dreamed that he would return my affection—not to the extent of marrying me, anyway. You see, Mrs Darcy, there was always Pemberley in the way, I certainly never presumed to be the Mistress of Pemberley. I always assumed that Julian would marry either his cousin Louisa or Amy Fitzwilliam, who were the two most beautiful and eligible girls in the district," she said, and Elizabeth smiled, amused at her words.

"Julian has always been a good friend; when he visited me while I was recovering from my illness, I assumed he was being kind, as usual. I was completely astonished when he proposed, and indeed, I told him that I did not think I could ever be Mistress of Pemberley."

"Why ever not?" asked Elizabeth, who understood Josie's qualms but was anxious to reassure her.

"Because I am not accustomed to great houses like Chatsworth and Pemberley and all the finery that goes with them," she replied. "Growing up in Matlock, between these two great estates, I always regarded them as beautiful, historic places I loved visiting; but I never contemplated living in one."

"Neither had I, Josie," said Elizabeth, gently interrupting her. "Longbourn, where I grew up, was every bit as modest as your family's property in Matlock, with even less to recommend it in terms of scenic beauty. We were an unpretentious family, as Mrs Collins, your grandmother, will tell you, with far less fortune than you could expect to inherit, and believe me, Josie, I was just as surprised when Mr Darcy proposed to me," she explained.

Josie, astonished, could hardly believe that the elegant and handsome Mrs Darcy, who always looked every inch the Mistress of Pemberley, could ever have had similar reservations.

Elizabeth continued, "In any event, Josie, you shall, God willing, have many, many years to prepare for it. Mr Darcy is very fit and well, and likely to remain so. Meanwhile, as you can see, we do not stand on ceremony at Pemberley."

Josie, who had started to smile and relax, said quickly, "That was exactly what Julian said," and they laughed together as they went downstairs to join the others, stopping only to let Josie admire the new portraits of Cassandra's children, which adorned the wall opposite.

"Perhaps the most wonderful part of all this is that Cassy will be my sister. I shall love that. I have never known the joy of having a sister," Josie said wistfully, causing Elizabeth to recall another time, when a young woman had said something similar.

The memory of her first meeting with Georgiana Darcy brought an indulgent smile to her lips; they had become good friends and remained as close as two sisters could be. "A sister's love is very special," she said as they descended the stairs.

Looking up, Darcy saw them laughing together; Josie's parents, following his gaze, saw the change in the nervous young woman who had reluctantly accompanied them to Pemberley. Quite clearly, Elizabeth had put her at ease.

A week later, Josie came to Pemberley, alone, to say farewell before leaving for London. This time, she was far more composed than before and spent a very pleasant afternoon with Elizabeth. Discreetly, Elizabeth avoided pressing her young guest regarding their plans and instead allowed Josie to see as much of the house and its environs as she wished to, without in any way wanting to overawe her.

Josie, who had not been through the private areas of the house before, could not help but admire the light, spacious rooms, elegant furniture, and the splendid works of art. Later, as they took afternoon tea together, she made it clear that she thought Pemberley was quite the most handsome house she had ever seen and she would be very honoured to be part of its great family.

As she rose to take her leave, Elizabeth placed in her hands a little velvet box.

"Give it to Julian; he is expecting it. It used to belong to his grandmother, Lady Anne Darcy. I have written to him and suggested that he place it on your finger at the earliest opportunity," she said.

Josie begged to be allowed to open the box, and when she did so, there lay within it a fine gold ring set with a perfect diamond. Exclaiming at its beauty, she impulsively embraced and kissed Elizabeth, thanking her for her kindness and promising to write as soon as she reached London.

Josie arrived in London, accompanied by her father, who had business in the city. They went at once to her aunt's house in the area of Regent's Park.

Julian had been informed of the time and date of their arrival; consequently, they had very little time to wait before he arrived, having travelled overnight from Cambridge. Mr Tate introduced him to his sister, Miss Beatrice Tate, and he was immediately invited to stay to dinner.

Later, Mr Tate left to keep his appointment in the city, and Josie's aunt declared that she was going upstairs to "curl up on the sofa with a book." This left the young couple to their own devices, and they decided that the excellent weather deserved to be celebrated with a walk in the park.

A few hours later, they returned looking exceedingly happy, and Lady Anne Darcy's ring had been felicitously transferred from its velvet box onto the appropriate finger of Josie's left hand. Both Mr Tate and Josie's aunt Beatrice admired the exquisite ring and declared that a celebration was definitely in order.

Anthony Tate had been too busy to notice that his beloved daughter and Julian Darcy were falling in love. However, now that it was all settled and they were engaged, he was very pleased indeed and played the role of the father of the bride to perfection.

Julian and Josie found themselves in London at a time of remarkable political change. Lord Palmerston, who had only the previous year won a great election victory following the successful end of the Crimean War, was defeated in Parliament and resigned, bringing to power the very conservative Lord Derby.

The sense of disappointment among the Reformists was almost palpable. Palmerston had been a Reformer, however reluctant, pressured by Russell and others to proceed with the changes that the people demanded. With Lord Derby leading a minority Conservative government, there were no such expectations.

Josie wrote to her parents:

A great groan has gone up all around London. No one seriously expects Lord Derby to bring about any further reform to help ordinary people.

We were invited by James and Emma Wilson to dine at their town house in Grosvenor Street and afterwards, repaired to the Commons to listen to the speeches. They were terribly dull and boring. James Wilson is very disappointed that the Conservatives are back, especially with Derby, who he says, only remains in power because the Opposition is so disunited.

Josie knew her father was vehemently opposed to the Conservatives and sought to cheer him up:

Papa, I know you will be exceedingly pleased to hear that James and many of his Parliamentary colleagues do not believe that Lord Derby's government will last. James predicts that they will be defeated on the floor of the

House and then Derby will have to resign, though no one is quite sure who will replace him.

Josie could feel the excitement of London already. She longed to see more of the city. Her aunt, aware of her interest, had introduced her to a literary group, but Josie found it all too tame.

The ladies are all extremely keen on writing "poetic prose," since they cannot produce real poetry! Much of it is in the old Gothic style, and it is either highly romantic or melodramatic in content. Nobody wants to talk or write about the ordinary people of this city. There are millions of stories to be told, and no one wants to hear them.

Dear Papa, I know you will, and I am ever grateful to have my articles appear in the Review *and the* Chronicle, *but it would be nice to be taken seriously, just once, by the Metropolitan press.*

We have been going out a good deal, too. Aunt Beatrice and I have been twice to the House of Commons, twice to the Museum, and once to drive in Hyde Park with Emma Wilson, whose beautiful daughters, Victoria and Stephanie, must be the envy of every other woman in London. Yet they are such modest, unspoilt girls, both very accomplished, too. I wish I had half their talent!

Tomorrow we are to have a very special treat. Julian is to join us and we are to attend a reading by Charles Dickens, after which we are to go to Standish Park at the invitation of the Wilsons. I am looking forward to visiting Standish Park. Julian says it is a very fine estate and, being in Kent, quite different to Derbyshire.

I cannot sleep for the excitement of actually seeing Mr Dickens in the flesh! I promise to write all about it next week.

Your loving daughter,
Josie.

Josie's excitement continued to grow until they were actually at the hall where England's most beloved and popular author delighted his audience with readings from two of their favourite novels, *The Pickwick Papers* and *A Christmas Carol.* The superb dramatic and comic elements in his material, and his own amazing histrionic skills combined to make a most satisfying entertainment. Josie was enchanted. She had never experienced anything like it before.

Sitting near them was a very smartly dressed woman, tall, blonde, and enthusiastic. Catching Miss Beatrice Tate's eye, she waved an elegantly gloved hand, and Josie's aunt waved back. She whispered that she had met her at one of the meetings of her literary group but, unhappily, could not recall her name. During a short break in the performance, Aunt Beatrice revealed that she did remember that the woman was an American writer, and an enthusiastic admirer of Charles Dickens.

Julian noted she was certainly that; she was manifestly overwhelmed with admiration and left no one, including those of the audience sitting beside and in front of her, in any doubt of her response. So keen was she to convey her adoration—mere appreciation seemed inadequate to describe her feelings for the author—that it seemed she did not mind how much of a spectacle she made of herself.

When the performance was over and Mr Dickens, whose skill and charm had completely captivated his audience, had left the hall, the tall woman made her way over to them, enthusiastically greeted Josie's aunt, and demanded to be introduced to her "friends." She seemed determined to make the acquaintance of the young people with Miss Tate.

Julian had slipped away to talk to a young man he had recognised across the hall, leaving the unfortunate Josie with her Aunt Beatrice.

Marian Thurber, for that was her name, introduced herself and, on discerning Josie's interest in literary matters, she was immediately curious to discover more about her and was about to press her for information when a young man in a black overcoat approached the group, plainly keen to attract her attention. Seeing him, Miss Thurber thrust her card into Josie's hand and, after promising to "be in touch," left in a great hurry, closely followed by the man in the black coat, who appeared to be remonstrating with her.

Rejoining them in time to see the rather bizarre exit, Julian raised an eyebrow and appeared about to comment when the woman was seen returning. To his great relief, the target of her attention was another group of people who were still discussing the performance. Seizing the moment and Josie's arm, he guided her out of the hall and, having secured a hansom cab, conveyed them to Miss Tate's house, where they were to wait for the Wilsons, with whom they were travelling to Kent.

Josie was tired and fell asleep on the way, waking only when they reached the inn at Rochester, where they dined and broke journey for the night. Emma Wilson, ever conscious of her responsibilities, ensured the maintenance of proper decorum by having Josie share her bedroom, leaving the gentlemen to their own devices.

The following morning, they left soon after breakfast and made excellent time, arriving at Standish Park in the afternoon. Josie, who had never been to Kent, was all eyes and ears, absorbing every new sight and sound.

Writing that night to Elizabeth, she expressed her appreciation:

> The lovely woods and meadows that clothe the countryside delight the eye, as do the quaint villages with thatched cottages and conical oast houses. The landscape seems to be sleeping in the sun, as are the dreaming herds of cattle in fields filled with the prettiest wild flowers I have ever seen.
>
> In addition to this rich feast, I have the most delightful room, overlooking the park that seems to fall in gentle terraces to the river far below. Ancient trees in green meadows and clumps of irises by the water all combine to make a veritable heaven wherever I look.
>
> Emma agrees that they are very fortunate to live in what must be the most enchanting part of England.
>
> It is all new to me, and I cannot imagine how I have lived for nigh on twenty years and not known the sheer beauty of Kent...

James and Emma made time to take Josie around the orchards, farms, and parklands of the Standish Estate. The more she saw, the more she loved them. For all her father's fortune and influence, both of which were considerable, Josie had never before experienced a style of life as it was lived at Standish Park. She loved its elegance, its leisured sense of space and time, which so contrasted with the bustle of her home at Matlock, where life was always run at a fairly brisk pace.

The Wilsons were clearly wealthy, but without the ostentatious trappings that bespoke a taste for opulence as at Rosings Park; rather, everything was elegant and tasteful, blending into an atmosphere of harmony and balance where nothing was overdone. Wherever she turned her eyes, whether to the lofty, handsome rooms or the acres of woodland and park, which seemed to stretch endlessly along the valley of the Stour, the prospect was universally pleasing. As they drove around the estate, Josie frequently begged that they stop so she could absorb the loveliness of a particular place or make a quick sketch, which on her return to the house, she would immediately fill out with other details.

In her personal notebook, she wrote:

> *I love this house above any other place I have seen. It has a most welcoming atmosphere and provides ample comfort in every room. Such airy, spacious rooms and graceful French windows, which I adore, surrounded by grounds so remarkable that, except at Pemberley, I have seen none to rival them. As for the weather, it is, as they told us it would be, perfect at this time of year!*

Before they had been three or four days at Standish Park, they were all teasing her that Julian and she would have to spend more time in Kent, seeing she was so in love with it.

Sitting on the terrace on a balmy evening, James and Emma Wilson watched Julian and Josie walk away from the house towards the Rose Garden. Deep in conversation they walked, their heads turned toward one another, and though not a word carried to the observers on the terrace, the degree of affection between the pair was unmistakable.

"Miss Tate seems a very engaging young woman," said James to his wife. "I can claim no great knowledge of the family, but I know her father is a very influential man in the Midlands. I believe his support for the Reform movement, through his newspapers, was crucial."

Emma agreed. "Certainly, Anthony Tate is a man of both influence and principle, according to my brother. Jonathan is very impressed by his support of many community causes, and I think I am right in saying that Josie's mother Rebecca has also given a great deal of time to the community. My cousin Emily is a particular friend of Josie's mother," she added. "She used to be Becky Collins, of course. It is a quite delicious irony that her daughter Josie seems destined to be the Mistress of Pemberley."

They recalled with amusement the circumstances of the entail upon Longbourn, the Bennet family home, which had caused Mrs Bennet so much anxiety, as she lived for many years in fear of being dispossessed by Josie's grandfather, the lugubrious Mr Collins, beneficiary by entail.

"It was the untimely death of Mr Collins and the wisdom of Mr Bennet that resulted in my brother Jonathan inheriting Longbourn, where Josie's grandmother, Charlotte Collins, now lives as a house guest," said Emma.

"Mrs Collins must surely contemplate the prospect of Josie's marriage with some satisfaction," James observed. "I would say with a good deal of satisfaction, but, quite clearly, it has not weighed heavily upon the minds of Mr and Mrs Darcy, if they have consented to the engagement."

Emma smiled. "Charlotte," she said, "is Lizzie's oldest friend. Furthermore, while he does not have his father's reserved manner, Julian does share his determination and strong will. He would never want to hurt his parents' feelings, but I do not think he would let them thwart him if he really loved Josie, and I think it is quite plain that he does."

James leaned across and took her hand. "One would have to be blind to miss it, Dearest. But it cannot be considered an unsuitable alliance, surely?" he asked.

"Hardly," replied his wife. "The Tates are a well-respected family in the Midlands. Anthony Tate's mother was the sister of Sir Edmond Camden, neighbours and friends of the Darcys. Their fortune is quite considerable, even without the newspaper empire Anthony has built."

By the time the day arrived for them to part, the Wilsons and their guests had grown very fond of each other. Emma told Julian that she thought he was a very fortunate young man to be engaged to such an intelligent and charming young woman. It was a judgement he heartily endorsed.

On their last evening, having spent a pleasant hour after dinner in conversation and musical entertainment provided principally by the two young misses Wilson, Victoria and Stephanie, Josie begged to be excused, since she still had some packing to complete.

Entering her room a short time later, Emma found Josie packing her trunk and offered to help. She had brought her a gift of embroidered linen for her dressing table, which Josie admired for its fine work.

As they folded and packed, Emma casually informed her that Victoria and her governess, Miss Fairfax, would be travelling with them to London.

"Victoria has to present herself for a music examination," she explained. "They will travel with you as far as Grosvenor Street, and when you break journey for the night at Rochester, would you mind if Vicky shares your room?"

Josie was conscious of her gaze as she spoke, "Of course not. Why should I? I would love to have Victoria's company."

Emma smiled very sweetly and said, "I know you are both thoroughly sensible and aware of the need for decorum; however, my dear Josie, it is very important to avoid any opportunity for untoward gossip when you and Julian are travelling together. Believe me, I speak from personal experience. I think the presence of Vicky and Miss Fairfax will ensure that you are well protected from any hint of impropriety on your journey."

Josie, grateful for Emma's concern, embraced and thanked her sincerely. Emma, who had had to exercise an exemplary degree of restraint in her own relationship with her brother-in-law after the death of her husband David Wilson, was ever conscious of the need for decorum. Like her mother, Jane, even though she let her feelings engage quite deeply, she had been determined never to permit their devaluation through gossip or malicious prattle. Her present advice to Josie was no different than the high standards she had always set herself.

On returning to London, James Wilson conveyed Josie to her aunt's house before taking Julian to the Darcys' town house at Portman Square, where he was staying the night prior to returning to Cambridge.

Josie's aunt informed her that Miss Marian Thurber had called twice and left her card. Tired from her long journey, Josie was not fit to pay much attention and went directly to her room, seeking only a bath before bed.

Julian had barely retired to his bedroom when he was disturbed by sounds downstairs, which suggested the arrival of some late callers. Minutes later, the butler appeared at his door to inform him that two gentlemen, a Mr Henry Wickham and a Mr Philip Wickham, were downstairs.

Julian, recalling his mother's advice to stay well away from the Wickhams, was quite bewildered by their sudden arrival. Going downstairs, he took them into the sitting room, where they fell into chairs and proceeded to explain that they were stranded in town, having missed their friends with whom they were to return to their barracks some miles out of London. They were only in need of a bed for the night, they claimed, and promised not to inconvenience anyone.

"We shall be gone at dawn, before you are awake," said one, and Julian thought it would be very churlish to refuse. How could he throw them out? He sent for the housekeeper and asked that a bedroom be made ready, and that they be served an early breakfast on the morrow. Expressing profound gratitude, the Wickhams were ushered upstairs.

Still rather confused, Julian returned to bed, not expecting to see them again—which was why he was totally surprised to hear, when he came down to breakfast, that the two Wickham brothers were still fast asleep. He assumed they would soon be gone and set about his own business.

Returning to Cambridge, having first called on Josie and her aunt, Julian soon forgot about the Wickhams. A fortnight later, however, he received news of them from Mr Johns, the butler, who turned up at his rooms one evening to say that the two gentlemen had not departed for several days.

"They returned to the house every night, sir, and expected to be served a late breakfast each morning. Cook has been really cross," he said, adding that they had only left after he informed them that an officer had arrived in their absence and asked questions about their whereabouts. Johns, the soul of discretion, had given as little information as possible, except to say they had left the house that morning and were not expected to return.

"They seemed rather worried and left soon afterwards, sir," he explained, then revealed that after they had gone, the maids clearing the room had noticed that a silver snuffbox and a set of tortoiseshell combs were missing from the dressing table.

"Sarah was very upset, sir, and I thought it best to inform you as soon as possible. I don't think the master will be very happy about it," he said gloomily. Julian was grateful for his concern and absolved him of all guilt, taking upon himself the responsibility for permitting the Wickhams to stay the night.

"I should have insisted that they left that morning before I did. None of this is your fault, Johns. I will write to Papa and explain everything. We should try to replace the snuffbox; it must have been quite valuable. I shall look for one when I am next in London," he said and sent Johns away, assuring him that all would be well.

However, two weeks later, the electric telegraph brought an urgent summons from his father, who expected to be at Portman Square on the following day. The Wickham brothers were back, and this time they had a few friends with them, including a couple of young women. They had virtually taken over the rooms upstairs and were ordering the servants around. Johns, in great distress, had sent an express to Pemberley requesting Mr Darcy's intervention. Short of calling in the police, he could see no way to be rid of them and hoped his master would be able to solve the problem.

Julian left immediately for London. Arriving at Portman Square, he was flung into the middle of a most undignified contretemps. The Wickhams were out, but the debris of their stay was everywhere. The servants had finally refused to take orders from the Wickhams and their friends. Knowing Mr Darcy was expected, they were bustling around getting the house back to normal, but there was a sullen atmosphere in the place. The parlour maid had complained that she had been importuned by one of the Wickhams and later harassed by his lady friend, which had driven the girl into hysterics. The cook had flatly refused to provide them with food at all hours, and the footman had grown weary of running up and down the stairs to attend to their demands for drinks and was threatening to leave.

Poor Johns—with a possible mutiny on his hands, he was at his wit's end when Julian arrived, to be followed soon afterwards by Mr Darcy, his manager, and a lawyer.

When the Wickhams returned without their friends, the brisk, businesslike manner in which they were dealt with left Julian quite amazed.

He wrote to Cassandra later that week:

The threat of being handed over to the police as well as being reported to the army for their disreputable, disgusting behaviour must have had the desired effect. They were clearly impressed by Papa's lawyer, who detailed to them the crimes they had already committed, including trespassing and stealing, the witnesses who would testify against them, and the sentences they were likely to receive from the magistrate. The very least would be several years in prison—more probable, if the case were pressed hard, would be transportation to Australia!

Of course, through all this, Papa stood aloof, looking very stern indeed!

Can you believe, Cassy, that these stupid men would continue to place themselves in jeopardy, without a thought for the consequences of their actions, behaving like highwaymen in the very heart of London?

I know that Mama warned me against the Wickhams, but nothing prepared me for their effrontery and insolence. We are fortunate indeed that we have not lost the services of several of the staff at Portman Square as a result of this debacle. However, it is now settled, and I sincerely hope it will never happen again.

I hope you and Richard are well. Do give the children our love.

Josie and I expect to be back in Derbyshire by the end of Summer, when I am sure we shall all meet together at Pemberley in happier circumstances.

He concluded his letter to his sister with the usual felicitations and added a postscript reminding her of a promise to visit him at Cambridge.

Meanwhile, Josie had been visited by Marian Thurber, who, on discovering her interest in writing, became even keener to assist her progress. She had, in fact, arranged a meeting between herself, Josie, and a man she called "my agent," who turned out to be the young man in the long black coat who had appeared at the Dickens readings.

Curious though cautious, Josie had gone along and initially, at least, she was willing to take their plans seriously. Miss Thurber claimed that she and her friend in the long black coat, whom she called "Georgie" as if he were a pet dog, were actually involved in publishing. They were, at the moment, she said, collecting material for a new anthology. She claimed that they had already published several such collections in the United States.

"All we need are some exciting new writers, preferably young writers, who will speak from the heart," she declared grandly. "Georgie" nodded vigorously but said nothing, leaving all of the talking to Marian Thurber.

She then urged Josie to let her read some of her own work. "Not that I am unsure of its quality; mind, I know it will be excellent, but I should like to know the genre in which you write. I cannot think of anything better than helping younger, struggling writers to publish," she cooed sweetly.

At first, Josie was quite impressed and promised to let Miss Thurber see a recent piece of work. However, she warned that she did not write fiction. "You may not like my work, Miss Thurber," she said.

"Marian, please," she begged, and Josie continued, "You see, I have no talent for fiction and no real inclination, either. My work is almost all factual and documentary. I wish to write about the problems ordinary people face, and the consequences for their lives of forces they cannot control."

Once again, Miss Thurber rolled her eyes and spoke encouragingly, "My dear Josie, that is what readers are crying out for. Any scribbler can pen a romance; but to argue a case, now, that is rare, especially in a woman writer."

Josie spoke of Charlotte Brontë, one of the three tragic Brontë sisters, who had died but a year ago. "I admire their ability to conjure up fascinating tales out of the mist on the moors, but I could not do it. I can only write about real people."

Marian Thurber assured her that writing romances was a very commonplace thing and urged her again to let her see some of her work.

Writing to Julian, Josie told him of Miss Thurber's ideas. Despite the need to concentrate upon his work, Julian was sufficiently concerned to write her a hasty note begging her to be cautious, and make no commitments.

My dearest Josie,

Please beware of those who will promise you fame and fortune. Do not give away any of your work to these people, of whom we know very little.

He had been working diligently through most of the Summer on a dissertation which had to be presented for evaluation soon. There was a great deal at stake, including the opportunity for further research, and a Master's Degree. Meanwhile, he had not been neglectful of Josie's interests. He had approached two or three persons involved in the publication of journals. One, a fairly progressive journal with the rather unlikely title of *The New Radical*, was based on *Cobbett's Reviews*, and seemed a likely prospect.

Josie's article on the mining disaster—which opened with two lines of poetry and closed with what Julian called "a great rant against the greed of mine owners"—seemed appropriate material. He was delighted when the editors expressed an interest in it.

The arrival of another letter from Josie, mentioning an invitation to a dinner party at the house of a Mrs Freeman, caused Julian to decide it was time to go to London forthwith. Arriving unannounced at her aunt's house on the afternoon of the dinner party, he was enthusiastically received by Josie but not quite so happily by Miss Thurber when she called for her. There was no mistaking her disconcerted expression when Josie asked if Julian could accompany them. Though she made a great show of generous hospitality, it was plain that Miss Thurber was somewhat put out by his presence.

On arriving at the house of her friend and fellow countrywoman, Gertrude Freeman, who was introduced as "a dramatist and free thinker," Julian had his suspicions confirmed. He did, however, attempt to keep his thoughts to himself for a while.

It transpired that the man in the long black coat, who appeared at the party more fashionably attired and, amazingly, minus his coat, was in fact a hopeful poet who had adopted the style and enthusiasms of John Keats with little evidence of similar talent. He was encouraged in his presumption by both Miss Thurber and her friend Mrs Freeman with no indication that anyone wanted to read his work, much less publish it.

There were others present who neither wrote nor, it would seem, read poetry, but had become part of the coterie of the two women and hung around on the fringes of the gathering. Miss Thurber spent a lot of her time actively encouraging "my protégés," as she called them, and reading out scraps of their work at intervals.

After dinner, which was a dull affair, the true purpose of the gathering became clear when Mrs Freeman produced her plan for the new publication, somewhat naively named *The Treasure Trove* (because, as she claimed, it would contain the hitherto hidden treasures of the contributing writers). *The Treasure Trove* would be published in America, and would cost each of the contributors a mere thirty pounds, for which, of course, they would receive copies of the publication—presumably in addition to fame and glory. There were, however, no legal documents, no guarantees of anything; everything had to be taken on trust.

Standing beside Josie as the plan unfolded, Julian could clearly see her early enthusiasm waning as the true nature of the enterprise was exposed. Despite the best efforts of both Marian Thurber and her friend, it appeared that not too many of her writers were either willing or able to part with that much money. For some, like the hungry-looking poet with lank blonde hair, whose main interest appeared to be the food on the table, thirty pounds must have seemed like a fortune!

When Miss Thurber asked in an eager voice for people to speak up, one or two young women, who appeared to be wearing more jewellery than one would expect to see at a ball, seemed to think they would have no trouble finding the money, while an older man claimed that he would be happy to sell some of his shares in the railway to pay his portion.

Julian prayed that Josie would not commit herself and indeed when she was asked directly, she did exactly as he had hoped and declared that she needed to think about it and talk to her father.

Miss Thurber, who knew exactly who Josie's father was, did not look very pleased, saying in a rather false, bright voice, "But Josie dear, thirty pounds would be no more than pin money to you."

That was absolutely the wrong thing to say, and, seeing Josie's expression harden, Julian knew he need worry no more.

They left soon afterwards, and when they were back at her Aunt Beatrice's house, he told her the editors of *The New Radical* had liked her work and what was more, they wanted to see more of it.

"I know it is not *The Times*, Josie, but it is a serious journal, and your work will at least be read with interest," Julian explained.

Josie could hardly believe her ears. Exasperated that he had not told her earlier, she pretended to throw a tantrum, but only briefly, before she turned to Julian and thanked him most sincerely. She was delighted.

As the Summer of 1858 waned into Autumn, the political situation in Europe began once more to concern the people of Britain. While the movements for the unification of Italy and Germany gathered pace, the lack of confidence in the government of Lord Derby created considerable nervousness. This was exacerbated by the signing of a remarkable pact between Count Cavour and Napoleon III at Plombieres, which made them allies and sought to link dynastically the kingdom of Piedmont with France.

Initially, it seemed the strategy had failed when the young Princess Clotilde of Piedmont stubbornly refused to cooperate. But when, in September, she decided that Napoleon's cousin, Jerome was "not so repulsive after all" and she would marry him, the nervousness turned to paranoia as British distrust of its former ally increased considerably. Dissatisfaction with the government and a desire for stronger leadership had led to efforts to bring together a united opposition party that could contest the next election.

Dining with the Wilsons at their town house in Grosvenor Street, Julian and Josie met Jonathan Bingley, who was in London for a meeting of what he called "a new force in British politics"—the Liberals. Both James Wilson and Jonathan were convinced that the only way to defeat Derby and the Tories was for all liberal-minded men to unite. They were certain that Palmerston would join them.

"Britain needs a leader who is strong on foreign affairs, at this time. Considering the chaotic situation in Europe, with a dynastic alliance between Victor Emmanuel and Napoleon III, we cannot afford to have a nobody leading the British government," declared Jonathan, who, despite retiring from Parliament, had been persuaded by his colleagues to retain membership of the party.

"He remains an active campaigner for reform, even though his wife seems to have surrendered to the attractions of Rosings, where the word reform does not appear in the lexicon," wrote Josie to her parents.

James Wilson was equally certain that the country needed a stronger leader and a better-directed foreign policy. "Ever since the resignation of Palmerston, we have had no clear direction in foreign affairs. It is essential that we rid ourselves of the deadwood and get some sound policy in place. Palmerston had a personal rapport with many European leaders—Derby does not. As a consequence, he flounders and so does Britain," he said in his usual, logical way.

"Do you think there will be war?" Josie asked nervously.

James was reassuring. "In Europe, perhaps, but I cannot see Britain becoming involved. Though there is no knowing what perils we may stumble into with the type of weak leadership we have."

Listening to their conversation, Julian felt a strong desire to return to Pemberley. Josie was staying with the Wilsons that night, and he was returning to Portman Square. He had completed and submitted his dissertation; there was a possibility he would be recalled to the college in Spring to continue his research. His plans, at the moment, were quite open. He was anxious, however, about Josie. He realised that she, for all her common sense and intelligence, was still young and impressionable. He had felt her deep sense of disillusion with Miss Thurber and her friends, who had sought to exploit her youth and enthusiasm.

The following day, he returned and found her still deeply ashamed at being deceived by the two women. "How could I have been so stupid as to believe them?" she cried, but Julian was unwilling to let her indulge in fruitless outrage and recrimination, which would only serve to increase her depression.

"How would you like to go home, Josie?" he asked. "Your brother will be back from College, and it is almost time for harvest home."

Half expecting her to protest, to be disappointed at the prospect of leaving London, he was unprepared for her response. Rising from her chair, she walked over to the window and looked out at the trees across the street. Their leaves were brown and the wind was stripping them away, already. Josie turned and said brightly, "Oh, yes, I would like it very much, indeed. Let us go home, please. I think I have had enough of London for this year. Perhaps in the Spring I may wish to return, but now, yes, Julian, I believe I would like nothing better than to return to Derbyshire."

Elizabeth awoke, hearing the sound of rain. She almost turned over and went to sleep again. It was too depressing to contemplate. Darcy had already risen, and she forced herself to get out of bed and, pulling on a robe, went over to the window and looked out at the grounds, sodden with almost a week of unceasing rain. With the Festival of Music only a few days away, she was desperate.

"Oh please, please let it stop," she said, in the forlorn hope that someone would hear. Someone must have heard, or else there was no more water left in the skies above the peaks and moorlands, because by midday the rain had begun to ease and a pale sun had pushed its face out of the dreary grey clouds.

Downstairs and around the grounds preparations continued apace. This year they had called in a professional team to organise the occasion. Darcy had insisted that it was too much for Elizabeth and Emily to handle on their own. "I cannot have you falling ill, Lizzie," he had said firmly, "and Emily has not been in the best of health, either. Besides, if we are to invite our distinguished neighbours, we may as well impress them."

It was left to her to arrange the program, which was something she enjoyed immensely. Together with Emily and Caroline, she had worked out the order of the items and arranged for the performers to be accommodated so they could practice before the festival.

"I am glad the choir is back from Bristol," said Emily. "I was afraid we weren't going to hear them at all this year. They've been so busy."

Caroline agreed that they would have missed the choir, which now performed at several venues and frequently won prizes in competitions. Occasionally, Elizabeth would have to remind herself that this was the choir that had started with a few children from the estate singing carols for her very first Christmas at Pemberley. Caroline, whose children were all very talented performers, remembered, too, and the cousins smiled as they recalled memories of those happy days. How much had happened in all their lives since then.

The centrepiece of the festival program was a recital by a group of singers from Coventry who had won national acclaim; but for the family, the highlight would be the performances of the two Courtney children, William and Elizabeth, and the young Matlock chamber music group. William was to play Chopin, for whose work he seemed to have a special gift, while Elizabeth, accompanied by her brother, would sing an aria from *The Marriage of Figaro*.

Mr Darcy came to remind them that Julian and Josie, who had arrived from London and stayed overnight with the Tates, were expected any time now.

Elizabeth smiled and reassured her husband, who seemed unusually anxious. "I had not forgotten, my dear," she said, as they went downstairs. "I am very pleased that they are going to be here for the festival. I think it will help Josie understand what Pemberley really means to all of us."

Darcy agreed, but he was less concerned than his wife was about young Josie Tate, knowing that Julian's own attachment to Pemberley would be the means of drawing her into its circle. "I am confident she will soon discover it, if she has not done so already," he said, recalling how easily Elizabeth had moved into her role as the Mistress of Pemberley, triumphing over those, like his aunt Lady Catherine de Bourgh, who had doubted that she would be worthy of the position.

The sound of a carriage drawing up at the front of the house heralded the arrival of the travellers, who were warmly received. Julian's pleasure in bringing his prospective bride home to Pemberley was plain to all, and Josie was especially delighted with the warmth of her welcome. Everything had been done to make her comfortable in what was to be her future home.

The day of the festival was fine but pleasantly cool, as early Autumn days are in Derbyshire, where the leaves turn to glowing gold and rust as the north wind begins to probe the woodlands and parks. Many of the performers had arrived and were accommodated in the nursery wing.

Elizabeth, having spent all morning downstairs attending to a myriad of things that simply had to be done, was feeling tired and, coming upstairs, rested awhile upon a couch in the sitting room, which overlooked her favourite corner of the park. She could see the servants bustling around making preparations for the evening, and Mr Darcy with Julian and Josie walking down to inspect the big marquee on the west lawn, where refreshments were to be served for everyone from the Pemberley estate before the performance.

She remembered how eagerly she had run to inspect all the arrangements, when they had first begun to hold the music festivals at Pemberley. How she had wanted everything to be just perfect. They had been very proud of her achievement. Musing upon those early days, she fell asleep.

She did not know how long she had been asleep, but she was awakened by the sound of the piano in the music room. She listened and realised that someone was playing the Mozart sonata that William had played on that Autumn day so many years ago. As the haunting *andante cantabile* flowed through the house, Elizabeth could not believe she was hearing it; she knew of no one who had played it since. Rising from her couch, she hurried down the corridor to the music room and, eager to discover the identity of the pianist, gently opened the door.

William Courtney leapt up from his seat at the pianoforte, "Aunt Lizzie, did I disturb you? I am sorry. I had no idea you were upstairs." He was most apologetic.

Elizabeth realised that William had come over to practice for the evening's performance, as he did quite often before a recital. The Courtneys did not have an instrument as fine as the one at Pemberley, and William had a permanent invitation to come in and play on it. Both Elizabeth and Darcy welcomed it.

She sought to reassure him. "Oh, no William, there is no need to apologise, not at all. I heard the music and I didn't know it was you. I was tired

… I must have dozed off and on awakening, I was surprised because I could not think who would be playing the Mozart …"

She seemed puzzled, and he explained, "It is not part of my program for this evening. I had almost finished practising when I saw it lying on the music stand, and thought to try it out. It's beautiful, but maybe too difficult for me just yet."

She smiled, wondering how the music had come to be on the stand— she could not remember seeing it there for years. "Would you like to play it … I mean, as a concert piece?" she asked.

"Very much; it has a most haunting theme. But I shall have to practice long and hard. Look, let me show you how complex the *andante* is," he said as he sat down and played through a part of the second movement.

As he played Elizabeth recalled, more calmly this time, the enchanting slow movement that her William had played with a tenderness that was almost too much to bear. William Courtney was dark and taller than her son had been.

He finished the movement and came over to her. "Did you like it? I'm afraid I cannot do it justice without much more practice."

He was very modest, but she smiled and said, "You did very well, William. But if you wish to master it, please do come back and practice some more. You know you are always welcome."

The door opened and Darcy entered with William's sister, Elizabeth. "Ah, there you are, Lizzie. We have been looking everywhere for you. Elizabeth is here to practice for this evening."

"William has been playing for me," she said. "We shall leave you two to practice together.

"I am looking forward so much to this evening," she said as they went out.

Darcy guessed she had been moved deeply by William's playing. He could not avoid seeing the irony in their situation. "Are you all right, my dear?" he asked, solicitous as ever, but she reassured him she was perfectly well. Darcy had heard a part of the music William Courtney had been playing and recalled it vividly himself. It always stirred deep memories.

Elizabeth realised that he had heard it, too. "I was startled to hear it at first, but William said he had seen it lying on the music stand and wanted to try it. He plays it well." She did not say, "But not as well as our William."

She did not need to. He knew exactly how she felt and was grateful she was no longer distressed by the music.

"Josie and Julian have gone up to the gallery," Darcy explained. "I understand Josie wanted to see your collection of miniatures."

Elizabeth was pleased. She had hoped Josie would take an interest in Pemberley and its treasures. Julian had hinted that Josie, eager to continue her career as a writer, was in no hurry to be married. Elizabeth was somewhat concerned, and though she did not wish to exaggerate her disquiet, she could not help voicing it. "Do you believe their feelings are deeply engaged? Are they strong and enduring enough to weather all that life will throw at them?" she asked anxiously. "I should be content if they were to settle upon a date. I can see they are in love, but I am concerned there is a lack of serious intention. Do you believe there is?"

Darcy's voice was quiet. "I certainly hope there is, with all my heart, but I cannot really tell. I am no judge of the inclinations of youth," he said.

Elizabeth challenged him, her voice teasing, "But surely, dearest, you are a good judge of feelings; can you not tell?"

Now he knew she was teasing him again. "No, truly I am not, Lizzie, and you know it. I never even knew how well I loved you and when I did discover it, the manner of my approach to you was so reprehensible that I was certain I had made you hate me. No, I am quite hopeless at making such judgements," he confessed ruefully.

This time, she laughed out loud and took his hand. "I do recall something to that effect; though in these matters, my memory is, fortunately, far from reliable! But, surely, you can have no doubts on that score now?" she asked as they went out into the garden.

"No, indeed, and I doubt there is cause for anxiety regarding Julian and Josie either," he replied with a smile that transformed his serious face.

Everything was in readiness. The weather had cleared to a perfect evening, and Pemberley looked spectacular in the late afternoon sun. Soon, it would be time to dress for the performance.

Julian and Josie came out of the house and walked towards them. They met at the foot of the stone steps leading to the rose garden and Julian said very quickly, "Mama, we have something to tell you and Papa. Josie and I have decided that we would like to be married in the Spring."

Elizabeth was delighted. As they kissed and embraced one another, of their happiness there could be no doubt at all.

There were dozens of questions Elizabeth wanted to ask, but she well knew that this was not the moment; there would be many days and weeks ahead and plenty of time for all that. For the moment, there was little need for words, except to express their heartfelt joy. She had been anxious that Josie's reluctance to be married sooner rather than later represented a lack of seriousness; the news just received and the happiness of the young lovers had set her heart at rest on that score.

As they walked through the rose garden towards the house, the delightful sounds of the young chamber music group practising for the evening's performance drifted out through the open French windows and across the lawns. Julian and Josie went indoors; Elizabeth took her husband's arm, and they walked around to the front of the house.

"There, Lizzie, are you content now?" Darcy asked gently.

Elizabeth smiled. "Yes," she said, "perfectly content."

An epilogue...

THE WEDDINGS ARE OVER. There are rose petals everywhere.

Jane and Elizabeth have seen their two youngest children married on a fine Spring morning in the year 1859: Louisa Bingley to Dr Matthew Ward, the scientist in charge of the research laboratory at the new Matlock hospital, and Julian Darcy to Josie, the only daughter of Anthony Tate and his wife Rebecca.

Emma Wilson's two daughters, Victoria and Stephanie, are bridesmaids and, like most bridesmaids, seem to attract even more comment than the brides.

The two sisters, Jane and Elizabeth, are almost inseparable these days, and together with their husbands, who continue to be close friends as well as business partners, enjoy an intimate and affectionate relationship. As they stood together on the terrace at Pemberley, watching the large party of friends and relations greet the newly wedded couples, they were joined by Charlotte Collins, Josie's grandmother and Elizabeth's closest friend. The weddings had brought them together again, reviving memories of the way they had been in Hertfordshire, many years ago.

❦

With the last of his daughters married, Bingley was in a light-hearted mood. "It will be your turn next," he said to Emma and James Wilson. "I cannot honestly remember an occasion, since we went to Netherfield and met the beautiful Bennet girls, on which I have heard so many compliments for two young women as I have heard today for young Victoria and Stephanie. I am sure it will not be long before you have their suitors beating a path to your door."

Both Emma and James laughed. "Oh dear, I do believe you are exaggerating, Papa," said Emma modestly. "I acknowledge they are pretty and they are both accomplished and very well taught, but anyone who expects them to wed in a hurry is bound to be disappointed. Vicky is eager to complete her studies in music. As for Stephanie, who is not yet seventeen, her schoolmistress, Mrs Harris, informs me that Stephanie is her brightest pupil. She excels in Literature and History." Having had an education at one of the best ladies' seminaries herself, Emma had always encouraged her daughters to read widely. It was plain that Emma, unlike her infamous grandmother Mrs Bennet, was in no hurry to be rid of her daughters.

The wedded couples having finally got away, the rest of the guests wandered around Pemberley's beautiful grounds while they waited for their carriages. As they departed and the servants began to clear away the remains of the wedding feast, the family moved indoors.

The Tates, Anthony and Rebecca, now bound to Pemberley by the strongest of family ties as well as friendship, joined them in the drawing room.

An hour or so later, Charlotte bade her dear friends farewell. "I must leave, Eliza. I am to stay with Rebecca and Anthony for a week or two, while Mary goes to Ashford Park with Jane and Mr Bingley," she said, and as the two women embraced, it was hard for both to hold back the tears.

They had grown up together and, despite occasional disagreements, had remained faithful friends, now brought even closer through the marriage of Josie and Julian. Charlotte was surely aware of the ironies that surrounded this happy event, for it had been through the Bennets that she had met and married their cousin, Mr Collins. Later, her invitation to Elizabeth had led to the meetings with Mr Darcy at Rosings, where the feelings he believed he had successfully suppressed at Netherfield had been rekindled and had led ultimately to their engagement.

Elizabeth was certainly sensitive to them, and while she gave no sign of it to her friend as they said goodbye, when she went upstairs with Jane and her Aunt Gardiner to take tea in her sitting room, there was no shortage of amusing comment on the subject.

Ever the romantic, Jane could not resist the attraction of an incipient love affair in their circle. "Lizzie, I am sure Amy Fitzwilliam will be the next bride in the family; she is so much like Caroline used to be. I did notice she had several admirers today, including young Mr Grantley."

Mrs Gardiner, who was Amy's grandmother, agreed she was indeed a beauty, much as her mother had been, but added, "I think there may have been some disappointment there, Jane, for while I cannot vouch for it, I have felt that Amy had a soft spot in her heart for Julian."

"Now there would have been a match after Mama's heart, God bless her soul," cried Elizabeth, pouring out the tea, "and if I were to be absolutely honest, I would have to admit to being quite partial to young Amy myself. She is not only beautiful, but though she is just eighteen, she shows remark-able intelligence and good sense. She also works very willingly for the community at both the parish school and the library. You might say a daughter-in-law after my own heart, in fact."

"Would you have preferred it, Lizzie?" asked her sister.

Elizabeth answered, with a degree of circumspection, "I cannot deny that I had hoped Julian might have been interested, but sadly, it was not to be. Since last Christmas, he has had eyes for no one but Josie, who we must acknowledge has a good deal more to say for herself, though she is nowhere near as pretty as Amy. Darcy believes she and Julian are well suited," she said. "Poor Mama, can you imagine how angry she must be at Charlotte's granddaughter marrying her grandson? She was barely civil to Charlotte when she became engaged to Mr Collins, and so desperately did she fear that the Collinses would throw us out of Longbourn, that she never invited them back after they were married. Oh Jane, what complaint we would have had to endure, had Mama lived to see this wedding day?"

"Mercifully, she was spared having to see my Jonathan marry Amelia-Jane," said her sister, recalling Mrs Bennet's plans for her grandchildren. "She was quite determined that Jonathan should marry into a county family, at the very least. She would never have been satisfied with a mere clergyman's daughter!"

"Especially if that clergyman happened to be the reviled Mr Collins!" said Elizabeth, warming to her subject.

Mrs Gardiner reminded them that their mother was not always wrong. "And yet, Jane, it must be acknowledged that in your case at least your Mama was absolutely right," she said.

"Indeed, she was," said Elizabeth brightly. "Dear Bingley had hardly set foot in the county before she determined that he was going to marry one of her girls, and soon there was no doubt at all which of us it would be. 'Oh, I knew you could not be so beautiful for nothing, Jane,'" she said, mimicking Mrs Bennet, whose dearest wish had come true when Bingley and Jane became engaged.

Jane blushed at the memory, even after all these years. "But Lizzie, you cannot pretend that she was not equally pleased by your engagement to Darcy," she said and Lizzie's riposte was swift.

"No, indeed, she was completely overwhelmed, even though she had, only that afternoon, commiserated with me for having had to put up with 'that disagreeable man' for two days in a row, while begging me to remember it was all for your sake, Jane."

Jane did not mind being teased, but preferred to divert attention to her sister-in-law. "Lizzie, how do you suppose Caroline Bingley must feel about Charlotte's daughter marrying Mr Darcy's son?" she asked with a degree of mock innocence that Elizabeth found vastly amusing.

"Oh, Jane, you are quite right to be concerned. Among the denizens of Bath, there must have been great outrage! The very thought that the shades of Pemberley could be even further polluted must have brought on an attack of the vapours," said Elizabeth mischievously. "We were not at all surprised that neither the Hursts nor Miss Bingley could make the journey for the wedding. Lady Catherine is genuinely unwell, and Mr Hurst's gout must present a problem, but Louisa Hurst and Caroline Bingley must surely have had no good reason except snobbery. They were so unforgivably rude to both Charlotte and Sir William Lucas that it must be mortifying indeed for Caroline, who once had high hopes for herself, to acknowledge that young Josie will one day be the Mistress of Pemberley."

Jane and Mrs Gardiner could only agree.

There were so many happy memories to recall that the afternoon was spent in the greatest merriment. Content in their own marriages, which had brought them both love and happiness, while enhancing considerably their well-being and material security, they needed only to pray that their hopes for their children would be similarly fulfilled.

Jane had known the agony of seeing a daughter suffer the pain of an unhappy marriage. "My greatest joy, Lizzie, is that Emma is now happily settled with James. I had always thought well of him, but since they have been married, he has proved to be quite the best man I have known since Bingley and your dear Darcy, of course. He has so remarkably changed their lives, there is not even the faintest shadow left of her former unhappiness."

As Elizabeth and Mrs Gardiner nodded agreement, Jane continued, "You were so fortunate with Cassy and Richard."

Elizabeth agreed readily. "Indeed, we were. There is not another man in the world to whom we could have entrusted her with so much confidence. There is so much joy in their home that Julian declares there should be a tax upon it!"

Their laughter reflected their own contentment, yet their aunt reminded them that there were those for whom there was little certainty of happiness, since marriage had become something of a lottery for many young women, with or without fortune.

"Why, only last week, my brother's wife told me of a most miserable situation in which a very respectable young woman from Staffordshire finds herself trapped in a terrible marriage with a feckless husband who will do nothing to support his family. Since he has run through her fortune, she must beg for help from her relatives to feed her children. Our daughters have been spared such privation," she declared.

"Except for poor Lydia," said Jane, whose soft heart would not let her forget her errant sister, whose unfortunate alliance with Mr Wickham, compounded by their subsequent stupidity, had turned them into an embarrassment and virtually cut her off from the rest of her family, except when she needed their help.

Elizabeth was more severe. "Poor Lydia's problems are largely of her own making, Jane. She leapt into an affair with Wickham having no thought for the consequences, and their contrived marriage seems to have done nothing to improve the characters of either Lydia or her husband," she declared.

Mrs Gardiner appeared to agree and more may have been said on the subject, but Robert's appearance at the door curtailed the discussion. Robert had arrived to take his mother home. Mr Gardiner had been weakened by illness recently and could not stay out too late. Mrs Gardiner, ever conscious of her husband's comfort, prepared to leave at once, but not before she thanked her niece and through her Mr Darcy for his kindness to Mr Gardiner.

"Dear Lizzie, please do not forget to thank your husband for his kindness. His concern for your uncle is deeply appreciated."

After they had gone, Jane turned to her sister. "Lizzie, I could not ask you in the presence of Aunt Gardiner, but I do worry about our uncle," she said, her eyes expressing her concern.

Elizabeth concurred. "He is weaker since his last illness, and our aunt is very concerned, but Richard has had the best physicians from London examine him and they can find very little wrong with him. His mind is as alert as ever, and Darcy, who spends some time with him each week, declares that he cannot see any deterioration in his faculties at all," she said.

Jane looked grave. "Aunt Gardiner is very grateful to him. I know our uncle looks forward to Mr Darcy's visits and appreciates them very much, indeed."

Elizabeth knew this to be true. She recalled her aunt's words. They had always been close, but since Mr Gardiner's illness, they had drawn even closer, more as friends than as aunt and niece. It was a great comfort to Mrs Gardiner. Elizabeth and Darcy, who had never ceased to be grateful for the Gardiners' part in their own happiness, were delighted to be able to repay some of their kindness.

Even as they talked of their friends and relations, their thoughts returned to their children, who had been married on this day. Jane's only concern was that Louisa and Matthew Ward had insisted on continuing to rent a house in Matlock to be near the hospital instead of moving to Ashford Park. "I shall miss her very much, Lizzie, especially now that Sophie and Daniel are gone to live with Mrs Lambert in Derby."

Elizabeth smiled. "Dear Jane, you are missing your girls," she teased. "I am fortunate to have Cassy living at such an easy distance from Pemberley."

"Will Julian and Josie return to live at Pemberley?" asked Jane and was immediately sorry she had done so when Elizabeth bit her lip and shook her head.

"No, at least not for a while, I do not think. Julian must return to Cambridge to complete his research. He has been offered a place on the team of a Professor, a preeminent scientist and a man of huge reputation. He cannot afford to miss the opportunity. As for Josie, you know how determined she is to get some of her work published in London. We are not entirely sure that her work is mature enough, and, of course, she has the added disadvantage of being a woman," Elizabeth explained.

Jane was outraged. "A woman writer is disadvantaged? You cannot mean that, Lizzie."

"Indeed, I do. Had she been a man, or used a man's name as a nom de plume, her chances of success would have been greatly enhanced, just as it was with the Brontë women, who all used male pen names at first."

Jane was aghast at the unfairness of it and said so. "I cannot believe it. And will they live in London?" she asked.

"Oh, no, neither of them like London much," Elizabeth replied. "They will take a house in Cambridge, within reach of the College. I have agreed to go down and help them with furniture and window draperies and other details. Meanwhile, they will stay at Portman Square. But it will not be for long; they are determined to be independent and find their own place."

Jane shook her head. This was very different than Jonathan, who had gladly accepted all his father could do for him, using the house in Grosvenor Street until they had finally decided to settle in Kent. "At Rosings, of course, where they spend most of their time, they have to maintain an appropriate standard. Lady Catherine has insisted upon it," Jane said.

"She would!" scoffed Elizabeth, and memories were revived of encounters with the formidable but frequently ridiculous Lady Catherine de Bourgh, provoking much mirth.

Elizabeth was about to ring for a fresh pot of tea, when, without warning, Jane's expression changed and she said, "Lizzie, I do wish I could be as certain of Jonathan's happiness as I am of the girls'."

When Elizabeth looked up at her, startled and confused, for she had no inkling that Jonathan was anything but happy with his Amelia-Jane, Jane explained that she had had reservations about the move to Rosings Park.

"Indeed, I have been concerned ever since they moved to Kent. I believe, Lizzie, that Amelia-Jane is still very impressionable and easily influenced by all the grandeur and status of Lady Catherine and her minions. I fear she places more value upon them than on her husband's position and work. Bingley was not surprised when Jonathan decided to retain his position in the party after leaving the Parliament; he could well be bored at Rosings when he is not busy with business affairs. Neither Amelia nor her sister are interested in Parliamentary matters."

Elizabeth had listened with concern. "Has he said anything to you?" she asked.

Jane shook her head. "Oh, no, he has not. I doubt that he would, he is too loyal to her," she said and added quickly, "I do not mean that he no longer loves her or that they are miserable together, Lizzie, but I wish I could see the kind of marriage that Cassy and Richard have or the felicity that Emma and James have found together. Regrettably, while they are always dutifully considerate of each other, I feel there is little warmth between them, except when they are both with the children."

Elizabeth was saddened but not entirely surprised. Amelia-Jane had always seemed to her to be the least interesting of the Collins girls, with neither the talent of Rebecca nor the strength and common sense of Cathy. She was certainly very pretty and, having married very young, appeared to have lost interest in all but the most superficial aspects of her husband's work. There was none of the intelligence and excitement that characterised the partnership of Caroline and Fitzwilliam. Indeed, Fitzwilliam himself had remarked that it was a great pity that young Jonathan Bingley had decided to leave Parliament, and Fitzwilliam had blamed it upon the fact that his wife was bored by his work.

"She does not value the work he does, and her conversation seems limited to her servants and her children, in that order!" he had said.

Jane did point out that Jonathan's wife was indeed an excellent mother, devoted to her children, but Elizabeth was not deceived. She could see her sister was unhappy, but there was very little anyone could do. Elizabeth was desperately sad for her nephew.

There were footsteps in the corridor, and Cassandra appeared at the door. She was warmly welcomed by her mother and aunt, who had promptly changed the topic of their conversation.

As she sat down, Jane noticed an anxious little frown and asked, "Cassy, my dear, are you not feeling well?"

Cassandra protested that she was very well, perhaps a little tired at the end of a long day, arousing immediate suspicions in the minds of Elizabeth and Jane. These were confirmed when Cassy asked, "Mama, would you mind very much if we did not stay to dinner? I think I should like to go home."

Elizabeth was concerned. "Why Cassy, my dear, what is wrong? Of course you need not stay if you are unwell, but tell me, what is worrying you?" she said.

Mother and daughter were very close, and Cassy could not keep her secret long, revealing that she was expecting their fifth child in the Autumn. After much delighted hugging and kissing and a great deal of good advice, her mother and aunt finally released her to return to her husband, but not before they had begged her to take great care of herself.

"I am so glad Richard is such a good doctor; it relieves me of the need to worry about you. I can simply enjoy the anticipation, knowing he takes such good care of you," Elizabeth said.

Cassandra laughed. "I assure you, Mama, he is sufficiently anxious for all of us. I am under so many instructions that I cannot possibly remember them all."

Cassandra was a favourite with everyone. Her devotion to her own family had never precluded her involvement in community work, and she and her husband, whose skill and integrity had earned him a great reputation in the district, were constantly available to those who needed their help. Elizabeth had always regarded her daughter as the ideal, modern young woman—accomplished, intelligent, and devoted to her heritage and her family more so than herself.

Modestly, she admitted to Jane that Cassy would have made an excellent Mistress of Pemberley. "Better by far than myself; she knows so much about the estate," she said.

"You cannot mean that Lizzie," Jane protested, but Elizabeth was quite adamant. "Dear Jane, do not misunderstand me, I love Pemberley; it is our home and I would never leave it. But Cassy was born here and knows every nook and cranny of the place. She used to ride everywhere with Darcy and his steward when she was a little girl, and after William's death, she made it her business to learn everything she needed to know while Julian was still a baby. As Julian grew older, she taught him all she knew. She remains interested not only in the estate, but in all of the people who live and work here. She knows most of them by name—a task that would certainly defeat me.

"It is to Cassy's persistence that the people of this area owe the free health service that the children of the Kympton and Pemberley parish schools receive. After the dreadful fright we all had with little Laura Ann, who almost died of croup, Cassandra was determined that all the children should be seen regularly by the doctors at Littleford, to avoid outbreaks of disease among them.

"Darcy is immensely proud of her, and I know that had Julian not been born, he would have been perfectly happy to have Cassy inherit Pemberley. He has told me so. We are not burdened with an entail, of course," she said.

Jane was suitably impressed. "Perhaps Cassy will teach Josie, too, and help her understand what it is to be the Mistress of Pemberley one day," said Jane, who had sensed that Elizabeth was disappointed that Josie and Julian would not be returning to Pemberley, at least not for a while.

Elizabeth seemed unsure. "Perhaps she will. Jane, I do not doubt Josie's ability to be the Mistress of Pemberley, only the depth of her commitment to this place and its people. I know that when I was engaged to Darcy, I soon became as obsessed with Pemberley as he was. I do not know if Josie will ever feel the same sense of responsibility."

Jane tried to reassure her. "She is still very young, Lizzie; they both are. I am quite sure, when the time comes—which God willing may not be for many years—Josie will understand the importance of her role at Pemberley."

"Oh, dear Jane, I do hope so, for it will surely break Darcy's heart if she does not."

Hearing footsteps outside, she rose just as Darcy and Bingley arrived and Bingley declared, "There you are, Darcy, I told you we would find them here, engrossed in their reminiscences, quite forgetting the rest of us."

"Well, we have been sent to invite you to join the party," said Darcy. "Our little group of musicians is ready to entertain us. Victoria and Stephanie have been persuaded to sing, and Bingley is so prodigiously proud of his grand-daughters, nothing will satisfy him but that we are all there to hear them."

As they went downstairs, Bingley and Jane leading the way, Elizabeth held her husband back and told him Cassandra's news. Darcy was delighted and revealed that there was more good news. His sister Georgiana had arranged for young William Courtney to return with them to Oxford, where he would study the organ with one of the finest organists at the university.

"For William, who has played the organ at the Kympton church for several years, it is a splendid opportunity," he said and Elizabeth agreed, very excited by the news.

"Emily must surely be delighted," she said and was soon assured that she was, by Emily herself.

"Oh, Lizzie, it is such a wonderful opportunity for William. I do not know how we can thank Georgiana. It was entirely her idea. She has often heard him play in church and thinks he will do very well," said Emily, almost unable to comprehend her son's good fortune.

As for William, it was typical of him that in the midst of the excitement, he alone worried about who would replace him at the organ in the Kympton church on Sunday!

❧

When it was all over and most of their guests had gone home or retired to the visitors' rooms, Elizabeth and Darcy went upstairs. It had been a day bright with new love and hope, warm with affection and friendship.

Looking out over the park, Elizabeth watched as Pemberley, which had been ablaze with light, its rooms resounding with the sounds of music and laughter, grew dark and quiet. A waning moon hung low in the sky, and the familiar shadows and birdcalls of the night took over the grounds. Here there were no deserted villages or starving poor; where industry and trade had brought prosperity to some, a dividend was paid to the people through schools and hospitals for their children. Elizabeth felt great pride in the involvement of her family in all of this.

As she waited for Darcy to join her, she thought again of William and Emily and their great happiness, but her mind returned to Cassandra with a warm rush of love mixed with concern. She had had no trouble with any of her children, but this time, she was older and her mother was anxious. More than anything in the world, Elizabeth wanted everything to be just right for her daughter. The pleasure of that longing was almost like pain.

When Darcy returned to the room, she told him of her concerns. He understood her anxiety. For many years now, he had been able to anticipate her wishes. So clear was the understanding between them, there was no need for her to ask.

"Lizzie, tomorrow, after all our guests have returned home and we have Pemberley to ourselves again, we could send the carriage for Cassandra and Richard, so we could celebrate their happy news together. Would you like that?" he asked, and he did not have to hear her reply to know it was exactly what she had in mind.

"Thank you," she said. "Nothing would give me greater pleasure."

He smiled and put his arms around her; it was as if he had read her thoughts. They, neither of them, felt the need to say much more. There was no better way to close the day.

Postscript

Julian Darcy and his wife Josie continued to live in Cambridge for a few years, during a period of constant turmoil with demands for reform and change coming from a variety of groups around Britain.

Everyone in England seems to belong to some group or movement, Josie wrote in her diary.

> *And they all want reform, whether it is Votes for Women, Freedom for Slaves, Secret ballot, more money for hospitals or public education for all children, there is no dearth of good causes. Unfortunately, the men who have the power are not listening!*

Julian Darcy did well, gaining a Doctorate in Science for his work; but, sadly, Josie never did achieve her ambition to get her work published in the Metropolitan press. She continued to write for *The New Radical* and her father's journals and was finally persuaded to provide a regular column for *The Matlock Review*. She lost none of her enthusiasm, and copies of all her articles were carefully collected and placed in the library at Pemberley by her father-in-law, whose respect for Josie's opinions and style increased by the day.

In the Summer of 1860, their son was born, whom they named Anthony Fitzwilliam Darcy. Determined to remain as independent as possible, they struggled on at Cambridge for a further year. But in 1861, following the death of the Prince Consort, the outbreak of the American Civil War, and consequent unrest in Britain, they decided it was time to leave.

"There is too much confusion and discord here for our comfort," said Julian in a letter to his mother announcing their decision, "for while neither of us objects to a robust intellectual debate, we would rather raise little Anthony in the relative peace and quiet of Derbyshire."

Not long afterwards, to the delight of their parents, they returned to live at Pemberley.

Appendix

A list of the main characters in *The Women of Pemberley*:

Emma Wilson—daughter of Charles and Jane Bingley

David Wilson MP—first husband of Emma Bingley

Victoria and Stephanie—their daughters

James Wilson MP—David Wilson's brother

Emily Courtney—Elizabeth's cousin, daughter of Mr and Mrs Gardiner (was married to Paul Antoine, deceased, now married to James Courtney, Rector of Kympton)

William, Elizabeth, and Jessica Courtney—their children

Robert Gardiner—brother of Caroline, Emily, and Richard Gardiner

Rose Fitzwilliam—marries Robert Gardiner.

Cassandra Darcy—daughter of Elizabeth and Fitzwilliam Darcy

Julian Darcy—son of Mr and Mrs Darcy

Richard Gardiner—husband of Cassandra (son of Mr and Mrs Edward Gardiner)

Edward, Darcy, Eliza, and Laura Ann—their children

Isabella Fitzwilliam—daughter of Caroline and Colonel Fitzwilliam

Dr Henry Forrester—a young doctor who marries Isabella

Josie (Josephine) Tate—daughter of Anthony and Rebecca Tate

Jonathan Bingley—son of Jane and Charles Bingley

Amelia-Jane Collins—Jonathan's wife (daughter of Charlotte and late Mr Collins)

Anne-Marie Bingley—their daughter

Louisa and Sophia Bingley—daughters of Jane and Charles Bingley, and sisters of Jonathan

From the pages of *Pride and Prejudice*:

Mr and Mrs Darcy of Pemberley

Mr and Mrs Bingley of Ashford Park

Mr and Mrs Gardiner

Colonel Fitzwilliam

Charlotte Collins

Georgiana Darcy (now Mrs Grantley)

About the Author

A lifelong fan of Jane Austen, Rebecca Ann Collins first read *Pride and Prejudice* at the tender age of twelve. She fell in love with the characters and since then has devoted years of research and study to the life and works of her favourite author. As a teacher of literature and a librarian, she has gathered a wealth of information about Miss Austen and the period in which she lived and wrote, which became the basis of her books about the Pemberley families. The popularity of the Pemberley novels with Jane Austen fans has been her reward.

With a love of reading, music, art, and gardening, Ms Collins claims she is very comfortable in the period about which she writes and feels great empathy with the characters she portrays. While she enjoys the convenience of modern life, she finds much to admire in the values and worldview of Jane Austen.